ANNIHILATOR

BY TIMOTHY PRICE

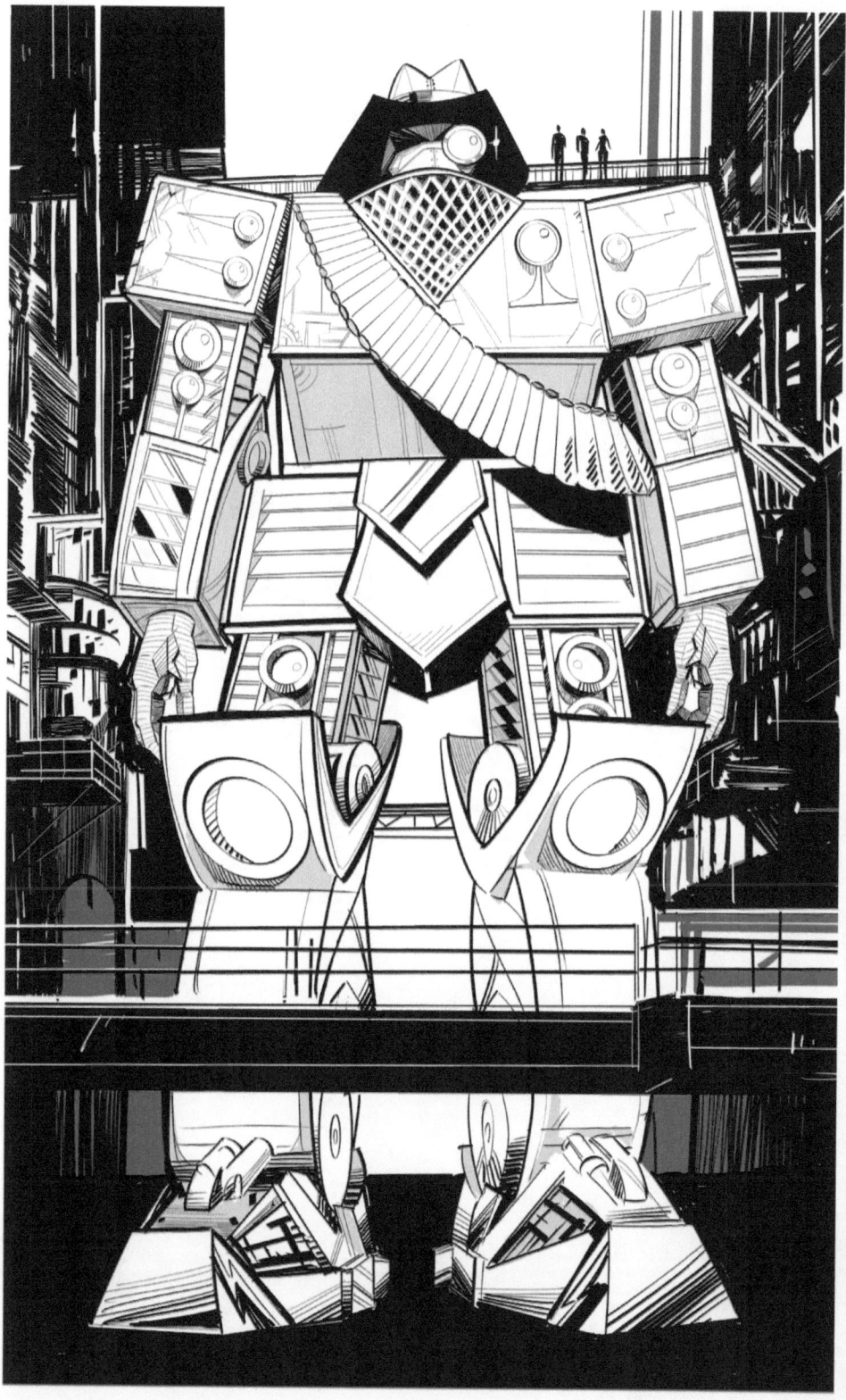

ANNIHILATOR

BY TIMOTHY PRICE

A NOVEL

by

TIMOTHY PRICE

WITH ILLUSTRATIONS BY
ALAN OW BARNES

Annihilator

Big In Japan Book 3

Additional Creative Input:

Alan OW Barnes, Wil Newman, Keira Barnes,
Jeffrey Price, Daniel Price

Special Thanks

Martin & Pam Arlt, Alan OW Barnes and family,
Benny Boynton, Joshua Brafman, Matt Dennion,
Robert Scott Field, Jeff Horne, Yutaka Ichimura,
Jas Ingram, Gary & Amanda Johnson,
Mark Justice, Derek M. Koch, J.D. Lees,
Sean Linkenback, Bambi Lynn, Shane Morton,
Nicholas Poling, Neil Riebe, Akira Takarada,
Jon Waterhouse, Ricky Zero

A very special thanks to my wonderful kids, family, and
friends. And last but not least, the love of my life, Alyce,
who never ceases to amaze me.

This book is dedicated to the loving memory, life
and career of Akira Takarada

Chapter 1

Noahmar

As I gaze up into the black, I am no longer overwhelmed by a sheer sense of awe and childlike wonder. Things are not as they were, a time when I looked to the skies with belief and hope. It is hard, but I must admit that my curiosity has faded. And now, all I feel is fear. At one time, I could get lost in these majestic and mysterious plains simply known as space. It was my sanctuary. But now a great terror harbors from beyond the above, and my refuge has become cold and unsympathetic. Instead of looking up, I now turn away. I despise the change. I wear a brave face, but I believe there is a war coming, a war between the heavens and earth, and it's one that we cannot win. It may seem impossible, but the eternal night that surrounds our planet is no longer so vast, and I am convinced that this amount of seemingly endless separation will not be enough to save us. The great annihilator is coming.

Private Log

Dr. Kyoshi Takarada
Earth Intelligence Organization (E.I.O.)

Across the great void, a mere 4.3 or so light years away, the ever-expanding rays of Alpha Centauri's triple suns reach out. From there, the two larger of these bright, burning stars, Alpha Centauri A and B, give light to a handful of barren worlds, and to one that is far from being uninhabited. For rotating in the center of these twin-orbiting suns, a small planet known as Noahmar spins peacefully around, blanketed in the fiery glow of each. There is also a third sun in this solar system known to most on Earth as Proxima B. It is what we would call a red dwarf or a relatively cool star. To the inhabitants of Noahmar however, it is only a glimmer to be seen within the sky of their purple dusk. It is merely a faint shimmer off in the distance, a dull sparkle to make wishes upon and nothing more.

Over millions of years the species of this planet, like their dominant duo suns, have evolved into a binary form of existence, a race where two entities create the individual. Not male and not female, and not like anything we've thought to exist elsewhere, but beings that are made up from one form, yet with two completely separate patterns of thought, duo nervous systems and hearts. Sometimes this is better, and at other times, it is not. But it is indeed something that most on our own world would not or would choose not to understand. For they are different from us, and different is a breeding ground for ignorance and fear. It's funny because these beings, as enlightened and advanced as they are, would typically be met with hostility and aggression should they ever come to Earth. Instead of being greeted by noble men and women of science, diplomacy and honor, chances are they would be met by angry mobs with torches and paranoid government officials wielding scalpels.

Think about it though. How would you react to seeing twin beings made up of thousands of lights from within one thin glowing outline? Can you imagine?

You're parked on some backwoods road making the moves on your best gal when some glow-in-the-dark freakshow bursts out from nowhere wanting to be your best friend? Well, even with the best of intentions, more than likely you're gonna panic. Because your mind is probably going to go straight to

Svengoolie reruns that boast a monster-sized serving of sci-fi with fries on the side. Or better yet, imagine coming face to face with one of these aliens that resembled something like walking television static. It would probably take a second to register, but as soon as you realized you weren't imagining something from the *Outer Limits*, you would probably freak. After all, it's normal. In the same way, the inhabitants of Noahmar would not understand beings such as us. Beings that not only insist on keeping our light on the inside, but ones who believe they can evolve while living a non-duo existence. It's absurd and can only lead to loneliness and despair.

And knowing this was what made the task of dividing one of their own into two so difficult. But this had to be done, because during times of war, when the threat of extinction is more of a probability than a possibility, life (any life, anywhere) will do what is necessary to survive.

It had been over a decade in Earth years since this small planet sent two soldiers born from one to our troubled world in order to save their own. It was also because of this bold risk and sacrifice that the threat of intergalactic extermination was thwarted, and since, they have known peace ... until now.

***

It takes a magnificent amount of mass to overshadow an immense city that is illuminated by the light of two suns. And to a world that only knows daylight and dusk, the darkness brought with it a morbid sense of curiosity to its inhabitants. Thousands, if not millions, of the planet's only populated region took notice and escaped to the bustling outside, gathering between the endless array of towering crystal skyscrapers.

The life-giving rays of each sun struggled to push through, but it was an impossible task. Soon the radiant glow of the transparent skyscrapers diminished, turning to a cool blue in the cold of the oncoming black. Many pondered the worst and wondered if this was indeed the end. Inhabitants of this great city gazed upwards, searching for the familiarity of their purple and orange evening sky. But it was gone, swallowed by the ever-growing gloom.

But as the black expanded, it started to take shape as two needlepoints of light glowed from within its ever-increasing form. Nobody knew exactly what was coming, but they knew it wasn't good. Then all at once, and quite instinctively, these beings began grabbing the hand of the one to either side of them. At first glance you may think they were preparing to die, but in fact it was just the opposite. They were preparing to fight.

From the ground, a tremendous hemisphere generated, pulsating high above the city, rising in conjunction with each beat of a million pounding hearts. The darkness faded, and the crystal city illuminated into a sickening neon green as the force field engulfed it. Upon ascending it dwarfed even the tallest of alien skyscrapers. It was truly magnificent.

Sirens screamed, and just like the inhabitants of our own earth, the very sound sent a tingling disruption down their static-induced spines. Their powers were indeed strong, but as the giant, clear, green-tinted shield magnified the silhouette of the oncoming horror, hopelessness began to consume the masses.

The gargantuan creature, still shrouded in its own shadow, slammed into the force field from the outer side. The shield held, but below in the city the impact was so great, the very ground they stood upon began to give way. Many lost their balance, falling to the ground and down between the shards of the shattering streets. The monstrous green dome flickered and shrunk as bursts of lightning ignited from it. White waves of electricity pulsated, and as they regained their footing, the protective shield immediately shot back up when the chain of alien hands linked back together.

KA-CHAAAAM! WHAM!

Again, the beast hit with the ferocity of a colliding world, and once more, the masses went down, this time feeling the pain of impact. It seemed the strength they needed to power the force field was a part of their genetic fiber, and when it suffered, they suffered. The invader reared back quickly to try to infiltrate the unsteady barrier while the Aliens attempted to get to their feet.

Some reached down for the hands of the ones no longer standing in order to reattach the link that generated their protective dome. In a blazing instance, a million beams of light began to weave the force field back together.

Again, it grew taller, rising up towards the very creature that was trying to break through. Then, in a blinding flash of white, they collided. A series of shock waves rained down from the skies, and the glowing inhabitants of this little planet known as Noahmar, again fell. The shield had been penetrated.

It was unimaginable. Two monstrous feet, each as big as battleships, hurled straight down towards the heart of the alien city! The creature spread its gargantuan wings to slow its approach, and like an eagle landing on the tallest of trees, it touched down onto one of the city's skyscrapers. Not being able to withstand the impact, cracks shot through the crystal structure, and it collapsed within itself with the brute still on top.

KA-CHOOOM! CRASH!

The illuminated Noahmarians scattered, and like a little boy squashing bugs, the creature began to slam its mighty feet down upon them, over and over. The beast gazed at the terrified masses below, seemingly enjoying what it was doing. Between the debris-clouded skies and the dusk to which their eyes weren't accustomed, the monster, although great in size, was hard to make out. It wasn't, however, hard to hear, and the giant abomination moaned out an eerie cry. It was low in pitch and bellowed with the deep sound of bending steel and steam. The mysterious space monster then swiped one of its three-fingered talon-like claws through an adjacent glass tower. The massive building didn't explode but shattered into a million shards of deadly rain.

Aliens stood tall, fighting the monster magnificently with exploding multicolored orbs created in their minds. Some joined hands again to magnify the power of the rising, glowing spheres as brilliant bursts of purple, green and yellow exploded on and around the beast. In smaller groups the aliens were not as powerful and due to toppling buildings, mighty feet colliding into the ground and explosions, separation was inevitable. It was almost as though the monstrous creature knew how to attack. The aliens met the behemoth with great resistance and synchronicity, some creating miniature force fields to protect the others as they launched one floating bomb after the other.

Great bursts lit up the sky as the monster made its way to the center of the city towards its tallest monument. The structure illuminated in a tone of gold that, with its great height, made it stand out from any of the other crystal skyscrapers. It rose towards the heavens of Noahmar and the top melded into two gigantic circles held within an even bigger triangle. It was more than just a structure though; it represented their entire society as a binary species. The huge beast paled in size, but that didn't slow it down in the least. The creature began pulling the gigantic and proud memorial up from its base. Inhabitants from inside were flung about as though they were ants being shaken from a dead tree branch. Some were able to float down in glowing shields, only to have the toppling structure fall onto them as the debris made its way to the shattered streets.

Pairs of aliens locked fingers and took to the skies like twin flying crosses, firing energy beams and launching orbs from the tips of their free hands. Their greatest advantage being that they were so small in comparison, it was as though the great beast was swatting at nothing but a swarm of electrified gnats. But still, with each swipe of its mighty arm, it would take out yet another handful. Obviously irritated at the feeble attempt to take it down, the angry monster clenched its three-fingered fists and flexed its arms to its side. Steam hissed through its porous and leathery armor, and in nothing shy of a millisecond, a great wave of pure energy erupted from it.

ZWOOP! FWOOOOSH!!

The force was so incredible and so vast, it leveled everything within the massive alien city, everything except for the monster itself. From within the center of a crater of its own making, it still stood, waiting for whatever else they had to offer, which was nothing. All was lost; this power-burst weapon of the beast was far beyond their fighting capabilities. They were but a mere peaceful planet, and although very powerful, they were nothing

compared to this immense devastator, this annihilator of worlds.

One final regiment took off in pairs, this time not to fight the beast, as they now knew it was futile, but to distract it. The plan was brilliant, and by creating a massive humanoid pinwheel of colorful spinning lights in the sky, it was drawn like a moth to a flame. The creature lumbered its way towards the edge of the flattened city, where the aliens circled high in the sky like a mass of multi-colored fireflies. It worked. They had lured it. But as they knew, it would be but a fleeting victory. However, it was about time, and a little was all they needed.

As brave alien soldiers sacrificed themselves from above, groups of the remaining inhabitants congregated below. All knew they needed to flee to designated structures within the city, the ones that led to subterranean canals that burrowed deep into the planet. Evacuating through the crystal rubble, glass debris, and alien carnage, they remained strangely calm and entered the shelters single file as their world died around them.

This would not be the end. This would not be their demise. This horrendous demon would not wipe out this species, one that took so long to find their peaceful place within the universe. Some had to survive, and that message travelled through each and every one of them. It was for the greater good of all, and therefore accepted. Maybe that's why panic and hysteria never ensued, for that would cause chaos and ensure their complete extinction. Many knew they would not make it, but that still did not deter them as they fled deep beneath the ground into the shelters. The thought was both noble, glorious and necessary with the driving need to survive forcing their every step.

Growing tired, or more so, irritated, the monster let out an ear-shattering bellow while it generated its internal power source to again fire its primary weapon.

With a great number of Noahmarians still on the surface, thick molten crystal began to seal in the entrances to the evacuation points. As it hardened, the ones that couldn't get in simply stopped. As their world crumbled, they quietly sat, forced out an illuminated smile to the one sitting next to them, held hands and generated small force fields for protection. They knew it would be brief.

SHOOOOOMM!!!

Whatever remained above ground exploded in a burst of bright blue and green. Only this time, the great creature followed the blast up with twin translucent rays fired from its eyes. The beast surveyed its surroundings and turned its head, navigating the red beams towards anything still moving or standing. The laser-like emissions of light appeared to go on forever, stretching to the furthest reaches of the horizon. The heat was so great that the lucent skeletons of the devastated crystal skyscrapers simply melted into heaps of liquified glass. No living entity on the surface or in the shelters had even a remote chance of survival. Still not satisfied, the creature again glowed and fired its main weapon. Their entire planet tilted at its very core, and a great shock wave created a massive tumbling canyon pulling the remnants of the city down into it.

The creature took a brief moment to survey its dirty work and, seeming satisfied, it stood erect and prepared for take-off from the crumbling surface of the planet. In a blur of twin jet streams, it simply rocketed back into the color-laden heavens from whence it had come.

FWOOOOOOOSH!

The dusk had passed, and again it was light. The shadows of the destruction cast a prism of bright hues high into the atmosphere when the rays of their twin suns began to cast down. The great alien city was gone and burned, not in fire and smoke, but in an array of a thousand multicolored rainbows. It was both devastating and beautiful.

What seemed eternal only lasted but a mere few seconds. It was reminiscent of the greatest of all disasters. It ended swiftly, leaving a million-year trace, or worse yet, no trace at all.

With tremendous speed, the creature made its way through time and the vast regions of space to the edge of Alpha Centauri. Its course, the spiral arm of Orion within the Milky Way. Its destination, Earth. The great Annihilator was coming.

***

Our world, the one we know as planet Earth, had undergone catastrophic changes of apocalyptic proportions over the last decade or so. It's no wonder the planet had even survived. The missing and the dead tallied into the tens of millions. To this day, Salt Lake City still remained a radioactive wasteland. Its only inhabitants being a few mutant inbred tribes that refused to leave after the blast but were then permanently quarantined due to sickness and disease. The earliest casualty in Daikaiju War One, Salt Lake City suffered the first war-based nuclear explosion since Nagasaki. Unfortunately, it wouldn't be the last.

The government, left to deal with the rest of the country, had little choice but to abandon Salt Lake City. People in the surrounding burbs were evacuated to a certain degree, but the rest were left to fend for themselves in their own nuclear prison. However, when some of the survivors decided it was time to move, they soon found themselves with a massive trench that completely surrounded the remains of the city, almost like a gigantic moat. But instead of water, the great ravine was filled with barbed wire, tank obstacles and landmines should anybody decide they'd like to leave after all.

The devastated parts of California were different. West of Fresno, as far north as Cape Mendocino and as far south as Tijuana, Mexico, there were no survivors. A giant creature (of the "intent" category) using an extreme heat source to burrow its way through the San Andreas fault triggered a 9.0 megathrust quake. But things went from bad to worse when this subterranean, travelling juggernaut surfaced in Los Angeles ultimately leading to the nuclear explosion of the USS Ford Warship. After that nothing remained, no buildings, no people, no land, nothing but boiling sea. San Francisco needed no further attention, as it too was now part of the Pacific.

Much of Tokyo and Yokohama had been rebuilt, as with most of London. However, the mighty Mount Fuji remained off limits as the mountain's northwest side was still sporting a monstrous crater. Luckily, in Antarctica, the devastation caused at Mount Terror was limited to Ross Island.

So much destruction and death. So many lives and families lost. So many longing for the way things used to be. In many ways, it was like a cancer infiltrating a body, and when battling it, everything gets destroyed in the process. But most would agree, when impending doom is kicking down your front door, more than likely you'll fight it tooth and nail. And that's exactly what the general consensus was with most proclaiming loudly and proudly, "On behalf of earth, we're gonna fight to the last man, baby."

But even Mother Earth seemed tired, beat up and bruised, and it was hard to pinpoint, but she was no longer the same. It was almost as though she had been knocked off her axis in some weird way. And maybe this would have some future repercussions, and maybe it wouldn't, but what seemed apparent was that she probably couldn't, or wouldn't, take too much more of the strain.

This wasn't about the shifting of continents, the changing of the weather or the decline of the atmosphere. No, this was more about the nuclear deserts, toxic seas, charred wildernesses and radiated skies. This was anger pure and simple. War after war, pollution, toxic dumping, atomic blasts, it was no wonder she began spitting out rogue monsters not only to battle the "intents" created by man and magic, but to also protect the planet.

These were the worrisome thoughts that now seemed to dominate his very being. They were ruthless, and soon the sound of his index finger tapping hard and fast on his desk snapped him out of the black of his mind. Even in the confines of his own head, his nervous finger-tapping habit now seemed to have taken on a life of its own. Tap, tap, tap, and the deeper he went, the louder and faster it became. His keen and finely tuned mind was suffering as all he could focus on now was the possibility of what could be, and what may be coming. So often our thoughts of worry and impending doom are nothing but concocted fears in our head, but this was different. This future, the one he couldn't stop ruminating on, surely had dire repercussions, but he still had to take control of his own mind in order to concentrate on a solution. Because he knew, and even though he didn't want to be right, Dr. Kyoshi Takarada knew all too well, what was on its way.

Chapter II

Funeral For a Friend

Dr. Kyoshi Takarada caught himself slipping again into his own self-doubt as the avalanche of the last ten years continued to crash down upon him. It's not that he was losing his mind, as it was still just as strong and sharp as ever. No, it was that he was dangerously preoccupied with his own thoughts. Getting lost in deep introspect was nothing new for Takarada, it was a trait he had always known, and if his old commander of the Earth Intelligence Organization (the E.I.O.), Sir Jonathan Winston, was still in charge, he'd order the good doctor to "Promptly pull his head out of his ass and get back in the bloody game." But his good friend Jack as he was known to many was gone. Towards the end of his illustrious tenure as the head of the E.I.O., Sir Jonathon had had enough. In the end, he may even had lost it a bit stating to Takarada in an angry tirade, "To Hell with all of this. I've had it with monsters, death, ruddy politics, smartass agents, rock stars and the whole bloody bit! I quit." That didn't even include the scars left on him by his ex-wife, who just so happened to be an evil Yokai She-Witch, spawned from the very pits of Hell itself. Jack did, however, have the opportunity to put a bullet through her brain, but even that didn't seem to ease his pain much. Takarada often wondered if that too may have had something to do with his early retirement. But in all reality, maybe Jack "losing it" was merely him coming to his senses. However, it didn't really matter, because in a few short years, General, Sir Jonathon Winston, retired chief commander and head of the Earth Intelligence Organization passed away after a massive stroke.

Shakespeare wrote that "A coward dies a thousand times, but the valiant taste of death but once." And though this may hold true for some, there are many of brave character who have encountered the reaper, or in Japanese folklore, the Shinigami not once, but twice in their life. This may be hard to understand, but for some in this world, life does not truly begin until after it is over. For Sir Jonathon this was not his first death. It was also nothing shy of an absolute kiseki that after taking four bullets to the back, that Sir Jonathon would live to die another day many years later. A proposition many of us would jump at should the opportunity ever arise. Because Jonathon, along with his gruff demeanor, round glasses, permanently un-straightenable tie and of course, that giant walrus-like mustache, left this harsh world with an abundance of treasures, wisdom, fulfilment and true friendship. Yes, he was indeed a warrior, a courageous senshi, but he was also a surprisingly gentle man. In the end, I truly believe that Jonathon realized something many never will, even if they had ten lifetimes to do it in, that the love you take, is equal to the love you make.

Rest In Peace Sir Jonathon Winston

These were the words that Takarada wrestled with, and he reached deep into the side drawer of his desk and pulled out the incomplete hand-written eulogy he was working on for Jack's funeral. It was tattered, smudged with scrunched sentences squeezed in where the previous had been crossed out. Takarada knew everything about Jack and who he really was and though others within the organization also did, he still didn't dare tread too far with his words. Especially ones being immortalized on paper. Due to its indecisiveness, it came across rather sloppy compared to his normal, almost calligraphic Japanese writing. But it didn't matter, because he was never able to read it anyhow. He couldn't seem to throw it away either.

The fact is, Sir Jack's second funeral was much like his first, in other words, that there wasn't really much of one at all. However, the first was at the request of his wife at the time (you know, the one he shot in the head) and the second of his own wishes. They would have come out in droves too for a memorial dedicated to Sir Jonathon Winston, one of the few who could truly claim, but never would that they had saved the planet on multiple occasions. A man who was worthy of ticker tape parades, news coverage, and a towering statue, but that was not who Jack was, at least not anymore and it only took dying to figure it out.

After a moment of silence, In My Life by The Beatles followed by Funeral for A Friend by Elton John echoed like a lonely ghost wandering through the halls of the last two E.I.O. facilities still in operation. It was haunting, quite ethereal and the extent of Sir Jonathon Winston's vigil. With nothing else to add, Takarada again folded up his departing words for his friend and returned it to its home deep within his desk drawer.

Sir Jonathon always seemed to make Takarada a bit nervous, but the good doctor had great respect for Jack, and over the years they had become quite close. It was obvious that when Sir Jonathon left, he took a little bit of Dr. Takarada with him. This may even have caused trust issues with Takarada, because even though the Earth Intelligence Organization still had quite a few card carrying members living on the premises, Takarada insisted on working with fewer and fewer people. Not because he was pretentious or anything, but because far too many had used much of his work and discoveries for greed and power. It seemed time, the loss of Jack and circumstances had taken a heavy toll on both Kyoshi Takarada and his trust.

The last ten years had been so surreal, so unexpected and so cruel, and the E.I.O. had undergone change after change as they sought to find their relevance in this new world. For hundreds of years, they called the shots and pulled the strings. The Earth Intelligence Organization was without a doubt the presidential puppet masters, the ruling majority, the king of kings. They were indeed what some would call, the high cabal. But not anymore.

Reduced to a shoe-string budget, The E.I.O. now ran more like a struggling nonprofit rather than a high-level government agency. The loss of lives was staggering during the kaiju conflicts, but that didn't seem to be the reason as every war has its casualties. It seemed it was more about the demise of every E.I.O. base around the world falling into the LOUDLY stated "billions of dollars wasted" category. But it was probably the gigantic apple bite left in Mount Fuji that was the last straw. Funny thing was, now that the kaiju attacks had stopped, so did the endless flow of money.

Tap...tap...tap

It seemed that Takarada's nervous finger tapping had become beneficial in the sense that the sound of it always brought him back to reality. Maybe reality wasn't the right word, because he wasn't slipping into fiction, he was slipping into solution. But either way, it took him somewhere else. It never took very long either and as the same old reel began to play in his mind for the millionth time, his comm system began to bark at him. He looked up from his not-so magnificent oak desk (the one he had inherited from Sir Jack) and saw he had a visitor.

"Yare yare daze," he mumbled in Japanese.

His first thought being it was probably Sir Jack's replacement, Commander Robert Jones. Even though Jones had been with the E.I.O. for some years now, Takarada still thought of him as the "new" guy. Sort of like the new keyboard player in Styx or the new guitarist in REO Speed Wagon. They were both going on thirty years with each band, and even though their time with said band had doubled that of the original, they were always and forever to be, "the new guy." And that's just what Commander Jones was to Takarada. It didn't matter though, because Dr. Takarada carried so much weight at The E.I.O. that if he said he wanted to work with less people, then so be it. They called him excentric, but he didn't care as long as the majority left him to his work. Truth be told, there were only two people he'd work with, and one had to be Commander Jones who he didn't even like. He has such weird eyes, Takarada thought as his *Star Trek* door swished open, but got stuck halfway.

Takarada smiled and sighed in relief as he was greeted with an uplifting, "Hey, Dr. T."

General Taylor slipped in through the crack of the doorway and sat down on the opposite side of Takarada's not-so magnificent oak desk. The air conditioner was again on the fritz and Taylor ran his left hand through his short, sandy-blonde hair to wipe the sweat from the top of his head. He then proceeded to twist and pull on that same hand in a very strange fashion. With a series of clicks and turns, it separated from his wrist, and he handed it to Dr. Takarada.

Takarada slipped on his glasses and observed the inside of General Taylor's hand from the opening where it connected to the wrist. It was apparent that Taylor had tried to take matters into his own hand as a few layers of duct tape were crudely wrapped around one of the appendages inner tubes.

As the doctor looked it over, he pulled a pen from his pocket protector and using the tip, yanked a saturated piece of the silver adhesive out of the intricate mechanism. While inspecting the hand further, Takarada made a bold and debatable comment. "You cannot fix everything with duct tape, Tommy-san." But even before General Taylor could counter, Takarada started shaking the hand, and as he did, it sprayed some foul liquid all over.

"Oh man!" Taylor shouted as he protected his face with his right forearm from whatever it was that was shooting out of the appendage.

Takarada smiled a little, maybe for the first time in a while, and he apologized. "So sorry, Tommy-san, it seems your hand is leaking lubricant into the main organic thorium artery."

General Taylor didn't really know what that meant, but he knew Dr. Takarada did, so it didn't concern him as much as something else.

"Please Dr. T., don't call me Tommy. I've asked you a million times."

Takarada stood up, bowed and asked General Thomas Lynn Taylor to please forgive him. Dr. Takarada wanted to respect General Taylor's request, but in all honesty, it was hard for him. Tommy, or Thomas as he now wanted to be called, was probably the closest thing to a son that Dr. Takarada had. It was also hard to believe he had known him for over ten years already and literally watched him grow up in the ranks of the E.I.O.

A montage of flashbacks ran through Takarada's head, and he almost giggled out loud when he thought of Tommy in the days when his robotic hand was brand new.

Takarada had saved Tommy's life when the E.I.O. rescued him from the debris of a destroyed building in Tokyo way back in the beginning. Like an aging father, it made him a little sad to think of how Tommy was no longer this naïve, rockstar-wannabe kid, but now a full general in the Earth Intelligence Organization. Of course he was proud, but like so many, time, war, monsters and death had taken its toll on Tommy, changing him at his very core. Takarada longed for the past, but it was that past in particular, maybe because back then the good doctor wasn't haunted by an uncertain future. Once again, Takarada's keen mind focused in on his troublesome thoughts. But before he could go too deep, Tommy, or Thomas or General Taylor or whatever, snapped him out of it.

"I'm sorry, Kyoshi, please forgive me, my friend." Takarada stood up fast, put his arms to his side and bowed again, only deeper this time.

"No, no, Tommy-sa ... General Taylor, it is me who must apologize."

Tommy sighed, "I'm not aging very gracefully," he admitted. Dr. Takarada again smirked, but knew Tommy had been wrestling with this and saw it as a prime opportunity to get the hell out of his own head.

"What is the matter, Thomas?" he asked as he sat back down in his chair.

Tommy sighed again and reached for his hand still sitting upon the desk. It was obvious he was fumbling to find his words as he played with the fingers of his robotic appendage.

"I don't know, Kyoshi. Maybe it's because I'm in my late thirties, but lately I've been wondering if I've made the right choices in my life." Takarada grunted out a concerned samurai-like, "Hmmm," and Tommy continued.

"Do you remember my first mission?" Tommy asked Takarada. "That day changed everything. That day made me realize there was a whole lot more to life than just becoming a rock star." Tommy shrugged and said "rock star" again with a demeaning tone. "It may have been the first time in my life that I truly put the needs of others ahead of mine. But my wants were just that, wants, and their needs were that they simply wanted to survive."

That day at Umihotaru had played in Tommy's head so many times that it now read just as clear and concise as the pages within a book. And he remembered ...

"I have a visual," Tommy said, and he gripped the joystick with his clammy hand, preparing to fire.

The giant crustacean was now on top of Umihotaru and heading towards the massive tourist attraction at the heart of the man-made island. The amusement facility housed a five-story parking lot, along with restaurants, shops and a few scenic decks. Hell, they even had a stage for live music, and Tommy couldn't help but think how cool it'd be to get a gig there sometime. The bridge that looped around in order to lead traffic back to the island was flat out smashed and littered with cars. Patches of fire and smoke climbed to the sky as some of them had burst into flames under the weight of the mighty creature.

The rogue reached the main building and slammed its massive claw down on top of it!

BASH-KARAAAM!!

It sounded like sharp, metallic thunder, and the structure began to collapse as the monster crab began ripping and shredding it to pieces to get to the toy surprises inside. The dust and debris dissipated a bit, and as it did, the daikaiju spied what it was searching for ... breakfast. A large group of sightseers cowered in the corner of the rubble crying and holding each other tight. It moved in closer, and its shadow ascended over the screaming crowd as its monstrous body blocked out the sun. Then as the creature reached down to scoop them up in its huge claw, a few fell to their knees, and the rest covered their eyes!

SHOOM! SHOOM! SHOOM!

Three missiles slammed one after the other head-on into the rogue kaiju!

BOOSH! KA-BOOSH! BAM!

"Three direct hits!" Tommy shouted.

SCOTT pulled back on the second steering mechanism, and the FU2 fighter jet rocketed directly over the explosions! The missiles knocked its mutated ass back into the water, and it looked like they had saved the lives of several people, at least for now.

All at once, Tommy's fear dissipated, and he got that same feeling he'd get on stage once in a while. It was the one that made him feel like what he was doing really seemed to matter and that he was maybe even making a difference somehow. Tommy struggled with a lot of things, but the only thing that ever-made sense to him was his love for playing the guitar. Even after agreeing to Sir Jack's crazy rock star offer, he still wrestled with how saving the world on a regular basis was going to cut into his practice time. Tommy wasn't quite ready to be kicked out of the nest yet, and maybe that's exactly why they sent him along with SCOTT and the Twins. Maybe not, but he definitely knew one thing, it sure as hell wasn't to wear that stupid helmet and fire missiles at a big crab, because any eight-year-old with a Play station could've done that. More than likely, it was all for that one, brief little glimpse he was given, a glimpse that would last a lifetime.

After the FU2 blasted the rogue into the water, Tommy had seen the crowd below and the looks on their faces just as they flew over. He saw them cheer, scream, and applaud, but then he saw them weep, hug their children, and help each other to safety. That feeling he got on stage couldn't hold a candle to this; it was strong (if not stronger) than any lick or any lyric.

*It made his old life seem puny, and Tommy realized this
was something very, very big and very, very important.*

Dr. Takarada smiled and sighed at the same time. Of course
he remembered. Sometimes it's easier for others to see the
changes in us before we see them ourselves, and Takarada saw
a change in Tommy from that day on. It was big, yet subtle, and
Tommy's dream of becoming a famous (and rich) musical deity
slipped down a notch after that.

But the fact was, there was so much going on in Tommy's life
then, that much of it was nothing but a swirling circle of vertigo.
After all, it's not every day you're offered "The Golden God" rock
star package from some secret government agency. You know,
one that guarantees you fame and fortune in exchange for
selling your soul to rock and roll. He thought about what
brought him to Japan in the first place and dealing with one
sucky gig after another. Not to mention the deaths of his
bandmates Mark and Billy when a live house in Tokyo collapsed
in on them all. As a matter of fact, and Tommy would never
admit it, but he still blamed himself for their deaths. And finally,
both finding and losing Akira Akemi in the midst of it all broke
Tommy's heart in two. Yes, Takarada remembered all of it,
because he was there for all of it. He stood behind Tommy and
placed his hand on his friend's shoulder.

"You know, Thomas, as we go through life, things change. It
seems the only constant in life is that there are no constants, and
that change is not just a possibility, but truly inevitable. But how
we choose to change, and grow is entirely up to us. You've made
hard decisions in your life. You've also made life and death
decisions that many will never have to face. But no matter how
you look at it, you have turned into a fine man, and I couldn't be
any prouder of you even if you were my own son."

Tommy knew that. He'd known how Kyoshi Takarada felt
about him almost since day one when the good doctor took him
under his wing. Tommy started feeling a little better. Dr. T. just
seemed to have a knack for that very thing. Tommy had also
recognized how Takarada had been acting lately, he knew
something was consuming his mind, his every thought. He

decided to get out of his own head and see if he could lend an ear to his friend.

Tommy started, "Man, I hate this place," and Takarada couldn't help but nod his head in agreement. "I sure miss the base back at Fuji." Takarada again nodded but kept silent. Not that Takarada really cared, but his inner turmoil had increased dramatically since the E.I.O. acquired its new location. Tommy knew that too, he also knew Takarada was no idiot and couldn't help but feel Doctor T. was evading him, so he tried a different approach.

"Kyoshi, what was your father like? I know this sounds funny, but for some reason, I've always pictured him looking something like Jack, only Japanese." Takarada shuddered, then tilted his head slightly, a bit astounded at both Tommy's question and the thought of his father looking like a Japanese Jack. In all the years they had known each other, Tommy had never really asked these things of him. Takarada sat, sank deep into his chair and scratched his head, seeming eager for once to talk a little about himself and his life, something that was definitely not in his nature. Besides, Tommy had been pretty curious him-damn-self for quite some time now.

Hiroshi's Story

Hiroshi Takarada was an exceptional engineer, a brilliant man of amazing generosity and great character. However, he knew it was his son, Kyoshi, who was destined to change the very world upon which we live. He recognized this early on and made sure this talent, this gift that his young boy held, was nurtured and given every opportunity to grow. But it wasn't for selfish gain, it was because he knew what was coming, something big. While others laughed and called him crazy, claiming the danger had passed, Hiroshi knew. He also chose to remember, where so many others decided to forget. Because as he often stated, "A world that forgets its past is surely doomed to repeat it."

Hiroshi came into this world sometime in the early forties and it was only a few short years later that his parents would return to Tokyo from Japanese-occupied North Korea. The tides of World War II were changing and planting roots back in a devastated Japan simply felt like the right thing to do. Much of his country was in ruins, and the Takarada clan felt a need to return to the homeland and help rebuild.

Hiroshi's son, Kyoshi Takarada, never knew his grandparents. He didn't know or remember his mother very well either, as she passed away when he was still quite young. Hiroshi Takarada loved Kyoshi very much, having almost an "us against the world" kind of relationship with him. Hiroshi was a loving but stern father who forced Kyoshi to spend the majority of his time studying. While still in his teens, young Kyoshi excelled in every class he took, graduating from high school at only fourteen. He often didn't understand this never-ending need to be driven so hard but always obeyed his father. He loved his dad very much but would grow tired and weary, and often he felt so very alone. One of his greatest refuges was to look to the stars above the Tokyo skies and imagine building great ships and vehicles that could travel to space and deep beneath the sea. He would get lost in his own thoughts, and according to his dad, he would "dream the day away." Little did Hiroshi know those "daydreams" were the first cornerstones to becoming what his father wanted him to be.

At the slightest sound, Kyoshi would withdraw from the open window and frantically pull out his books, scattering them about his desk whenever he heard his dad coming down the hall. He would stare at the door and developed a habit of tapping his index finger incisively on his desktop as he waited for it to open. That was the giveaway, the tapping, and of course, his dad knew. Kyoshi would get a pat on the back and his father would sit with him and ask what he was thinking about. It was usually some crazy idea about endless, clean power or great cities built within mountains.

His dad would laugh and say, "Like within the great Fujisan!" And no, he wasn't mocking Kyoshi. As a matter of fact, he believed his son was the only person on earth that could ever pull off such a marvelous act of super-science and achievement. Hiroshi would smile and simply peer out over the lit-up building tops of his son's open window. It was a magnificent sight, too, cranes resurrecting inner skeletons of steel as far as the eye could see. If it was a night like tonight, clear and cloudless, he could even see the mighty Mount Fujisan majestically towering to the skies far off in the distance. Tonight, Kyoshi stared at Fujisan and dared to dream.

Hiroshi Takarada's demands of his son were indeed great, and he knew it. He also knew it was in the best interest of ... well, everybody. Hiroshi had been left with many scars, scars from a war-torn Japan, an even deeper scar that left him without parents, and for a while, left him without hope or faith of any kind. Hiroshi had never told his son his reasons for driving him so hard, but as the world continued to change and his fine hair began to gray, he decided it was time.

"I was so very young, and now it seems like nothing more or less than a terrible nightmare, but it still haunts my mind. The bright full moon melded with the tremendous fires, and all of the color was sucked out of the city except for the dancing bursts of flickering red. My father hurried a few steps ahead clearing a path through the disjointed crowd as we made our way to the shelter. We followed close behind, and I remember feeling so very hot even though it was November. The sweat dripped down from my head and found its way into my eyes. I tried to wipe away the sting, but my mother was holding my hand so tight that my feet were barely touching the ground as we ran.

Through the screams you could hear thunderous booms of what sounded like giant footsteps amid the explosions and echoing machine-gun fire coming from the bay area. Beneath it all the sirens wailed as artillery bursts went off in rapid succession. I wanted so badly just to wake up safe in my bed. However, this was real, and even though I wasn't all too sure of what we were running from, I knew war had returned to Japan.

Civil defense soldiers, emergency vehicles and police officers attempted to navigate the evacuees to safety while pleading and shouting to the crowds to, "Please stay calm and do not panic!" But it was quite the unreasonable request. Hell was coming, and it wasn't merely radio theater, a show on television or a picture in the papers. It was here, right in our own neighborhood, pounding at the front door.

Families pulled rickety wooden carts carried screaming children and drug the elderly towards the fictional safety of the higher ground that surrounded the Shinagawa train station. It was terrifying as well as all too familiar to many. Then, as the chaos mounted, the oncoming smoke melded with the dusk, swallowing all traces of anything resembling color.

We resided on the second floor of a small two-bedroom apato within a slim, five-story building on our block not far from Tokyo Bay. I knew something peculiar had been going on over the last week or so, but my parents were protecting me from all outside communication. I didn't really understand at the time but being that soon after the war I guess I can see now why they did it. For the most part, they kept me in my small room where our still unpacked boxes doubled as furniture. We had a radio, but my dad accidentally (yeah, right) severed its chord, so I couldn't have plugged it in even if I wanted to. What was happening around me could've been anything, and not knowing made it the scariest thing I could ever imagine.

Fear fueled my thoughts of yet another atomic blast going off as we scurried like scared rats into the sewers. I had no way of knowing; my parents never mentioned the bombings. It was something you simply didn't talk about. But sometimes the kids at school would tell me stories that their parents had told them. Even in the chaos I seemed to drift but was then pulled back to the harsh reality and truth of what was happening. I heard something I had never heard before, like the bellow of some giant, wounded creature. You could feel the pain within its body with every scream it made.

I was instantly out of my thoughts and back into the fast-flowing crowd when it came to an abrupt stop, and I stumbled over my parents as they hit the ground. The deafening sound drew me, and I looked straight up at something as it ripped its way through the building that stood above the shelter. It was big, and it was terrible, its lumbering body blending in with the smoke in the air and the black of night. For a brief second, I recall seeing the yellowish-red of its unsympathetic eyes as they cut through the haze like two beams from a lighthouse. It looked right at me, and that's all I remember. It was also the last time I ever saw my parents.

I woke up from a concussion-induced coma in a small military hospital a few miles outside of Tokyo some ten days later, left an orphan from a war I couldn't explain and didn't want to believe. I had survived, just another number in the endless stats of human wreckage, from something that was destined to be forgotten and destined to resurface in some way, shape or form."

***

Dr. Takarada's eyes glistened on the verge of tears, but he took a deep breath, regained his composure and held them back. "That is the story my father told me when I was a very young man. That is why he drove me as hard as he did. It is why I accepted this as my fate, my duty and my destiny, General Taylor."

Tommy didn't say a word as he seemed to ponder what had happened to Dr. Takarada's father, then after a brief pause, he finally replied, "Oh my God, that sounds so weird. You know what, just forget it. Let's just stick with Tommy." This made Kyoshi smile. He was happy there was still some of the "old, young" Tommy left. He didn't say it out loud but also thought that "General Taylor" sounded kind of funny, like someone who made breakfast cereal or something.

It had been a long afternoon, and Takarada decided that General Tay ... Tommy had helped him enough, so he changed the subject to something he had been wondering, or maybe for some reason needed to know. "Tommy, how long has it been since you have spoken to Nathan?" Tommy made a what-the-hell-does-that-have-to-do-with-anything kind of face before blurting out an angry, "Not nearly long enough!" Following it up with a quick and sharp, "Why?"

Takarada simply smiled and said, "I am just curious. I have not talked with him or Olivia in quite some time." Tommy just shook his head as he was, without a doubt, carrying a daikaiju-sized chip on his shoulder over his prior bandmate and ex-best friend and lead singer, Nathan Fox. Takarada looked at his watch and again changed the subject as he now knew what he needed to know.

"Tommy, don't you have a gig tonight?" Tommy looked down at his handless wrist and gasped, "Crap! I forgot!" Dr. T. picked Tommy's hand up from the desk and assured him that it would be ready for his big show at the local coffee house in Akiota tonight, without the use of duct tape.

Upon arriving at The Goku a few years back, Tommy made cute little promo packages and hit coffee houses all over Akiota and northern Hiroshima looking for gigs. Never anything too far out of the way, just places around the E.I.O.'s new makeshift and more than likely permanent base within Mount Gokurakuji.

No matter what happened in Tommy's life though, something that had always remained a constant was he couldn't, or wouldn't, stop playing guitar. It flowed in his veins like the organic thorium that ran through his robotic hand. It was also quite possible that's why he was pondering if he had maybe wasted his life in the E.I.O. It was something that Tommy often thought about, wondering, if maybe he could've made it on his own, without the Earth Intelligence Organization. These, however, were not new thoughts. Tommy had grown so much over the years, but it was obvious he still struggled with that whole "not knowing just how good things are" thing. Sure, he had suffered tremendous loss, but nowadays there wasn't anybody on planet Earth who hadn't. Tommy had many bouts with the ol' "coulda, shoulda, woulda," syndrome, when deep down he knew that there was no turning back after Umihotaru. Maybe that's why he also struggled with the whole, "I'm a General, I'm not a General," thing too. But he did know one thing, when the images of those people he saved would come into his mind, he was always reassured about his choices.

Tommy had done and sacrificed many things for the lives of others, but make no mistake about it, he was still no saint. The fact of the matter is that he had a bit of his own kaiju lurking around deep within him, one most of us are familiar with, the green-eyed monster.

Yup, in some ways, the superficial ways, Tommy was jealous of Nathan Fox. Even after leaving the E.I.O., Nathan went on to a brilliant solo career as a singer. He had become rock-and-roll royalty and donned his stardom like a long-flowing regal robe. So, while Nathan was playing to sold-out arenas, Tommy couldn't even get twelve freakin' people to come watch him play at a stupid coffee house. But as Dr. Takarada had pointed out to him many times, "Don't judge how you are inspiring people with music by the size of your audience." This was hard for Tommy as these little gigs brought in about the same amount of people as the early days of his former band, F-Bomb. But in all fairness, it'd probably be hard on anybody when you get accustomed to playing for thousands of people all over the world, or what was left of it.

Truth of the matter is that Tommy rarely even played electric nowadays, opting for acoustic fingerstyle and classical styles of guitar. Something he initially started doing for one reason and one reason only, stating, "I never want to have to trust my music in the hands of others ever again." So even though his playing had grown by leaps and bounds, his audience had shrunk by those same leaps and bounds. Tommy, however, usually didn't really care, as playing is what always mattered to him. Best yet, there was no more vampire sucking the life out of him. No more trying to figure out everything "musical" around him either, like lazy, drunk singers, sleezy managers, producers, angry club owners and such.

This whole Nathan thing though, it messed with him, and Tommy had no one but his ego to blame while these crazy, but surprisingly typical thoughts consumed him. "Freakin' Nathan Fox. He's still kickin' ass, sings great and looks amazing. What a loser." It was funny too, that since Tommy gained some weight, began wearing glasses, cut his hair off and started going by Thomas Taylor, most people didn't even know him as the once mega-huge rock star, Tommy Lynn Taylor. It was a little hard to believe, too. It was sort of like Clark Kent being unrecognizable as Superman until taking those dumb glasses off. Tommy wouldn't admit it, but he missed his red and blue jumpsuit, the one with the cape and the big "S" on it. Regardless though,

Superman suit or not, coffee house or arena, playing guitar was still what kept Tommy sane, and for better or worse, some things will simply never change.

Chapter 3

Message From Space

Over the last few months as Takarada went deeper and deeper into worry, he was having more and more trouble sleeping. Even though this was nothing unusual as of late, this time something was different. A sharp ring seared throughout his head, and after lying in bed for a while hoping it would simply go away, he abandoned the idea of sleep and forced himself to sit up. He put his left palm to his ear and pumped his hand like a plunger in an attempt to suck the noise out. It didn't help, and the pain was approaching unbearable as it grew louder with every passing second. Takarada tumbled out of bed from his quarters at The Goku (as most called the "not so" new E.I.O. base within Mount Gokurakuji) and made his way to the bathroom. He opened the mirrored medicine cabinet and, upon a quick inspection, opted for the limited selection of his liquor cabinet instead. Like a snake, his wrist twisted past the wine and grasped the unopened bottle of Johnny Walker. He had intended to give the scotch to Sir Jack next time their paths crossed, but that day never came.

He held the bottle and grimaced as both the piercing sound and the pressure grew to an unbearable level. The pain mounted and sliced like a sharp razor through his bloodstream to the rest of his body, and his arms became weak. After failing to open the bottle with his hands, he put it up to his mouth and cracked the seal with his teeth. Takarada never drank hard liquor but forced himself to take a healthy swallow in an attempt to ease the pain. He made a face as though he had just bit into an angry lemon, coughed, and the bottle slipped through his fingers. He anticipated the shatter but could only hear the painful ring over the bottle breaking as it collided with the hard floor. Takarada lifted his heels, and like a ballerina, stepped over the fresh shards of glass as he made his way towards the door. Something was definitely wrong, he knew he needed to get to the infirmary to get some relief from the growing ring and increasing pressure. He could barely speak and forced out a painful "Open!" Takarada's door creaked and slowly swished to the side. Standing just outside of it ready to kick it down was Tommy, also holding both his hands up to his head.

"You too?" Tommy grunted between his clenched teeth. Takarada tried to answer but instead fell to the floor in the hallway outside of his quarters. Tommy tried to catch him, but it was hard as he was also on the verge of passing out from the combination of sound and pain. He dropped to his knees clutching his head, and even in his weakened state still managed to eke out the words, "Code 54." The hallway erupted in red and white swiveling lights, and even though neither men could hear it, the accompanying siren wailed beneath the ring.

Fweet! Fweet! Fweet!

Takarada had passed out, and Tommy laid on the floor clutching the back of his head within his interlaced fingers. As Goku guards and medical officials arrived on the scene, Tommy thought he heard a voice, one he had not heard in quite some time. The words were barely audible, and he couldn't understand how it was capable of infiltrating the noise in his head, when in fact it was part of it. It was soft and shrouded within a distant echo that merely emphasized his thought that it must be coming from a million miles away. The pain was unimaginable, but Tommy still squeezed his eyes tight and strained to hear. He also figured he was either hallucinating, or that this was something big. So big that whoever or whatever was on the other end must have been reaching out from the furthest and deepest ends of space and time. A message from the very gods themselves! It was small and barely recognizable, but Tommy hung on, and even though the pain was excruciating, his resolve was stronger, and he listened, and he waited …

"Duuuuuuuuude?"

Tommy for a brief moment forgot about the horrendous noise in his head, and his eyes sprang open just before he passed out.

***

The music came to an abrupt stop, and all went black to the screams of almost twenty thousand people. A bright yellow beam appeared from high above and expanded in circumference as the rumble of a low growling Moog Synthesizer swelled to an arena-sized volume. It was reminiscent of that retro sci-fi sound from the eighties that John Carpenter used in *Halloween* and *The Thing*. Only it was loud, really loud, and the note was long and also kind of creepy.

"*BWAAAAAAAAAAAAAAAA*"

The lone bright light expanded to a perfect circle about fifty feet in diameter and cast down upon the giant wavy curtains that draped from the trussing behind the drums. The synthesizer moaned, rising in parallel with the growing noise of the crowd when it finally crescendoed to a complete stop. All went black, then all went silent, but just long enough for the bright light to reappear, only now with something occupying the inside of it.

From within the great light, a large silhouette of a lanky, long-haired lad with something like dinosaur fins and a spiked tail appeared! The dark figure also had its hand stretched high in the air and was clutching what appeared to be a microphone. The audience roared! Yeah, it looked pretty weird, but they knew exactly what it was and what was coming!

"Good evening, Maddison Square Garden! Let's Go!"

The drummer clicked his sticks, and with the strike of the guitar's first power chord, the band kicked in to its first song of the evening, Superstar! It was spectacular and the stage ignited in lights and explosions as the back curtains dropped revealing eight giant jumbotron screens proudly illuminating the name, Nathan Fox!

The crowd exploded, and before they could even catch their breath, Nathan shot up through the thick, illuminated fog that blanketed the floor of the stage! He strutted, grabbed his microphone and started spinning it like a propellor by its cable. For a brief second, Nathan was taken back to his earliest days at the E.I.O. when he and Tommy walked onto a "real deal" rehearsal stage for the first time. He remembered spinning a mic then, almost killing somebody after the cable snapped. It was a good feeling though, and he also remembered Tommy showing him how to use duct tape to adhere the microphone to the cable, stating, "This is how Roger Daltrey does it." Nathan pulled the cable tight retracting the microphone, clutched it with his right hand, put it up to his mouth and belted out the first chorus ...

You ask me and I'll tell you
From the back of a long black car
I was born to rock, got boots to knock
I'm a superstar!

Since his solo career began, Nathan had a tradition of opening his shows with "Superstar". True, it was a song originally recorded by his old band Vinyl Crush, but he always thought it set the perfect tone for the evening. So even though Vinyl Crush was no more, the music could still live on from the band's ex-lead singer. At least that's how Nathan looked at it. After-all, he did write the majority of their lyrics.

The song ended in a succession of exploding flash pots, and the stage went pitch black at Maddison Square Garden to the roar of the thunderous crowd. Nathan loved playing the "Garden" as New York City was one of the few places not devastated by the wars of the last ten years. Actually, there were still quite a few places to play in North America and even the U.K. as well as Japan. Sure, things weren't perfect, but were they ever? It also seemed the more the planet fell on hard times, the more people begged for entertainment. But this was nothing new, probably dating as far back as prehistoric man playing instruments made from turtle shells to forget about their best friend being mauled by a seven-foot sabretooth tiger. Another

reason Nathan enjoyed New York City was that it was where he lived now, having moved there shortly after leaving the Earth Intelligence Organization. He figured that since both his dad and California were gone, maybe he and his new wife could make a go of it in the Big Apple. And that's just what he did, Nathan and his new bride, Olivia.

Nathan had been touring solid over the last six years and even managed to release three albums within that time. His latest record, however, was his favorite as he felt it best represented his almost fanatic feelings for Jim Morrison. He also loved the new album's name and its title song, "Son of The Lizard King." Not to mention the cover artwork that featured a silhouette of himself within a yellow circle, sporting dinosaur fins and a spiked tail as he held a microphone high up into the air. "Son of The Lizard King" also just happened to be his next song. Nathan curled his upper lip and grinned like the Cheshire Cat himself, basking in the heat of multiple spotlights that lit him up high above the masses like some sort of golden god! The audience roared and chanted "Lizard King! Lizard King!" over and over, and just as Nathan went into the first word, an abrupt and loud ring pierced his skull.

***

Dr. Takarada eased one eye open and scowled knowing that he was waking up in the E.I.O.'s infirmary. He couldn't quite remember what had happened, but the hospital bed and flickering florescent light above made it pretty obvious. Not thinking, he sat up rather fast, only to be pulled back by the IV tubes that had him chained down. He was still in a little pain, but the sharp ringing and pressure in both his and Tommy's heads had disappeared. Besides, it seemed now there was an even more pressing matter at hand.

He squinted and saw Tommy in the next bed over, along with Commander Jones hovering just above him. Takarada had such disdain for Jones and growled, "Kare wa totemo kimyōna me o shite imasu." under his breath.

Tommy followed Takarada's lead and soon woke up as well, only to a pair of mismatched eyes about two inches from his face. Tommy let out a squeamish "Yeesh." and Commander Jones backed off and stood erect clasping his hands behind his back. Tommy always thought Jones looked like a new wave Gestapo agent, with his long black leather jacket, pants tucked into his boots and gray tinted hair piled up uniquely high for a man of his age.

Sort of a cross between Morrisey from The Smiths and Fearless Leader from Bullwinkle. He was tall, tailored, clean shaven and trim, the complete opposite of Sir Jack. And maybe that's why both Tommy and Takarada disliked him, because he simply wasn't ... Jack. They also thought Jones was hard to read. He had this aloof, smug, too cool for school kind of thing going on and even if he wasn't that way, he sure looked it.

Like his predecessor though, Commander Jones did speak with a British accent. However, it was much more refined than Sir Jonathan's Liverpudlian inflection. "General Taylor," he asked, "do you remember, or know what happened to you and the doctor?" Tommy was also wired up to about ten machines, so Commander Jones summoned a nurse over who loosened his tubes and helped him to sit up. Tommy was still a little fuzzy, and Jones literally breathing down his neck with his rancid onion breath didn't help much either, but he did his best to focus.

"General Taylor," Jones repeated. "Do you remember or know what happened last night?"

Tommy sat up even further, pushing himself up upon the bed's mattress with the heels of his hands. He smacked his mouth a couple of times as he was suffering from a case of the "zactlys" (that horrid condition where your mouth tastes "zactly" like your ass) and grabbed the bottled water sitting next to him on the nightstand. Tommy downed the majority of it and poured the remaining drops into his palm, dropped the empty bottle and rubbed his face with his wet hands. He took a deep breath, squinted and looked up as though he were searching for the answer above his head. Commander Jones began to grow impatient and ordered his general to "Please, spit it out, Taylor."

General Taylor quickly went all Tommy, giving Jones that ever popular, "Dude, chill, I'm in a freakin' hospital bed after almost dying from possibly the worst migraine ever known to man," kind of look. Of course, he didn't actually think he almost died, but he did take a much longer time to answer Jones for the sole purpose of irritating him. But now it seemed that everybody else in the infirmary also wanted to know as their ears were all pointed towards Tommy. He looked around the room, thought long and hard, then finally answered …

"Titties and kaka."

Having no patience whatsoever for this, or any kind of juvenile foolishness, Commander Jones just glared at Tommy in complete disbelief. Jones then looked in Takarada's direction and the good doctor quickly closed his eyes and pretended to be asleep once again proving he was the smartest one in the room. The commander stood up and turned his wrist to look at his gold, Longines watch. He didn't even have an ounce of the patience Jack did but chose to compose himself rather than get angry. Jones cleared his throat and in typical old school English fashion, ordered General Taylor to get out of bloody bed, put on adequate attire and meet him in his office for a private meeting. Sure, Tommy was groggy and wasn't quite himself, but he still wasn't sure why he said what he said. It's like opening your mouth and the worst thing that could ever come out is exactly what comes out. Either way, he felt compelled to follow his commanding officers order and after his nurse yanked a few tubes out of him, that's just what he did.

Chapter 4

Suzy

With his tail tucked firmly between his legs, Tommy held on to what was left of his butt and beat a hasty retreat from Jones's office after their little private soiree. There was no doubt, he was getting pretty damn sick of Commander Jones and his strict by the book policies, not to mention the constant ass chewings. "Sure, there's protocol, and he's entitled to run his ship how he sees fit. But does he have to be such a dick about it? I don't think he believed a damn word I said." Tommy growled to himself as he limped to the sanctity of his quarters. This particular problem, though, wasn't anything new as Tommy was never one to follow the rules anyhow, then or now. "Yes, I've made mistakes," he thought, and then his ego countered that with a, "But I've also saved a lot of lives, and some even say I've saved the world, not once, but two times!" Truthfully, though, what it really boiled down to was Tommy's tiresome problems with anybody in any kind of authoritative position, and of course, his stupid pride.

Now don't get me wrong, over the years Tommy had made amazing progress with those crazy voices in his head. No, not the ones that tell you to shoot the president or that you're God. Just the ones that tell you things like you're not good enough or that you'll never amount to anything, those kinds. Tommy had learned that with proper medication, therapy, diet and yoga, that he could rise above anything or any situation. But when your business is saving the world, you see a lot of shit, and Tommy had. And who could ever stick to a strict lifelong regimen of fish and leafy greens … uhm, no one. And the only thing he liked about yoga were the hot babes in those skin-tight pants. But all in all, Tommy had learned not to believe every foul thing his head told him anymore, and just that alone had made a world of difference. Okay, so he wasn't perfect, and maybe his ego did mess with him once in a while. But as Nathan used to tell him, "Tommy, you may not yet be the person you want to be, but Dude, you certainly ain't that guy you used to be either." Such wisdom to come from freakin' Nathan Fox. Heck, Nathan even carried around a business card that said that very thing, well sort of.

No, this more than likely had something to do with the arrival of a brand-new board member on the committee within his head, and its name was aging. Tommy was almost forty now and the inner battle between General Thomas Taylor; rock star, Tommy Lynn Taylor; and respected fingerstyle guitarist, Thomas Taylor, was waging. Most would say it was probably just a mild case of the mid-life crises, but with Tommy there always seemed to be more to it. He was also viewing every single stupid aspect of his past with a freakin' high-powered microscope, scrutinizing every little mistake he ever made. He also thought it was kind of peculiar that these feelings only seemed to flare up when he was speaking with Commander Jones. At least that's what that damn committee was telling him. But in all fairness to Jones, he viewed Tommy as nothing but a total smart-ass, and it'd been that way since day one. If it were up to Jones, Taylor probably wouldn't even be a general. However, it was one of Sir Jack's last recommendations before retiring. But when your commanding officer doesn't think much of you in the first place, it's usually not a good idea to respond to him with the words, "titties and kaka." Even if it was the right answer, Tommy was becoming more and more convinced that he and Dr. T must've had some bad sushi, and he decided to put it out of his mind.

Before meeting with Jones his headache was just lingering, but now it had kicked up a few levels to the verge of pounding.

The thought of a cigarette, a strong drink, maybe picking a little guitar and spending some good, quality alone-time with Suzy seemed to ease his troubled head.

Tommy stood at the door of his quarters, adjusted his lapel and pulled the wrinkles out of his jacket. One thing was for sure, the E.I.O. uniforms looked pretty cool, and Tommy always felt a bit movie-starrish in his: a sleek, long, dark coat with gold buttons down the middle, a slimming belt on the outside and a tieless shirt with a high mandarin collar underneath it all. It was kind of a cross between Kato on the old *Green Hornet* show and Neo from *The Matrix*. Tommy often thought a blaster hanging low on his left side would be the cherry on top, but Commander Jones would never allow something as untailored as that. Instantly Tommy's thoughts went back to Jones, and he couldn't help but shrug as he soon discovered he was, once again, wasting valuable brain space on the guy that bugged him so much. So he shook it off, thought about Suzy and spoke the magic words, "Open please." His door staggered sideways, and he practically sang her name as he stepped in.

"Oh Soooooooozie, I'm home."

Like a sultry high-stepping showgirl, Suzy pranced out from the dark of their bedroom, and Tommy sighed. It was obvious that she'd been sleeping, but it didn't seem to matter much. Her eyes were so big, brown and mesmerizing that Tommy was an absolute slave to them. She also had a knack of somehow sensing when Tommy had had a bad day, and she ran to him. Tommy held her tight and nothing else seemed to matter anymore. He looked deep into those seductive eyes, brushed her hair back and they collapsed together onto the couch. Tommy held Suzy even closer and with her mouth almost upon his, he giggled as her long tongue waggled a symphony of saliva all over his blissful mug. Tommy lifted Suzy up above his chest and the weight of her big head brought her face to his. If a man could purr, that's exactly what he would've done, and he started talking like a baby as he rubbed his nose against hers.

"Who's a good girl? You are Suzy Woozie! That's right, you are!" Tommy pulled her up to his face, put his mouth up to her short, pancake-tan hair and proceeded to blow a big, wet raspberry on her witto tum tum. Suzy howled in total ecstasy! Tommy was in the moment. He wasn't thinking about Jones, the past, or the future. The only thing he was thinking about was Suzy and the love he felt for her, and if he could've bottled up that feeling and sold it, he'd've been a kabillionaire. It seems that we're ALL looking for relief from our past mistakes, and sometimes we even build a future of fear in accordance with those very blunders. And Tommy was no stranger to his share of mistakes. As a matter of fact, his most recent one being that he had neglected to tell his voice operated door to close.

A gasp of, "Oh my God" came from the hallway, and just before Tommy could order his door to "Please Close," a voice interrupted him. "Damn, dude, be sure to name the first puppy after me." Suzy jumped off of Tommy's chest, snarled and ran up and sniffed the lower leg of Tommy's uninvited guest. The hair on her back stood up, and she growled, reared back, and then in an eloquent voice promptly told the intruder to get bent.

"And it talks too!" was the quick response and Nathan Fox made his entrance from the low lights of the hallway into the yellowish glow that illuminated Tommy's quarters. As Tommy laid there on the couch, he actually seemed excited, for maybe a second. "No way, Nathan, is that you?" But before Nathan could respond, that happy, excited feeling soured, and soured fast. "Just what in the hell are you doing here? What's it been, about eight freakin' years? What, you and Olivia have another fight or something?"

"No, Olivia and I didn't have a fight," Nathan hissed back, sounding more like a spoiled three-year-old than a multi-millionaire rock star. If there's truly any difference.

Nathan opened his mouth to speak, but instead of the usual garbage Tommy was used to, he gained his composure and politely stated, "No, Tommy, Olivia's here too. She's just taking care of a little business first." Tommy raised his right eyebrow and said, "Wow, I'm impressed. Working those stupid 12-steps of Triple A must be having some actual kind of impact on you beca..." Tommy stopped hard on his words. Then, looking just like his witto Suzy-woozy, he squinted his eyes and stared Nathan down. "You ARE still clean, right?"

Nathan smirked, reached into his pocket and with his thumb, flicked a silver-dollar-sized coin in Tommy's direction. Tommy caught it but didn't need to look at it to know what it was. It was one of those medallions from triple A that you get for staying clean. He also remembered Nathan's dad had one too. As much as they had been fighting over the last ten years or so, Tommy still couldn't be prouder of his oldest friend. He looked at both sides of the bronze medal and saw Nathan had been clean for over nine years now. Tommy got a slight lump in his throat but didn't say a word, maybe because he was speechless, or maybe because if he had talked, he would've started to bawl. So instead, he stood up, and like a good general, he nodded in approval and handed Nathan back the medallion. Nathan smiled. "By the way Tommy, it's not Triple A, it's just A.A."

Tommy laughed out loud, "Not with the way you drank!" And just like that, after almost six years of silence, no words, no calls, no nothing, it was, for better or worse, as though they had never been apart. It was also pretty obvious that as much as Tommy and Nathan hated each other, they loved each other more.

Nathan joined Tommy on the couch with Suzy sitting in the middle. She still wasn't quite sure of how to take Nathan Fox, so she jumped down and disappeared back into the bedroom. Tommy just sighed, and in a bit more of a pleasant tone, again asked Nathan why he and Olivia were at The Goku.

Nathan was still wide-eyed and fixated on Suzy as she strutted back into the black of Tommy's bedroom. "Oh no, General Taylor," he said with a bit of a funny emphasis on the word, general. "Not 'til you tell me all about your new girlfriend." Of course, Nathan was referring to Suzy. Funny thing though, Tommy had no problem telling Nathan about Suzy, he just didn't appreciate the condescending tone when he'd referred to Tommy as General Taylor. It did two things: one, he felt it was a total lack of respect, and coming from Nathan, it probably was, and two, it had been quite obvious Nathan didn't think Tommy's career move to go full time with The E.I.O. was a good decision. So, in spite of their little happy-ass reunion, Tommy's committee held a quick board meeting in his brain, and the fact that Nathan made him again question his life choices (even if he didn't) irritated him.

Tommy's lips tightened into a sneer, and he fired back in a very subtle way. Standing up, he headed towards the quaint little kitchen in his quarters, "Sure, I'll tell you all about Suzy, but first I need a beer." Then Tommy went pure evil on Nathan and asked his friend with nine years clean if he'd like one too.

Nathan just laughed and shouted to Tommy as he walked away, "You're still such a dick. That's cold man." Tommy grabbed a beer, turned and kicked the fridge door shut with the back of his heel, placed his index finger on the pull tab and gave it a little tug.

SPLOOOOOSH!

He then chugged about half of the can, let out an "Ahhhhh ...," then wiped his mouth. "Yeah, it's cold ... but not as cold as this beer," capping it all off with a monstrous kaiju-level belch like only Tommy could do.

"Buuuuuuuuuuuuuuuuuuuuuuurp"

All Nathan could do was crack up, and when he did, Tommy forgot all about being irritated and cracked up too. As he laughed, he took another swig, but the frosty beverage seemed to find its way down the wrong tube. Tommy started coughing, then he started gagging, "Cack! Cack! Cack!" Nathan's eyes began to tear up, "Good Lord Man, can I get you something? You sound like a damn chicken!"

Tommy tried to clear his throat and cacked out a, "No ... I ... Cack! ... I ... Cack! Got this ... Cack-Cack!" He then reached into the side pocket of his super-cool General's jacket and pulled out a pack of smokes. Nathan was stunned to silence, and anytime Nathan is left speechless, that's a mighty tall feat.

"I thought you quit!" Nathan blurted out two octaves higher than normal.

"I did," Tommy responded with the cigarette hanging from his bottom lip.

Nathan had a slight aha moment. "I get it, you're just gonna' *Barretta* it," a term Tommy and Nathan used to use when it came to sucking on unlit cigarettes.

Tommy pulled out his Zippo from another pocket, and when he opened it, it made that metal clink sound that's so unique to those lighters. In regard to "Baretta-ing" the cig, Tommy reassured Nathan with a well thought out, "Uh-Huh," lit the cigarette and proceeded to inhale the smoke deep into his lungs.

"Holy Flirkin Snit!" Nathan shouted. "How ...? What ...? Since when can you even smoke in here? And what's with the AC being on the fritz, the fully stocked bar and beers in the fridge? Man, this place has really gone downhill."

Tommy just nodded and exhaled a long beam of thick, white smoke like the devastating breath of some sort of monster. He sat down in the chair next to the couch and, remembering he had a headache, rubbed his eyes with his thumb and index finger. He pulled the cigarette from his mouth and tapped the long ash into his now empty beer can.

"So, you wanna' know all about my new girlfriend, huh? Well, first off, she's not that new. She's already over five years old, and I guess in dog years, makes her almost my age." Tommy couldn't help but throw a little zinger of guilt in Nathan's direction. "Not that you know much about the last five years of my life." Nathan got up, walked out of the room and started rummaging through the fridge for something to eat. From the kitchen you could hear the rustling of drawers and the clanking of silverware, and in a loud voice he stated, "Yeah, but that ain't no ordinary dog."

Nathan returned to the couch along with a peanut butter (the crunchy kind) sandwich and a warm bottled water and waited to hear more.

"You're right. Suzy is no ordinary dog. She was a gift from Doctor Takarada," and that's all it took. Nathan wasn't so perplexed anymore, and Tommy continued. "She's a lot like SCOTT, an android powered by organic thorium. Only a whole lot cuter."

A montage of memories played in both Nathan and Tommy's minds at the mention of SCOTT's name. Nathan also remembered that, android or not, SCOTT was the closest thing to a friend that Tommy had after arriving at The E.I.O. all those years ago. Nathan thought about the time he walked in on

Tommy while SCOTT was holding him in his arms as he was helping him learn to walk again.

"Wow!" Nathan smirked. "Seems it's twice now I've busted you doing questionable acts with one of Takarada's robots! Is there something you need to tell me?"

Tommy ignored Nathan and went on.

"It was late, and I found her outside after playing a coffee house in Hatsukaichi." Nathan didn't say anything, but the thought of Tommy playing for about six people at some coffee house in the middle of nowhere just didn't sit right in his gut. Tommy didn't notice and just kept talking. "I don't know what the hell happened to her, but she was pretty beat up and bleeding. I figured something must have attacked her. She was wearing a heart-shaped dog tag so I figured she must belong to someone. I tried to pick her up, but she was so terrified, she wouldn't let me near her. So, I reached into my "to go" bag and lured her in with a leftover piece of karaage. Before she could even eat it, she went cold in my arms. I read her little tag. It said Suzy, and I damn near cried. I thought for sure she was dead, but if she wasn't maybe Doctor T. could do something for her. So I slipped off my guitar backpack, she fit right into its little accessory pouch, and I brought her back to The Goku."

Nathan pictured Tommy walking with his backpack guitar case and a little doomed doggy head sticking out of the accessory pouch. He was on the edge of his seat, and upon getting all verklempt he demanded to know, "What happened next?"

"Well as you know, Takarada couldn't rebuild SCOTT after our last mission, and since all of you decided to take off and leave me here, I guess Doctor T. sensed I was feeling a little abandoned, so he ..."

Nathan wiped his eyes, cut Tommy off and went on a bit of a rant, "Whoa, wait a minute! What do you mean we left you here? We were all psyched to put the band back together! YOU were the one that said no. You were the one that went off about some stronger life-calling or something." Nathan paused, looking like he was about to get angry or maybe even take a swing at Tommy, but he didn't, opting for a deep breath instead. "The only times I went solo, Tommy, was because I had to. I never wanted to do any of this whole music thing without you, but I still wanted to do it, even when you didn't. That stupid golden package The E.I.O. offered us was great, and yes, we were desperate. But did you ever stop to wonder if we could've made it on our own? I've told you this before. If you didn't constantly have your head so far up your ass, you'd know these things."

Tommy's face started to heat up, and completely forgetting that he was talking about Suzy, he exhaled the last puff of his second cigarette out his nose. But the thing that really frustrated Tommy was that he knew deep down, or maybe not so deep down, Nathan was right.

"Nathan just doesn't get it," Tommy thought, and he started to think of all the reasons "WHY" Nathan was so wrong. "He just doesn't understand the level of loss and the sacrifices I've had to make." However, somewhere in the midst of Tommy playing his own personal victim card in his mind, he jumped up from his chair and went from thinking to yelling.

"All you've ever cared about is yourself! You've never given a frog's fat ass about anybody unless it was about getting whatever you wanted!" Tommy went into a complete rage and with both hands, grabbed Nathan by the collar pulling him up from the couch. Without thinking, Nathan sideswiped Tommy at his ankles with his right leg, and Tommy fell on his butt. Nathan assumed a fighting posture and reminded Tommy of the fringe benefits of being married to a fourth degree, black-belted, ex-E.I.O. agent for so long.

"And that's another thing!" Tommy hollered, "You didn't even invite me to the freakin' wedding!"

Nathan sighed and lowered his arms, and his guard. "I didn't think you'd come."

And without hesitation, Tommy fired back. "I wouldn't have, but that's beside the point! You could've at least invited me." And while on his back from the floor, Tommy followed it up with a blow to Nathan's privates.

Nathan collapsed into the fetal position, and as he laid there in pain, the cavalry rushed out of the bedroom barking and commenced to chewing up the cuff of his pants.

Tommy just laid there in pain, and Nathan (who was clearly about to blow chunks) tried to shake Suzy off while simultaneously holding onto his package. It was pretty pathetic. It was also then that the door to Tommy's quarters swished open and standing there in the entrance was none other than Mrs. Laughs herself!

Olivia pushed her glasses up and surveyed the scene. "Un-freak-in-be-leviable ... You two are still ab-so-lute morons, aren't you? I don't know why this should even surprise me." Nathan forgot about his boys because he knew that whenever Olivia started separating her words into tiny pieces, whatever she was mad about would far exceed any physical pain.

Words weren't gonna work, not this time, so Olivia just squatted down at the knees and snapped her finger a few times. Nathan responded with a timid, "Coming, dear," and tried to pull himself up. Olivia moaned. "Not you, genius, the dog."

Suzy instantly let go of Nathan's pant leg, hightailed it into Olivia's arms and she started talking like Tommy. "Who's a good witto doggy-woggy."

Tommy picked himself up and sat himself down at one end of the couch, and Nathan did the same only at the other side. Olivia, while still holding Suzy, plopped down between them, and the four of them just sat there. It seemed like an eternity, and Olivia couldn't stand the awkward silence.

"Soooo, Tommy, how you doing? Long time no see. I can't believe you're a general! Wow. Good for you ... Good for you." Tommy just grunted, turned and pulled Suzy out of Olivia's arms and held onto her like a pouting, selfish child. She then turned to Nathan, her husband, and asked, "Soooo, how'd it go with Tommy, hun'?" Nathan also grunted, but at least he replied.

"I'm not really sure. We fought, we made up, I met his dog, we fought, made up again, I knocked Tommy down, and he kicked me in the nads. We both wound up on the floor, Suzy attacked me, then you walked in. Basically, it was just like old times."

Olivia pushed up her glasses, then leaned over to scratch the witto doggy-woggy's head, and Tommy pulled Suzy just out of her reach. "Yup," Olivia grumbled, "just like old times."

Tommy was about to say something not so profound but was interrupted by the blinking of the egg-shaped light next to his door. He seemed even further irritated and, looking up from the couch, mumbled something about Jones, Grand Central Station and freakin' Nathan Fox before instructing his door to, "Open please." The door jerked, came out about six inches and stopped, allowing Takarada just enough space to slip in sideways.

It was apparent his head still hurt, as for a second, Takarada thought he was hallucinating when he looked over to see Nathan, Olivia, Tommy and Suzy all sitting upon the couch. He'd had a hunch they might be showing up, but not being agents anymore, was surprised at how fast they had arrived at The Goku. Takarada extended greetings to both of them, first with a bow, then a three-way hug. "I knew you would be coming," he admitted, "But how did you get here so fast?"

Nathan broke away, "It's easy, Doc, when you're rich as shit."

Takarada backed up, bowed for a second time and with his thick Japanese accent, responded, "Yes, yes. Forgive me Nathan-san, I forgot that you are rich as shit." Nathan grinned from the side of his mouth and decided, now that Takarada was here, it was time to get down to business.

"I'm going to assume, Tommy, that both you and Dr. T. know what happened last night? I mean my head hasn't pounded like that since I woke up after a night of debauchery and Drano. Man, I thought I was having a stroke on stage in front of an arena full of screaming people. I wouldn't have thought too much of it either, after all, what a way to go! But I could have sworn I heard what sounded like a thousand voices asking for help. But here's the kicker, Olivia was also rushed to the hospital at the same time for the very same thing."

Tommy looked past Olivia and glared at Nathan, "That's why you're here? Why didn't you say something?" and Nathan reminded him that it had slipped his mind after being kicked in the nards and all. Tommy smiled at the thought but also knew something had to be up. "Yeah, that's exactly what happened to me and Kyoshi! But when I told Jones, he either A, didn't believe me or B, thought I was out of my mind." Then Nathan added, "Or C, he just thought you were being your usual dick self."

Tommy quietly replied, "There's that too." Tommy paused for a second. "I know he thought I was being a smart-ass, but I can't seem to shake this whole titties and kaka thing." Nathan almost exploded.

"Me too!" he shouted. "Titties and kaka! Oh. My. God. Titties and kaka! Just what the hell does that mean?" Dr. Takarada tapped his index finger against his chest and nodded to himself as he thought. He squeezed his eyes shut, maybe trying to get more brain power, and whispered over and over, "Titties and kaka ... titties and kaka ... titties and ..." He stopped and his eyes burst wide open.

"Aramu Muru!" he exclaimed. Tommy and Nathan had absolutely no idea what he was talking about, and Takarada turned to the obvious higher intelligence in the room, again exclaiming, "Aramu Muru ... Gateway of the Gods!"

Olivia gasped when it hit her and lit up upon making the connection. "Of course, Gateway of the Gods!" She looked at Tommy and Nathan, and they grunted like cavemen not knowing what either Takarada or Olivia were talking about. She sighed out an "Ugh," pulled her phone out from her back pocket and talked into it, "Gateway of the Gods." They all hovered around Olivia's screen, waited for the spinning beach ball of doom to disappear and then ... they waited some more. "Man," she said, "You guys got horrible service here." And before anybody could further comment, a small voice responded ...

"Aramu Muru or Gateway to the Gods was discovered in the early 1990s. It is believed to be an abandoned Incan construction project used for paranormal or alien teleportation. It is located in Peru at Lake Titicaca."

"Holy crap!" Tommy shouted, and all at once they knew. Almost like telepathy, they all realized what this was about and the significance of this truly important and esteemed task. Tommy added, "We gotta' go, and I mean like right now! Door open, please!" Tommy's door jerked out, again stopping around the halfway point. And just like that, they were off. Almost as though they had been summoned to the gate by the very gods themselves, and one by one, they squeezed through the small crack of Tommy's broken door.

Chapter 5

YETI Institute

In the early morning hours from northern Nepal amidst the Himalayas, a squadron of the world's largest radio telescopes began to illuminate every screen within the Yeti Institute. It was at 0300 hours when a signal from beyond the orbit of Neptune seemed to burst right through the tremendous, icy objects within the Kuiper Belt.

Feet scrambled amidst the alarm as unbelieving scientists and astronomers resorted to paper and pencil to double-check the signal. Eyes widened and jaws dropped as the truth rang louder than the eerie 1420-megahertz frequency that was dominating the control room. Even with the extraordinary circumstances of the last decade, the question, "Is there life beyond earth?" had still yet to be answered ... at least honestly. Then, when California tumbled into the sea, SETI went down with it, and in the aftermath, nobody really seemed to care anymore if E.T. existed or not. Plain and simple, there was far too much going on down here to be worried about what was going on up there. And maybe that was a mistake.

There was also the chance that this new research facility in Asia was somehow experiencing some sort of glitch. After all, it had been almost fifty years since any kind of interstellar radio waves even registered. Now it seemed as though that too had been all but forgotten, just more theories and useless hot air wrapped up in a vast conundrum of hydrogen. But one thing they did know, they needed to be at least one hundred and ten percent convinced before going all Chicken Little to the rest of the world.

The Yeti institute was only a few years old and had nowhere near the popularity of its predecessor. It was much smaller, a million times more secretive and only consisted of a few of the brightest minds from all over the still-populated areas of the planet. Similar to The E.I.O., they were funded through individual anonymous entities, companies and even some countries. But (and also like The E.I.O.), much of their funding had been cut off and redirected to the world's rebuilding campaigns. And though that's probably the way it should be, it's always a good idea to have a plan "B" so to speak. Maybe somebody keeping an eye on the flock just in case a wolf or, Heaven forbid, something much worse, should decide to crash the party. One thing was sure though, neither organization could afford a mistake, especially one of such magnitude. One more budget cut would probably mean the end of the road for organizations such as The Yeti Institute and The E.I.O., leaving the third rock from the Sun basically defenseless. But if it were true, a quick response was in order, because something was heading to Earth and fast.

***

Commander Jones's side-swiping door seemed to work just fine and Takarada led the way into his office as Tommy, Nathan and Olivia followed close behind. It seemed they had a better idea as to what happened to them and desperately needed the commander to listen. At least this time Dr. T. was leading the troops, and when anything involved Doctor Kyoshi Takarada, Jones, along with most people, were far more apt to pay attention.

Doctor T. bowed deep to the commander who was perched behind his desk. Jones was just hanging up his bright red James Bond phone, but before Takarada or anybody else could say a word, he revealed the nature of the call. He placed his palms on the edge of his desk and pushed himself up. "Well, that was quite an unusual call I just finished from The Yeti Institute."

Nathan eased over close to Tommy, and even though Jones was still talking, he whispered a question to him from the corner of his mouth. "The Yeti Institute? What the hell is that and what does Yeti stand for?"

Tommy whispered back from the corner of *his* mouth, "It doesn't stand for anything. They literally converted an old shack up in the Himalayas that for a while was used to search for and study abominable snowmen."

For some reason Nathan thought this was quite funny, and even though his next question was legitimate, he couldn't help but snort it out. "You mean like ... Bigfoot?"

Tommy, not feeling like another ass chewing, elbowed Nathan in his side and hissed out a quiet, "Shut up, man." And of course, Nathan just kept going, only louder.

"Folks, we have Earth-shattering information coming in from the prestigious Institute of Sasquatch! We've captured a hairy, twelve-foot alien from the planet Hoth, hell-bent on world domination! It's true! How could it not be! Oh, and something even more ground-breaking, after an hour of tiresome research, we at Yeti have also discovered that Bumbles bounce!"

The Commander looked fast in their direction, and even though Tommy thought Nathan's "Bumbles bounce" comment was kind of funny, he wasn't about to push it. Jones gave both men a dirty look and simply continued.

"It seems, like all of you, The Yeti Institute (Jones put a strong emphasis on the word Yeti) has been picking up strange frequencies themselves. They are claiming that something has broken through the Kuiper Belt and is heading to Earth at around 80% the speed of light. They are not quite sure, but are speculating that whatever it is, it must have come through the Oort Cloud from a point unknown in Alpha Centauri."

Nathan was about to make another dumb comment but soon found himself fearing for his life. Not from Commander Jones, but from Olivia. Just before Nathan could say anything else about Yeti, Bigfoot or freakin' Bumbles, she mumbled something that only he could decipher, and he clammed right up. Olivia pushed her glasses up and asked Jones what Yeti thought it might be. Jones explained they had no idea, and though it was quite large, it wasn't of E.L. size.

"Okay, again with the funny words! Just what in the hell does E.L. mean?" Nathan demanded.

Takarada softly replied, "Extermination Level."

"Well then, with whatever this is and not being E.L. size, that's good news. Right?" Nathan asked, and Takarada again responded.

"I would think anything not of extermination level to be a very goodly thing Nathan-san."

Even though Takarada's English was not perfect, very goodly was still enough for the entire room to let out an enormous sigh of relief. But before the last bit of air could leave their lungs, Commander Buzzkill made yet another comment. "I would not recommend breaking out the champagne just yet, as Yeti has also determined that this is quite peculiar and still potentially dangerous. It may also be a living organism or a craft of some sort."

"How do they know that?" Tommy asked, and Jones stated that whatever it is, it has changed direction twice in order to stay on course with Earth.

Takarada invited himself to the empty chair in front of Jones's desk, rested his forehead in his left hand, and with his right began tapping its fine wood top with his index finger. "How is this possible?" he asked the air, and Takarada closed his eyes to work out the math in his head. Tommy tried to keep up but couldn't as Takarada mixed words with thought while navigating the vast plains of his mind in both English and Japanese. Plus, the annoying finger tapping wasn't helping much either.

"At 80% the speed of light ... Tap, Tap, Tap ... Coming to Earth from the Kuiper Belt ...Tap, Tap, Tap ... An object would need to travel at 53649330350.752 ..." Tap, Tap, Tap ... He paused ... "536 million miles per hour over distance, plus speed equals time ..." Takarada's finger stopped, and he looked up. "Whatever this is, it will be here in approximately 504 hours."

An overwhelming feeling of frustration glossed over Tommy. Ever since his position at the E.I.O. they've always had the means to deal with such cases, but now he felt completely helpless. As a general he was feeling somewhat responsible, as a guitar player he didn't really care. Obviously Takarada was feeling something similar as Tommy noticed him tapping his finger on his own hip. Either way, it seemed everybody was thinking the same thing. If this was some sort of invasion, we won't be ready and if the changing of the object's direction was just a fluke and some sort of asteroid, E.L. level or not, we still won't be ready. And if it's of the "something much worse" category ... well ...

"Damn it!" Tommy glanced at Dr. T. and blurted out what everybody was obviously thinking. "We've been on a shoestring budget for over five years now. How can we prepare for the freakin' worst when we don't even have the means to fix my damn door?" What the hell are we supposed to do?" Tommy asked, and Jones replied without hesitation.

"There's not much we can do. Whatever it is, all we can do at this point is hope for the best and try to prepare for the worst." As Jones stated this, a very slight, but odd look seemed to overtake his face. Tommy looking right at him would've bet the farm that he saw him crack a smile, but decided his hate for Jones was simply getting the best of him.

Rational thought was taking a quick second to the mounting fear and tension, so Jones ordered that the meeting adjourn and to reassemble "full force" in the control center in thirty minutes. On their way out, Tommy hesitated and stopped. "Wait a minute!" he shouted, "Aren't we forgetting something?"

Since the last few minutes were all spent discussing frequencies from the great beyond, their initial reason for going to Jones's office seemed to get lost in the outer-space shuffle. But whatever Yeti was reporting, it was far different than what he and Takarada had experienced. Not to mention that both Nathan and Olivia had some sort of close encounter them-damn-selves, or they wouldn't even be at The Goku. Tommy knew that Jones would probably chew him a new one for even bringing it up again, but that's why they were in his office in the first place.

This new discovery from Yeti was just additional news, and from the sounds of it, additional bad news at that. Tommy didn't like the idea, and if he truly thought he had a choice, he would have gone back to his quarters to catch up on *Attack On Titan*, but he knew what he had to do.

"Sir, I still believe contact is trying to be made by another and completely different entity."

Jones sat hard and fast back into his chair and sighed. "Let me guess Taylor, more aliens from the planet of Titties and Kaka?" Though Tommy could appreciate Jones' smart-ass remark, now wasn't the time, and before he could again state his case, Takarada interrupted him.

"No sir, not the planet, the place, Lake Titicaca in Peru. We all believe that some entity is trying to reach out to us using The Gateway of The Gods. We believe that whatever it is, or whoever they may be, some form of telepathy is being used to send us a message."

Jones for the first time looked concerned over this particular matter and asked, "Dr. Takarada, do you think it may be a warning or somehow connected to what the Yeti Institute has reported?" Takarada couldn't say for sure, nor could Tommy, Nathan or Olivia. Because the fact of the matter was that nobody knew exactly what had happened, and as more time went by, the less convinced Jones was. Plus, it now seemed that the commander had a much larger fish to fry, and he weighed out the options first in his head, then out loud.

"Look," he stated, "I understand something obviously happened with all of you. However, and mainly due to Earth's current news from Yeti, The E.I.O. is now on high alert. If something foreign is on its way, we must be ready. And with our budget and obvious time constraints, it's going to be an almost impossible task. I'm not saying no, but I am saying not yet. It is simply going to have to wait as I need all hands on deck here."

Tommy and Nathan both puffed up like a couple of angry peacocks, and Jones promptly put them in their places before either could so much as utter a word.

"Taylor, stand down or I'll demote you back to the bar band status we found you at! And Fox, you are a civilian guest, and I swear I'll bounce you out of here so fast that incoming messages in your head will be the least of your worries!"

Tommy made a particular sound only found in cartoons when he snapped to attention, and surprisingly, Nathan also backed off. "Wow," Tommy whispered, "I've never heard him raise his voice." Jones kept his game face on and finished up in his normal speaking tone.

"It's simple, and I need to make the best decisions I can in regard to the E.I.O. and our current situation. I don't owe you any kind of explanation, but I am still going to offer one."

Jones paused, "I am faced with two situations. I have your concerns about what happened to all of you and the possibility of what that could mean, then I have this news from Yeti, which is indeed happening, and that is where I need to focus. Besides, every yen we have is going to be needed, and we cannot afford to have doctors, agents, civilians and their wives going on million-dollar holidays to Peru or wherever. We simply do not have the funds."

Takarada still didn't care for Jones much, but he also knew he wasn't an idiot, and he faced his commanding officer. "Then you have a responsibility which no man has ever faced, you have the concern over something we can't explain which might become reality, and you have your current data from Yeti, which *is* reality."

A slightly glazed look washed over Commander Jones's face, and even though he was usually hard to read, Takarada knew he had made his choice.

Jones hesitated, took a deep breath and spoke. "As stated, we will reconvene with Yeti online. I expect to see you all in Control Room One in thirty minutes, sharp. Normally, Mr. Fox, I would ask you and Olivia to leave, but you are already in the know, and I believe the brilliance of your wife could possibly lend a hand. So, I ask you to please stay."

Even in a desperate time such as this, Nathan still managed to be offended by Jones's compliment to his wife and lack of even one word about himself, but he let it go. Olivia also knew this was something that often got under her husband's skin. The constant "Gee, Nathan, your wife is so awesome, but you ..." kind of comments. She grabbed Nathan's hand, and with her eyes she spoke to him, "Jones is just a jerk. Good job letting it go." Nathan smiled; he knew exactly what she was saying without as much as a syllable. He gripped her hand a little tighter, and that feeling of "less than" was replaced with a strong feeling of love for his wife and best friend.

As they exited to the hall, Jones's door perfectly swished shut, and Nathan dug his heels in deep. "Is it really that screwed up around here?"

Of course, both Nathan and Olivia knew about the financial woes of The E.I.O., they just never imagined that it was as bad as all this. Tommy could see it in their faces and "as a matter of factly" stated, "No monsters, no money."

Takarada acknowledged Tommy's comment with a frustrated nod and elaborated, "Due to there not being even one kaiju sighting since Mount Terror almost eight years ago, The E.I.O. has lost much of its funding. But in the past Sir Jonathon would always make sure that we were always prepared. If I remember correctly, we once went almost ten years without a sighting but that made no difference. We also had four bases in operation, and agents stationed around the world ready for attacks of any nature. Over the past two years, the majority of the world's high-ranking officials have been leaning far more towards rebuilding than protection. I believe their mistake is in thinking the crisis has finally passed. I also believe I have made the same mistake, because I do not believe ..." Takarada paused before continuing, "No, I am certain, it has not."

Nathan's heart fluttered, and he whispered "Good Lord" to himself because it was a rare occasion indeed when Kyoshi Takarada was wrong about such things. Still holding onto Olivia's hand, Nathan Fox suddenly donned a look of grave concern. "Let me take a wild guess, doc. I'm betting you know something we don't and by the look on your face, I'm thinking that you're thinking we may even be on the verge of another war." Takarada didn't even flinch, and Nathan pushed out a quick explosion of air that somehow managed to form the words, "That just figures." A rush of cold fear shot through his veins. Nathan forced out a fake smile, and with eyes even bigger than Suzy's, placed his hand on his wife's stomach and said, "I've been kind of hoping it was over myself." Olivia put her other hand on top of Nathan's and forced out a similar kind of smile.

Caught up in the moment, everybody gazed at the floor, and out of the blue a lightbulb seemed to go on above Tommy's head. He looked back up and pointed the index finger of his super-duper roboto hand at Kyoshi, "That's it!" That's why you've been acting so freakin' weird lately!" Takarada was still looking down at the floor, lost in his unusual, and of late, disconnected, state when Tommy's truth infiltrated his head.

He backed up, acknowledged Tommy and begged for his forgiveness in the form of a very deep bow. "Oh my God, Kyoshi," Tommy said to his good friend, "Why did you keep this to yourself? I can't imagine what you've been going through." Takarada seemed to deflate as the stress of this enormous secret exited his body, and Tommy added, "Why didn't you tell me?"

Takarada lifted his head and said, "Since knowing you, Tommy-san, I've heard the American phrase, 'to go all Chicken Little' many times. And even though I have had no proof, something in my stomach has not been right. A constant feeling of destruction on an apocalyptic level that I cannot explain has been haunting me. It is as though something from beyond has been trying to warn me of an inevitable war between the Heavens and Earth. But as you have just witnessed, without any evidence, without any facts, my fears could not be justified. You heard how Commander Jones acted. But with all of this, the news from Yeti, Nathan and Olivia coming to The Goku and our trip to the infirmary has given me all the proof I need."

"Proof of what?" Olivia asked.

"For the last few months, I have been noting all of this in my daily log. Part of my job, my life, is to constantly watch the skies and the endless plains of space. All four of us know the truth about what is out there. But these visions of fear and feelings of catastrophe have absorbed my every thought. And truthfully, I did not know if I was losing my mind or if it was real.

Now that whatever has been plaguing me is now plaguing you, I am convinced. The great Annihilator is coming … and it will be here in approximately 504 hours."

Olivia shuddered, then let Tommy and Nathan know that 504 hours is only about three weeks, and then they, too, shuddered themselves.

"Kyoshi", Tommy asked, "Why didn't you tell Jones?"

"What, about the messages we were receiving from the land of titties and kaka?"

Tommy was impressed, as a part-time teacher at the late night school of sarcasm, he felt he had taught Dr. T. well and responded with a simple, "Point taken."

"That is not all," Takarada continued. "We need to get to Peru. It is more than just a feeling now. It was the same thing with Organic Thorium, I know when I am right. Not to prove this to Jones, but to get the help we are going to need. Because I am convinced it is there, at the Gateway of the Gods, where we will find some answers to what is happening. However, I have no idea how this is even possible."

Nathan cleared his throat. Not because he was congested, but because he knew of a way, and of course, it was quite obvious.

"Dr T., I may have an idea." Takarada for the first time in many weeks actually smiled as this answer had already popped into his head. "Is there something you can do Nathan-san?"

And Nathan replied, "Remember doc, when you're rich as shit, you can do just about anything."

Chapter 6

Peru

Takarada was not happy with Jones's orders. He felt helpless, and to him that was even worse than his recent plans of simply waiting to see what happens. He now knew that putting the inevitable on standby often wasn't the answer. But in Takarada's defense, if you're ready to take action and ready to strike, but for some reason cannot, it becomes like that Tom Petty song where the waiting is the hardest part. Because that is exactly what Takarada did, and he felt like he had done nothing but waste valuable time. He knew their best bet was to get to Peru, as he had a hunch the cavalry could be waiting within the mountain caves at the Gateway of the Gods. And if Dr. Takarada was willing to be a part of one of Nathan Foxes hair-brained schemes, times were tough indeed.

It's a fact that when you're a world-renown rock star making heaps and heaps of cash, the impossible indeed becomes quite the possible. Yup, there's definitely a lot you can do with a kabillion dollars in the bank, not to mention the perks, or even the trouble you could buy yourself out of. Because when the going gets tough, the rich write a check. However, Nathan preferred using cash. It must be nice to say things like, "Man, I gotta' get me one of these!" and back it up with a wad of Benjamins so thick that it could choke an elephant. But after Nathan's second solo album followed suit with his first and went double platinum, Nathan bought himself a little gift, a brand-new Bombardier Global 7500 gray and silver luxury jet. And it was a total steal at a cool eighty mil. His expertise piloting Fuji Fighters and FU2's while battling giant, nasty kaiju seemed to spark a love for flying, even after he retired from the E.I.O. As a matter of fact, after talking with his good friend Bruce (who also piloted his band's touring jet), Nathan now usually flew both him and his band members to the majority of their gigs around the world.

By the time Takarada, Tommy, Nathan and Olivia had arrived at the E.I.O.'s garage, checked out one of the few remaining big, black SUVs and reached the gated guard shack at the foot of Mount Goku, it had easily been thirty minutes. Takarada was hoping they could slip past the guards, as they more-than-likely wouldn't have had any clue that the group was dodging the upcoming mandatory meeting with Commander Jones. After bypassing the guards, they could then head to the nearby airport in Hiroshima where Nathan's jet was being prepped and refueled.

Two guards stood in front of the red-and-white striped gate, and one more was sitting in the small shack that had windows on all sides. Tommy shut off the headlights and proceeded to a point where he could see the guard station, but they couldn't see him. At least that's what he hoped. He pulled in close to the trees on the side of the dark, wooded road and watched. The wait was a short one as the guard from within the shack picked up the phone, slammed it down and joined the other two, cocked and ready to fire from the front of the gate.

Both Takarada and Tommy knew they were just guards following orders. They were not the enemy. As a matter of fact, Tommy had even, well, kind of, become friends with one of them, Toshiyuki, who was usually stuck on late night patrol. Tommy would often join him for the occasional cigarette when returning back to the Goku from a gig. Olivia whispered, "They wouldn't actually shoot us, would they?"

Tommy shook his head and whispered back, "I don't think so, but you never know with Jones. Besides he doesn't like me much."

Nathan agreed and responded, "Nobody likes you much."

And Takarada chimed in, "He hates you, Nathan."

So, the consensus being that most people did not only dislike Tommy or Nathan, but were probably capable of shooting them, indeed merited the need for a plan. They had to simply get past the gate without anybody getting hurt. But how...

The guards looked nervous, and Tommy's smoking bro, standing between the other two, lowered his weapon in order to fire up a cigarette. He lit it and handed it to the guard on his right, then did the same for himself. The smoke, the yellow lights of the shack and the muggy haze of a hot Japanese night created a creepy scenario, similar to one found in an old Mario Bava film. They looked up, and the high beams of a big, black beast caught the guards, well, "off-guard" and rushed towards them with a thundering battle-cry! They dropped their cigarettes and raised their weapons, but it was too late. The metal monster was upon them! Two jumped to one side, and Toshiyuki, who was standing by the shack, was able to raise his gun. It was obvious that the night monster was nothing more than an SUV, but Toshiyuki aimed his weapon and prepared to fire. He looked through the telescopic sight of his machine gun, placed his index finger on the trigger and began to squeeze. Before it could fire though, Toshiyuki pulled his weapon from his face and blinked repeatedly, as he had never seen a beagle driving an SUV. The black vehicle sped past, and over the commotion he could have sworn that he heard an elegant, soft voice say, "Bite me."

Tommy who was hiding behind the passenger seats watched the guards from the SUV's large back window. They were a bit discombobulated, but all in all just fine. He hoped Toshiyuki wouldn't get into any kind of trouble and vowed to himself to pick him up a carton of smokes after everything was said and done.

"Holy Flirkin Snit!" Nathan yelled. "That was awesome!"

Takarada gave a proud-papa nod, knowing that Suzy would indeed come in handy.

Nathan looked at Suzy who was still driving, and not really sure just how she was doing so, started talking the same way both Tommy and Olivia had before.

"Who's a good-witto girl? You are Suzy-woozie … Yes, you are!"

Nathan reached up from the back seat to pat Suzy on the head and she began to growl, indicating to Nathan that he could "get bent."

Tommy decided the coast was clear and asked Suzy to pull over so he could resume driving. As he climbed back into the front seat, she lost her footing on the slippery leather upholstery but still managed to force her way into Tommy's lap.

He scratched her floppy ears and started talking the same way both Nathan and Olivia had before.

"Who's a good-witto girl? You are Suzy-woozie … Yes, you are!"

Suzy pushed her nose up and started licking Tommy's face clean, repeating "Hello Thomas!" between each wet, sloppy, doggy kiss. "Okay, okay," he giggled. He opened the compartment between the two front seats and instructed Suzy to climb in and go to sleep, which she promptly did.

Tommy's pants started to vibrate, and soon Kashmir by Led Zeppelin filled the front seat. He reached down and fumbled around in order to pull his cell phone out of his front pocket. He looked at it, and the name "Dickhead" illuminated on his screen.

"Uh-Oh … It's Jones. What should I do?" "Don't answer it!" Nathan yelled, and as he did Tommy's phone stopped playing Kashmir, and Takarada's phone took its place with a haunting melody … "If you like pina coladas and getting caught in the rain." Tommy, Nathan and even Olivia gave Kyoshi a perplexing look, and he defended his ringtone with his middle finger. Nathan smiled, "There's hope for you yet, Doc!"

It was a fast drive, and the tarmac glistened with the reflective lights of a moist evening as Tommy pulled up to the hangar where Nathan's jet was waiting. But before opening the door, he rolled his window down, looked around and stated, "I thought for sure there'd be a welcoming party awaiting us courtesy of the E.I.O."

Nathan did the same and added, "Maybe they didn't have enough money in petty cash for an uber cab to pursue us." Like a twin pair of wings, four doors sprung open, and they disembarked from the SUV.

As they climbed the stairs leading into the plane, Takarada stated the obvious. "Hai" he agreed. "I too am not sure why Commander Jones did not pursue us. It is obvious he has either decided not to do so or is planning on shooting us down while we are in the air."

And on that lovely thought, they were cleared for takeoff and took off into the purple-and-gold-streaked sky on their long flight to Peru.

***

The morning sun cast sparkling images of light upon the deep blue water of the Irish Sea that separated the coast of England from Ireland. Even further in, on the banks of the River Mersey, there stands a rather large structure over one hundred years old that is known as one of the city's Three Graces, the Royal Liver Building. Almost resembling a Victorian era castle, its main rectangular stone structure encases an extremely large courtyard with two three-hundred-and-fifty-foot massive clocktowers on each end of it. From the inland-facing tower, Bertie, a four-ton, copper-winged fowl, watches and protects the residents of Liverpool. From the other end of the large, stone building, Bertie's mate, Belle, sits high atop the seaward-facing clocktower making sure the good sailors of this coastal city return safely home.

Upon its completion in 1911, the Royal Liver Building, although technically not a skyscraper, was donned England's tallest structure at the time. Not because of its frame-like shape that encased its oversized foyer, but due to its enormous and lofty clocktowers, each standing much taller than London's Big Ben.

But similar to an iceberg, oftentimes there is much more that you don't see lying beneath the surface than what you do see above it. And this could not be any truer than with the Royal Liver Building, because before work started above ground in 1908, highly classified construction began beneath it a few years earlier. Sure, some buildings go deep, but not almost a quarter mile, and not with spiraling veins and arteries running below the city it was built upon. To the public, it was a massive and noble structure that housed multiple insurance brokers and the like. But to the Earth Intelligence Organization, it was their first complete, modern complex. It was also the only pre-WWI E.I.O. base that still remained intact and was now known as E.I.O.H.Q.

When The Fuji, London and San Francisco were still in operation, the LP (as the Liverpool branch was affectionately known) was reduced to a mere training and research facility, but that all changed when the majority of E.I.O. bases around the world were wiped clean from the Earth. So, along with the LP, only one other base still remained intact, and that was the newer makeshift base at Mount Gokurakuji. When the Mount Fuji and San Francisco facilities were nothing more than a gleam in their proverbial daddy's eye, the LP (along with the now buried London base) were fully functioning. As a matter of fact, some of the best E.I.O. valedictorians came from the LP. Elvis Presley, Jimi Hendrix, Otis Redding and even Sir Jack had the honors of becoming full-fledged rockstar agents out of the little Liverpool branch that now headed up all operations. And it was from that very base where the wall within the high command office opened from the middle and parted wide to a performance of noise and static. As the signal found its way, a message scrolled to the left from the center of the screen,

... SIGNAL SECURED ... SIGNAL SECURED ... SIGNAL SECURED ...

When the gray flicker subsided, a thin-faced man with mismatched eyes and uncommonly perfect hair came into view. Of course it was Robert Jones from the Goku, and he began to speak. "This is high command. Takarada and Taylor have joined up with Nathan and Olivia Fox and have gone AWOL. If I am correct, they will return to Mount Gokurakuji with the package we had discussed. Move forward and implement all necessary arrangements from your end." Jones, not even waiting for a response, cut off the communication, replacing his visual with the quick and abrupt message.

... SIGNAL TERMINATED ... SIGNAL TERMINATED ... SIGNAL TERMINATED ...

***

Nathan's jet looked more like an angry, super-sized pterodactyl compared to the other planes when it touched down upon the ground at the Inca Manco International Airport. The good news being that, albeit small, the Inca Manco still boasted the longest runway in Peru. And even better, it was also the closest airport to their destination at Lake Titicaca. The bad news, however, was it seemed that every police car in Juliaca (all three of them) was awaiting their arrival. Nathan taxied to the end of the runway, and as the engines cooled down, he opened the safe that was concealed beneath the cabin floor. He had a hunch after radioing the tower about landing that the word would quickly get out. And it did, because soon most knew that a dumb, rich American with a big jet and an even bigger bank account was going to be giving out money.

Chances are the Peruvians spoke English, but Nathan knew Olivia spoke Spanish just in case. Plus, he even remembered a little from high school. But if that didn't work, he also knew that the U.S. dollar spoke much louder than any possible language barrier that may arise. Just before Nathan closed the safe, he pulled what seemed to be a small radio receiver out of it, held it to his mouth and spoke, "Light My Fire," into it. Unlike the Goku, the secret panel in his private jet worked just fine, and it opened up to an arsenal of weapons adhered to the wall behind it: a few handguns, a semi-automatic rifle, an Uzi, a couple plasma grenades, and even a photon blaster.

"Holy crap!" Tommy yelled. "What'd you do, join a militia or something?"

"No," Nathan replied, "just a few parting gifts from the E.I.O. when I retired."

Tommy was stunned, but also a little relieved, and as he read Nathan the riot act, he pulled down the semi-automatic rifle and made sure it was loaded. Nathan pulled up his shirt and stuck a Glock in the back of his jeans just above his butt, then placed two revolvers in the front. "Just call me the Duke!" he joked, and Takarada winced, thinking it wasn't funny at all.

Nathan opened the cabin door and proceeded down the mobile flight stairs that the local federales had placed against the plane. Tommy peered out of the oval-shaped window closest to the door and prayed he wouldn't have to shoot anybody. Nobody could hear a word beneath the dissipating whine of the jet engines, but as Nathan reached into his pants, Tommy lifted the rifle and placed his finger on the trigger. Only instead of pulling out one of his weapons, Nathan pulled out a wad of cash and gave it to the man who seemed to be in charge. Even from the jet, Tommy could see the police officer smile, and his gold tooth glistened as he put the money in his pocket. Nathan walked with the others over to one of the idling squad cars, and Tommy followed them with his sight. A cop stepped out of the vehicle with what appeared to be a map, but before he even opened it, he simply pointed south. Takarada stuck his head out the door and looked past the horizon to what seemed to be a pulsating light coming from the other side of the Haya Marcu Mountains. He recognized its unique shade of purple and green and instantly what he had believed from the beginning was verified. Takarada, now more than ever, knew that time was of the essence, and he yelled down to Nathan,

"Nathan-san, this is it! Can we get a car?" Nathan conversed with the cop for another brief second, handed him even more money and turned back toward the jet. As he climbed the stair the Peruvian federales shouted,

"Amigo, los caballos esteran aquí en diez minutos!"

Nathan entered the jet and Tommy lowered his weapon. "Everything good?" he asked, and Nathan nodded.

"Did they speak English?" Takarada asked, and Nathan replied, "A little."

Tommy then asked, "Did we get a car?"

And Nathan responded, "I don't think so. It was hard to understand him, but it seems that big, pulsating light is coming directly from the Gateway to The Gods, and nothing electrical can get within twenty miles of it." He then added, "I couldn't even get a guide, they're terrified."

Takarada added that the light must be emitting some sort of massive EMP, and how fortunate it was that they arrived from the opposite direction.

Tommy shook his head and made a sideways comment about just how fortunate they were and tagged it with, "Well, I sure ain't walking." And Nathan added,

"Yeah, me neither. I gave that guy a ton of cash, too. My Spanish is really rusty, but he did say something about getting us a Mustang or some cabello ... or something."

Takarada and Olivia looked at each other, and Olivia assured both Tommy and Nathan that he probably wasn't getting them hair, maybe mustangs, but only if they were ...

"Horses!" Nathan yelled, and he ran back down the stairs to the oldest man in the world who was driving an older pickup truck while pulling an even older still, but nonetheless quite long, trailer.

Tommy looked at Olivia, "Wow, he really likes horses."

"He should," Olivia said, "He has like twelve back home."

Tommy had an undeniable look of puzzlement on his face, and he said, "I guess I never figured Nathan as the horse-riding type."

Olivia laughed, "Whoever said he could ride, I just said he had a bunch." Olivia made her way down the stairs, and as she did, she added, "I, however, LOVE riding!" and she joined Nathan at the back of the trailer.

Olivia mounted up with her usual grace, and even Takarada seemed to do all right. Tommy stumbled a few times but eventually made it up and felt the need to wrap his arms around the animal's neck and hold on for dear life. Nathan, on the other hand, made it up rather effortlessly, which kind of surprised everyone. It was a bit odd, Nathan taking the lead as he did, but that's just what happened. Maybe since he now had a large sum of skin in the game, he felt he needed to protect his investment.

Reminiscent of his old friend, Sir Jack, he even felt the need to make a brief speech as he sat tall in the saddle upon the back of this majestic beast.

"Okay, it's over thirty miles, but if we stay on the old highway out of the airport it'll take us over the mountain range, and we should be there by dawn. If I understood correctly there's usually not much traffic, if any, at night, and lately, there's been none due to that."

Nathan pointed at the dancing lights up in the sky. They seemed to cast an eerie glow for them to follow. He yanked on the reins, and the beast stood upright upon its back legs. As it did, he pulled the two revolvers still lodged in the front of his pants out and shot a few rounds into the air. "All right! Let's ride!" he shouted, just before falling off his horse.

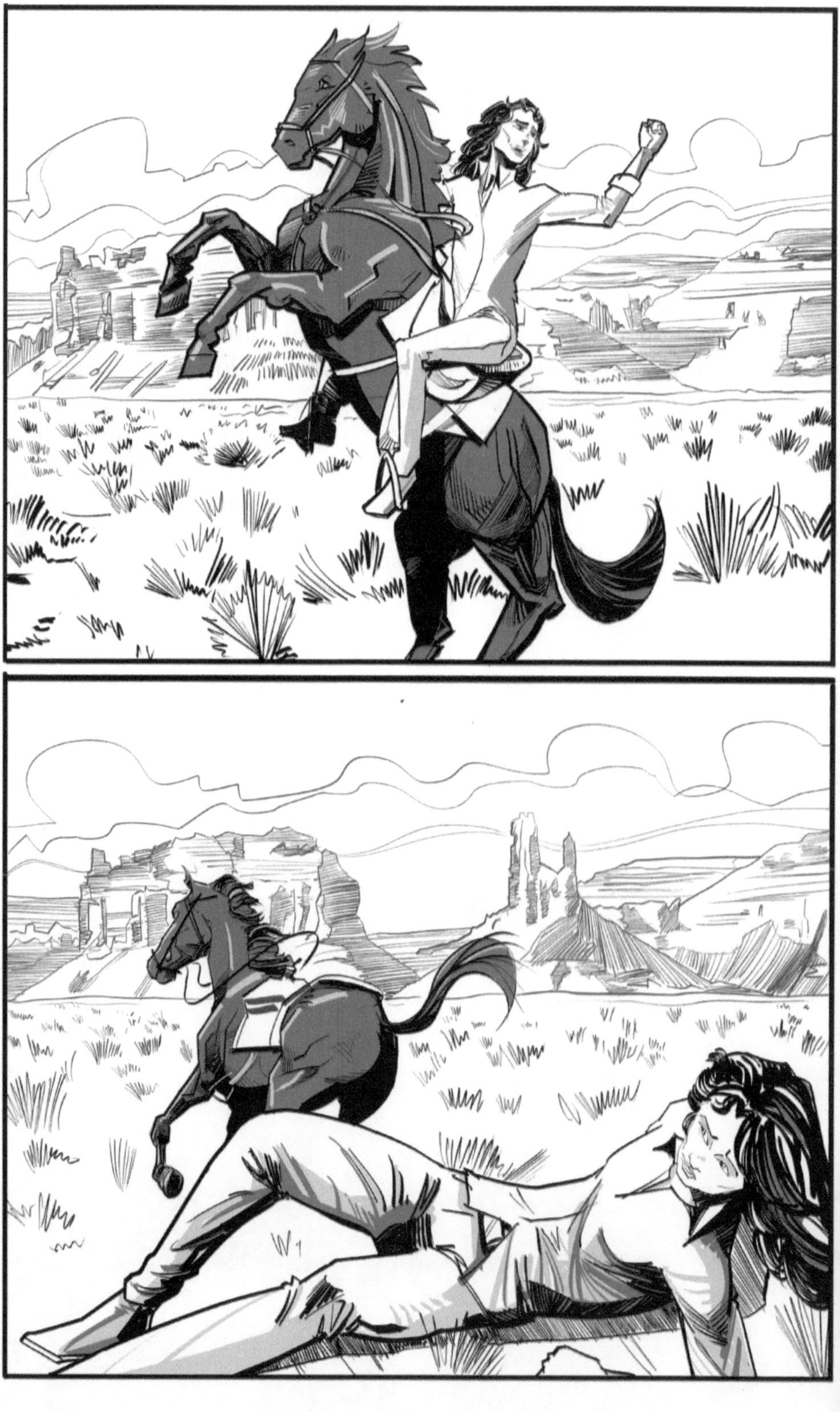

Chapter 7

The Last Leg

A creepy kind of bright, one like you'd see just before a wicked storm, illuminated the old highway that Takarada, Tommy and the Foxes had followed all night. It was almost four in the morning, and the shimmering glow coming from the Gateway of The Gods had turned it, and everything that surrounded it, to an eerie green. From its epicenter, Takarada concluded it probably lit up the whole region for well over twenty square miles. He also concluded that anything within its radius was probably being affected by the electromagnetic pulse, the very one that had so many locals terrified. It was an odd kind of light, intense and brilliant, but still sort of dark with black overtones. It was hot, too, Africa hot, and the horses passed tired many miles ago. Olivia led the others to one of the many scattered farmhouses that speckled the bleak desert countryside. It was empty; however, the well was not. She stopped, floated down from her trusty steed and led it by the reins to the deep, dark, water-filled shaft. Tommy was still clinging to his horse's neck, and Nathan was fast asleep upon his. Takarada jumped down, and the sand from the charred red earth burst into an explosion of dust beneath his boots. The moon was full but could barely be seen due to the lime green glow. It was like an oven, and he wiped the hot sweat from his brow. He reached behind, removed his backpack, unzipped it and set it down. Like Olivia, he led his horse over towards the well, and from the ground his backpack jerked a few times and then started to follow him.

Nathan moaned, scratched his head and opened his eyes just enough to see what was happening. He screamed for Takarada to "Look out!" and reached for the Glock stowed in the back of his jeans.

"No, no, Nathan-san!" Takarada yelled, and when the backpack came to an abrupt stop, Suzy stuck her head out of it. Nathan groaned at the extreme cuteness of it all and mumbled "Damn dog" under his breath. He then eased his foot down towards the stirrup of his saddle only to miss it by a mile and fall to the hard gravel below. It's rare indeed when a dog actually seems to smile, but that's just what Suzy did when Nathan hit the dirt with a painful thud.

Olivia turned the large crank on the well, and the frayed rope brought up some refreshing, brown, glorious, bug-filled water. The contents leaked through the cracks of the wood bucket, and she held it over her head for the closest thing to a shower she could get. She offered a palmful of water to Suzy but was quickly snubbed. The little beagle then trotted out of sight towards the main event, the entrance carved into the red jagged ridges of the Haya Marca Mountain. "She okay?" Olivia asked.

"Yes, my dear." Takarada answered. "Suzy is going ahead to make sure the air is goodly to breathe before we get any closer."

Nathan joined Olivia and Takarada at the well and dipped his hands in the bucket to cool his horse down with a wet pat. As it drank, he looked over at Tommy who was still asleep on his saddle. He noted how tired he must have been because Tommy was usually never able to sleep much when they traveled. Olivia clicked her mouth making that universal, animal-calling sound, and Tommy's horse made its way to the morning gathering at the water cooler. Tommy, still clutching his horse's neck, opened his eyes and asked the $64,000 question, "Are we there yet?"

"Yes, Thomas, we are," Takarada answered.

Tommy looked around, while suffering from an extreme case of morning discombobulation, and then asked, "Where's Suzy?"

Takarada pointed towards the mountain range about a quarter mile off in the distance, and Tommy knew. He tightened his lip and showed the slightest sign of worry, but ultimately knew what Suzy was and why they brought her along. He dismounted his horse and placed his palm gently on the side of its long nose. "Good boy," he said in his Suzy voice and held the bucket underneath its mouth so it could drink. "We don't even know your names," he stated, looking at the four animals, and decided for his, "Jack" was as fitting a name as any.

As the early morning sunrise melded with the glow emitting from the gate, both the temperature and light rose to an even higher level. Takarada saluted to block out the light, and from in between the waves of heat he could see Suzy coming back from her recon mission. He grabbed his horse by the reins with the plan of meeting Suzy half-way and then continuing on to the gate. But the beast would not budge. Olivia did the same, and her horse, too, did the same. She gently ran her hand down the frightened steed's mane and noted, "They're scared."

"Maybe they know something we don't," Tommy added.

Clearly it didn't matter, as even before Tommy could say another word, Suzy was back. Takarada pushed on her butt, and she sat. He then pressed her side, and a fur-covered panel popped opened over her ribcage revealing a small screen and a series of buttons. His fingers did a quick little dance on the micro console, and Suzy spoke in a sexy voice.

"Hello Thomas. The local air is primarily composed of 78% nitrogen and 21% oxygen. I am also registering trace amounts of argon and carbon dioxide. It is perfectly suitable for human breathing. I am also registering gamma rays that have ionized the air molecules, producing both positive ions and recoil electrons."

"What the hell does that mean?" Nathan asked looking slightly worried.

"It's just as I thought, Nathan-san. Goodly air, but there is an electromagnetic pulse generating from the gate of Aramu Mura." Takarada assured him that since they themselves are not electrical, that there should be no reason to be concerned.

Nathan tugged on his horse's reins and said, "Somebody should tell them that, because they still ain't budging. Either way, looks like we're walking." Nathan looked off towards the mountain range, kicked the dirt around and made a bold statement to his wife. "Olivia, why don't you stay here with the horses." But as soon as he said it, he wished he hadn't, as the awkward silence and her glaring look made the obvious, obvious. Nathan squirmed and jumped ship. "By the way, Doc," he asked changing the subject, "Being a robot and all, why isn't Suzy affected?"

"Well Nathan," he proudly explained, "Suzy is powered by Organic Thorium, the same chemical element that powered both the Duke and SCOTT. It acts almost like fuel that passes through her microfiber veins." Takarada also added that Suzy should be all right, but EMP's can also be quite unpredictable.

Nathan nodded. He felt smart. He'd been hearing the words Organic Thorium for over ten years now, but never admitted he had no freakin' clue what it meant, or what it was. But what really made him feel smart was that he had dodged the repercussions of telling Olivia she should stay behind. Olivia gathered the horses and tied them to the well. "Hopefully they'll be okay," she stated, and Nathan added, "Hopefully *we'll* be okay," and they set out on foot with the gate looming off in the distance.

Anxieties were high, making the walk go quick, and Nathan was the first to approach the giant gate sculpted into the side of the seven-meter, solid granite mountain. He crept up to the ancient carving, then eased into the doorway within the stone frame and just stood there waiting for something to happen, but nothing did. Takarada joined him and started feeling around the sealed door first, then the wall itself as though he were searching for a secret passage, but there wasn't one. Tommy and Olivia did the same but neither found anything either. A chilling thought ran through Takarada's mind, "*What if Jones was right?*" If there was a table, or even something flat, he probably would have started tapping on it with his index finger. It wasn't nearly as big as they thought it would be, and Tommy mentioned for that very reason it reminded him of Graceland.

Nathan put his hands up against the wall within the frame of the doorway that supposedly opened the so-called portal and claimed, "Well, I don't know about this weird glow, but the rest of this sure seems like a total bust."

With that remark, Takarada's nervousness started to rear its head, and he said he absolutely refused to believe that this was nothing more than a wild moose chase. Tommy hated seeing Takarada all flustered but stated, "I agree with Nathan. If there's nothing here, we need to head out, cuz' we're a hell of a long ways from home." Funny thing though, he wasn't eager to get back to The Goku, as he had become quite attached to his butt, but he also knew the longer he was AWOL, the worse it was going to be. Nathan then started ranting about the heat and his chapped thighs from riding a damn horse all night, and Takarada demanded he stop and be quiet.

Nathan couldn't believe Takarada yelled at him like he did but chalked it up to the good doctor simply being old and tired. He then started going on about the effects of extreme heat on the elderly, and Tommy also told Nathan to "Shut the hell up!" Not because of his jabbering, but because of what was happening to his freakin' head! Nathan started to pull his hands down from the sides of the doorway, and Takarada said, "No, no, put your hands back up!" Nathan looked terrified but still did what the doctor told him to do without hesitation. With his hands placed against the walls of the indented doorway, it seemed Nathan had become some sort of human conduit. He winced as the flowing currents of energy lifted each hair on his head one by one until he was sporting what seemed to be a large fro of static electricity! Tommy cracked up, but then a bolt of purple lightning blasted through Nathan's body launching him about ten feet into the air. Olivia ran up, dropped to the ground and held him in her arms. Nathan groaned, mumbled something about Ace Frehley, getting electrocuted and giant spiders, and proceeded to cough out a puff of black smoke. "Whoa," he proclaimed, "I really am the Lizard King." Olivia rolled her eyes and stood up. Nathan's smoking head hit the dirt, and she stated he was just fine.

However, whatever Nathan started (even if he didn't) grew, and the entire carved-out seven meter by seven meter square face of the gate erupted in a violent series of colorful electricity. For a moment, it was like watching Animal Planet on the world's largest TV as it showed a documentary about illuminated, purple-lightning-spitting cobras. Of course it was dangerous, but there was also something beautiful and hypnotic about it. Takarada watched as the colors reflected on his face, and he wished it would never end. But unfortunately, it did, and within a few seconds, the streaks of electricity retreated into the large indents that framed the mountain door. Takarada turned to Tommy with a childlike look of, *Did you see that?*, and Tommy answered him simply with the call of the Keanu ... "Whoa."

The ground shook, and boulders of red granite, dirt and earth started crashing down. Tommy and Takarada each grabbed one of Nathan's arms, and they and Olivia literally ran for their lives. Nathan found his feet, and they climbed onto an island of rocks and dead trees as the avalanche of debris rolled past them like a fast-moving river. Tommy and Kyoshi held onto the deep roots of a dead stump while Olivia and Nathan held onto them. A large rock slammed into their inselberg and exploded into a thousand pieces of stone shrapnel with a tremendous crash!

The same rays of purple light that had vanished found their way to the top of the gate, and with nowhere else to go, shot straight up into the air from the tip of the mountain. At first, the beams were waving about like Medusa's hair, and as they did, they changed from purple, to green and finally to yellow. Then all at once, the lights stood erect resembling the golden bars of an illuminated spinning birdcage. As they spun, its base grew and took the shape of a fat-bottomed vase still upon a potter's turning wheel. Then, as though the beams of light were taking a deep breath, it all at once exhaled, turning into one towering ray that shot clear above the clouds and into space.

SHOOOOM!

Takarada watched in amazement, as this was something he had never witnessed in all of his life, and he had seen some pretty weird stuff. It was indeed a portal, and it looked as though the endless beam of light was some kind of cosmic elevator shaft. There was a hum in the air, and everyone's body tingled with that same sensation as when your arm or leg falls asleep. Then, like Nathan, their hair began to stand up from the electricity. With their short cuts, Tommy and Takarada didn't look that bad. But Olivia, with her long locks and the lights reflecting in her glasses, looked like a sixties flower child who had taken the brown acid. The electric sound in the air grew louder, and Nathan covered his ears. Just as everybody else was about to do the same, it stopped. Their hair went flat, and the only thing that remained was the glowing, yellow stream climbing to the heavens. White and purple floors of light descended one after the other within the beam. It was kind of like a celestial crazy straw in reverse, and a whole lot of something was coming down through it. Takarada watched in both fear and amazement, and he knew beyond any shadow of a doubt that the skyward ray of light was a wormhole. But what troubled him the most was one simple question, who or what was filling up the waiting room within the mountain portal?

Takarada needed a closer look, so he slid down one of the giant, round boulders from the protruding formation of rocks they had climbed on. He ordered everyone to stay put and cautiously walked back towards the gateway, and of course, Tommy followed, and so did Nathan and Olivia.

The door to the gateway portal was covered in debris, and he began pushing and pulling away at the fallen rock that now covered it. The electric hum in the air had subsided, but Olivia still kept her distance while clinging to Takarada's backpack. Tommy and Nathan approached the gateway to help Doctor T. remove the mountain remnants. The door was completely covered, and even though there were a couple of larger rocks, there was nothing so big that they couldn't handle it.

Any fear they may have felt had now been replaced with hope and curiosity, and Takarada shouted out an almost gleeful, "Dig!" Even Olivia moved in closer, kicking away the excess of what they had already removed. Nathan and Tommy together tugged on one of the larger stones, and it seemed it was acting as load-bearing support. It wouldn't budge. Takarada braced his back against the remaining rubble and pushed with his legs, and Tommy and Nathan pulled. It wouldn't budge. Olivia brought over a large branch and suggested they use it as a lever. They did. It wouldn't budge. Sweat and dirt covered their faces, and Tommy blew out an exacerbated sigh of frustration; they couldn't move it. Tommy, Nathan and Olivia looked worn out but knew they had come too far to call it quits. Little did they know Takarada had another trick up his sleeve.

The good doctor whistled, and Suzy eagerly popped her head out of his backpack. "C'mere girl!" he said in that traditional dog-calling timbre. Takarada then asked everyone to follow him to a safe distance and to please stand behind a large boulder and to shield their eyes. Tommy did exactly what the doctor told him to do, but before he did he caught a glimpse of this cute little beagle puppy facing this mighty wall of rock and debris and simply wondered, "How in the hell is ..."

ZZZZZZZZZZZZ ZAP!

CHOOM!

Tommy covered his eyes with his forearm, and Nathan yelled out, "Holy flirkin snit! What just happened?" Four heads peered around the boulder in bewildered amazement, and through the haze Suzy just pranced over and back into her backpack.

Takarada smiled and whispered, "Good girl."

The smoking gateway portal was still covered in fallen rock, but now nothing more than the size of a clenched fist remained. Dr. Takarada could see an opening! He ran over and again started yanking and pulling away the stone. His fatigue turned to excitement, and as he lifted one of the bigger stones, an open hand from within the gate shot out! Takarada locked fingers with it and pulled. Tommy and Nathan brushed away anything that was in the way and with one final yank, what was just an arm was now an entire body. Takarada fell backwards on his ass, and both Tommy and Nathan nearly popped out of their skulls when they laid their eyes upon the hideous creature. And then, as if things weren't bad enough already, it spoke.

"Dudes!"

Olivia ran up, and it was almost as though they had practiced it when the quartet sang out, "Michael!" And if Michael was here, more than likely, so was ...

"Liberty!"

Liberty and her dirt-and-dust-covered body started crawling out of the rocks, and Tommy pulled on her so hard, for a second he was worried he may have hurt her. Of course, she was just fine, and for the first time in over ten years, the band was back together! But what was truly awesome was that for those brief few seconds, they (including Takarada) felt nothing but joy. As they reminisced, Tommy just happened to look down and saw yet another hand coming up from the opening. While still laughing, he asked Michael if he had forgotten something ... or someone. "Shoot!" Michael gasped, and both he and Tommy reached down to pull up yet another Michael.

"No way!" Nathan yelled. But yes, it was surely another Michael, dark hair, ebony skin, about 24 or 25 years old. No doubt about it, it was him. At least until he spoke.

"Hello, my name is Michael. I am so glad to meet you. This is indeed such a pleasure for me. All of you are quite well known on Noahmar. Now if you would please be so kind as to help pull up my sister as you did for me." Nobody moved as they obviously hadn't processed all that was happening.

Michael (the first one, you know, the one from the other books) then snapped them back to the here and now by reminding them that others still needed their help. And he did so with one word, "Dudes?"

Doctor Takarada was the first to respond. "Hai! I mean, yes, of course, Michael." Reaching down to help another Liberty out, Tommy peeked into the long cave-like portal and swore he saw about 1000 identical pairs of Michaels and Libertys waiting in line to exit.

Whoa, this is going to take a while, Tommy thought, and Michael knew what he was thinking by stating that they could probably speed things up. He grabbed Liberty's hand, and they both closed their eyes, but nothing happened.

"Oooops," Michael stated, "wrong Libs." Liberty (the right Liberty, you know, the one from the other books) shook her head and grabbed Michael's hand. All of the remaining rocks and earth that still covered the portal glowed in a putrid green and in an instant were pushed aside.

"Now we're talking!" Nathan yelled, and Tommy asked them why they just didn't do that from the inside of the portal.

"Dudes, we tried," Michael answered, "but it didn't work." It was at that very moment that Michael realized that he may have grabbed the wrong wrist in the portal as he just did. But before he could say anything, Takarada spoke,

"Maybe after you were brought down, the influx of electricity in the air had some effects on your telekinetic abilities."

Sounds good to me Michael thought, and he acknowledged Takarada's explanation with a thumbs up and a, "Mahalo, Dr. T."

After removing the remaining fallout, The Gateway of The Gods was open wide, and the survivors of Noahmar exited at a calm pace in twos. From deep within the cave, the light of the Noahmarians who had not yet changed into their human form lit up the back of the ancient portal.

"Wow," Tommy thought, and he placed his hand on Dr. T's shoulder and quoted a line from one of his favorite movies. "Kyoshi, old friend, I do believe we're gonna need a bigger boat."

Chapter 8

Intergalactic Survivors

At last count, Takarada had tallied almost 1000 Noahmarian refugees that had escaped to Earth through the portal in Peru known as the Gateway of the Gods. And even though 1000 was a large number, it was but a minute fraction of what they once were. If not for Michael and Liberty using the stargate to travel from Noahmar to Earth over the years, there might not have been any survivors at all. It was amazing the amount of Noahmarians the alien twins had saved, but it was hard for them to focus on the positive after the total annihilation of their little planet.

The exodus from the Aramu Maru Mountains flowed like a swarm of ants over the dirt and gravel desert. It was a good thing the farmhouses were still abandoned, as it was going to be home to the Noahmarians for at least a day or two, or until a transport could arrive. Like humans, they ate, slept and even drank water, so the empty little village would be the perfect refuge. Maybe Takarada could even get Jones to quarantine the town to keep out intruders and locals for the time being. Obviously, the villagers were staying somewhere else, plus they were totally freaked out by the surrounding light of the mountain gateway, so it wouldn't be too difficult.

Even though the EMP that pulsed from Aramu Maru had diminished, the cell service still sucked, and there was no way to make contact with anyone shy of drums or smoke signals.

They needed to get to the airport, or at least a phone or somewhere with good reception, and get a hold of Jones. Some sort of plan had to be put into action. There was no time to rest, and according to the twins, Hell was coming to planet Earth. It was agreed that Michael and Liberty would accompany Takarada and Tommy back to the Goku. Olivia was eager to help as well, but Nathan shut her down and quick like. She gave Nathan the Olivia glare of death, and usually that would have worked, but Nathan stood his ground and said, "NO! Not this time and maybe not ever again!" To everyone's surprise, Olivia backed down. She nodded in hesitation but agreed with her husband.

Michael and Liberty put Michael and Liberty in charge of the Michael and Liberty collective and informed them that they needed to stay put for a few more days. Of course they understood. Michael told Michael to feel free to transform into their true form should any of the locals happen to show up and that should do the trick.

The horses were still tied up close to the well, and even though Nathan may have liked them, he definitely did not want to ride one all the way back to the airport. He was a bit sheepish about it but still asked the twins to please fly them back to the jet in one of their floating orbs. However, fate was on his side, and his request just made sense. Because as stated before, time was indeed running out. Not to mention that all four of them (including Olivia) were suffering from extreme saddle-sore, giving new meaning to this whole trip being "a monumental pain in the ass". Michael and Liberty were happy to oblige. But never actually seeing horses in real life, they approached the beasts and gently rubbed their long necks. Their kindness and compassion were almost overwhelming, and everyone seemed to take note with a contagious smile. Tommy sighed and proclaimed that maybe there was a lesson here to be learned by us silly humans. Michael nodded and added that these creatures would be a great form of sustenance should any of the Noahmarians become hungry. There was a chorus of multiple gasps, and just before Olivia could say, "Please don't eat the

horses," a rare shade of lime green generated from the alien twins and quickly engulfed everyone in a perfect circle.

The force field made a "SHOOMP!" sound, almost like you were hitting your palm on the end of a steel pipe, and they ascended towards the heavens in their green, glowing ball. It was cushy and quite cozy on the inside. Takarada even liked the smell which would be way too hard to try to explain. Nathan leaned back, placed his interlaced fingers behind his neck and in a funny voice said, "It's the ooooonly way to fly!" mimicking that bird that rode against the tail of a plane in those old television commercials.

What took them all night on horseback now took only a few brief minutes, and as Nathan looked down upon the airport, he could see his beautiful, wonderful jet. A few of the federales were also there leaning against their squad car with rifles in hand. Nathan blew out a heavy burst of air and sighed in relief that it wasn't up on cinder blocks and determined it was money well spent. However, the police officers had never seen a fast-moving, flying green orb and immediately opened fire. The bullets had no effect, and as their floating chariot landed next to the jet, the officers jumped in their car and sped away.

Nathan ran up the boarding stairs leading to the open door, and everybody followed. He beelined for the cockpit, plopped down and started flipping switches in front and above him. The slow whine of the jet's engines grew as the turbines picked up speed. Nathan looked down and saw his new Peruvian friends had even remembered to fill the tank. He thought for sure they would have jilted him on that as fuel was a pretty penny in itself. The airport wasn't empty, but it was pretty dang close to being so, and as luck would have it, the runway was vacant. Nathan contacted the tower and said, "Ready or not, we're leaving." The radio spit back in static, and a treble-induced voice instructed them they needed to wait. Nathan pulled the ol' "Sorry, I don't speak Spanish" card. He taxied the jet to the long stretch of empty runway and floored it. Two squad cars made their way to the foot of the lengthy tarmac, but instead of chasing the plane, they just sat there. It seemed no one at the airport really cared that much about the big jet avoiding protocol and taking off without confirmation, they simply wanted them gone. Nathan pulled back on the yoke, and as they climbed, he was grateful to be leaving without a freakin' posse close behind in high pursuit.

It wasn't long after taking off that everybody on board began to vibrate in a series of colorful tones as their cell phones indicated the numerous messages they each had received. Tommy looked at his and saw he had one hundred and eleven messages from Dickhead.

Takarada had about the same, and even Olivia had a few. Nathan had one, a message letting him know his car warranty was about to expire. Tommy didn't even bother to listen to his as he had a good idea what they were about. He hit return call, but even though they were able to retrieve their messages, they weren't able to call out. Takarada noted that it may take a while before they actually hit a patch of usable cell service. Nathan was able to reach the airport in Hiroshima from the jet's radio, but they were unable to put them through to the Goku, so they simply had to hurry up and wait, something Takarada was sick and tired of doing.

Takarada looked at his watch, joined Nathan in the cockpit and made a suggestion. "Nathan-san, due to our lack of both time and communication with Mount Gokurakuji, would you mind changing course?" Nathan looked puzzled, but ultimately didn't really care, stating he had nowhere in particular he needed to be until his concert next week. Takarada nodded and said, "Very goodly. Please set a course for Liverpool, England."

Nathan programmed the new flight path into his jet's GPS and responded in his best British accent, "Rot awayee cappin'!" He was also happy to see that Liverpool was only half the distance of Hiroshima.

Nathan and Tommy had both been to London before, as had the twins a little over ten years ago, and Olivia had been there numerous times. Nathan played the tape in his mind of when they were all dangerously close while two monsters battled in the Thames from opposite sides of London's iconic Tower Bridge. The scene was unnerving, and one he'd brought up to his therapist on many occasions. It wasn't so much the behemoths themselves as the uneasy feeling it gave him of being insignificant and completely helpless. Glaucusidious in one corner, and Spike (the name he eventually gave to an atomically mutated and oversized spider crab) in the other. This often haunted him in his dreams, always ending the same way with the kaiju smashing the London landmark to a mere heap of historic rubble. But that was nothing compared to the scars left on him from King Taraxian, a terrifying, towering tarantula created by the madman who killed both of his parents. Nathan started to freak out as he always did when he went far too deep into his own head. But thankfully, he had learned in A.A., or "Triple A" as Tommy called it, how to deal with these things. He reached into his pocket, pulled out his trusty sobriety medallion and held it tight. Nathan then took a deep breath, recited the "Serenity Prayer" to himself and could feel the chaos of the freakin' committee in his mind break for coffee. A bead of slow-moving sweat left a trail down Nathan's forehead and, being lost in his own thoughts, he completely forgot Takarada was sitting next to him in the cockpit. He looked at Kyoshi and in a trembling voice said, "You must think I'm crazy, Doc."

Takarada stood up and did the same thing with Nathan that he had done with Tommy many times. He placed his hand gently on his shoulder and simply said, "I am so very proud of you Nathan-san." He then bowed deep and exited.

Nathan brought the jet up to almost 1000 MPH, placed it on autopilot and in a few minutes joined the others in the expensive and only slightly gaudy cabin area. He, like everybody else, looked tired, and he sunk down deep into the plush, red-velvet couch with a sigh. He rubbed his eyes and stated that they had about 8 hours to England and everyone should get some rest.

Tommy was stretched out on a green recliner, that looked more like a lawn chair covered in astroturf, with Suzy nestled on his stomach. He was bug-eyed awake from the amount of anxious energy swirling around in his stomach. He had no doubt about the greeting he was sure to get upon his next encounter with Robert Jones. He wondered if he even had enough ass left for Jones to take another chunk out of it. In his head, he started making plans for his life as a buttless civilian if he was lucky enough not to get court-martialed.

Maybe he could dedicate his life to music again, continue his highly-acclaimed acoustic tour, playing coffee houses for tips, java and audiences of about six people. It would just be him, Suzy and a little place of their own. He liked Imizu, a small, quiet fishing town just off the Sea of Japan he had stumbled upon during an assignment. The thought actually slowed his fast-beating heart down to the point where he could finally sleep. It sure sounded good, and just as he started to drift, he was snapped out of Wonderland by Takarada's snoring. Tommy looked at Nathan and tilted his head sideways in the doctor's direction. Nathan acknowledged the snorting beast by smiling and slipping on a pair of headphones.

Tommy knew the pressure that Doctor T. had endured over the last few months. He was a little miffed at him for not confiding with him that he knew the end of the world was coming, but also knew that Takarada was of the strong, silent, no-nonsense type. It would have surfaced when he was sure, and now he was. The fact that Michael and Liberty were indeed in need of help in Peru proved it. It also gave him some reassurance that maybe Jones would understand why he went AWOL. He thought the Doc looked tired, not just now, but in general. He was super thin, and you could see his eyes were heavy when he wasn't wearing his glasses, which was most of the time now. He wondered if the doc would ever be able to call it quits. Probably not, because there was absolutely nobody like Kyoshi Takarada. Nobody.

Tommy then jumped from that thought to another, and his mind went to Akira Akemi, the love of his life. She was also the good doctor's assistant way back when Tommy first met her. He thought about Akira every day. As a matter of fact, he still wore her necklace religiously, even though he had an identical scar forever burned into his chest. That, however, is a different story, and of all the craziness of the last decade or so, his love for Akira was the one thing he couldn't seem to shake.

Tommy made the rounds and looked at Michael and Liberty who were sleeping, or shut off or whatever the hell it was that they did. He couldn't help but notice that neither had aged at all in the last twelve years. It wasn't that they just looked good for their age, they literally had not changed, not one bit. But after seeing what Noahmarians really looked like, he knew their earthly form was nothing but an illusion. It always had been. And deep down, knowing they were aliens, everybody kind of knew. But after becoming friends and colleagues nobody really thought about it that much. And as far as being bandmates went, they were like most musicians, never caring if somebody was green, yellow, red, black, white, freakin' aliens or whatever, as long as they could play.

Michael's "Surfer Dude Drummer from Outer Space" vibe used to make Tommy wonder if all intelligent life beyond the stars was like him. But thankfully Liberty was nothing like Michael, and after meeting his first collective of aliens, he knew it was some sort of alter-ego persona. He imagined after Michael and Liberty were split that Liberty hit the books and Michael gravitated towards Led Zeppelin and multiple viewings of *Fast Times at Ridgemont High*. Little did Tommy know just how spot-on he was. He looked around the cabin and thought about all of the changes in both his life and his friends. Nathan had nodded off, but then again, he always had the ability to fall asleep anywhere, at any time. At least he wasn't passing out anymore from too much Jack Daniels. Tommy would never admit it, but Nathan had really done something with his life, probably changing more than anybody, inside and out. So much of the vanity that once made up Nathan Fox had truly turned to humility once he sobered up. Physically, he was in the best shape of his life, and he looked great. Olivia looked pretty dang good, too. She had put on a little weight, but it was no deal breaker. You'd never think that two people so incredibly different like Olivia and Nathan would have ever hooked up, let alone get married. But that's the way it is sometimes, and Olivia was Nathan's ying to her yang.

Tommy had never been vain or envious of anybody's looks, talent, social status or even money. Sure, like Nathan he had his bouts with that damn committee in his head from time to time, but being jealous just wasn't his thing. His battles were more with himself than others, and simply being a confident musician seemed to fill in the "I'm special" category for him. Once in a while he needed to defend that role, but only when some snobbish jackass made himself feel like a better player by repeatedly telling Tommy he wasn't. But it seemed (at least for the most part) that those idiots never really bothered him, especially when he had a dang gold record hanging up on his wall.

Tommy snapped out of his own thoughts and hadn't even noticed that Nathan was gone and that Suzy had retired to her backpack. But before he could sit up and look around the cabin, he felt the headstock of an acoustic guitar tapping on his shoulder from behind. He sat up. Nathan placed the guitar in Tommy's hand and said, "Figured you might have a problem sleeping. This oughta' help kill the time." Tommy felt a warm fuzzy for his oldest, but not always dearest, friend. He tuned the guitar and started playing an instrumental version of his all-time favorite song, at least one not by Led Zeppelin, "Over the Rainbow." It was as hypnotic as only that song could be, and Tommy seemed to effortlessly bring it even more to life. Nathan closed his eyes and listened. It was the first time he'd heard Tommy play in quite a while. Sure, he had multiple recordings of him and Tommy jamming, his Vinyl Crush albums and even a demo of their first band, F-BOMB, but there's truly nothing like hearing a musician work his craft live. He complimented Tommy on his new fingerstyle approach to the guitar and secretly imagined them doing an all-acoustic record someday.

Nathan stretched, gave up his spot on the red velvet couch and snuggled up to Olivia who laid across the cabin on her own. Olivia welcomed Tommy's music, and as he settled in from behind, Nathan placed his hand on her stomach, and she covered his with hers. This was the second time Tommy had noticed this, and as he played, it became obvious.

Chapter 9

The Yeti and Dr. Wang

In the Himalayas, everything at the Yeti Institute came to an abrupt stop when the Earth-bound frequency of 1420 MHz just up and disappeared. There was no warning whatsoever, it was simply ... gone. It was becoming even more apparent that Yeti had indeed either been suffering from faulty equipment or it had been some sort of celestial mirage all along. Regardless, there was an undeniable feeling of relief that it was maybe nothing but a false alarm. So, after running yet another scan on their systems, it was officially determined to be some sort of cosmic space glitch. Dr. Chen Wang, the head scientist at Yeti, picked up the phone to place a personal call to Commander Jones of the E.I.O. with what seemed to be good news. However, he was quickly drawn back to the viewing screens within the control center of the institute.

Somewhere between Earth and the moon, the black of cislunar space seemed to be at odds with itself, and Yeti, with no hesitation whatsoever, zeroed in on the disturbance. There was nothing wrong with their computers, and soon they would learn that there never had been. It was showtime, and being this close to Earth, their high-powered telescopes were able to lock onto a satellite feed and tune in for the big broadcast. The scientists within the Yeti witnessed as the darkness distorted and spun in violent succession, leaving what looked like some weird, spinning, interstellar fisheye. Silent lightning sparked from the hurricane within as the circle grew to a massive circumference. All at the Yeti had become hypnotized as every screen, computer and frequency-measuring monitor erupted in a loud cacophony of rings, clicks and beeps. Wang's jaw almost hit the floor; his eyes had become glued to the viewing monitors that surrounded the entire circular-shaped room. Forgetting he was holding the telephone receiver, it slipped through his fingers and down to the floor. It was a wormhole.

Similar to its appearance in the purple atmosphere of Noahmar, Dr. Wang could see two red pinpoints of light growing as they came closer, getting larger as whatever it was on the inside made its way from the opposite end of the long, spinning vortex. The storm from within spat and spun, and as it increased the wormhole became unstable. In a series of violent flashes, space clashed with time itself, and the traversable tunnel collapsed into a brilliant explosion of great light! As the vacuum of space swallowed up all remnants of the clash, only one thing remained ...

With the butt-end of his coffee cup, Wang smashed the glass case that enclosed the "you'd better be damn sure" first alert alarm system and pulled down on the lever. It was an archaic messaging system, using strategically placed towers to transfer ham radio signals in the event of an EMP or something equivalent. It was designed for that very purpose, should any kind of catastrophic event result in all systems shutting down. Or to be on the safe side, should someone ... or something decide to invade. From inside the Yeti it didn't look like much, but from all points around the globe, every remaining military branch on our planet was now on high alert and ready to deploy.

The great Annihilator was here.

***

From high above the clouds, the rapid blinking of its towering beacon could be seen from all ends of the horizon. Climbing over a half mile into the air, the Burj Khalifa in Dubai called out to the heavens with its illuminated invitation. With the surrounding buildings gathered at its feet, its famous height was soon to be its complete demise. The mammoth beast burst through the atmosphere that shielded Earth, and as the flames parted, it set its sights on the first thing it saw, the lights high atop the world's tallest skyscraper. Earth was much, much larger than Noahmar, and even the city of Dubai was on a grander scale than the inhabited regions of the twins' destroyed home. However, grander scale or not it didn't matter, because it was all merely bantha fodder to the oncoming space kaiju.

Even before the stratosphere had been breached, the emergency call from the Yeti Institute went out all over the world, including the United Arab Emirates. The UAE military took to both land and air, and Dubai went dark as multiple searchlights shot towards the sky. Annihilator had the Burj Khalifa in its sights and jetted with immense speed towards the tower from above. Like on Noahmar, the dark skies made it difficult to make out the details of the beast, but there was no denying how massive it was.

The form appeared to have thick, claw-like feet as well as matching hands consisting of three digits and a thumb, each with razor sharp nails as big as a bus. They were immense and almost looked too big for its armor-plated legs and arms. Even though the finer details were hard to make out, its silhouette was not. As it broke through the calm evening clouds, two veined sets of jagged, almost fly-like wings burst out wide like demonic parachutes to slow its rapid descent. Its torso looked to be full, muscular and massive. Its head, shrouded in the dark, almost appeared to be part of its body, with enormous red, oval eyes. It seemed to be eighty meters or so in length and looked quite small compared to the half-mile-high structure that awaited its call, but it didn't matter.

Annihilator descended headfirst and fast on the towering monolith with its paired wings streamlined behind its body. With immense speed, it spiraled like a threaded needle in and out of the skyscraper as it made its way down. When it reached the bottom the monster pulled up, bursting from the base of the building in an explosion of smoke, blue glass and steel. It rose up, then landed feet first on the ground with such an impact that

the entire planet shook, causing the now honeycombed Burj Khalifa to collapse in on itself!

BWAM! KA-BOOSH!

The monster flexed, clenched its claws and shrieked at the remains of the building while the flames and dark gray dust climbed to the sky. It then raised its left leg and brought its enormous foot straight down upon the adjacent Khalifa mall with a thunderous crash! Mighty girders of iron and steel bent like mere licorice twists as it caved in on a countless number of screaming shoppers and tourists. An expanding spill of terrified people escaped to the streets in all directions, and the horrific beast began picking them off one by one with quick, short beams of light from its eyes. In a split second, their lives were gone in a single little poof. Their riches, influence and power meant nothing, and now they were just ... dust. It turned, kicked itself out of the rubble and made its way to the streets, stepping on and destroying one kabillion-dollar car after another. Like the people it vaporized, none of this "status" stuff meant a damn thing to this horrible creature from the stars.

Multiple lines of tracer rounds fired like glowing phosphorous dots through the smoke, immediately trailed by three Mirage 2000's bursting through the blackened haze. In a triangle formation, they shot over the skyline and came about with their Vulcan cannons blazing hot red from the rapid machine gun fire. The cavalry had arrived! People in the streets cheered the jets on as they unloaded their payload into the chest of the steel-armored monster, only to no avail. They immediately upped the ante and switched to a succession of air-to-air missiles that blasted from the wingtips of their jets.

SHOOM! SHOOM! SHOOM!

But just before impact, the beast's wings came forward, wrapping itself in some sort of sinister shield! The missiles exploded against it but couldn't penetrate the veined cocoon. Like some sort of pissed-off vampire, it hissed and opened its wings revealing its morbid, spider-like head that was actually part of its upper thorax. Its eyes lit up red, and twin glowing beams took out all three jets in one fell swoop!

The UAE military responded, and a fleet of fast-moving Leclerc battle tanks thundered down the streets in two lines. These mechanical marvels were monsters within themselves, each at almost ten meters long with a 120mm cannon belching twelve rounds per minute! The tanks were soon within firing range of the Annihilator, and their guns erupted! The first two pummeled the beast with everything they had, then after exhausting their ammo, each turned in opposite directions to make room for the next two in line!

CHOOM! CHOOM! KA-CHOOM!

It was a bombardment of epic proportions! Annihilator advanced on the fleet, bringing its entire weight down upon the next tank with the heel of its tremendous foot. It folded like a mere aluminum can, then exploded beneath it. It reached down with both claws, picked up the next tank in line and lifted it above its body with an iron scream! Multiple lines of bright morse code dots filled the beast's back with hot lead as the second fleet of Mirages descended. With one jet taking up the rear, the front two rocketed towards the beast from behind with their gatling guns working overtime. The skill and precision of these pilots was amazing, especially when they parted to the left and the right at the back of the monster just before impact. The third jet continued the assault as the first two went ahead just far enough to come about for another attack. With great strength, the creature hurled the tank at one of the oncoming jets, and they collided in midair sending a rain of exploding shrapnel to the streets below. Almost an entire city block detonated, and as the tar and concrete gave way, so did the buildings that were caught up in the horrific explosion.

There was no escape for those caught in the trenches of war-torn Dubai as the masses took to the streets like a horde of depressed zombies. It was hard to imagine that only a few minutes ago people were going on with their lives, jobs and vacations in the world's richest city. Covered in white dust, dirt and blood many marched towards the sanctity of nothing as they tried to wrap their little heads around what just happened. At least on Noahmar, they had the portal allowing escape for a few. Here (and on who knows how many other planets) there was no escape. Earth had not achieved anything even close to that kind of technology. We had no stargates, wormholes or ships that could travel the galaxies. We instead had cell phones, TikTok, Facebook and enough weapons to blow ourselves to kingdom come.

The military of the United Arab Emirates fought valiantly, but they were no match for the annihilator of worlds. One attack after another proved to be futile as the massive monster countered them on every move. This thing wasn't like any daikaiju before; it was quite intelligent and had the means to back up its devastating arsenal with well thought out strategic precision.

From about a mile away, the mobile commanding officers, press and growing crowd witnessed the mass destruction as the fires now illuminated the skyline of Dubai. The cameras rolled, and the world observed as cannons, tanks, guns and bombs had no effect whatsoever on this horrible behemoth. Funny ... with all of its great wealth and riches, neither its sticks nor stones could bring this abomination down. Another emergency call went out around the world, but now it was requesting more reinforcements as this branch of the UAE military dwindled down to nothing.

The planet watched in horror. It had been over ten years since the last attack, and many thought the wars were over. Yes, Earth was a mess, but there was something about World Kaiju War One and World Kaiju War Two (WKWI and WKWII) that brought the planet together for the sole purpose of survival. Now, people seemed to be more about people and less about self. Many petty disputes among bickering countries had not necessarily been resolved but put on permanent hold. It was a magical metamorphosis, and probably one that could only happen as the result of war and catastrophe. But now as the significance wore off, the human race did what it always does ... it forgets.

Nothing could save the city, and as the rest of the world tuned in, they knew that WKWIII was upon them.

Just like on Noahmar, it was time to call it a day. The angry monster clenched its three-fingered fists and flexed its arms to its side as though it was curling weights. Steam hissed through its leathery skin while thick veins protruded from its biceps, and in nothing shy of a millisecond, a great wave of pure energy erupted from it.

ZWOOP! FWOOOOSH!!

An underwater silence replaced the screams, chaos and wailing sirens as the city was engulfed in a brilliant display of subatomic particles. It didn't look like a typical explosion, but more like a magnificent dome that destroyed everything within its growing confines. It was hard to take your eyes off of it, and the commanding officer from the nearby outpost watched in sheer horror. First, because of the total annihilation of the city, and second, because of the oncoming wave of energy that was charging at them like an enraged tsunami. In the precious two seconds they had left, the crowd took cover, only to be vaporized in their third and remaining second.

Chapter 10

Liverpool

Both remaining branches of the E.I.O. were beyond frantic, exploding in a frenzy of cavalcading chaos. Forgotten for nearly ten years, the world again turned to the Earth Intelligence Organization, looking for answers primarily on how to destroy the Annihilator before it destroyed us, if such a thing was possible. Nukes were even on the table, but with the E.I.O. suddenly regaining much of its control, Jones immediately put the kibosh on all nuclear or atomic weapons.

After landing in Liverpool, Takarada strapped on his backpack from the confines of the cabin and collected his thoughts. He knew that for the majority of the planet everything was about to change, if it hadn't already. Dubai had become world-wide knowledge, and even when you're travelling at forty thousand feet, news travels fast. Dr. Takarada looked and admired this little group of ragtag misfits as they exited the jet. He couldn't help but smile. He loved all of them, even Nathan. They were his family, and he would fight tooth and nail for each and every one of them.

It was goodly to have Michael and Liberty back too, he thought. Goodly, however, may not have been a strong enough word, because he was convinced they would probably wind up saving all of our asses. Their telekinesis abilities will no doubt be useful in the war, the one that was now upon them. Even though he knew this, his brain still hadn't registered that Earth was now their home. It made him think of the stories his father told him so many years ago about the towering creature that took his family away from him. He started to wonder if aliens had parents, and it occurred to him the loss everybody had suffered over the years. He wondered why all of this was hitting him now. He had over ten years to figure this out, and now the floodgates were crashing open. But that's what war of any kind will do. It makes you think and prioritize what's truly important. It was then he realized that they were all the same, they were all orphans of the beasts. Now they were up against the kingpin of them all, and he had no idea what they were going to do. In all the excitement of the past few days, Takarada forgot to worry. Now in this brief downtime, the weight of the world was back on his shoulders. But instead of letting it get the best of him as it had over the last few months, he just shook it off, drawing strength from his friends.

Upon arriving at the LP in England, Takarada made his way through the pandemonium with the Scooby gang in tow. Tommy was relieved that he didn't have to deal with Commander Dickhead at the Goku and knew this would give his ass a fighting chance, at least for the time being. He was eager to pitch his side of the story to anybody as long as it wasn't Robert Jones. It'd been a long time since the Liverpool base had seen this kind of action, years as a matter of fact. There was a heavy feeling in the air, only it wasn't one of excitement, but one of fear and uncertainty. Last night the world watched as this massive alien from space took out a city, decimated an army and killed thousands of people. Who was next? An attack could be anywhere, including the town or metropolis that you yourself live in! Nobody knew, not even the E.I.O. The only thing they did know was that the alien kaiju had headed back into space and was now slumbering somewhere on the dark side of the moon.

Practically kicking down the door of the base commander's office, the first thought to run through Takarada's head after their bold entrance was one of complete disbelief. He looked at the figure behind the magnificent oak desk and was stunned. It was Robert Jones, and he wasn't happy to say the least. Tommy held on to what was left of his butt, and in a vain attempt opened his mouth to defend their decision to go AWOL. Without the slightest hesitation, Jones cut him off at the knees.

"Quiet Taylor," Jones hissed in a rather low monotone and emotionless timbre, and it wasn't just Tommy who was about to lose a chunk of their derriere. "I warned you, I warned all of you not to go galivanting around the planet on some personal mission of mercy." And as he said this, he peered at Liberty and Michael with a foul gaze. He stood up from behind his desk stating there were multiple facets as to why he couldn't just shoot them down, but if he could've had his way, that's exactly what he would have done. Six jaws hit the ground as they listened in complete and total disbelief. Tommy figured it'd be bad, but not this bad. He wondered if Jones was using some sort of scare tactic to forever cure him of his rampant insubordination. Tommy looked at Jones and asked him if he had completely lost his mind, then lied, proclaiming that he forced Takarada to leave the base. Jones shook his head, letting him know that it was a good thing that they did, because it was one of the reasons they didn't blow them out of the sky. Tommy's eyes widened in bewilderment, and he again questioned Jones's mental stability. "Are you freakin' nuts?" he demanded.

"Had you not gone AWOL, we may have had some sort of fighting chance against last night's invasion. However, you, Taylor, along with the others, were all having a grand time getting reacquainted on Mr. Fox's private jet." Typically, being the strong, silent type and one to never lose their composure, Dr. Takarada started tapping his index finger against his own hip. He knew the absurdity of this and also knew he needed to respond.

"So, Commander, you are blaming Tom … General Taylor for the devastation caused in Dubai? This creature wasn't even supposed to enter our atmosphere for another few weeks. Yes, General Taylor disobeyed your orders." Then added, "As did I. But I am concerned not only about your reaction, but your sanity, because the Noahmarian survivors may be one of our greatest defenses against this beast, the one I am calling The Annihilator."

Commander Jones didn't as much as flinch at Takarada's common sense. Instead, he pushed up on a tiny red button that was concealed beneath the lip of his desk. "General Thomas Lynn Taylor, you are under arrest and are to be escorted to a cell within the confines of this base, where you are to await trial. You are being held for high treason, endangering lives, disobeying direct orders, stealing E.I.O. property and anything else I can think of."

Tommy and everybody else were stunned beyond comprehension, almost bordering on shock. This was wrong on so many levels, and Tommy freakin' knew it. He needed to do something. So he did, he panicked. He lunged fists-first at the commander, and as he did, the office door swished open. He somehow managed to tag Jones in the face just as two big LP gorillas grabbed him by the shoulders and pulled him struggling towards the door. Nathan started to freak, and just like Tommy, he panicked. Not knowing what to do, he jumped on the back of one of the guards, and they began to spin around. Olivia stepped back and away from the chaos as four more guards paraded into Jones's office. One reached for Takarada, and Dr. T. spun around and kung fu kicked him in the chest. Jones then slithered up from Olivia's side and wrapped his forearm around her neck. Normally he'd be no match for her, but for some reason she did nothing, and upon seeing this, Nathan yielded.

Michael reached for Liberty, and Jones motioned the index finger of his free hand back and forth sounding like Newman in Jurassic Park with a subtle, "Ah, ah, ah." He then added, "I would not do that, as a few rather large E.I.O. transports have just landed to see to your fellow travelers in Peru. They were so grateful, they even let us separate them by their new earthly genders. They're as helpless as you're about to be when I put you in two different cells." Micheal and Liberty, like Nathan and Olivia, had no choice but to yield. Jones then looked at Tommy and Takarada. "Well?" he asked, and both men simply raised the palms of their hands in surrender. Jones gave an approving nod, then padded the bustle out of his uniform and said something they never say in the movies. "I will accompany the guards to make sure nothing goes wrong." As they exited, Jones put his hand on the back of Michael's shoulder to let Liberty get ahead of him. He then reminded the guards to keep them separated.

For being over one hundred years old, the Liverpool base was still quite impressive. It was also mind-blowingly huge. With his right hand next to his sidearm, Jones took up the rear as they entered the elevator that would bring them deep down into the bowels of the LP. As they descended, Tommy was hoping this was just a set up and that Jones would knock out the guards, apologize for the charade and they'd all become besties. Tommy waited, but it didn't seem like it was going to happen. Knowing the LP inside out, Olivia commented that they were going far deeper than the holding cell level, and as soon as it came out, a cold chill ran down her spine. Jones grinned, "I know what you are thinking, and you would be right. However, I need all of you for the time being. I would just like to show you something. Since you are so fond of reunions, I'm going to reacquaint you with another old friend."

The elevator stopped, and a second set of doors parted from the other side of the lift revealing a long hallway with two guards at the end. They filed out and made their way down the hall. Seeing Jones, the guards stepped aside, and the top-secret bay opened for them to enter. As they walked through the doorway, they found themselves on a metal catwalk encased in thick glass that circled the top of an enormous bay. Nathan and Tommy at first weren't quite sure what they were looking at, but Takarada instantly recognized the mammoth round monocle that was staring them down. "Nanite kotoda," he uttered as he covered his mouth in both shock and surprise. It only took about a second, and soon everyone knew just what they were looking at. It was The Duke! The freakin' fifty-some meter, organic thorium fueled, six-gun photon blasting cowbot in all his ass-kicking glory!

Tommy and Nathan cracked up, as uncontrollable laughter was typically their response to seeing the large cowboy mech that they had piloted so many times. It was contagious too, as soon Olivia, Michael and Liberty couldn't help but giggle a bit themselves.

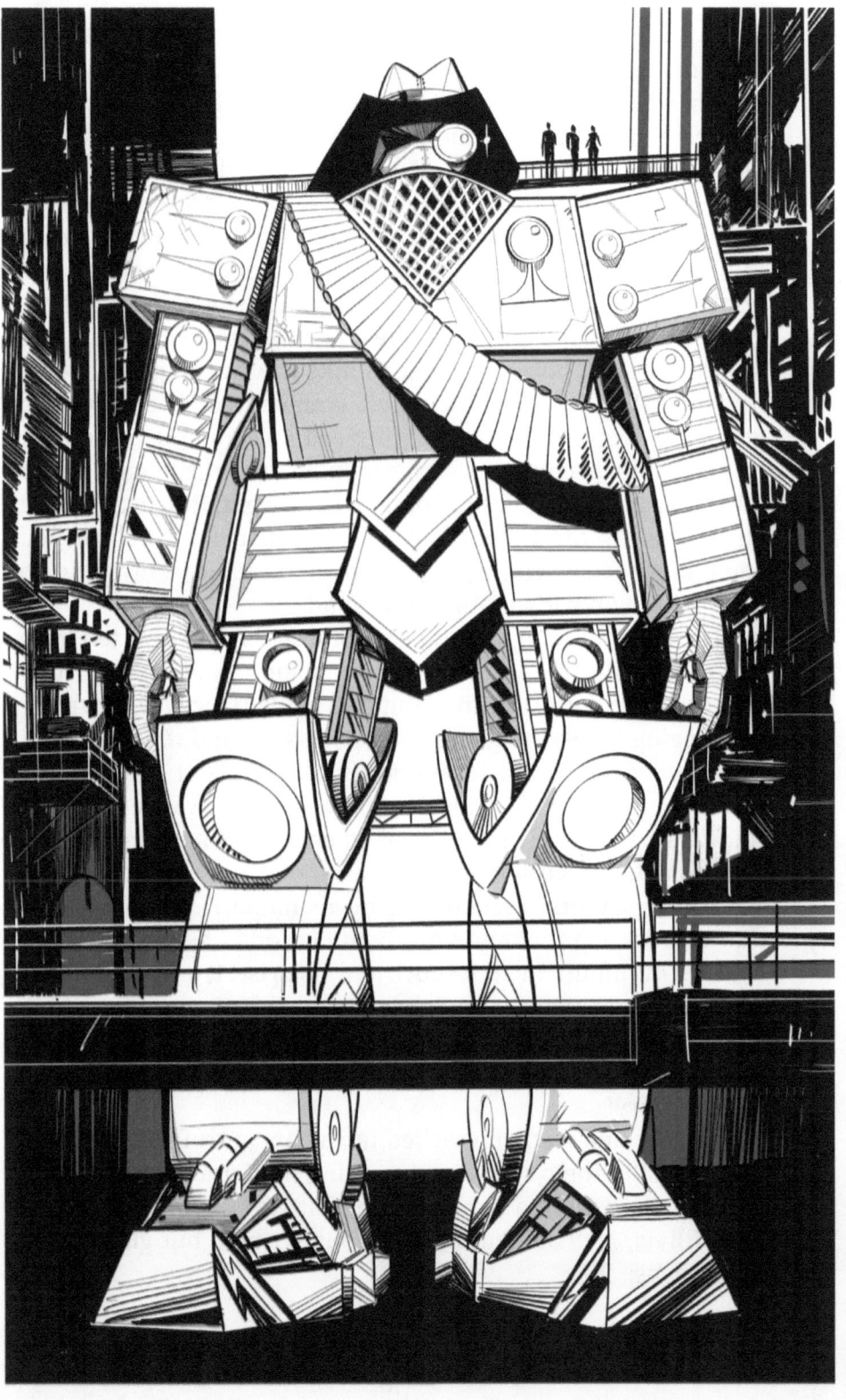

Olivia pushed her glasses up and stated that she never understood why a giant cowboy robot would wear a fedora instead of a cowboy hat. Even Takarada, who designed the thing, couldn't help but grin at the comment. As they pondered, Jones became furious as this was clearly not the response he was hoping for, which of course made it even funnier.

Nathan (while still laughing) then stated the next obvious thing that was probably running through everybody's thoughts. "It'll be a cold day in Hell when I step back into the head of that thing. I have enough problems keeping my own mind straight." And he was right for thinking so, as the giant cowboy mech worked off of each of their subconscious minds. Each member of the now defunct band, Vinyl Crush, had their own role to play in the working and functioning of the towering mech. While placed in an induced coma known as the sleep state, Tommy, Nathan, Olivia, Michael and Liberty each contributed a vital role in the Duke's operations. And as quirky as this thing was, make no mistake about it, it was deadly. Sporting an array of weapons and agility, it had been Earth's best defense against daikaiju and other giant nasties. The six-foot-in-circumference monocle alone that stood in front of them could shoot a beam of pure organic thorium capable of taking out a complete city block. And they knew this, because that's exactly what had happened just a few years ago.

Metal echoes rang throughout the bay deep within the Liverpool branch as E.I.O. workers performed an array of last-minute preparations. Geysers of steam burst through the metal, and sparks fell to the ground from high above as welders worked to seal up the remaining cracks. Thinking the Duke had been completely decommissioned after battling King Taraxian in Antarctica, Dr. Takarada was at a complete loss for words. He was shocked that this could have gone on without his knowledge or input. Something was wrong here, and it only solidified his decision of not trusting those who are capable of stealing your thoughts and ideas. Of course, it had nothing to do with ego. It did, however, have everything to do with his inventions being used for sinister purposes, and this reeked of just that. Not quite knowing what was going on, Tommy agreed with Nathan out loud, claiming neither he nor his friends will be getting back into the Duke for any reason. "Such arrogance," Jones sneered. "Nobody is expecting you to."

From the opposite end of the bay, five figures entered and walked single file across the metal bridge that led to the back of the Duke's head. Tommy remembered when SCOTT helped them in for the first time from the roll bar just below the brim of the cowbot's massive hat. He was glad to see Takarada's android creation, known as SCOTT, wasn't with them, because whatever was happening here wasn't right. Tommy almost inquired, but Dr. T. shook his head with a look of, "Do not say a word," and fortunately Tommy picked up on it right away. It was odd though, as the new robotonauts who were climbing aboard the Duke looked more than just familiar. It was them to a tee. Nathan nudged Tommy and said it was like watching a rerun of their past lives. Then he shuddered as he often did when he thought about those days, especially the ones he couldn't remember. Finally, Doctor Takarada demanded to know the meaning behind all of this, and Jones remarked that it was simple.

"We rebuilt the Duke here at the LP, and these are our new robotonauts. They may look familiar to you. Well, that's because they *are* you, twelve years ago. Not too long ago, they played you in the Vinyl Crush sanctioned touring act, Superstar. Each one will be taking on your individual duties within the Duke that you have all made so clear you'll have no part of."

"Wait a minute," Tommy demanded, "They're a tribute band?" Instantly Nathan, Tommy and Michael broke out in uncontrollable laughter. "You got a freakin' Vinyl Crush tribute band to pilot the Duke?" Not seeing the humor in this whatsoever, Jones turned a few shades of red and put an end to the preshow highlights by ordering them to their cells. As they were escorted out, Michael and Tommy argued about which of their replacements was better looking, and Nathan commented that even though the idea was super lame, he still liked the name Superstar far more than Vinyl Crush, which he always hated.

Jones was true to his word and brought them all to the LP's holding cells. There were six in total, three on one side and three on the other. They were dark, musty, smelt of wet stone and must have been as old as the LP itself. The guards placed Tommy, Nathan and Michael in the furthest jail and put Olivia, Liberty and Dr. Takarada in the one closest to the exit with an empty cell in between. In the middle cell across from them, Tommy noticed a person buried under the gray, wool blanket of their cot and wondered if they were even still alive. This place sucked, pure and simple. This had to be some sort of nightmare, it was so hard to fathom. Court-martial? Jail? The Duke? And worst of all, a Vinyl Crush tribute band? This was getting far too real, and with the slamming of the iron doors and clanking of the turning keys, they were all prisoners of the E.I.O.

Chapter 11

An Old Friend

Hours passed and little sleep was had. Takarada laid on the cold floor and may even have drifted off for a bit as he was able to prop his backpack under his head for a makeshift pillow. If he was sleeping though, it didn't last long because Tommy, Micheal and Nathan must have formed a new band sometime during the night. Their few hours in the joint must have been laying deep on their souls, and they were suffering from a serious bout of the blues. Singing an old tune Tommy and Nathan used to do in F-BOMB, soon the entire cell area was ringing out with a less than stellar version of "I'm A Man" by Muddy Waters. Nathan took lead vocals, Michael played lap drums and Tommy sang the signature riff. Soon everybody was wide awake, like it or not.

Dah-Donta-Dah-Dunt ... "Now when I's a young boy"
Dah-Donta-Dah-Dunt ... "At the ol' age of five"
Dah-Donta-Dah-Dunt ... "My Mutha said I was gon' be"
Dah-Donta-Dah-Dunt ... "The greatest man alive"
Dah-Donta-Dah-Dunt ... "But now I'm stuck in this cell"
Dah-Donta-Dah-Dunt ... "With my idiot friends"
Dah-Donta-Dah-Dunt ... "I should be back at home"
Dah-Donta-Dah-Dunt ... "Sleep in my rich-ass bed"

At this point the girls joined in from the other side of the cell and echoed Nathan on the words of the chorus, "He's A Man."

Dah-Donta-Dah-Dunt! ... "Cuz' I'm a man" (He's a man)
Dah-Donta-Dah-Dunt ... "Way past twenty-one" (Twenty-One)
Dah-Donta-Dah-Dunt ... "Stuck in this cement tomb" (Cement Tomb)
Dah-Donta-Dah-Dunt ... "With no bathroom" (No bathroom)

And quicker than you could sing "I'm A Man," they were again making sweet music together. Okay, so it wasn't the greatest, but it still seemed to come so naturally. It was the same chemistry that propelled them to stardom in the first place. It wasn't the E.I.O.'s Golden Rock Star Package, because there were plenty of other bands and artists that were offered the same deal that never amounted to anything. Tommy used to believe the old record executive theory of "They'll like whatever we tell them to like," but learned that "that" is not necessarily the case. It's not the juice behind the band, it's not the money, it's the music they create, it's the stories, it's the personal connection with the fans, a common bond. Whatever that may be.

Upon the next verse, Nathan switched to rhythm guitar giving Tommy the Dah-Donta-Dah-Dunts to play over. Tommy stood up and broke into an air-guitar lead and sang a wonderful solo that even ol' Muddy himself would have been proud of! Nathan then came back in singing with a second verse ...

Dah-Donta-Dah-Dunt ... "Now when I's younger"
Dah-Donta-Dah-Dunt... "Thought I knew it all"
Dah-Donta-Dah-Dunt ... "From the bottle to the gutter"
Dah-Donta-Dah-Dunt ... "Just a shitfaced, mother fu ..."

"God blind me Nathan, you're going flat again!" Bellowed from the middle cell across from theirs, and if they were holding real instruments they would have surely fallen to the floor. An awkward silence took the place of the music, and everybody looked around the holding area attempting to pinpoint the source. The main security door hadn't been opened, and there were no windows whatsoever, just six individual cells with a walkway between each side of three. The only place it could have come from was the blanketed cot in the other cell, but it hadn't appeared to move even once the whole time they had been there. Nathan wrapped his hands around the bars, squished his face in between the rods of iron and attempted contact ...

"Hey you! Clump on the cot! Hey! I'm talking to you!" Nathan turned towards Tommy and raised both his palms and shoulders up indicating he hadn't a clue. He also felt the need to defend himself and his flat vocals, but before he could utter another word, the clump on the cot sat up. Still shrouded beneath the gray wool blanket as though it were an overgrown hoodie or something, it spoke again.

"You've always had that problem, my boy. When you relax you go flat, when you get excited, you go sharp, but when you focus, you get it right." There was only one person whoever said that to Nathan Fox before. It was word for freakin' word, and Nathan never forgot it. But it was impossible, because the person who said it was gone. Not just gone, but dead. Dead as in left this realm, moved on to another plain of existence, singing with the angels, you know, dead. Takarada approached the bars, because impossible or not, he recognized the voice and knew right away. His eye's swelled up, and with a trembling voice he said the name of an old friend out loud in the form of a question.

"Sir Jonathon?"

Everybody approached the bars of their cells in order to get as close as they could to the source in question. They waited with bated breath, and after a brief but lengthy pause, Takarada's old friend answered him, "Hello Kyoshi." The room erupted in varying screams of disbelief that reverberated off the cement walls from all present. That is from all but Takarada, who remained quiet as he fought to hold back the tears. In addition to being overwhelmed, he also had an onslaught of mixed feelings running through his head, everything from joy to frustration to anger. Even so, Takarada still kept his composure, as he often did, and simply asked Sir Jonathon for an explanation before passing judgement.

Jack, however, was not as good at composing himself as the good doctor was, and the cheers from the others prompted him to shed his cloak and jump up from his cot, which was usually not an easy feat for a man in his eighties. But to everyone's amazement, Sir Jonathon (or Jack as he was known to his friends) looked totally awesome! He was much thinner than he used to be, even looking to be somewhat buff. Jack's infamous walrus mustache was gone, and though he was a bit scruffy, you could now at least make out his pencil thin lips, hook nose and broad chin. That stoic, brigadier appearance everybody had come to associate with Sir Jonathon Winston was gone, and he now looked more like an aging rockstar. The change wasn't too much of a stretch though, and Takarada even saw it coming a few years back as Jack readied himself for retirement.

However, for Kyoshi Takarada, it wasn't about Jack's studly new look, it was more about him still being alive when everybody (including Takarada) thought differently. Now for the E.I.O. that's old hat. After all, when you use rockstars as agents, the first thing you have to do is tell the world they're dead. Overdose was always a popular favorite, but plane crashes and the occasional terminal illness worked just fine in most cases. But this wasn't even remotely the same, as Takarada himself was told something different, or to put it bluntly, was flat out lied to. So, the big questions for Jack (if this really was him) were why, how, and who, and before he could even think, he was hit with a bombardment of rapid-fire queries. It was understandable, but nonetheless frantic and overwhelming, and Jack barked out an abrupt, "Enough!" like only he could do. The cells echoed with Jack's commanding voice, and everyone instantly and instinctively shut the hell up. Yup, it was Jack.

Sir Jonathon pulled his flimsy cot up to the bars and squatted down upon it. It creaked and moaned, but like a birch tree, bent, but didn't break. Everyone else mimicked Jack either by doing the same or simply sitting upon the cold, cement floor. Either way, it appeared to be story time.

"First off, Kyoshi," Jack explained, "even if I had been ordered with the possible threat of execution, I would never ... NEVER ... leave you out of the loop my friend. I know your heart has grown weary of others, and trust is hard for you to come by these days." Takarada was the only one still standing and shifted his gaze from the cracks in the floor up to Jack. "I know this because our betrayals are similar. So know, Kyoshi, if I would have had any way to let you know I was still alive, I would have." Takarada nodded, and Jack continued.

"As far as I can tell, I've been here for almost two years. Shortly after my retirement I was ordered here to meet with Robert Jones, and I've been a prisoner ever since."

Tommy couldn't help it. Like a little kid he blurted out, "I knew it! I knew Jones was crooked!"

Jack answered with a contradicting "Hurumph!" and boldly stated, "That's not Jones." Tommy's jaw just about hit the cold hard floor, but it wasn't because he was shocked, but because he'd always had a feeling in his gut.

"How did you figure it out?" Tommy asked, and before Jack could answer, Takarada shook his head, sighed, and answered for him when he came to the realization.

"The eyes."

Jack nodded, "Yes, the eyes. Robert Jones, the one I knew for years, had a condition called anisocoria. One eye was blue, and his other pupil never became dilated, giving him the appearance of two different colored irises."

Nathan again raised his palms outwardly asking, "So?" and Takarada, feeling a little ashamed for not noticing this either, once more answered for Jack.

"They got it backwards."

Jack nodded and repeated what Kyoshi said, "They got it backwards. His right eye had always been blue, and my misfortune was not keeping my mouth shut upon noticing."

"They? Who the hell is they, and if it's not Jones, who is it then?" Nathan shrieked, and both Michael and Liberty responded at the same time from their different cells.

"It's more than probable that they are Velatians from the Luhman 16 System located in the constellation of Vela."

Nathan glared at one twin, then the other with a bit of a confused look on his face. "The whose-it's from the what's-it's?" Normally Michael and Liberty found Tommy and Nathan's brand of humor somewhat pathetic, but still amusing. This time though, not so much. Not because of Tommy or Nathan themselves mind you, but because they now knew it was without a doubt the inhabitants of Velatian that destroyed their home.

Takarada stated he didn't think that the two brown dwarfs of Luhman 16 were capable of sustaining life or even a planet for that matter, and the twins again responded in unison.

"They are not. However, they used to be, and every planet in that system fell prey to the Velatians. Now it is nothing but a galactic graveyard of smoldering worlds. Thousands of years ago as the suns began to cool, the Velatians knew they would need to find another planet to ensure their survival. Nobody is exactly sure how old their species is, but they far exceed Noahmarians. While quite advanced, there is still something barbaric and undeveloped about them. And to the best of our knowledge, no one is quite sure what they look like, as they always take the form of the apex species of whatever world they are conquering. They are like a terminal virus going from planet to planet. But they don't travel by ships, they travel by portals held within the tapestry of the universe. They have been known to take over governments, religions, corporations and such, using Annihilator as little as possible until they are through."

Tommy then broke into the conversation. "So, they put their little plans together, infiltrate, start draining the planet's resources, then bring in this annihilator thing to flex its muscle and mop up when they're finished?"

Michael grimaced and replied with a, "That's pretty much it, dude. They had a hard time getting past the Noahmar elders and couldn't make any headway, so they just opted to destroy our planet. They're not the brightest stars in the galaxy, if you get my drift, but neither are Earthlings, so they've assumed control of much of your world's governments already."

Tommy nodded and stated, "Yup, we're pretty much the trailer park of the galaxy."

"What is the Annihilator?" Olivia asked. "I mean is it alive? Is it a machine?" The twins again replied together,

"We believe it is both. It is a cyborg of immense size and strength that was designed to defend Velatian centuries ago. Our elders stated that once the Velatians created this living weapon, they realized they had also created the greatest power in the universe. The elders of Noahmar also believe that this is when the Velatians went from using the Annihilator as a source of planetary defense to something much more sinister. The Velatians discovered they could not only save their species but also dominate the entire galaxy by exterminating all other forms of life." For Dr. Takarada it was all coming together, and as a cold wave of fear overwhelmed his senses, he whispered those infamous words of Oppenheimer beneath his breath.

Tommy started freaking and pacing his cell, repeating that they needed to somehow break out of this damn cement tomb. Like Takarada, he was beating himself up. However, for Tommy it was about simply not seeing the writing on the wall. For Dr. Takarada it was about seeing it, but hoping his conclusions were wrong and therefore not doing anything sooner. Neither were at fault, but one thing's for sure, they had both become much wiser when it came to trusting their guts.

As he walked back and forth, Tommy started naming all the things that had been directly in front of his face the whole time. "No new weapons or E.I.O. locations in over ten years, the extreme budget cuts, Jones being an absolute impossible dick, no new recruits, the cheesy, makeshift base at The Goku and last and probably least, his broken door and crappy Wi-Fi. it was just one thing after the other. Tommy's anger mounted, and in his frustration, he began punching the bars of his cell with his robotic hand. The steel chimed upon the metal hitting metal, but it was no use. They weren't budging. Soon he was kicking the bars as though he were trying to find some sort of resolve within his rage, but it just wasn't there.

"Taylor!" Sir Jonathon shouted from his cell. "Stop acting like a spoiled brat rockstar and start acting like a bloody general of the Earth Intelligence Organization! Last thing we need is to go all willy-nilly! Action my boy! Not fear! We'll figure a way out of here. We need to stop that bloody team of robotonaut wannabes from setting foot in The Duke." It had been some time since Tommy heard Jack's thundering walrus roar, and it was still just as scary as ever. There was also something reassuring in it too, because unlike Commander Jones, he always trusted Jack. They had been through too much together and seen each other at their best as well as their worst. Tommy stopped, placed his palms against his eyes and with his back against the prison bars, slid down into a squatting position. He took a deep breath, reached into his inside jacket pocket and pulled out a pack of cigarettes.

As he lit up, Tommy asked Michael in a foul tone why he and Liberty didn't tell them this earlier. Michael simply stated, "Because we didn't know dude. But as soon as Sir Jack mentioned that 'They' got it backwards, both Libs and I knew it could only be the Velatians. That's their galactic calling card compadre. And who knows how many people they've taken over." It was funny that with his "surfer dude" alter ego, people often forgot (or didn't know) that Michael was an alien and much smarter than your average bear. Sort of like when people confuse kindness for ignorance, and Michael was far from ignorant.

Olivia asked both Michael and Liberty if taking over their bodies was the Velatian's plan for them also, and they replied together, "More than likely, it is." Nathan and Olivia glanced at each other through the iron bars that separated them, looking a bit more worried than normal. Olivia then cleared her throat, and as nicely as possible, asked Jack why they hadn't killed him yet. Jack responded,

"As far as I can tell, for information. I believe they can take on physical aspects such as your voice, body and looks, but not your mental ones, so they need to learn your memories. Every once in a while, they'd drill me for information, and I'd give them nothing but rubbish. Bloody body snatchers."

Tommy took a long drag of his cigarette and, as he exhaled, asked a question while Nathan flapped his arms to clear the all-consuming smoke. "You told them to bring in the tribute band, didn't you?"

Jack responded, "Absolutely not, my boy. I don't know what the plan is, but they won't survive in the Duke even if they're just taking him out for a bloody Sunday stroll. It isn't designed for impersonators, it's designed for you five, and you five alone."

Takarada nodded. "I have to believe that so far all of their training has been simulated, and they've never actually gone up."

Olivia was confused, stating, "I don't get it. Why do they even need the Duke?" and Nathan shook his head in agreement.

"Yeah, why all this fuss?" he asked while still waving away the smoke from Tommy's second cigarette. "I mean why not just have this Annihilator thing come in and take care of everything in one fell swoop?"

"It's not that easy, my boy." Jack replied. "Chances are they are infiltrating the powerhouses of the planet to destroy as little of it as possible. After all, they want our resources, and a charred wasteland is probably not in their best interest. My guess is that's the only reason Jones was so opposed to nukes. Trust me when I talk about how best to manipulate the masses. This way they can even try to overtake all of our bodies so Earth will better accommodate their needs. This whole bloody escapade with The Duke is probably nothing but a ruddy dog and pony show. Just like the E.I.O. is nothing now but a front. And one more thing ..." Jack suddenly stopped talking and focused in on Tommy who was about to light up yet another cigarette.

"God blind me! Taylor, you're smoking!"

Tommy looked at the cigarette, held it up, turned it a few times and responded, "Yes Jack. I am smoking." Then he made a "So what?" gesture with his face.

"Didn't they search you guys when you came in or when you were in Jones's office?"

Takarada, who was again laying on the floor with his backpack as a pillow, immediately sat up, kind of like Michael Myers in Halloween, groaned, face-palmed his forehead and (referring to himself) grunted, "Watashi wa hontōni oroka desu." He then unzipped the backpack and out jumped Suzy.

About a thousand things were running through Jack's head. One being, "What the hell is a bloody beagle doing in Takarada's backpack?" and another was, "How in the world did these boneheads ever get along without me?" Nathan started laughing and stated what everyone was thinking, "Wow, you're right Jack!

For being the scourge of the universe, these aliens sure ain't too bright."

Sir Jonathon smiled, thinking something similar in regard to present company, but held his tongue and simply acknowledged Nathan's comment, "Indeed they are not, Mr. Fox. Indeed, they are not."

Suzy scanned the area and located Tommy in the far-off cell that was holding him, Michael and Nathan captive, then went into action. She stared at the bars, and two thin slits of green light casually projected from her eyes.

ZZPPPTTT

The steel gates that separated the cells turned red-hot and Suzy simply stepped around the molten metal of their cage as it dripped to the floor. She pranced through the empty cell in-between (the one that made sure the twins were at a good distance from one another) then proceeded to repeat the process.

ZZPPPTTT

"God blind me!" Jack yelled. He knew Suzy had to be one of Takarada's Organic Thorium androids. For the first time in years, Jack's big ol' walrus stache' wasn't covering the entire lower half of his face, and you could see his teeth when he smiled. Tommy picked up an ecstatic Suzy and blew a giant raspberry on her witto' tum tum. Nathan ran to Olivia, and Michael approached Liberty. The alien twins grabbed each other's hand, and every bit of steel that made up and separated all of the cells began to hum. In a split second they looked more like glowing purple light sabers than jail bars, and then they just disappeared. As did the twins.

"Whoa!" Nathan exclaimed. "Where'd Michael and Liberty go?"

Tommy had a slight smile on his face as he thought about what the twins would do to whoever was holding the remaining survivors of Noahmar captive. He knew they couldn't take the lives of anybody on any planet, but he also knew they could make things quite uncomfortable for those who crossed them. His slight smile then turned to an evil sort of grin when he imagined Michael and Liberty teleporting Jones into one of those flying orbs of theirs and floating him into deep space ... naked, with a clown's nose. Tommy cracked himself up and then thought, "Too bad they couldn't do the same for the Annihilator," not necessarily the clown nose part, because that'd have to be one damn big nose, just the floating it back into deep space part. But he knew the twins didn't have that kind of power. Besides, there really wasn't such a thing as deep space for this creature. He then started to imagine the Annihilator not only with a clown's nose, but also sporting a red afro and wearing a black and yellow polka-dotted outfit while doing a little jig. As strange as this sounds, it's simply how Tommy's mind worked, and before he could take it any further, the twins reappeared. Tommy looked at his watchless wrist. "What'd that take, like two seconds?" He then looked at Michael who was also sporting a sinister grin, and Tommy wondered what he did to those poor bastards.

Kyoshi asked the twins if everything was "goodly," and they responded together with a simple, "Yes." He then walked over to shake Jack's hand. Jack rapped his muscular arms around his old friend and just about squeezed the life out of him.

It was almost as though Jack's tight grip snapped Takarada out of a long funk. He knew he hadn't been at his best, but now he felt as though he could see some light at the end of the tunnel. These Velatians that had consumed his mind with troublesome worry for so very long had their weaknesses. Not to mention, it didn't seem they were too bright. The cloud of haze in his head cleared, and he felt a strong confidence, one he hadn't felt in a long time. Maybe because the Scooby Gang was back together, maybe because Jack was still alive, or maybe it was because he needed to stop living in fear and get back to just ... living. Back to dreaming and having a little hope that maybe, just maybe, things will work out. Takarada smiled to himself, and Jack leaned down and whispered to him, "You know Kyoshi, we've made mistakes. But just because we've made mistakes, it doesn't mean we are one."

"It is time to kick some of the ass!" Takarada boldly stated! Everybody cheered and raised their hands in the air, then just stood there in an awkward kind of silence.

"Well, what now, Sir Jonathon?" Takarada asked. Jack laughed deep, a little like Santa Claus, and quickly answered him,

"Well, we can't just sit around waiting for the next ferry. We need to get out of here."

Olivia pushed her glasses up and asked the obvious question, "And just how do we do that?" Jack responded,

"Why, we steal the Duke, of course."

Chapter 12

Good News & Bad News

The good news was that the Velatians didn't seem too concerned about Takarada and company as they made their way through the lower ancient halls of the Liverpool base. Olivia pointed out the archaic cells at the LP were over a hundred years old and rarely used anymore so they weren't really even monitored. More good news was that both Jack and Olivia were well acquainted with the LP, so they knew just where to go. And even better news still was that they had Suzy, and the twins could again use their telekinesis abilities. So, it seemed their luck was changing for the better.

The bad news, however, was that the further they ventured out from the cells, the more guards they had to ditch. Worse news was that the bay area that held the Duke was infested with them. There was no way of telling who was or was not a Velatian. Some of these men and women were just LP flunkies following orders. And even worse yet still, as Tommy peeked out the door of the small closet they were currently hiding in, he saw the Vinyl Crush tribute band wannabes coming out of an elevator and right towards them. Tommy did a double take because it was really weird seeing his twenty-seven-year-old self coming down the hall. Wow, they were dead ringers, he thought, except he was convinced he was much better looking than his poser stand-in. He also thought Nathan's double was much better looking than the actual Nathan. They were being escorted by two guards single file down the hall and were no doubt heading towards the Duke. And to top it all off and unbeknownst to them, the Annihilator had awakened from the dark side of the moon and was heading back towards Earth. So, it seemed that maybe their luck hadn't changed after all.

Jack's hugeness consumed most of the space in the closet they were hiding in, and his elbow was pushing straight up into Nathan's nose. "Damn, Jack," he loudly whispered, "get your freakin' arm out of my face." Jack grunted and moved forward pushing Michael into Liberty and Liberty into Tommy when the door busted wide open and they exploded like dominoes into the hallway. Aside from looking like a scene from an old Marx Brothers movie, they were now all on the floor looking straight up at their doppelgangers. Tommy grinned at a guard with quite the synthetic smile, and as he reached for the comm unit at his side, Suzy jumped out of Takarada's backpack and attacked. It was as though the leader of a foxhunt sounded the horn, and its cry called everyone to action.

Jack jumped up, and with his right forearm sent the other guard to La-La Land with just one hit, and the battle commenced! Tommy yelled to Nathan, "I'll take Tommy, and you take Nathan!" For a split-second Nathan looked puzzled, but when the fist of his double made contact with his face everything became crystal clear. Nathan shook it off and immediately spun and landed a reverse roundhouse kick to Nathan's head. Nathan went down, and Tommy jumped over Nathan to get to Tommy but was blocked by Michael. Tommy went down, and Michael pounced towards him. Liberty grabbed Michael's hand, and a rubbery green force field engulfed Tommy, causing Michael to bounce off Tommy and land on Nathan. Olivia made her way over to Olivia. Olivia face-palmed her and in a calm demeanor simply said, "Sorry girl, but I am NOT playing." However, that didn't seem to stop Olivia, and she lunged at her but came up short when Suzy latched onto the cuff of Olivia's pants with her teeth. Michael grabbed Liberty's hand and absolutely nothing happened, probably because they weren't Michael and Liberty, and Liberty then grabbed Michael's hand, and a purplish-green orb erupted knocking Michael, Liberty and Nathan to the ground. Tommy jumped over the three and managed to peg Michael square in the head with his heel. Michael lost his grip with Liberty and hit the ground. Takarada, who deemed himself more of a lover than a fighter, joined Jack and Olivia against the wall of the hall and watched in amazement as each band member fought their double, except for Olivia, of course, who was still preoccupied with Suzy the wonder beagle.

"God blind me!" Jack yelled. "I know they have their physical differences, but at the rate they're fighting, it's still bloody hard to tell the good guys from the bad!" Olivia squinted and pointed out that Tommy had shorter hair than the other Tommy and also sheepishly mentioned that the real Tommy was better looking. Just then Nathan slammed head-first into the wall next to Olivia and sunk to the floor in a sitting position. Olivia knelt down and stated,

"This is the real Nathan, Sir Jonathon." Jack asked her how she could tell, and Olivia (agreeing with Tommy) said that her Nathan isn't quite as good looking as the fake.

Nathan, beat to a pulp, uttered, "Thanks a lot," through his fat lip and immediately returned to the brawl.

"By the way, Olivia, my dear," Jack asked of one of his all-time favorite E.I.O. agents, "how come you're sitting this one out?" Olivia gave Jack a warm and heartfelt smile and placed the palm of her hand on her stomach. Jack gasped and let out a hearty chuckle. "Well, I'll be. Who's the father?" he joked. Olivia punched Jack in the arm, and as Nathan again slammed into the wall next to him, Jack shouted, "Congratulations, my boy!" He then picked Nathan up by the scruff of his neck and threw him back into the fight.

Olivia hugged Jack hard and began to weep, "I'm so happy to see you." Jack returned his affection and tightened his grip on Olivia. "I'm scared Jack," she whispered with her face buried in his not-so-sweet smelling shirt. "After mom and dad were killed, I kind of just shut off emotionally. It's makes for a great agent, but not much else. I can't believe it took Nathan Fox for me to see how much more there was to life. I kind of feel like now that I understand, it's all on the verge of being taken away."

Sir Jonathon sighed; he'd always had a very special place in his heart for Olivia. It wasn't long after both her parents were killed that she moved to London and worked under Jack at the very building they were now trying to escape from. Jack backed away from Olivia and put his hands on the sides of her upper arms.

"It seems like it was a lifetime ago, and sometimes I forget that your parents were from Salt Lake City. The truth, my dear, is that there are no promises or guarantees that we'll be given another day, or even another hour. And I don't say that just for us, because it's like that for everybody, every ruddy day of the week. In my life, I've discovered the trick is to not take any of it for granted. Because the moment you do, it's gone." Olivia pulled back, wiped her eyes and looked up at Jack. "We'll get through this, Mrs. Fox, and those Velatians are going to be sorry they ever trifled with the likes of Sir Jonathon Winston." After that no more words were necessary.

Tommy jumped and landed a flying elbow smash into the back of Tommy's head, and the last of the Vinyl Crush posers went down face first. He wiped the sweat from his forehead and looked down at the human clump that laid beneath him. He then noticed something and wondered if maybe this human wasn't actually human. He called Michael over and put his index finger on a small X-shaped incision on the back of Tommy wannabe's lower neck. "Look familiar?" he asked. Michael squatted down giving it a closer look and nodded his head. He then asked Nathan to turn not Nathan over to see if he had the same mark. He did, and he did. Michael stood up, and he and Liberty stated in unison, "They are not human. They are Velatians."

As Nathan stumbled over to Olivia, he stated that since they were Velatians, he didn't feel so bad for kicking their asses. But as he said this, he had a horrible thought. "So," he asked of Michael and Liberty, "does this mean the real members from the Vinyl Crush tribute band are already dead?" They replied,

"Unfortunately, yes Nathan. It does."

"Why would they need to kill them?" Nathan asked. "I mean at some point they must have been willing."

Michael and Liberty explained, "Remember Nathan, it is the Velatians' intent to exterminate all Earthlings. They have already stolen many lives, and this is just the beginning. There will be no slaves, they will not use us as cattle, there will be no survivors. It will be complete and total annihilation."

Takarada then interjected, "Maybe they resisted the Velatians, and as a result were replaced. Or maybe it was the Velatians' intent all along to simply learn what the doubles' knowledge of each band member was, absorb them, then hope they, too, could operate the Duke." Tommy then interrupted Takarada ...

"Or maybe they needed pilots because they're bringing in the Duke as a tag-team partner for the Annihilator!"

Michael and Liberty again interjected, "Another thing to consider is that the Duke is also one of Earth's greatest resources, and simply utilizing its power is beneficial to them. There may also be another reason, but as of yet, we do not know what it is."

Then Jack, assuming control as he so often did, summed things up. "Right. We don't know the reasons as to the why, but this just made our jobs a whole lot easier. Take their gear. Kyoshi and I will put on the guard's uniforms, and everybody just act like we own the place. These Velatians aren't too bright, and by the time Jones figures out what's going on we'll be rocketing through the stratosphere in that wretched cowboy robot!"

"With a pissed off Annihilator hot on our trail!" Nathan added. Jack nodded his head,

"More than likely."

The launch bay that held the Duke was bustling with a mix of LP Flunkies and Velatians as they prepared the cowbot for departure. Only it was hard to tell who was who from a distance, and those (who were actual humans) had no idea the others were not. After taking the elevator up, Tommy and the others strolled right up to the sentries watching the double doors that led to the entrance of the towering mech. They stood erect, opened the doors and saluted the two guards leading the way. They didn't seem at all concerned that one uniform was a bit too tight, and the other was a bit too large. They did, however, eye down the five robotonauts as they walked by single file onto the catwalk that encircled the cranium of the robot. So far, so good. From their prior training, Tommy knew to take the lead and bring the other four to the back of the Duke's head where they would enter the control room to take their positions. One after another they swung in from the roll bar, and just before Tommy followed suit, Jack casually told him where they would meet as he gave him an "All systems GO" pat on the back. Tommy looked stunned, but before he could say anything, the thick metal hatch slammed shut, and the wheel upon it spun, sealing them in.

The seating arrangement within the head had changed, and instead of five separate cubicles, there were now seven forward-facing seats. The two pilot seats in front had twin yokes for maneuvering and steering the cowbot, along with three seats in the middle and two in the back. The circular catwalk that encased the cockpit area was also gone, and with the way the seats descended towards the main viewing monitor, it reminded Tommy of a movie theatre. The giant screen was tall and curved, almost completely outlining the inside of the Duke's cranium up to about where his ears would be. Tommy soaked it in, thought how awesome *Attack on Titan* would be from here and wondered if he could stream it. Yup, it was that cool. "Wow," Nathan said, as he and everybody else looked around amazed (and a bit worried) at their remodeled digs. "They've even added passenger seats! Too bad we didn't know, Jack and Doctor T. could've joined us!" Tommy noticed an array of small, circular lenses built into the walls of the cowbot's cockpit. He stepped beneath one and raised his index finger to his closed mouth indicating the Duke's head, like his own, was full of bugs.

Tommy surveyed the area and finally whispered, "This is totally different," admitting he was a bit relieved that he didn't see any of the helmets that induced the horrid sleep state that allowed them to operate the mech. However, he was a bit concerned, as it looked to be completely manual now. In the past, the Duke's main computer that linked them into the system was accomplished by SCOTT, Takarada's android creation, that in a sense tied everything together. But it seemed SCOTT was the missing puzzle piece, and they had to devise a simpler way to operate the fifty-some-meter cowboy mech. So obviously, making it manual was the Velatians' answer, and now they only had a few precious minutes to figure out how to fly this damn thing.

Tommy wished they had Suzy. Had he known of the new luxury layout within the Duke, he could have brought her and maybe tapped into the mainframe. In a sense though, he was glad they didn't because the way Jack and Takarada looked in those dumb uniforms, they were going to need all the help they could get. "Besides," he thought, "should anything unpredictable happen, we have ..." Tommy stopped, and with a calm demeanor looked at Liberty and Michael. In a voice, just above a whisper, he stated, "the twins."

Michael tilted his head and responded with a well-thought-out, no-nonsense, right to the point, "Dude?" Tommy, in an instant, went into General Thomas Taylor mode and, not knowing if anybody was listening, told the twins his plan in a very soft, almost inaudible voice. He then told Nathan to sit next to him in the front and for Olivia, Michael and Libs to take the middle three seats. The control panel was so different, and for Tommy and Nathan who were both expert pilots, they still couldn't make heads nor tails out of it. There was writing on the panel, but it was in some ancient Arabic sort of text filled with odd shapes, eyes, cats and weird-looking people (or whatever they were) holding vases. But if his idea worked, it wouldn't matter.

Static consumed the massive viewing monitor that surrounded them, and Tommy instructed everybody to strap in, look down and pretend to know what you're doing. It flashed as the screen projected a badly animated image of a world atlas and an Egyptian-looking Duke following a series a dotted lines to Paris, France. Nobody was quite sure what it meant, but they soon knew without a doubt when the cheesy cartoon Duke decimated the Eiffel Tower. It was the trajectory of the Duke's first mission as a Velatian weapon. Nathan was right, the cowbot was to aid in their destruction of the planet. A voice came through the comm system, but it was like nothing anybody had ever heard. It had to be Velatian. It was harsh and sounded as though it had just eaten a gravel sandwich, with each sentence ending in a loud, sharp grunt on the last word. The in-flight movie of the Duke's trip to Paris faded, and the voice of the Velatian seemed to chirp as though it were laughing.

The screen again flickered, but this time switched to a digital windshield, giving the pilots a panoramic view as though they were looking at the world from the eyes of the cowbot.

From the Duke, nobody dared say a word. The Velatian then said something else that sounded just like what it had already said, and there was a long pause. A bead of sweat rolled down Nathan's nose as everybody just continued to look down towards the control panel in front of each seat. It was taking too long. The silence roared, Tommy looked up with just his eyes and his brain went into overtime. "Crap," he thought, "this was a bad idea. We're so dead." He started to freak and unstrap his safety belt, but a sudden series of metallic echoes and thunderous clicks from the outside bay pulled him out of his panicking mind.

From the viewing screen it seemed the walls of the massive rectangular-shaped launch bay that housed the robot began to lower. Tommy wasn't sure, but it seemed the Duke was on some sort of platform, and the giant hangar around them was descending. From above, the electric sound of moving steel and rotating metal could be heard as a beam of light flooded their large monitor in a wash of white. It was the sun creeping in. The walls weren't going down as he had thought, they were rising up!

Outside the air raid sirens screamed as the entire city block that surrounded the Royal Liver Building began to shake. People stumbled about, while others lost their balance and fell to the sidewalk. Liverpool had experienced earthquakes in the past, and this felt like a foreshock at about a 4.0 on the seismic scale. Which means it has the potential to get ugly, but this wasn't a quake.

The ground-level garden courtyard located within the four sides of the Royal Liver Building trembled as it began to part in the middle. As it did, the mammoth platform on which the Duke stood rose up in conjunction with the ceiling as it opened from above. From the streets, terrified people screamed and ran, while some watched in curious horror. From the center of the building, the lift on which the towering robot was perched creaked as it ascended towards the sky. The mech's shadow cast down upon the city and grew taller as it went up, leaving a long black silhouette of itself at least ten city blocks long. Then, when the platform was level with the top floor, it stopped with a thunderous jerk and a loud clank. In a heartbeat the shaking stopped, the sirens quit, and everything went silent. And there, while still upon its perch, (but looking as though it were standing on the roof of the Royal Liver Building) the Duke stood tall and mighty while steam hissed from various parts of its iron-clad skin. The twin clocktowers that donned each end of the Royal Liver Building stood much taller than the roof, giving it the look of an old castle. But as lofty as they were, they didn't even come to the mech's knees. From below the onlooking crowd was no longer scared, as a matter of fact they cheered, recognizing The infamous Duke. Like Vinyl Crush, it had become a legend in its own right. It gave everybody a sense of hope and confidence knowing that it was our turn, knowing that Dubai would be avenged.

Though this wasn't the invaders plan for the bot, it had indeed become just that, and the Velatians were in for a big surprise as the Duke prepared for flight ...

And the Velatians were in for a big surprise as the Duke prepared for flight ...

and the Velatians were in for a big surprise ...

"What the hell's the problem?" Tommy bellowed at the twins.

Michael, almost crushing Liberty's hand as he held on to it, gnashed his teeth and let Tommy know that he wasn't helping in the least. The inside of the Duke's head, where they were sitting, shook and glowed a dim, putrid, pinkish purple. Tommy looked around and wondered if this was going to work after all, thinking that maybe the twins didn't have enough power. From outside the giant robot hadn't lifted off but was shaking as a glow of the same hue as inside the cockpit began to spread all over its steel body. Nathan grabbed Olivia's hand and squeezed, almost hoping he could give the twins that little extra jolt of electricity they needed. A loud ringing filled the head of the cowbot, and Tommy recognized it from when he and Takarada wound up in the infirmary. It became ear-shattering. Everybody screamed, and as they did, the dim, putrid, pinkish purple turned to a bright neon green. When the noise stopped, the Duke jettisoned into the sky!

SHOOOSH!

Everybody cheered, (except for Michael and Liberty who were a little busy) and Tommy told the twins to head due west. He was hoping they had enough juice to get them over the Atlantic and to the United States. In the meantime, he, Nathan and Olivia started going over the controls in an effort to hopefully figure a few things out about the all-new-and-improved Duke.

As Tommy fumbled around, he felt his pants vibrate. He pulled out his cellphone, and the caller I.D. displayed the word, "Dickhead." He held the phone up, stated that it was Jones calling and Nathan snatched it out of his hand.

"Hey Dirtbag!" he yelled into the cell, and Tommy corrected him,

"It's Dickhead, not Dirtbag." Nathan cupped the phone with his palm,

"What?"

Tommy repeated, "Jones is a dickhead, not a dirtbag." Nathan looked a little perplexed, un-cupped the phone, asked Jones to hold on, covered it again and went back to Tommy.

"What's it matter? Dickhead? Dirtbag?"

Tommy replied, "Jones is a dickhead." Then he asked Nathan if he remembered the sleezy manager of the Flooid Zoo in Tokyo, Nathan sneered as he nodded and Tommy casually stated, "He's a dirtbag."

Nathan thought about it, then responded with the long, "Oh," of understanding and went back to the phone.

"Sorry for making you wait ...," Nathan giggled, "Dickhead," and immediately hung up on Jones.

Olivia rolled her eyes and thought for sure Jones would call right back. But instead of the sound of Tommy's ringtone, they heard a loud boom from behind them, and the Duke shook and rattled. Michael tightened his grip on Liberty's hand, but creating a giant floating orb around something as big as the Duke was hard enough. The only thing the twins weren't controlling was the massive viewing screen that the Velatians kicked in before they took off. Tommy could see something approaching fast from the starboard side of the cowbot and, though he wasn't sure, he still had a pretty good idea what it was. He told Nathan and Olivia they had company, and when they looked, whatever it was, was gone. Olivia told Tommy to quit freaking out. He looked out again and she was right, it was nowhere to be seen. He rubbed his eyes, looked forward and shrieked when he saw that what was beside them was now directly in front of the screen and coming right towards them. Nathan and Olivia saw it too. It was a terrifying, not to mention incredibly huge, massive, nasty, bug-like creature at least thirty meters taller than the Duke.

"Oh my God, that's the Annihilator," Nathan said softly. "That's gotta' be the scariest thing I've ever seen. And considering Nathan had once come face-to-face with a twenty-story tarantula, that meant something. Again it disappeared, and nobody knew what to think. Olivia started to frantically go over the controls trying to figure something, anything, out.

BWAM!

It was another explosion from the rear, only its impact was much heavier this time! It must have hit the Duke somewhere, and it was so intense that everybody went flying about the cabin. Michael groaned as he flew out of his seat, and as he did, he lost his grip on Liberty. The green hue that illuminated the cockpit of the mech vanished; the orb was gone. In that very second, the cowbot immediately started plummeting head-first towards the Atlantic.

Chapter 13

It's Up To You, New York, New York

Thanks to their telekinesis abilities, the twins were able to manifest a green, glowing orb that engulfed the Duke in an outer layer of irradiated skin. Pushing the limits of their powers, the field they created enabled the metal, monstrous mech to blast off from Liverpool in (as they say) the nick of time, once again saving our heroes butts! And because of the amazing speed the alien-propelled Duke was traveling at, they had already flown halfway to New York. However, keeping something as big as the Duke airborne was still quite the task, even for the alien twins. Yes, getting the cowbot the hell out of Dodge was their main priority, and even though the mech packed an arsenal of mind-blowing weapons, they had access to none of them. Of course, that's when tall, dark and creepy decided to show up.

From about 40,000 feet the Duke descended like a missile straight down towards the North Atlantic Ocean with the Annihilator hot on its trail. After being hit on the left boot, the creature blew off one of the cowboy mech's giant spurs and sent Michael flying throughout the cockpit. He struggled against the G-forces to get back to Liberty's hand and regenerate the force field that kept them afloat. As the cowbot nose-dived towards the sea, Olivia, Tommy and Nathan frantically pushed buttons and flipped switches hoping for something to happen. Michael grabbed onto the top of one of the cushioned seats with his right hand and stretched his other arm towards Liberty. She grimaced as she reached for him, extending her arm just about out of its socket. Michael screamed and forced his hand forward while pulling himself closer using the seat as leverage. Liberty stretched even further, and she, too, screamed in both pain and determination. If one could even as much as touch the other, they could resurrect the surrounding orb. Liberty's index finger trembled and was only about a millimeter away from her twin's. Michael tightened his lips, and in a burst of resolve, he pulled himself even closer as the tips of their fingers danced while trying to make contact.

CHOOOOOOM!

The Annihilator, still following close in the wake of the Duke managed to tag the bot with a short laser burst from its eyes. This time, the back of the cowboy robot's left upper thigh blew into a million pieces of raining steel! Michael once again went flying, nailing his head on the wall as the cockpit shook from the shock of the explosion. He was out cold. From their altitude, it would only take a few short minutes before they crashed into the ocean. And at this speed, it wasn't going to be pretty. Both Tommy and Nathan each instinctively yanked back on their yokes, but nothing happened. Olivia continued flipping switches, but it was useless.

Now it's not like Olivia to lose her cool, but there were definitely a few hormonal-type changes taking place within her body. With the exception of confiding in Jack, she thought she had done a pretty good job of not letting the proverbial cat out of the bag. Or in her case, the proverbial bun out of the oven. But of course, it was obvious to everyone. Nathan was even sworn to secrecy and had been chomping at the bit to tell somebody, anybody, but valued his life more than his need to blab. So, Nathan promised Olivia he would keep his mouth shut until she thought the time was right, and apparently the time was right.

The cockpit of the Duke shook and creaked with massive bursts of turbulence as they fell at a rate of 10,000 feet per minute. Olivia wobbled to stand up and began shouting at the top of her lungs, "I am freakin' (only she didn't say freakin') pregnant, and I don't want my baby, my husband or my friends to die in the head of this God-forsaken robot!" And that's all she said. You can't blame anybody for not stopping to hand out the cigars as they just kept fumbling with the controls in what seemed to be a futile effort. Of course, the nonresponse made her that much angrier, but what did she expect? Besides, Tommy and the twins had figured it out long ago. Concerned for her friend, Liberty, who unlike Michael was still seated, put her arm around Olivia's waist and tried to get her to sit back down. Olivia, however, wasn't as sad as much as she was just plain mad, and as Liberty eased her down, Olivia side-kicked the back of the front row seats.

CRACK!

She kicked so hard that Nathan's head flung forward and nailed the panel just to the right of his steering mechanism with a tremendous thud. With that there was a series of flashes, and the inner cranium of the cowbot's cockpit went from the dismal, gray of a cloudy winter's day to that of the Norway Spruce that lit up Rockefeller Plaza on Christmas Eve.

From the left side of Tommy's control panel, a circle of a hundred or so lights were now blinking in a sequence leading to a large, red glowing button within its center. It looked pretty obvious, but Tommy was still a little uncertain. After all, maybe it was a self-destruct switch. He looked up, and the viewing screen that pretty much acted as the Duke's eyes had become consumed by the blue of the sea. It was also impossible to tell just how close they were to colliding with it, but they were approaching at a breakneck speed. Whatever this button meant, it was now or never. "Screw it!" Tommy yelled as he mashed the button with his fist.

Flames erupted from the bottom of the bot's boots as a heavy thrust sucked everybody deep into their seats. FWOOOOOM! Even more lights appeared within the cockpit as a series of almost animated readouts appeared on the viewing monitor. Nathan rubbed his forehead. It was bleeding, and Olivia knew it was her fault. She was sorry, but somehow nobody felt bad about it in the least, not even Nathan. The double steering mechanisms clicked, moved forward, and neither Tommy nor Nathan hesitated. In no less than a heartbeat, they both grasped the yokes and yanked them back. Michael, still out cold, flopped about the cabin as Liberty and Olivia screamed, holding onto each other as they were sure that this was the end.

"Pull Tommy!" Nathan yelled. "Pull! Everybody freakin' shut up and hold on!"

Tommy and Nathan gave it everything they had, bellowing in a strong fixity of purpose as they almost pulled their helms right out of the cockpit's front panel! But it was working, they were starting to ease up. The brim of the bot's hat cascaded with the surface of the sea, but just before impact, they rocketed up leaving nothing but a pair of vapor trails behind them! Then, before climbing too high, Tommy and Nathan instinctively and together pushed their steering mechanisms forward. The cowbot descended back down to just above the surface of the water, leveled off and continued on at about Mach 1.

Nathan blew out a mammoth sigh of relief, following it up with a "Holy crap, that was close."

Tommy analyzed their surroundings through the Duke's viewing screen and said he couldn't see the Annihilator anywhere. He also suggested staying just above the water to avoid any possible radar surveillance. They still had no idea how the Velatians controlled Annihilator, but they weren't taking any chances. They were also increasing in speed and even now hadn't a clue about the cowbot's weapons or how to fire them. But now, thanks to Nathan using the old noggin, they at least had power and could steer the dang thing. Oh, and being alive to do just that was also another perk.

Michael sat up, rubbed his head where it had collided with the inner wall of the Duke's cockpit cabin and eased himself back up and next to his twin sister. He, Liberty and Olivia continued investigating their front control panels for any clues whatsoever as how to gain full control of the bot. Tommy wished Takarada was there but also knew just how damn smart Olivia was. And because they weren't on the verge of colliding with the Atlantic Ocean from freakin' 40,000 feet, he wasn't quite as worried about it. He was however, a little concerned to where the Annihilator had disappeared to.

***

As the sun set on the city that never sleeps, its vast array of towering skyscrapers began to contradict the dark. Over the East River, the majestic Brooklyn Bridge, like a child straggling behind its big-building parents, was the last to light up. And that was the first thing the Annihilator homed in on when it appeared from out of nowhere in the early evening skies of New York City. As it did before, it descended straight down feet first towards the metal giant that connected one land to another! The rush hour traffic traveling in and out of Manhattan still consumed the three-laned highways that ran in both directions on the lower level of the bridge. It was also loaded with cyclists and pedestrians. But none of them saw it coming, and the Annihilator landed directly in the center of the bridge between its two 84-meter, stone gothic towers.

KERAAAAANG! CRASH!

Screams of terror ignited from those witnessing the beast's crushing feet as they pulverized a mass of people into the pavement of the upper deck. Its tremendous weight crushing them to a horrible death just before breaking through the top level to the traffic below. The historic monument didn't stand a chance, and in less than a second it started to crumble. The almost 16-inch galvanized steel suspension cables made a hollow metallic sound as they snapped one by one like mere pipe cleaners. The Annihilator broke through the lower deck of the Brooklyn Bridge, and it, along with hundreds of cars and pedestrians, plummeted into the East River. Cars sank, and the cold, murky water pulled those trying to swim straight down into its depths. The river, however, didn't even come to the Annihilator's waist, and it eyed Manhattan with vicious intent from the center of the collapsed bridge.

It's monstrous pair of double wasp-like wings were still extended, but it chose to wade through the river to the shore of Lower Manhattan. It lifted its massive leg out of the water, slamming its foot down onto the FDR Parkway. The majority of the cars still upon the highway had been abandoned, as it seemed running was simply a better option than waiting to die. The impact was horrendous, creating muffled explosions from beneath the soles of the beast's flattening feet as cars burst into flames. Then with one more step, the Annihilator left the banks of the East River making landfall in the financial district of Manhattan Island.

It was almost as though the city had created a clear route of wide streets and smaller buildings that would allow the creature easy access to downtown. However, there were a few towering obstacles in its path, the first being 8 Spruce Street, the tallest residential skyscraper in the world. The shimmering monolith of glass and steel stood at 73 stories, almost three times as tall as the Annihilator. But not only did it house thousands of New Yorkers, it was completely inclusive with stores, entertainment and even a public school.

The wings of the monster folded up and retreated back into its cockroach-like shell, and it eyed the building as though it were picking a fight. The brute, with obvious malice, crouched down, almost like an 80-meter, 40,000 metric ton football player and rammed into the building with its shoulder! Glass rained down upon the city streets, and the skyscraper rocked, but it did not fall. The surrounding city streets filled with an expanding lake of horrified men, women and children. People screamed in sheer and unbelieving horror as they took to the streets in a vain attempt at saving their own lives. The individuals were of all races and religions, old, young, gay, straight, good, bad, whatever, it just didn't matter. The monster played no favorites as it crushed them into oblivion. To the creature, we were nothing but an assortment of various chocolates all within the same box. We were one thing and one thing only, the enemy, and we needed to be exterminated.

Once again, the beast backed up and charged, trampling hundreds in the process before crashing into the majestic tower. *WHAM!!!!!*

The steel girders just above the skyscraper's deep foundation bent and started to give way within its foyer. Pressure blew out the street-level picture-glass windows, and dust and debris followed as the manmade mountain started to tip. It was loud, sharp and harsh, and the only thing louder were the people it was about to fall on.

Its slow tilt turned to an all-out fall, and the building toppled sideways towards downtown and onto the adjacent Woolworth building. The historic cement and limestone skyscraper pancaked as a result of both the horrendous impact and utter weight of its falling neighbor, and they both collapsed to the ground. A thick, white smoke of burning solid materials spread throughout Lower Manhattan as it simultaneously erupted into the night sky. It was a nightmare of unbelievable proportion, reminiscent of that foul and treacherous September day many years ago.

The Annihilator screeched at an ear-piercing level, and through the haze it cast its gaze upon its next victim, One World Trade Center.

***

Almost as though they were traveling on a cushion of air, the Duke parted the water beneath them as they hauled ass over the sea. Tommy and Nathan kept a firm grip on their steering mechanisms, but it was getting harder and harder as the cowbot continued to increase in speed. At this rate, Tommy didn't think the twins could even stop it. Olivia continued to scrutinize the controls all around them, but nothing seemed to work. They were rocketing towards New York City and Nathan and Tommy both knew they were going to have to climb back up before colliding with the coast. Neither one wanted to expose themselves to radar surveillance, but chances were the Velatians knew their exact location. But what nobody in the cockpit knew was that the Annihilator had beaten them there, already taking a significant bite out of the Big Apple.

Tommy's pants vibrated, and a rectangular glow could be seen through the fabric. He looked down, and soon the head of the Duke was reverberating with the song, "I Think I'm Turning Japanese."

"Dude!" Michael roared, "I love that song!"

Tommy squealed, "Oh my God! It's my phone, and it's Takarada!" Tommy in his "hesitant" ways was a little reluctant to answer. Like usual, his committee immediately kicked in, ever convincing him that it had to be something extremely bad, something along the lines of Jack was dead and Dr. T. was calling from the LP as Jones held a knife to his throat.

"Good Lord, Tommy! Answer your freakin' phone!" Nathan demanded. "I got this," he added, referring to steering the mech.

"Hello?" Tommy stated in a fashion that came out more like a question rather than a greeting. He didn't say a word as he listened with a puzzled look. After that, he simply nodded and handed his phone to Olivia. "It's for you."

"Hello?" Olivia stated in a fashion that came out more like a question rather than a greeting.

"Yes, this is she ... Okay ... Okay ... Good-Bye." Olivia concluded the call by pressing the red button of Tommy's cell and then stood up next to him.

She handed him back his phone, and Tommy, Nathan and the twins all bombarded her with a series of queries. "Well? Are they all right? Where are they? What about the Duke?"

Olivia didn't say a word, she just reached down, between Tommy's legs, eased his seat back and flipped four adjacent switches. It wasn't particularly mind-blowing, or seemed like that much of a big deal, but it was. The bot had become fully operational. Olivia squealed and began a quick diagnostic.

"I tried those switches!" Tommy defended.

"According to Dr. Takarada," Olivia stated, "everything the Velatians do are in sequences of four, and he said to try this. Nobody had noticed, but every button, lever, or knob were all laid out in even sets of four. He said whatever direction you go: up, down, sideways, diagonal, in-between, it doesn't matter as long as you go from one to four to three to two.

Both Tommy and Nathan grunted out a confused, "Huh?" and the twins immediately went to town, pressing the sequence and consuming information from the Duke's computer banks.

"Okay, I get it," Tommy responded, and he tried it. Using the fingers of his left hand, he cautiously depressed a series of buttons on his control panel in the one, four, three, two sequence. Instantly a 4D image of The Duke flying horizontally apparated in mid-air from the center of the cockpit, precisely demonstrating what the cowbot was doing at that particular time. "Hmmm," Tommy mumbled out loud. He tried another set of four buttons using the same sequence, and the cowbot pulled its two massive six-gun photon blasters out of their holsters and pointed them forward (as the 4D image demonstrated).

"WOW!" he exclaimed. "I get it. How the hell did Takarada figure it out?"

And Olivia responded, "I have no idea, and he didn't say. But he did also want to let us know that the Annihilator is in New York City."

Nathan gnashed his teeth and snarled. "Oh hell no. Not now! Not ever!"

"Okay then," Tommy sighed, "looks like we got a lot to learn in a very short amount of time."

He then announced that he could see the black and gray smoke of New York City over the sea's horizon from the Duke's monitor.

"We're coming in fast; we'll be there in less than two minutes. Do we got this?"

Right as Tommy asked this, a series of displays appeared on the viewing screen showing the Robotonauts in complete detail their power level, adjustment attenuators, velocity, everything! But most importantly, it showed the arsenal of weapons they were packing, and it was, well ... a lot! And Olivia said, "Yeah, we got this."

The payload the cowbot was carrying further demonstrated what those slimy Velatians had in mind, and little did Paris know the massive bullet they just dodged.

"Mr. Fox, please prepare the Duke for battle and arm all weapons."

The one, four, three, two sequence was odd, but Nathan was getting the hang of it. He wondered how the hell his head could have hit that freakin' panel in such a way that it mashed all the right buttons in their proper order. "Somebody or something must be watching out for us," he thought as he punched various buttons. The viewing screen blinked followed by four rising levels appearing on the monitor, the Duke was completely jacked. Nathan smiled.

"All weapons at full capacity General Taylor," he proclaimed.

A feeling of confidence surged through the cockpit. They now (for the most part) knew what they were doing or least knew how to figure it out. Not to mention, they had the twins should things go completely awry. They were now soaring north over the Upper Bay, and through the massive fires and heavy smoke they could see lower Manhattan via the Duke's wide-angle viewing screen. In the thick of it, they could also see the Annihilator, and it could see them.

Chapter 14

The Duke VS. Annihilator

Even though its bottom boot booster and metallic upper thigh had been damaged, the cowbot rocketed photon blasters first into Lower Manhattan. Looking like a caped superhero shrouded in steel, the Duke made its way through the smoke that lingered in between the buildings of West Street. They needed to get to Freedom Tower and fast, as in their minds there was in no way, shape or form going to be a repeat of 9-11. Both Tommy and Nathan were kids when terrorists brought the World Trade Center down, killing thousands. Olivia was too, and like most people, none of them ever forgot that terrible Tuesday morning. They couldn't let the new tower fall, they just couldn't. The planet had seen so much destruction and death over the last decade, and New York City had remained completely unscathed, at least until the Annihilator showed up. Now, hundreds of New Yorkers had perished, the Brooklyn Bridge was toast, and two towering skyscrapers had already fallen, and that was two too many. They couldn't save those poor bastards or prevent the devastation that had already happened, but maybe they could stop the brute before it killed any more people.

Through the Duke's viewing screen, the United States' tallest building, One World Trade Center, was coming up fast. They witnessed its seventeen hundred and seventy-six-foot majesty rising high above the smoke that filled the surrounding blocks like snakes in a maze. The only thing between them and it was the Annihilator, and the creature did not hesitate. But neither did the Duke.

Green bursts of photon plasma blasted from the cowboy robot's revolvers one after the other.

CHOOM! CHOOM! CHOOM! CHOOM!

At the same time, the Annihilator fired at the cowbot with rapid spates of red from its eyes! The Duke veered straight up, barely missing the neon rays of destruction, while its own beams tagged the foul beast directly in its face! "HAH!" Nathan triumphantly yelled! "Take that, beyotch!" And Tommy noted that the Velatians' armaments seemed even stronger than Takarada's organic-thorium-fueled weapons. The Annihilator went down! Tommy and Nathan came about to get another hit in ASAP-like, and as the debris cleared, they could see it licking its wounds. While it regained its senses, it cleaned the burnt and smoldering remnants of charred skin from its bug-like mug. Its head twitched like that of a fly, looking freakishly similar to something that had been filmed in stop-motion animation. Not only was it creepy, it was downright disgusting to say the least, and the cockpit within the Duke erupted in a chorus of, "Ewwww."

As they descended, the Annihilator rose to its massive feet as they fired the Duke's six-shooters once again. This time, however, the beast was ready, and as it did in Dubai, it wrapped itself in its enormous wings absorbing the deadly rays.

Tommy mumbled a soft, "Uh-oh," and Nathan followed that with his best imitation of Graham Chapman as King Arthur shouting ...

"Run away! Run away!"

The Duke flew to the right of the creature and circled back from around the Freedom Tower. With its guns still leading the way, it pummeled the monster with the front barrels of its blasters!

BWAM!

Again, the Annihilator went down. It seemed it was having a hard time understanding what was happening. Apparently not being accustomed to pain, it just stood there for a second and then tumbled down onto the massive imprints of the World Trade Center memorial.

"I don't know what all the fuss is about," Nathan stated. Then added, "This thing's going down easier than an ice-cold mug of frosty root beer on a hot summer's eve."

Tommy gave Nathan a, "What the hell, Jethro?" kind of look, right before seeing the Annihilator vanish from the face of the earth. But even before Tommy could gather his thoughts, the beast reappeared right in front of them in midair like it was being suspended by wires or something. It then grabbed the Duke from the bot's extended arms, and while grasping the tips of its guns, spun around profusely. Both became nothing but a blur, looking like a massive tornado in the sky. Then it just let go. Like a flimsy rag doll made of steel, the cowbot hurled over the bay colliding into the base of one of New York's most precious monuments, the Statue of Liberty. The perch from which the copper-clad statue stood crumbled, and even though Lady Liberty may have fallen, she hadn't fallen. Steam poured from the cowbot who was buried within the wreckage of her stone pedestal. From there, the larger-than-life icon laid on top of the downed Duke, and although bruised, she was remarkably still in one piece.

The inside of the cowbot's cockpit head flickered and hissed. Tommy looked over at Nathan, asking him if he was hallucinating or did the Annihilator at one point just up and vanish? Nathan nodded and reassured Tommy he wasn't having a flashback, and that he saw it too. Olivia leaned back and placed her hand on her stomach, and Nathan knew they needed to get her out of there. Hell, they all needed to get out of there. Because even though they were figuring out the Duke's new system, they were, by no means able to operate the bot as efficiently as they would have liked. Nevertheless, getting back in the fight was their only option, because that was their only way out. Not to mention the Annihilator, more than likely, was moving towards wiping New York City from the face of the Earth, right after it took care of the Duke along with those pesky kids inside of it.

Olivia barked sequences of four at Tommy and Nathan, and they followed her orders to a T, trying to get the bot to once again take off. Even though they had both already become pretty good at figuring it out, this wasn't an earn-while-you-learn type of situation. They weren't getting it fast enough to save themselves, the Duke or New York. Tommy looked back and asked Michael if they could somehow divert all weapon operations to him, Liberty and Olivia. Michael and Liberty pressed a few buttons (all in sequences of four of course), and both stated in unison, "It is done." Tommy then asked the twins for another favor.

The Annihilator circled Liberty Island from above, veering down upon its ruins, watching and waiting for any sign of its new foe. As it did this, and as though it were mere target practice, the beast started blasting the barges and ferries that were still in the harbor, one by one. Then it set its sights on Ellis Island, destroying every last building with the bright beams of death that erupted from its eyes. Within the massive fires of the burning historic buildings, the Annihilator screamed and touched down from the center of the blazing inferno. Not knowing the Duke was incapacitated, it continued to urge the cowbot out into the open by lighting up Liberty Park and the iconic Central Railroad Station on the Jersey shore. It went up like a thousand napalm bursts and within seconds was turned into a smoldering wasteland.

The beast then took to the inlet of the sea, wading through the firelit bay of the harbor, back towards New York, the Manhattan waterfront and the World Trade Tower. But from the center it suddenly stopped, stretched out its arms and clenched its massive fists. It was done fooling around and was preparing to fire its primary weapon.

On Ellis Island, the massive heap that now littered its landscape began to rise up and down as though it were trying to catch its breath. The island trembled causing boulders of mortar and steel to roll down the several tons of the stone-debris grave that buried the Duke. The slight tremble turned to more of an earthquake as a multitude of bright puke-green rays escaped through the cracks and crevices. A distinct hum could be heard over the ongoing explosions, fires and screams that was immediately followed by a massive shockwave. The ruins of the statue's base that once covered the giant robot blasted in all directions, and in its aftermath stood the Duke!

The jagged, white glow that pulsated around the Annihilator reflected off the water, and what was coming next was pretty obvious. The people still in the city, and even from the shores of New Jersey, more than likely had witnessed via the news and social media what the creature did in Dubai. It also seemed they had the same fate in store. Crowds of evacuees and injured poured onto the paths and lush grass of the Manhattan Greenway. From there, an almost calm serenity seemed to overtake the masses. Strangers held hands and comforted people they didn't even know, some even hugged others they had never met. It wasn't like the inhabitants of Noahmar in the fact that holding one another's hands wasn't going to produce a shield or help them in any way whatsoever. They simply knew they were going to die, and all of life's stupid, petty differences no longer amounted to a hill of beans. It was like Jack told Olivia: you never know when your number is up. Maybe some realized they had pissed their lives away. Maybe some realized that, though they were rich, they crushed others to get there. And maybe some used their few remaining precious seconds to ask for forgiveness. Either way they watched, and they waited. The sea from where the Annihilator stood began to boil, and most watching from the sidelines squeezed their eyes shut just before the blinding flash.

KA-CHOOM!

The beast went down in a mighty explosion, and the sea, although somewhat shallow in the harbor, still pulled the creature beneath the water. The people opened their eyes, and straight above the Duke flew over like a bright green neon sign! From both shores they cheered! Tommy once again got that feeling, the one that made everything else feel puny. But this time Nathan was by his side, and he looked at Tommy as though he finally understood. Nathan turned back to Olivia who now knew how to fire the Duke's monocle ray and said, "Whoa! Nice shootin', Gene." And she responded in her best southern drawl, "All in a day's work, Roy."

The bay churned, and the Annihilator broke through the surface of the sea firing twin laser beams at the Duke from its eyes. It missed the cowbot by a mile, and with one quick motion its massive wings burst out of its shell, and it took to the skies after the metal mech! The evening dusk had turned to black streaked with the glistening red of the out-of-control blazes coming from the fires below. And although New York was under a massive attack, many of the city's skyscrapers were still saturated with multiple lit-up windows. The Duke was also lit as the alien twins generated their trademark green force field around the bot.

Tommy and Nathan came about, rocketing out of New York City towards a less densely populated area. The Annihilator followed close, and both Tommy and Nathan slalomed the bot to the left and right avoiding the beast's barrage of laser fire. The twins tightened their grip on each other pushing the orb well past Mach 1, and Olivia yelled the last thing a Youtuber influencer often says, "Okay, watch this!"

She flipped a few switches (in sequences of four), and the front monitor screen went to a rear camera shot showing them their reverse view of the Annihilator close behind. She then hit another series of buttons, and the screen split to a satellite feed of the Duke from above! Both Tommy and Nathan let out an impressed, "Whoa." Even Michael, who was busy with Liberty generating their force field, did the same. Then Olivia said,

"All right, let's see what this does."

The Duke, who was flying with its arms tightly by its sides, lifted its shoulders, rotated its hands and locked onto the twin photon blasters from its massive steel holsters. It made a sound like churning steel, and both arms from their boxy bases rode a track that guided them to the cowbot's back. It now looked as though the giant mech was sporting a rocketeer-style jet pack. It's massive, metallic revolvers clicked and started shooting exploding pulses of energy in its wake!

CLICK! CHOOM! BOOM! CLICK! CHOOM! BOOM!

Both shots nailed the Annihilator smack in its creepy face, and though it didn't stop the creature, it sure looked like it hurt. "Wow!" Nathan yelled. "What the hell did you do?"

Olivia pushed her glasses up the cleft of her nose and replied, "I have no idea. But I think the bot knew we were being chased by a hostile, and certain buttons (in sequences of four of course) began to glow. So, I started pushing them. To be honest, I don't really know what I'm doing."

Both Tommy and Nathan smirked, because truth be told, they were pretty clueless them-damn-selves. Tommy, looking at the split screen images, noted that the Annihilator was up to its old tricks and that it had just disappeared. He was also quite sure where it would reappear, and sure as shit, it did. Right in front of the bot. The Duke, with absolutely no time to turn, slammed into the floating beast with tremendous force. From the mech's cockpit they were tossed about like damp clothes in a dryer! Sparks flew, steam hissed and their viewing screen, along with all the other means of light within the Duke's head, went dark. The green orb that surrounded the bot dissipated, and the monster wrapped its elongated arms around it. Like some form of alien bearhug, it clutched its prey tight and descended toward the land below.

Tommy hoped they put some distance between them and New York City, and fortunately, traveling over the speed of sound, they had. He was also hoping for an unpopulated region, and unfortunately, that wouldn't be the case. He pulled out his Zippo, flicked it twice and it cast a small glow within the darkened cockpit. Minus a few scrapes and bruises, it seemed everybody was all right, but for how long?

The Annihilator slowed its descent and hovered directly above the Huntington Bank Field. It then let go of the Duke, and the cowbot plummeted straight down.

It was as though all gravity inside the Duke's head was gone, and they floated straight up to the ceiling of the cockpit as the bot dropped. Liberty quickly grabbed Michael's hand and yelled for everyone to do the same.

The Annihilator disappeared, then reappeared below the falling bot on the parking lot of Cleveland's open-air stadium. Towering twice as tall as the structure, it waited in sweet anticipation for the arrival of the Duke.

KA-BOOOSH!

A magnificent explosion of earth and building debris erupted high above the grandstands from within the circular arena! The Annihilator watched, then screamed in a fashion similar to that of a mad cackle and kicked its way through the walls of the stadium. It picked up the Duke by its neck, raised the cowbot into the air and yanked its steel leg from its body with its mouth. It then slammed the bot into the shallow harbor of Lake Eerie and began beating it with its own leg. The Duke didn't move; it just lay there taking hit after hit as though it had been paralyzed. The Annihilator reared its mighty arms back and unleashed yet a new weapon. An array of bright blue lightning bolts ignited from its fingertips, and with them it lifted the Duke high into the air. Reminiscent of a sorcerer casting a spell, it guided the cowbot up and out over Lake Eerie and then reared its arms back. As though it snipped the strings of the steel mech, it fell like a broken marionette into the sea and sunk like a rock to its muddy bottom. The Duke was gone.

From the shore, the Annihilator turned and cast its glare upon downtown Cleveland and started its advance towards the heart of the city. Anything that as much as moved was taken out with the red heat ray that blasted from its eyes. Like New York, Dubai and even Noahmar, it seemed the puny Earthlings hadn't a chance in hell against power such as this. Especially now with the Duke at the bottom of Lake Eerie, it seemed nothing could stop the beast. But what the Velatians or their infernal creature didn't realize was that Earth's inhabitants weren't going to simply roll over and die. And with that, the distant rumble of the calvary could be heard like an oncoming storm from the west. But it wasn't mere jet fighters, oh no. It was a squadron of FU2 Fuji Fighters coming to the rescue. They swarmed around the monster like a swarm of angry wasps stinging the beast with hundreds, if not thousands, of 50mm organic-thorium-infused bullets. The monster, however, wrapped itself in the cocoon of its wings and absorbed the rounds. The FU2s ascended up in tight formation to come about, and the Annihilator pinned one with its heat ray.

KA-BWAM!!

It blew into a million pieces of nothing, and as the explosion subsided, the sound of even more FU2s could be heard coming from the west. With their guns a-blazing, they opened fire, but not at the beast, at the other fighters. Spotted lines of red lit up the Cleveland sky as the interceptors fired upon each other. The jets from the east attacked as the FU2s from the west tried to lure the others far out over the great lake. It didn't work. Instead, they flew at head level with the advancing beast taking out buildings, people and anything mobile. Then, as the others came about, the FU2s aiding the monster broke out of attack formation and hightailed it out of town. For a second, the pilots were confused as to why the other fighters would just up and leave. Then it became obvious, and the reason hit them like the force of the blinding white flash that leveled Cleveland.

Chapter 15

Akira

Tommy was dying for a cigarette, but the pink cushy pod that literally saved their lives was running low on air. He also knew it wouldn't be too good for Olivia to breathe in that crap with their limited surroundings and all. But truth be told, he was surprised they were still alive. Thank God for Michael and Liberty. They may have bounced around a bit, but that magnificent glowing shell they manifested at the last second saved their lives. It was like riding inside a giant, rubber beach ball, and had circumstances been different, it might've even been fun. Speaking of Michael and Liberty, they were almost completely spent from the combination of powering the Duke and then having to generate the lifesaving orb within the cowbot's cranium. The back hatch was almost beyond recognition, and if it had dented in a bit more it would have busted right off. However, that wasn't the case, and now it was nothing but an iron door that sealed them into their watery tomb. Both Nathan and Olivia looked worried, and they sat close to each other in a knees-up fashion. Nathan held her tight with both arms, going on about all the wonderful things they were going to do after all of this was over.

The glowing cocoon flickered every time one of the twins started nodding off, only to be nudged awake by the other. Everybody was so tired, and nobody remembered the last time they ate or had any water. Tommy wasn't even sure where they were, but he knew they were at the bottom of a lake or an ocean or something along those lines. Tommy talked Michael and Liberty into getting up and moving in closer to Olivia and Nathan. They agreed but made sure they kept a tight grip on the other's hand as it was hard to move about within the rubbery orb. Tommy got the ball rolling. "Remember our first concert in Osaka?" he asked with a sincere gleam in his eye. "That was probably one of the best nights of my life, the lights, the roar of the crowd, you know, everything. It was all so exciting ... so new."

Michael chimed in, "Dudes, I loved the first time we rode down that bitchin' weird tube thing at The Fuji right after we met."

Tommy got excited, "Yeah, you pulled out your weird crystal MP3 player, and I remember EXACTLY what you said. You said, 'This, amigos, is the best thing about planet Earth ...'" And before Tommy finished the phrase, everyone joined in on the final word, laughing as they all screamed, "Led Zeppelin!"

"Damn straight!" Michael added, then he turned to Libs and speaking almost like a normal person said, "I'll also never forget when we stepped off the bus, and all those fans swarmed around you as though you were everything they'd ever want to be." Liberty smiled, but only slightly as that kind of attention still made her a bit uncomfortable.

The bubble was consumed by a still hush that brought with it an obvious uncertainty, so Olivia broke the awkward silence. "I'm so thankful I got to meet your dad before he passed," she said to Nathan who felt the same way. He started to get all misty-like because he knew how fortunate he was to have reconciled with him. And also, because he knew they weren't going to make it.

Nathan didn't talk much with Olivia in regard to her losing her parents in the "Great Salt Lake City Blast," not because she wasn't willing, but because it was just so damn depressing. But it seemed everybody was baring their soul, so he stepped up to the plate, "I would've liked to have met yours." And he wasn't lying, he really would have. He also knew the baby not having any grandparents whatsoever ate at her a bit, too. But of course, none of that mattered now.

The orb flickered; Liberty was fading fast. Michael squeezed her hand, "Wake up, sis." But it was no use. The air was so heavy that, tired or not, they were all on the verge of passing out. Tommy peered through the pink force field. He didn't say anything, but the water outside the orb was eager and waiting to get in. It hadn't filled the entire cockpit, so maybe the remaining bit of oxygen lingering in the Duke's head would be enough. But enough for what?

Olivia started crying. She placed her palm flat upon Nathan's face and smiled through the tears. "I love you so much, Mr. Fox. Jack was right, we're not guaranteed anything. I don't know how we managed to stay alive on so many missions during the years either." Olivia took a deep breath of heavy air. "For so long, I was nothing but a hollow husk and probably wouldn't have cared either way. But now I do. I don't want to die. I don't want our baby to die." Nathan held her close, and the orb faded. The cockpit went black, and they were now up to their necks in the icy-cold water of Lake Eerie.

All was dark and Tommy had gone numb, no longer feeling the cold, the pain or anything. Then something happened that hadn't happened for a very long time. The kanji pendant Akira Akemi had given him so many years ago was suddenly hot and began to glow. It wasn't unbearable, but there was no denying it. He placed his hand over it and a bright yellow, almost star-like glow illuminated the darkness. His eyes widened as he continued to clutch the necklace. The light was bright and beautiful. No, it was more than that, much more, and a strong, overwhelming sensation of love filled his heart.

"Hello Tommy," a soft voice whispered through the radiant glow. He squeezed his eyes shut, and the pressure forced out a stream of tears. It was Akira, at least that's what he thought as he could barely make out her face within the illuminated light she cast. But he had to be hallucinating. Maybe he was already dead, but then again, Akira was a Yokai princess. So, who knows either way.

"I miss you," escaped his lips, and Akira smiled without showing any teeth.

"I miss you too," she replied, "and we'll be together again. But not yet." Tommy grinned, and as the radiant glow dissipated, he closed his eyes and drifted off.

***

It was quite cold, but the early morning sun was beaming. Dr. Takarada peered through his porthole as the spinning shadows of two massive rotors danced upon his face. The transport was not only gigantic, but it was loud and made a thunderous whir as its twin blades sliced through the air. From his round window he could see the other three choppers in their formation. Two were double-bladed juggernauts like the one he was in, and one was a single-rotor heavy transport copter. Only one was E.I.O. tackle. Two were U.S. Military, and the fourth was a Russian-borrowed Mi-26, the largest cargo-carrying helicopter in the world. It was a magnificent sight, and his eyes followed the array of thick, galvanized steel cables leading down to the payload below, the Duke. His upper torso was, for the most part, intact, but both of the bot's steel legs were gone, completely ripped from its body in the brawl. However, 'brawl' might not be the right word, because it was more like a complete and total ass-kicking.

Jack, lost in thought, stood behind Takarada and peered into the nothing. The destruction to the United States had been devastating. Thousands of people were dead. Takarada turned from his window and looked down the tunnel of the helicopter's long cabin. Medics from the U.S. Army had turned it into a makeshift hospital, and the pilots of the giant cowbot in toe were resting with the aid of some strong sedatives. Takarada didn't know if they would even remember the divers breaking through the Duke's back hatch with their plasma cutters. Like Tommy, he was surprised they were still alive.

Jack sat down next to Takarada on the long bench that ran most of the cabin's length and placed his palms on his knees. He let out a heavy sigh. "Well Kyoshi, I have no bloody idea as to why they're not all dead. In addition to keeping that blasted thing airborne, I don't think the twins could have sustained them for as long as they were down there." Takarada shook his head. He was just as puzzled, and Jack turned to look out the window. He gazed down at the Duke as the ground rushed by from beneath them. "Thank God for the Yanks though," he continued. "We never would have pulled this off without them." Jack was appalled at the state of the E.I.O. but knew it was all part of the Velatian's plan. "One ruddy helicopter, two FU2 fighters and this worthless hunk of steel. We're up to our necks in it, my friend."

Takarada looked at his watch and asked Jack how long it would take to get to the base. Jack answered, "Well, not long, the challenge will be getting into it. It's been abandoned for quite some time." Takarada pressed his lips together and let out a burst of air from his nose.

"I'm still not too sure of this, Sir Jonathon," he admitted. Jack replied,

"Me neither, but I don't think we have much choice. We don't even know who we can trust. I mean, God blind me, are they human or are they Velatian? It's not like we can ruddy examine the back of every Tom, Dick and Harry's neck to make sure." As he said this, Takarada snuck a peek at the back of Jack's neck as he was still looking out the porthole. And as though he had eyes in the back of his head, Jack let Takarada know he had nothing to worry about and that he was still 100% human.

Jack turned, and Takarada looked up as they both witnessed the blanket on Tommy's cot rising up like an inflating pup tent. It would have been odd too, if not for the long, black nose protruding out from the draped fabric. Suzy yawned, then began clawing at the sheet with her paws. She spun around twice, moved in even closer to Tommy and laid back down. Jack almost looked irritated, then shook his head, "Are you sure that things a bloody robot?" and Takarada just shrugged his shoulders. Either way, she had awakened Tommy. Dr. T. and Sir Jonathon went and sat next to him.

"How are you feeling my boy?" Jack asked, and Tommy answered,

"I'm alive." He added, "How's everybody else?" and Takarada responded with a reassuring,

"They are all fine, Tommy-san."

Tommy let out a long and deep breath of relief, then noticed Suzy. "Hey girl," he said just above a whisper. He lifted his hand and started scratching between her ears. It only took about two seconds for things to sort of catch up with him, and he sprang up from above the hip.

"Oh my God, how did you guys find us? What happened in Liverpool? Where are we?"

"Calm down," Jack said with a somewhat lifeless tone. "It was obvious where you were." Tommy chilled and Jack explained. "Anyone with a ruddy smart phone, TV or computer watched that winged nightmare tear the Duke limb from limb outside of Huntington Bank Field. It saturated the airwaves until all signals from that area terminated. However, after New York and Dubai, most had a good idea as to what happened."

Tommy's gaze intensified, "So ....?"

Jack knew exactly what he was implying and answered, "Yes, my boy, last night Cleveland was annihilated." Tommy laid all the way down again and just looked up. Even though fighting the monster was not the plan, Tommy still felt deflated and weak. He stared at the curved ceiling of the helicopter, and it blurred into the black of his mind. Because that's where he was really looking.

Takarada reminded Tommy that stopping the Annihilator with the Duke was not why they stole it. He pointed out that it was indeed a good thing that they had, as the bot was completely armed to the pills. Tommy didn't utter a word about Takarada's English faux pas, but still knew he was right. A muffled, know-it-all-sounding "told ya!" came from beneath the blanket of the cot next to his. Tommy rolled his eyes and stated, "It's of the utmost importance to Nathan that you know he was right all along." Takarada and Jack looked a little perplexed, so Tommy and Nathan filled them in on the pre-flight movie involving the Duke, Paris and a bunch of explosives. The Velatians were indeed going to use the Duke to help them destroy the cities of the planet. This, along with infiltrating the E.I.O. and who knows

how many branches of the military would, without a doubt, assure the Velatians of complete and total world domination. This didn't make Tommy feel much better, because even though commandeering the Duke saved Paris, New York was a mess and Cleveland was gone.

All sorts of thoughts ran through Tommy's clouded head. He wondered about how the Velatians retrieved the remnants of the Duke from Antarctica after its battle with King Taraxian or when they took over Robert Jones. These things bugged him, but at least they were starting to make sense. What he didn't understand was why they'd even bothered with a tribute band. Takarada again stated that piloting the Duke with the original sleep-state operations system was probably their first intent, but without the members of Vinyl Crush, it was impossible to control. He wasn't positive but stated that this could have set them back years, as reconfiguring the mech had to be a next to impossible feat. He then concluded with, "They must be extremely advanced to do all of these things."

Jack chuckled, "Well, they can't be that smart. We bloody walked right out of the Liverpool office like we were off for ruddy fish-n-chips. Bleedin' wankers." In spite of everything, this made both Takarada and Tommy smile ever so slightly.

Nathan removed the covers from his head and asked, "What now, Jacky Boy?" Jack frowned at Nathan and replied,

"I had to call in a few favors from some old friends, but I know those who are helping us are definitely Earthlings, and they got us from England to the states in almost no time at all. Those bloody Velatians have stolen most of our munitions, so we don't have much of an army either. Hopefully they think the Duke is destroyed and that you all are dead. And believe me, I know what a pain in the ass you all can be, and Jones, or whoever or whatever he is, will be glad of that fact."

Tommy then pointed out to Takarada the Annihilator's ability to appear, then reappear, and though Dr. T. had never seen this, it made sense to him. He placed his index finger and thumb up to his chin, the way smart people do when they're pondering something, and he nodded his head. "I think I understand," he calculated. "That is why Annihilator was able to get to Earth much faster than we had predicted. It either can, or can come very close to traveling at the speed of light ..."

Jack interrupted, barking out a confident, "That's bloody impossible!" Then stopped, adding a not quite so sure, "Isn't it?" Takarada replied,

"Not if they can do it. It also explains a number of things and gives me an idea."

A treble-induced voice that was almost inaudible crackled over the speaker system housed within the large copter. "Sir Jonathon, we are starting our descent. Ten minutes to our destination. Repeat, ten minutes to our destination. Please buckle up."

"Right," Jack grunted, and as he and Takarada stood up in order to go strap in, Tommy asked him one final question.

"Just what is our destination, Jack?" And he replied,

"Salt Lake City."

Chapter 16

Salt Lake City

Jones stepped out of the heated infrared room that prepared his alien body for its human suit of skin. It's a bit unclear how the Velatians acquired these living garments, but chances are they came from the vessels they absorbed. Like that of Robert Jones, who was not anything like the alien who now occupied his body. Jones (the real Jones) was a good man, appointed head of the E.I.O. by Sir Jonathon himself. He was a man similar to most, married, divorced, married, two kids, you know, that kind of stuff, but also very talented and quite colorful indeed. And like Jack, most would've known who Jones was before he became a member of the E.I.O., the organization so versed in using as well as creating rock stars.

But this was not Robert Jones, this was an imitation, a cheap knock-off, a bootleg of the once great man. These "skin suits" as the Velatians called them, were hands down the ultimate act of identity theft. And although uncomfortable, it appeared that most of the aliens liked their human Buffalo Bill garbs as opposed to their own bug-like features. If the Velatians had indeed (as Michael and Liberty claimed) made the Annihilator, it was obvious that they created a god in their own image. Talk about ego. On most worlds the Velatians had already conquered, the species were always more uniform. Take the Greys for instance, Jones (or whatever his name was) always made the comment that he couldn't tell one from the other. He also found it easier to tell themselves apart when disguised as humans, because even he (or it) would agree that most beetles look alike.

But even though they were basically walking, talking bugs, they also sported a few humanoid qualities consisting of two legs, two arms and a head. Jones often stated that he liked the hands of the earthlings much more than their own four-digit palps. Probably because when in their true form, every console, control panel or array of buttons had to be pressed in a series of four to accommodate the length of their long, scarab fingers. Jones, as well as any Velatian who had ever assumed human form, never knew what a pain in the bug-butt their own operating systems were, that is until acquiring fingers with an opposable thumb. For that reason, and that reason alone, Jones always began his skin suit ritual "hands first."

Jones lifted his bony insectoid leg and guided it through the bottom half of his suit. He had to watch it because the spurs on his tibia were so sharp they'd often rip the skin. Then he pulled, carefully pushing his other tarsi down the other side like a pair of trousers made from delicate fabric. He put on his coat of skin like a finely tailored garment, then pulled the draping veil of Robert Jones's face over his head like a bank robber puts on a ski mask. It was disturbing and looked anything but human. He then returned to the infrared room for a few brief seconds, and when he exited, you would never have known that he was not who he was pretending to be.

What also wasn't known was Jones's rank and position as a Velatian. It seemed he, without a doubt though, was the one in charge, the big kahuna. But in charge of what, who, and just how many? If there were more aliens coming from the stars, it still remained to be seen. But without a planet of their own, it would stand to reason that the Velatians, as in every last one of them, were already here. And since most myths are often based at least in some degree of truth, it kind of makes sense. That weird hieroglyphic alphabet of theirs, a strong resemblance to the scarab-faced, Egyptian god Khepri, the Annihilator's giant cockroach qualities, that kind of stuff. Truthfully if we really thought about it, we'd probably figure out that maybe, just maybe, they've been here much longer than we thought,

probably even longer than us. But perhaps that was good in the sense that if they are already here, there would be no more surprise uninvited alien houseguests stopping by for a visit, at least not from the planet Vela.

***

From the ground, what sounded like the rhythmic thunder of a thousand taiko drums grew louder and louder as they approached from at least a hundred miles away. Both Takarada and Jack were concerned about attracting unwanted attention, but that was the least of their worries. It was more about the sight of four helicopters airlifting a busted steel robot through the sky like some sort of demented parade balloon that concerned them. However, they had no choice. What they really hoped for was that the Velatians weren't looking for them, seeing no reason to do so after the Duke's ass whooping.

Even if it hadn't been a time of war, the thrust of the large engines and chop of the mighty blades would still have demanded an audience. Sir Jack had the pilots avoid heavy populated areas as much as possible as their location would have been divulged by anybody with a smartphone. Though it was impossible to avoid each and every rubber neck, it still seemed as though they were safe for now. Not having the luxury of time, the convoy had to fly directly over the remains of Salt Lake City to get to the foot of the Cedar Mountain range. From a distance, Takarada could see the massive man-made canyon that kept the ruins of the city imprisoned. Differentiating from a moat around a medieval castle, one that would protect its inhabitants on the inside while keeping intruders out, this did just the opposite. It supposedly protected those on the outside while imprisoning its inhabitants on the inside. Takarada shook his head in disgust.

He was also surprised to see so many patches of lush, green vegetation that had melded with much of the ruins, turning some of the surrounding area into small forests or even gardens. It had been quite some time since any non-government traffic had entered the airspace above, around, or even close to Salt

Lake City. Takarada was discovering there was much more here than meets the eye, and the deeper they went, the more of a mystery it became. In addition to the threat of radiation, rumors of disease and cannibalistic mutated humans still ran amok, even if it was not true. Takarada in the back of his head often wondered if the actual level of poisonous emissions that permeated the air was still lethal. He didn't think it was, nor had been for a long time.

He felt the heat of someone's breath upon his shoulder as they readied the convoy for landing. It was Olivia. She peered over the doctor from behind and stared out the window in an almost hypnotic fashion. It had been years since she'd been to Salt Lake City, since she'd been home.

Jack stepped into the cockpit to direct the pilots to the charred edges of the city limits where the secret but abandoned base still hopefully resided. Immediately following the great blast, all operations were shut down and the base evacuated. But after sitting dormant for almost three years, it was again being scrutinized and secretly studied, only for a completely different kind of occupation. Draped in the radioactive rumors the government had created, Leopold Iscariot discovered the empty base would be the perfect lair. The once decorated doctor (who at one time worked hand in hand with Takarada) knew the threat of toxic air was nothing but a lie fabricated by the feds for control. So just as a mischief of rats would infest a cellar, he and his cronies did the same, knowing the threat of lingering radioactivity would be their best defense against unwanted company. He reconstructed the bases factories deep within the ground where he could further his experiments. Combining super-science and a bit of black magic, he used the spirit of Notawni Nonaashi after it was freed from the nuclear blast. Like the prison that embodied the survivors of Salt Lake City, Iscariot imprisoned the Native-American god in a monstrous eight-legged cyborg constructed of titanium steel. Fueled by organic thorium and veiled in synthetic flesh, course hair and a nightmarish exoskeleton, he called his abomination by its English translation, King Taraxian. But now Iscariot was gone, and again the base sat dormant, this time for close to ten years.

Takarada still wrestled with having ever shared any of his secrets, like that of organic thorium, with the sinister, and frankly quite mad, doctor. Obviously, it left a profound impression on Takarada, maybe even causing some of his borderline paranoia that now leads him to only work with a select few. Olivia couldn't help thinking about Doctor Iscariot either, but for two completely different reasons. One was Brandon Fox and the other was Pamela Fox, Nathan's parents whom Iscariot murdered.

Jack summoned Takarada to the cockpit, as he was pretty sure he had located the area below from which the base resided. So much of it looked the same, almost an ongoing desert wasteland where the surrounding rural areas had been wiped out. But even in its heyday the base was hard to locate; now the patches of thick green foliage made it even harder. But as Sir Jonathon looked down upon the area, he saw what made its whereabouts quite obvious.

From above, Jack could see the dancing vapors being emitted from the twin turbines of an idling FU2 fighter. He let out a sigh of relief upon seeing the mighty jet waiting for them on the ground. He didn't dare use the radio to signal, but the plan was obvious. Now everybody was up and gazing out the portholes as the Duke-toting helicopters hovered in anticipation. Much of the green that was now occupying the area below began to vibrate, and as the ground moved, grass, dirt and even trees were pulled down into the gap. An enormous rectangle floor opened and whirred with the sound of creaking, spinning cogs and rusted metal. As it widened, it briefly took the shape of a square. Then as it kept expanding, it eventually turned back into a rectangle. What Tommy thought was a floor was actually a ceiling, and beneath it he could see a large, blue-tinted hangar with its multiple rows of guide lights leading deep downward. It was an underground launch bay, and it was massive! Tommy let out a loud and unbridled, "Whoa!" at the sight.

The four transport copters moved in closer, suspending the Duke over the opening of the hanger. As they descended, they lowered the cowbot into the bay, and the choppers became level with the ground as it was so deep. Jack tapped the top of one pilot's white helmet, and he flashed his landing lights three times. Jack then looked at his watch and counted backwards from ten ...

"Three ... Two ... One ... Zero." He tapped the helmet again, but only once this time. Instantly a series of charges detonated, simultaneously separating the long steel cables that supported the Duke from the helicopters that held him up. Unfortunately, without its legs there was no way around the thirty-meter drop, and the mech crashed to the floor of the hangar. Fortunately, nothing exploded, and though in dismal shape, the giant cowboy mech was ready to undergo another complete makeover, once again proving to be Earth's best defense. Sheesh, it was Earth's only defense, and it wasn't looking too good as they were short on just about everything: supplies, fuel, time, and most of all a freakin' workforce, because it was going to take a lot of people to make this happen. You name it, they needed it.

After the "all clear" was given, the massive ceiling of the underground hangar moaned in a metallic bellow and started to shut. One by one the helicopters landed, and just to be on the safe side, around the outside perimeter of the monstrous bay door. As the subsiding rotors of each copter whirred like slashing swords, they exited the vehicles and congregated towards the center of the circled wagons. There wasn't many either, a few pilots, a few military and E.I.O. personnel, Jack, Takarada and the band. Oh, and one more...

"Ramsay!" Olivia shouted as she ran the best she could to her old and dear friend. Jack smiled, and Nathan demanded to know what she was doing there. Jack's smile grew even more, and he said, "I told you my boy, I had to call in a few favors from some old friends." And choosing fear and pride over gratitude, Nathan got all defensive,

"Yeah but, her?" he said as though the world's worst babysitter had just shown up for the evening. Beneath his bruised ego though, truth be told, Nathan was glad to see Ramsay. Next to Takarada, she was the "Q" of the E.I.O., both brilliant and resilient. He was just uncomfortable with how he had treated her in the past, asking her out again and again, even after being told, multiple times mind you, that she doesn't date

... men. Not that there's anything wrong with that. But as he (like everybody else) approached her with open arms, he did something he was getting better at every day. He thought about it before opening his big mouth and realized the best thing he could do was make amends with her. He had done this many times already on his recovery journey, and nothing truly says "sorry" like a sincere apology backed up by the proof of a changed person, and that he was. So, Nathan decided he would do just that as soon as he could.

The subtleties didn't last long, and the group, standing atop the closed hangar bay door, started bouncing ideas back and forth, each short-lived suggestion hitting one stumbling block or another. Jack realized that maybe the best plan was to first get into the abandoned base, get cleaned up, have a meal and get their shit together. Ramsay noted that she had already reconnected the mainframe and, using organic thorium, had enough power to light up a small city. Takarada nodded. He really appreciated Ramsay, and the look on his face made that perfectly clear. She also added that there may be a few things of interest to everybody within the massive empty hangars inside the base. She stated that their biggest challenge was going to be a shear lack of hands needed to get the job done, and both Jack and Takarada agreed. "We've got a lot to do and simply don't have the workforce to do it." She stopped and looked around at their little ragtag group and sighed. "Okay, let's get inside. Once in, I'll open the doors to hangars one and two. Pilots, please get your vehicles inside before we're seen. It seems we're not quite sure who we can trust." Ramsay pointed in the direction of a concealed entrance, and Jack took the lead. As they walked, Ramsay fell back to Tommy's side.

"It's good to see you after all these years. How's Rose?" he asked, and Ramsay nodded and smiled,

"Oh, she's fine. She sends her love."

He then asked, "How's Australia?"

And again, she nodded and smiled, "In spite of everything, it's still there."

Tommy took a deep breath to camouflage the awkward silence, and as everybody started to file into the base, Ramsay stopped Tommy and pulled him aside.

"Look, Tommy, I know I should've contacted you after Akira died, but that whole Oku Rikoku thing really messed me up." Tommy just kind a sneered, not at Ramsay but into the distance, as he was having a hard time making eye contact.

"I knew Akira longer than you did, Tommy, and for my own sanity, I had to get away. Far away." She paused, "I loved her too."

Tommy didn't flinch, but the teardrop that ran down his face showed he was listening. Ramsay hugged him. He hugged back, but the top of her hair didn't even reach the tip of his nose, and he just continued to look into the nothing.

With her face against Tommy's chest, she could feel the pendant Akira gave him against her cheek, and it made her feel good. Then with a soft, muffled voice she said, "I also have a confession to make."

And Tommy, still looking off into the distance said, "What's that?"

Ramsay hesitated, and started slowly, "Well ..."

"No ... what's that?" Tommy said again, pushing Ramsay to the side, followed by a quick shout to Jack.

Jack came back out through the secret door that was embedded in the side of a steep hill, and everybody followed. As predicted, the spectacle of the Duke-toting helicopter brigade brought some of the curious inhabitants of Salt Lake City out of the shadows and into the open. Even though the convoy was outside of the actual city limits, a parade of men, women, and even children could be seen through the lenses of Jack's binoculars heading their way.

"What is it, Sir Jonathon?" Takarada asked.

Jack lowered his field glasses, looked at Ramsay and let out a hearty laugh.

"You said you wanted extra hands? Well, here they come."

Chapter 17

The Noble Clan

Coming towards the entrance of the base was a large wave of about a hundred or so people: men, women and children from all walks of life with one thing in common, they had all been forced to live in the radiated remains of Salt Lake City. They were thin, scraggly and wearing tattered clothes made from an array of spliced fabric, but other than that, they seemed healthy. Not knowing just what to expect, a few of the E.I.O. and military personnel accompanying Jack and Takarada floated their unsteady hands just above their sidearms. They seemed harmless, but should anybody be approaching with any funny ideas they'd be ready. Of course, nobody on the E.I.O. end wanted any trouble, not to mention they were totally outnumbered.

Jack eyed the oncoming mass and cleared his throat. "Okay, Kyoshi, Tommy and Nathan, you come with me, and the rest of you hang back here. And for God's sake, keep your hands off those ruddy weapons!" The four men broke away and treaded lightly towards the mob. Jack spoke from the side of his mouth to his fellow comrades as they approached the mysterious group. "Right. Nobody go all willy-nilly now. Chances are they haven't seen any people outside of this area for quite some time. Let me do the talking and keep your chins up." As they got closer, Nathan looked deep into the faces of the Salt Lake City citizens, and his stomach did a flip-flop. He felt horrible, imagining what they must had gone through. He couldn't tell if they were friendly, angry or going to attack, because all he could see was sadness. Nevertheless, happy, angry, sad, whatever, they were still completely fenced in. Nathan, as well as everybody in their group, hoped nobody did anything rash. He was particularly concerned about Olivia, as he knew damn well what she was thinking. He gazed back towards the entrance to give her a reassuring smile, only to see she was tagging along from about a foot behind. Nathan rolled his eyes, stopped and waited for her to catch up.

As they walked, Tommy saw another group getting uncomfortably close to the "not-so-secret-anymore" doors to the base. He also noted that their new friends had formed human barriers around all four helicopters as well as the FU2. It was reminiscent of when Carl Denham and his crew were approached by the angry natives of Skull Island. But unlike the scene in King Kong, this group had thought to cut them off from all points and had them surrounded.

A large man along with two other men and a woman broke away from the mob. One was armed with a double-barreled, sawed-off shotgun, one was toting a rusty sword, and the other, a homemade spear or staff of some sort. The obvious leader (the tall one) donned twin bullet-filled bandoliers and two silver revolvers at his side. As the two groups approached each other, Nathan and Tommy looked timidly up at the man in charge. This guy had to be over seven feet tall, and they couldn't help but wonder if he was the inspiration for the Duke. All he needed was a stupid hat. When they came to just a few feet shy of each other, the small group that represented the Salt Lake City survivors stopped and encircled Jack, Takarada, Nathan, Tommy and Olivia.

Spotting this from the sidelines of the base's entrance, Michael instinctively grabbed Liberty's hand, and the sound of clicking firearms permeated the air. Upon hearing the choir of cocking guns, Mister Sawed-Off Shotgun placed both barrels up against Jack's cheek. Jack didn't as much as flinch, and the tall, Duke-looking-dude approached him with a skeptical glare. He got right in Jack's face, but Jack didn't even blink. Sir Jonathon

simply and slowly said one word, "Friend." But it was long and drawn out, as though you were trying to convince Frankenstein not to pull your arms out of their sockets.

The tall man backed up and scrutinized Sir Jonathon even further, so Jack responded with an even longer,

"Friiiiieeeeeeeend …" But added a desperate, "Do. You. Under. Stand?"

The stranger lifted his muscular arm up, wrapped his enormous hand around both barrels of the shotgun that was pointed at Jack and eased it down. Submitting to the apparent leader, the man holding the gun allowed this to happen. However, he and the others in their little recon team kept a firm grip on their weapons, just in case. Jack watched without moving his head even once and repeated another, but slightly modified, "We. Are. Friends. Do. You. Under. Stand?"

Obviously annoyed, the rather large man looked at Mr. Shotgun and exhaled a quick, "Jeez, can you believe this guy?" He then turned to a statuesque Sir Jonathon and replied, "Yes. I. Under. Stand." followed by a barely audible and quick, "Douchebag," from beneath his breath. Jack, who still hadn't flinched even once, kept one eye on their new friend, as he asked General Taylor to tell their fellow E.I.Onians to please stand down. He waited, then after Tommy got the "all-clear," extended the right hand of friendship towards this extremely big person. He sized up Jack as well as his open hand with caution, and it didn't seem like he was going to bite. Nathan watched, and for a brief second thought this guy was gonna' dis Jack and leave him hanging. Fortunately, it didn't happen, and after a brief hesitation, Sir Jonathon's mitt was engulfed by a monstrous paw. The tension that filled the air dissipated, and more of a celebratory feeling remained after a loud gasp from both ends. Jack finally exhaled, and the enormous man introduced himself.

"I am Noble."

Jack responded back with "I am Sir Jon …" He paused, then with a heavy breath changed his response, "I'm Jack." Noble smiled (sort of) as Jack continued to hold a tight grip on this insanely large gentleman's hand. Nathan nudged Tommy with his elbow and whispered,

"He looks like John Coffey from The Green Mile." And even though this was one of Tommy's favorite movies, he told Nathan to shut up.

Jack stated that he had a million questions for Noble, as did Noble for him. All at once, Olivia slipped into the conversation between the two men and asked how many were in his group. Noble replied, we have almost two hundred altogether. Olivia then asked if they were the only survivors. Noble shook his head and answered, "There are many villages scattered among the ruins of the city. Most stayed around their old neighborhoods and boroughs from the areas where they lived before the blast. These little chasms of people just sort of began to pop up. Most were good, but after the ravine was dug around the city and we knew we weren't getting out, some groups started stealing and killing." Nathan could see the wheels in Olivia's head turning, still knowing exactly what she was thinking. Noble continued stating that many of the survivors were gang members who attempted to control the populous through intimidation and violence. However, the people came together to rid the areas of most of what he called, "the vermin." Jack asked Noble how dangerous Salt Lake City had become since the isolation and Noble responded,

"We're mostly good people. Good people who at one time, had families, jobs and a mortgage and now we're just trying to keep ourselves and our loved ones alive. But I'll put it this way, you still don't want to go out at night alone. And I'll also tell you we can hold our own." Noble looked deep into Jack's eyes with a glare that said, "so don't try anything foolish." He was obviously still a little skeptical.

"The last time we had any kind of serious trouble was when this very base was commandeered by Dr. Iscariot. He kidnapped a lot of people imprisoned inside the ravine, and they became part of his group of minions. I don't know how he did it, but he was able to control them somehow." Noble then gave Jack a stern, hard look.

"I assure you, Mr. Noble, that is not our intent. But we are indeed in a bit of a sticky wicket and could really use your help."

Noble nodded his head. "I don't know who you are, but I do know who that giant robot cowboy is. We may not be able to leave, but we hear rumors and have a little contact with the outside world thanks to some old radios and a little ingenuity." Jack was blown away that they knew about the Duke, but more so, he was flabbergasted about something else and asked,

"Noble, is it really that hard to escape from here?"

Noble felt a little dissed at the question and gave Jack a look of, "are you kidding me?" "Let me explain something Jack," he said with a tinge of tude in his tone.

"First off, the only air traffic we see is when the black patrol copters scour the area within the surrounding ravine, usually once in the morning and once at night. If they fly over the ravine and see you trying to escape, they will shoot you. If they see you at the edge of the ravine, they will shoot you. We have fuel and even vehicles, but again there's no way through the ravine, and if they see you driving anything anywhere near it, they will shoot you. And then of course, there's the ravine itself, or as we call it, the pit: a treacherous deep canyon that holds us in, filled with land mines, tank blockers, barbed wire and even some rather nasty mutated creatures."

"Why on God's green earth would they insist on keeping you here? We don't read any signs of dangerous radiation anywhere. It just bloody-well doesn't make sense!" Jack blurted out.

He then asked Noble if anyone had ever escaped, and he replied, "I think so, but there's no way of knowing for sure. It's not like they're going to send any kind of rescue party for us. Chances are they died in the pit, but if they didn't, we'd have no way of knowing." It was clear that these questions were forcing Noble to dig up some demons, and frankly, he was getting a little irritated and rightfully so. "Listen Jack, you've never seen death like most of the people here have. Women and children fused into concrete, charred corpses of your neighbors and family, the radiation, the cancer, starvation, the tears. And no damn help from anyone, anywhere, we were just left here to die. And to make sure we did, they sealed us in. Tell me Jack, what part of that makes sense?"

Takarada's mind went to the distant stories he had heard as a child about Hiroshima and Nagasaki. Horrible, nightmarish and ghoulish tales that were absolutely real and not fabricated on some screen with CGI or from within the pages of a book. Jack placed his hand on Noble's arm, and with all of the sincerity he could muster, he apologized to him for all that they had endured. Then Jack did what he was good at, he changed the subject. "Tell me, Noble, who are these people with you?" Noble snapped himself out of his head and started to introduce his friends, beginning with the woman. "This is Ann, and this is Bruce." They both addressed the group with a nod. Then with a gesture of his head in the direction of the man carrying the sawed-off shotgun, he said, "This is Armstrong, but we call him the Professor. He is an MIT graduate who holds a doctorate and two master's degrees in science and agriculture." The Professor acknowledged Jack but bypassed him along with everybody else and beelined straight for Takarada.

The Professor bowed deep and offered greetings. "Konichiwa, Armstrong desu. Douzo yo ro shiko." Takarada lit up and surpassed stunned going straight for amazed. He too bowed, and both men started conversing at the speed of light in Japanese.

Jack grinned, "God blind me, it looks like Kyoshi has found a playmate." Jack turned on the serious and looked back at Noble. Well, Mr. Noble, could I invite you and your friends in for a spot of tea? We have much to discuss." Noble agreed. He whistled a loud tweet from between his teeth and raised his hand into the air with his index finger pointing towards the entrance of the E.I.O. As everybody in Noble's group made their way to the entrance, Jack mentioned that they might not have enough tea for everybody. Noble smiled (a real smile this time) and said he didn't care what it was, as long as it was cold and sweet.

A string of eager people formed a long line that led into the secret entrance. It was going to take a while even though there were eight elevators to take everybody deep down into the bowels of the subterranean base. It was quite the scene, and Nathan noticed two young children playing at the feet of what he assumed were there parents. Some of the sadness he noticed earlier seemed to have evaporated. A few were even laughing and joking as they walked towards what they were probably thinking was a whole new life. And they'd be right. They were in good hands as Jack, Takarada and Tommy weren't ones to let this travesty continue. Nathan got a big warm fuzzy and turned to Olivia to share it, only she was gone.

Chapter 18

Sightseeing

Nathan gazed down the long line of people waiting to get into the newly resurrected Utah branch of the E.I.O. but couldn't see Olivia anywhere. He murmured a pissed off, "Crap," because he knew perfectly well what she was up to. Nathan was just hoping he was wrong, but that feeling he had in his gut was telling him he wasn't. If he was right, he also couldn't blame her, because he would have done the same thing. Tommy, who was guiding Noble's clan into the elevators, noticed Nathan walking the line for the third time. He had a pretty good hunch himself. The noise generated by the excited group grew like their anticipation, but it was soon drowned out by the increasing whine of the FU2's engines. The sound drew everyone's attention towards the jet, including Nathan, who grumbled out an exhausted, "Damn it, Olivia."

The FU2 rose straight up and hovered for a few brief seconds as though it were having second thoughts, and both Nathan and Tommy ran towards it. The thrust of its vertical lift system prevented them from getting too close, and as it just floated, they could only watch. Nathan hoped that Olivia was coming to her senses. She wasn't. Jack and Takarada broke from the crowd and joined Tommy and Nathan just as the FU2 rocketed out of sight. Nathan gave Jack a "what now?" kind of look, and Jack pulled out his pocket watch, flipped it open and sighed. Nathan knew Jack was perturbed at not just one, but two of his agents (because of course Ramsay went with her) doing precisely what he had asked them not to do. He clicked his watch shut and officially declared them of going all willy-nilly. Noble ran up and asked where they were going. Nathan responded, "Bonneville Hills, it's where Olivia grew up. She's looking for her parents."

Noble responded with an unsettling look and simply stated, "There's not much there, nothing good at least." Bonneville Hills was close to ground zero and wiped clean from the Earth. Nobody goes that far east, it's too dangerous. If there's any radiation still in the air, it's there. It's not very safe." Nathan getting frustrated, again repeated himself,

"Damn it, Olivia."

Noble asked if they should contact them by radio. Jack looked at the line of eager people waiting to get into the base and said, "No, we need to retain radio silence. I have a bad feeling they may be listening, and the last thing we need is that bloody Annihilator taking us out before we even have a chance to fight back." Noble wondered who "they" were, but didn't say anything, figuring he'd find out soon enough. Jack paused. He knew there was nothing he could say that would stop Nathan, so he told him to take a chopper and bring them back. He told Nathan to take Tommy, and Noble gallantly offered his services. He proclaimed to know exactly how to get there, plus he'd never been in a helicopter before.

Noble asked Sir Jonathon if they could retrieve the rest of his clan, that is assuming they were all welcome. Jack, who had already been envisioning his new workforce, reassured Noble that, "Oh yes, you are indeed all welcome, but we're going to need your help." Somehow Noble knew this though, and he nodded, then said he'd send Armstrong back to fetch the rest. Jack, who was growing more and more impatient, looked at Tommy and Nathan and barked, "Well, get going! We don't have all bloody day!" Nathan, Tommy and Noble headed towards the smallest chopper (which was still huge), and within seconds they were on their way to Bonneville Hills. As they left, Jack saluted, not because he was showing respect, because in all sincerity, he was pretty irritated. He did it to shield his eyes from the wind, dust and debris caused by the spinning blades.

Jack was right to insinuate that they didn't have "all bloody day," because it was already dusk by the time they were hovering over Bonneville Hills. Noble was also right. It was a barren land, almost flat with rows upon rows of decimated houses and the outer skins of assorted charred buildings. Nathan had heard stories of Olivia's youth while growing up here, but of course, he never pictured it as it truly was, a wasteland. It was easy to spot the FU2 idling in the street below as its immense size made it stick out like a sore thumb. Without saying a word, Nathan tapped Tommy on his head and pointed towards the two figures walking around the shell of Olivia's childhood home. There was nobody there, nobody to be seen for miles. If there were people still living down there, they were waiting for the veil of night before creeping out from the shadows. Tommy noted that even though the radiation level was higher, it still wasn't dangerous, and they landed in an empty yard next to the FU2.

Olivia may or may not have noticed the large helicopter landing across the street as she was so fixated on her house, her past and her parents. Ramsay stood with her arm around her as she just stared into the abandoned and hollow abode. Ramsay, however, did notice the large copter and looked over her shoulder as Nathan, Tommy and Noble approached from behind. Ramsay removed her arm, and Nathan slipped in taking her place next to his wife and soon-to-be mother of his child. He didn't say a word and just stood there with her, offering his support in the form of silence.

The dusk had turned to dark, and almost as though he had some sort of sixth sense, Noble announced that it was probably a good idea to get back. Tommy agreed and eased Nathan and Olivia back towards the awaiting chopper. He also suggested to Nathan that maybe they should take the helicopter back for some "much needed alone time." Nathan wholeheartedly agreed. It didn't take long, and in a few brief moments Nathan and Olivia were airborne and heading back to the base. Tommy looked at Ramsay and Noble and sighed out a grateful, "Well, that wasn't so painful." Noble only smirked, pointing towards the FU2 as six figures wielding a few machetes and all sorts of funky homemade weapons were blocking their entrance to the craft.

Tommy groaned, and Noble stated that no good deed ever goes unpunished. They walked towards the idling jet. "Well, at least they can't get in," Ramsay declared as she squeezed the tiny remote control she was carrying. The FU2 made that car-alarm click and beeping sound. She then added, "Maybe they're friendly." And Noble, who knew better, grasped the grips of his sidearms as they moved in closer.

Tommy shouted a friendly, "Hi!" over the low whine of the FU2's engines. "Can we help you?" and the men said nothing, smiling as they tapped their clubs against the palms of their hands. Tommy sighed. He was getting a total "Baseball Furies" vibe from this Bonneville Hills gang of misfits. He realized the only way out was through, and knew they were going to have to bop their way back.

Noble drew his weapons, asking "Didn't your mamas ever tell you not to bring knives to a gun fight?" followed by a shot into the air from each pistol hoping it would deter them. It didn't, and the supposed leader reached behind his back, whipped out a small, Sig Sauer semi-automatic pistol and began firing. He, however, was not firing into the air. Both Tommy and Ramsay hit the dirt, and Noble, like Jack, didn't even flinch nor hesitate. He marched towards the gang with his pistols leading the way, firing one round after the other.

BWAM! BWAM! BWAM! BWAM! BWAM! BWAM!

From the ground, Ramsay shouted over the gunfire to Tommy (who was lying next to her), "I think he's the president of the Duke fan club." President nothing, Tommy thought. He IS the freakin' Duke personified! All six men went down one after the other, and Noble returned the hot pistols back into their holsters. They were all dead. Noble, however, unlike the Duke, had human feelings and never enjoyed killing. He wasn't a robot. This was a different world though, one that was simply of the "kill or be killed" philosophy, but that never made it any easier for him.

Noble walked up and started collecting the dead men's weapons, boots and clothes. A ritual he hated, especially when finding a faded and wrinkled photo in one of their pockets of their children. "What are you doing?" Tommy asked and Noble replied,

"We can't afford to let anything go to waste around here. We can use these weapons and clothes for my clan." Tommy understood, but instead of going into how they don't need to worry about that anymore, he just let it go. He knew Noble wouldn't have listened anyhow. After stripping the men clean like cattle, Noble said they needed to bury them. Tommy for a brief second thought to tell this mountain of a man that there simply wasn't enough time but knew that THAT probably wasn't a good idea. Ramsay said they had all sorts of tools and survival kits on the FU2, or that she could simply blast a hole in the earth. Tommy was surprised that Noble agreed to the latter, knowing an explosion of any kind would more than likely draw more from the shadows.

BOOOSH!

Noble grabbed from the feet while Tommy lifted at the shoulders, and they gently placed the men one at a time into the newly-formed crater. It was a hard scenario. It's one thing to see buildings, ships and structures destroyed. It was another to see or bury the ones who were inside of them. One of the men had fallen face-first onto the dirt, and as Tommy reached down to flip him over, he noticed something, something he'd seen before. He wiped away the blood, sweat and dirt and couldn't believe what he was seeing. He called Ramsay over, and Noble followed.

"See this?" he asked, but it wasn't a question, and he placed his index finger on a small X-shaped scar on the back of the dead man's neck.

Both Noble and Ramsay responded with a "Yeah, so?" and without looking at the others, Tommy predicted that they would more-than-likely have them too. Ramsay and Noble weren't following, and Tommy climbed into the grave and began flipping the bodies over. Noble thought this was extremely disrespectful, but before he could say anything, Tommy noted he had found another with the very same mark, and then another. He did the same with the three remaining bodies and was surprised to see that they were ordinary men. Neither Ramsay nor Noble knew what was going on, and as Noble reached his hand down to help Tommy out of the pit, he stated they're not human. Adding "at least those three aren't" referring to the ones where X marked the spot. Ramsay, who had been in Jack's confidence, started to catch on. Noble however, was still in the dark, and Tommy spelled it out.

From the rim of the hole containing the bodies, he pointed down towards three, "See those guys, they're human." He then pointed at the other ones, "Those three, they're not, they're Velatians." Ramsay's eyes popped wide open, and Noble, not knowing what the hell a Velatian was, was still confused. But it was becoming more and more clear to Tommy why, even after the radiation level had dropped, no one came to these poor bastards' rescue, why the surrounding moat was built, how Dr. Iscariot was able to build his army of minions, everything. Right then and there it dawned on Tommy that the Velatians had been involved all along.

Noble didn't believe it, stating that little marks on their necks didn't prove a damn thing, but Tommy knew. He had that feeling of "just knowing," the same one Takarada now talked about and vowed never to ignore anymore. Tommy reached into the pile of clothes and weapons that Noble had confiscated, picked up one of the machetes and jumped back into the hole. Noble tensed up as though he were not going to let this happen, but Ramsay placed her hand on his large arm begging him to listen.

Tommy took the knife and started cutting through the skin of one of the bodies, one with an "X". He cut two fine lines on the face and began pulling the skin back as though he were merely cleaning a fish. All three gasped at what lied beneath the thin layer of flesh that disguised the Velatian's true form. It was that of an insect, a beetle to be more precise, a scarab to be even more precise than that. After all Noble had seen, he had never seen anything like this before, and this giant man leaned over and vomited at the sight. Ramsay almost did the same, and although she had seen more than her fair share of tragedy, she'd never seen anything like this either.

Tommy threw down the machete, wiped the dirt and blood from his hands onto his pants and stated that "these" are the "they" we were talking about. Noble had forgotten he'd even asked the question. "We need to get back," Tommy added. Noble, who was still somewhat in shock, didn't help Tommy out of the grave this time. Not because he didn't want to, but because he was deep into his own head. Ramsay gently guided Noble, who was almost twice as tall as her, towards the FU2 with a warm, "C'mon, honey." And Tommy let on to both (even though Noble was probably not listening) that they needed to find out who is human and who is not. It's also fair to assume that the Velatians know we're here. It seems they have infiltrated far more than we ever thought possible.

Tommy picked up one of the small folding shovels Ramsay had pulled from the FU2's survival kit and began filling the pit. He definitely did not want to take the time to bury the ones that would have without a doubt killed them all. It was hands down more to appease Noble. As soon as Ramsay and Noble were aboard the idling jet, Tommy threw the last pile of dirt he was willing to shovel, as well as the shovel itself, into the still quite open hole along with a sharp, "Screw this."

They needed to get back and quick-like. Tommy knew time was of the essence. He was also dying for a cigarette and didn't know when he'd have another chance to have one. He sat on the rim of the crater containing the dead men and aliens, pulled out a smoke, followed by his faithful Zippo, which wasn't working. He flicked it repeatedly, but after spending a little time at the bottom of Lake Erie, it hadn't worked quite right since. He reached to his left, picked up a still-smoldering stick from Ramsay's blast and held it up to the cigarette. He sucked in a few times, and it lit up in a golden glimmer, followed by an exuberant burst of smoke. It was glorious, and Tommy exhaled his first drag in a long sigh. It'd probably been a day or two since his last one, and he even got a slight buzz from the tobacco. After the need for a fix wore off, routine kicked in and it started tasting like every other cigarette he had ever smoked in his life. His mouth was dry, and he smacked his lips a few times as he simply stared into the grave. His thoughts started running away as they so often did, and as he reached the butt of his smoke, he heard some shuffling.

He pretended not to notice, but knew someone or something was lurking about, just as Noble had said. Tommy took one last puff and flicked the butt into the hole, and it bounced off the beetle-face of the dead Velatian. It was time to leave.

The high-pitched whine of the FU2's jet engines increased, and if that explosion didn't bring the local "whatevers" this would surely do the trick. Tommy stood up and made his way towards the little retractable stairway leading into the massive jet. He knew he wasn't alone and had a feeling he was being watched. Even if he wasn't, he started creeping himself out and picked up the pace towards the FU2. He wanted to look back, but also didn't want to be turned to a pillar of salt, so he just kept his eyes forward. He moved even faster, though he was still walking, and upon reaching the stairs of the jet he stopped and placed his hands on the rails in a freaked-out fashion. Just as he lifted his leg for the first step, he felt something stop his ascent. He froze and slowly turned to look at what was grasping his left shoulder. It was a decrepit hand, and he screamed like Ann Robinson. A million retaliatory thoughts ran through his head, but before he could act on any of them, a soft, trembling voice begged him to "Please ... Stop ... Wait."

Chapter 19

Cedar Mountain City

Jack delegated the job of corralling Noble's remaining people into the Salt Lake facility to Michael, Liberty and Armstrong. Slipping away, he grabbed Takarada, and they ventured deep into the chasms of the subterranean base. Both men had been there before, many times as a matter of fact, but it had been quite a while. They knew what they were looking for too, anything that could aid them in their struggle against the Velatians. Of course they knew of Launch Bay 3, where the Duke was presently enjoying a little sabbatical. That was a no-brainer. Their hope, however, lied within the bases deep subterranean manufacturing plants. Two massive factories that opened up to the western part of the state from the side of the Cedar Mountains. Within these foundries, the E.I.O., the United States and the U.K. pumped out arsenals of special aircraft, vehicles and heavy machinery. And how would Takarada and Jack know all of this? Because Takarada designed the whole damned thing, not only overseeing its construction, but also overseeing the birth of the Duke. This was where the massive cowbot was erected by the Americans over a decade ago, not long after The FUJI was built. And as the kaiju situation outgrew the borders of Japan, additional E.I.O. facilities were created in the west. Yes, San Francisco had the submerged Pacific branch, but it wasn't built as a place to manufacture the tackle of which the world found itself in such desperate need. It was the same with the

Liverpool office, and though they had one hangar, the additional London division was created to manufacture and store organic thorium.

As they rode the elevator down, the thought occurred to Takarada that this base would have been a far better choice than their latest home at the Goku. He simply never thought to question the truth behind the ever-lingering radiation in Salt Lake City. He was not alone. Obviously, the facade was elevated, if not downright invented, by Dr. Iscariot to keep out those pesky people who would interfere with his plans of world domination. It was a cruel and ruthless hoax perpetrated in the name of power, and it had ruined countless lives. Takarada was surprised that the E.I.O. didn't think of it first.

The fast-descending lift stopped with a slight jerk, and its doors parted to a gigantic and magnificent warehouse. It was dark, but a few lights from above, that appeared to be as far away as the stars themselves, offered a shadowy glow. Dr. Takarada stepped out of Elevator Six and eased to his right, fumbling around for what he knew was there. Jack waited in the lift as Takarada searched for the nearby twin doors of what was once deemed "The Electric Company" within the super-structure. Jack heard a flipping of switches that echoed throughout the vast emptiness of the abandoned hanger, and he peeked out of the dimly-lit elevator. He looked up with somewhat of an unsettling feeling, and the flipping of switches was replaced by the sound of one large "click." An echoing sound that can only be described as a nuclear plant powering-up in an ascending tambor. Jack squinted because it was as though the sun had risen within the confines of the bay as soon it was ignited in light.

It was nothing short of a city beneath the surface of the earth, filled with its own offices, roads, living quarters and large warehouses within the mammoth hangar itself. Multiple runs of track for supporting monstrous cranes and assorted lifts garnished both the walls and ceiling that climbed to over eighty meters from beneath the ground. Even now, with the hangar fully lit, you still couldn't see the other side, and where the first one ended, the second began. Each plant also sported an array of vehicles designed for lifting heavy metal, steel and pre-assembled machinery. But none were as impressive as the treaded crawlers that literally weighed in at three thousand tons each. Designed after the NASA rocket transports, these were for carrying crafts or mechs (like our old friend the Duke) along the massive runway to their designated launch sights. Saying the hanger was colossal would have been a huge understatement as well as a disservice to those who built it. And anything big enough to create its own personal weather system, well, you get the idea.

The sheer size, however, was not the reason both men were in total awe, because as mind-blowing as it was, they had seen it all before. It was, without a doubt, because of what was inside. Takarada's jaw nearly hit the floor, and he voiced a surprised, "Nanite kotoda." While Jack simultaneously did the same thing, only in the king's English in the form of, "Oh my God!" Both men looked on in surprised shock, because it wasn't quite as abandoned as they had believed.

Suspended above the long runway that ran from bay to bay was what appeared to be an assembly line of enormous hanging metal exoskeletons. Due to their size, Jack and Takarada could only see a few before the continuing thread faded into the black of the second hangar. What they could see though, were four daikaiju-sized arachnid ligatures made of titanium steel. The tremendous weight of each had to be supported by three separate mobile cranes that crept along the tracks adhered to the ceiling. There, the hanging cephalothorax and combined eight legs waited lifelessly to be resurrected. But it had never happened, and now they just hung there like the skeletons of cattle within an abandoned slaughterhouse.

Jack's stomach turned upside down, but then his uneasiness was replaced by a lump in his throat and a sincere, overwhelming feeling of gratitude overtook him. "God blind me, Kyoshi," he whispered as they stared, still in disbelief, "Iscariot was making an army of these things. We were barely able to take even ONE down." He paused, "Can you imagine if he had completed even one more of these eight-legged abominations, much less an entire bloody battalion?" For a second, Jack's mind drifted as he imagined a cluster of giant spiders harboring death and devastation throughout a web-coated London. It was almost too much to bear, and he truly realized the massive bullet they had dodged. He put his hand on Takarada's shoulder and stated that even in the midst of it all, someone up there must like them, because it could've been a lot worse, if not the end itself.

"This is where we all need to be for the time being." Jack stated. "It seems somewhat safe, and we can house thousands down here." He stopped and pondered, "We need to get that blasted cowboy robot in here too." Takarada said it should be no problem. Jack then added that it would piss Iscariot off even from the grave if they could somehow use his arachnid cyborg technology to help them defeat the Velatians. Takarada smiled. He liked the idea too, but more so the part about pissing off Iscariot. Jack sighed, "But even with Noble's people, I don't think we have the manpower." It was then that a few of the skylight panels from above flickered twice, and they lost partial lighting. Jack's eyes looked up. "We also don't know what works down here and what bloody doesn't." It may have phased Jack, but Takarada was used to this kind of stuff from the Goku. He wasn't worried, and apparently that rubbed off on Jack because he stopped, grinned, then slapped Takarada on the back and triumphantly barked, "Either way, Kyoshi, it sure beats the hell out of that ruddy jail cell I've been wasting away in for two years." I say we give these blaggards what-for! What do you say, old chap?" Takarada didn't usually fall for one of Jack's signature pep talks, but what choice did they have?

"Yes, Sir Jonathon, I am with you all the hay!" he responded and returned his enthusiasm by slapping Jack on HIS back. Jack gave Kyoshi a stern look, and for a split-second, things got awkward. But the silence immediately subsided when both men burst out laughing as though they were in a poorly-dubbed Japanese film.

***

As Tommy, Ramsay and Noble returned, they could see the massive work lights casting mammoth shadows on the rolling

hills of the Cedar Mountain Range. Time was in short demand, and Jack immediately ordered the Duke to be transported to Launch Bay Two. From there the bot would be brought to the assembly plant section via the runway that led out of the mountain from its other side. Jack knew this is where they should have initially brought the giant mech, but he was cutting himself some slack as their plan wasn't written, it was merely unfolding as trials and opportunities presented themselves.

Jack still refused to break radio silence, but Tommy and Ramsay both knew to follow the Duke delivery service to the opposite side of the mountain. Even though Tommy had never seen or even knew about the massive factories within the base (other than what he had heard), Ramsay did. She told Tommy to pull ahead, and he blew past the choppers. Seeing four helicopters also told him that Nathan and Olivia must have returned safely. Tommy grinned; he felt like a giddy little schoolgirl when he thought about Olivia. He couldn't wait to see her.

The west side of the Cedar mountains shook, causing what had grown and accumulated on its majestic slopes to break free and tumble to its rocky base. The sound of gargantuan spinning cogs used to open its concealed entrance snapped and churned as the metal broke free from years of rust and corrosion. It was a miraculous sight to behold and amazing when you think about what the flipping of just one switch could do. Like most of the E.I.O.'s designs, it was a two-section door that parted from the middle. But it was nothing compared to the Launch Bay Three exit portal which opened from the top of the mountains two miles north. To Tommy, it was apparent that an extremely large amount of WD-40 would help things to go a little faster. Growing impatient, he jettisoned in between the still opening doors. The runway that burrowed through the mountain was not only long, but wide enough for a freakin' battleship. It was barely lit too, and Tommy gasped in awe when it opened to the subterranean plant where Jack and Takarada were waiting in an idling tread crawler. Like the space shuttle, Tommy landed and rode the runway instead of using the craft's propulsion system, because it used far less fuel that way. He, Ramsay and Noble gazed up through the FU2's windshield at the hanging spider skeletons above and knew without hesitation what they were looking at. "Good Lord," Tommy gasped, and he suddenly felt like Jack, grateful that Iscariot's plan never came to fruition. After the FU2 came to a full stop, the tread crawler, with Jack at the helm, made its way down the runway tunnel and towards the point of exit where the choppers hovered in wait. Tommy was surprised at how fast those things could move considering their massive weight and size.

Tommy unstrapped and stood up, but before exiting the craft both he and Noble offered assistance to their elderly passengers as Ramsay cut off the engines. They walked down the flight stairs and were overtaken by the size of the underground factory. Without even realizing it, Tommy ventured ahead, never once looking down. It was almost hypnotizing. It reminded him of The FUJI, only it was much, much bigger. He could see the eight-passenger elevators in the distance down at the end of what was basically a street surrounded by buildings. It truly was an underground city where engineers, workers, their families and their lives revolved around what was obviously an E.I.O. constructed community. At least that was the impression he was getting. But his thoughts were soon solidified when he saw a quaint sign from atop one of the base's underground housing compounds that said, "Welcome to Cedar Mountain City". It was overwhelming, and Tommy felt as though he had just stumbled upon Captain Nemo's long lost lair. He leaned up against the street sign next to him to take it all in and saw he was at the corner of 1st and Runway Boulevard. Tommy looked around, then pulled out a cigarette. He looked around again then pulled out his Zippo. He flicked it a few times, but it still wasn't working. Desperately, Tommy tried to find another source of fire, anything would do, but it was too late.

The elevators started opening one after the other, and waves of Noble's clan started filing out and heading their way. Michael and Liberty were leading the first group and Armstrong the second. Ramsay joined Tommy, and while they waited, they giggled as they searched for Nathan and Olivia in the crowd. Noble ran towards Armstrong and began conversing with him.

As they walked, Noble lifted up a young girl, kissed her on the cheek and placed her on his shoulders. It was the closest thing Tommy had seen to a family since he, Nathan and Olivia were at Nathan's dad's house all those years ago. He liked the feeling too, even though it was all warm and gushy-like.

There had to be at least two hundred people in Noble's group, and it seemed they had every intention of making the abandoned base their new home. Some pushed carts as others pulled wagons full of food, supplies and whatever else any good survivors of Armageddon would be toting. Michael waved and screamed from the other end of the block, "DUDES!" and he and Liberty joined Tommy and Ramsay. Tommy asked if they had seen Nathan and Olivia, and Liberty stated they were still topside, adding that Olivia was quite upset. Tommy knew why. He also figured Nathan was probably doing his best to console her and more than likely having a hard time with it. He giggled again and stated that he was going up before Jack and Takarada returned with the Duke, then asked his friends if they would like to join him. Tommy figured they had about fifteen minutes before the giant cowboy mech returned home riding high on the back of its trusty and noble tread crawler. Okay, maybe it was more like a heap of scrap metal piled up inside the bed of an old pickup truck, but nobody was splitting hairs.

*****

Olivia was outside leaning with her back against one of the metal-plated doors that concealed the ground-level entrance to the base. She was crying, and Nathan (as Tommy had predicted) was having a hard time consoling her. Olivia losing her parents had always been a touchy subject, and truth be told they didn't talk about it much. But obviously coming to Salt Lake City and being this close to her childhood home, of course it made sense that it'd rear its head. It was almost cruel she thought, to be shown a glimmer of hope after so long, all for nothing. Being pregnant had so much to do with it as well, and not because of the accompanying raging hormones. It was because she spent so much time thinking ... wishing, that her child would have had the chance to know at least one or two of its relatives. Both of Nathan's parents were already gone, neither had any other family and that's usually as far as she'd get before bursting into tears. Nathan walked Olivia slightly away from the four sets of gates built into the mountain to get a little privacy from the two men standing guard. Sure, they were polite enough, but they were poised right behind them in a foyer that separated the front set of doors to a second. They seemed concerned for Olivia, but it was obvious they didn't really care as they had their own worries. Nathan wanted to wrap this up, because he knew Olivia was tired and needed rest. He planned on taking her for a short walk, not too far out though. Through the whir of the spinning air vent fans, he could hear the hum of an elevator returning to the surface. Nathan ignored it, and he and Olivia slowly meandered off together, her face in her palms and his arm around her back.

It was funny, Nathan acting like a grown-up, responding to his wife in a fashion that showed not only wisdom, but love and tenderness. It was a far cry from the Nathan who ventured to Japan for the first time over a decade ago. It seemed most people in the world were a far cry from who they were then. So much had changed. But the changing happened to the individuals themselves, and that's how it has to work. The change in someone else usually occurs when it first happens within us. He sat Olivia down on a large rock and scootched his butt over to make room for himself. He said the only thing he could think of, "I love you," and nothing else. Olivia's crying subsided and became more of a series of heavy snorts as she inhaled the contents within her nose back up into her head. She took her glasses off, rubbed her eyes and smiled at Nathan.

"So, have you played around with any names yet?" she asked him in a still-crying sort of fashion.

Nathan thought about it and answered, "Well, if it's a girl, I was thinking Dextrose." Olivia burst out laughing, and Nathan responded with a "What?"

Joking or not, Olivia made sure that Dextrose was not a name in the running and then asked, "What if it's a boy?"

Nathan paused to think about it for a second, but before he could say anything, a trembling hand laid gently upon Olivia's shoulder from behind.

"How about Oliver?"

Nathan turned and followed the hand up the arm to the face of someone who looked familiar to him, but he wasn't quite sure where he had seen him before. It didn't take long. The Lizard King gasped, and like a pair of dashboard airbags, his eyes inflated into twin ping-pong balls. Olivia, not really paying too much attention, said she liked than name and reminded Nathan that Oliver was her dad's name.

Nathan couldn't speak and thought for sure he had just entered the *Twilight Zone* because this kind of stuff simply does not happen in the real world. He stood up so fast he didn't even notice that he had knocked Olivia off the rock he had so gently placed her upon. He spun around and found himself looking into the tired but gentle eyes of a man who may not have been as old as he appeared to be. From the ground, Olivia hadn't even realized they weren't alone as she was too preoccupied with trying to hoist her pregnant body back up. The man reached out and offered Olivia his hand while Nathan just stood there in shock. Olivia grabbed it, and once to her feet she finally noticed. It was truly one of the most awesome things Nathan had ever had the pleasure of bearing witness to. For a second, Olivia thought she had entered the *Twilight Zone* because things like this just don't happen in the real world. But this WAS real, and it was happening, and as though she were hanging on to the very essence of life itself, she embraced her father.

Nathan eased over, and both Oliver and Olivia pulled him in, and they held each other in a silence that said it all. Nathan couldn't help but think of his own dad and a similar situation, and his eyes, like an exploding dam, burst into a flood of flowing tears. With his face buried in Oliver's shirt, he peeked over his father-in-law's shoulder and saw not just Tommy and Ramsay watching from the entrance of the base, but also Jack and Dr. Takarada who was holding Suzy the wonder beagle. Nathan felt a flood of emotion that warmed his insides like the smell of homemade beef stew coming from the kitchen. This was his family. He would fight tooth and nail to hold onto them and this feeling that was worth far more than all of his riches. It also occurred to him that no matter where he was, if these crazy people were alongside him, he was home.

Chapter 20

The Return of Wang

The long day finally reached its peak, and both Sir Jonathon and Dr. Takarada had to retire for the evening. It's hard to believe, but the last twenty-four hours seemed like a lifetime, and tomorrow would prove to be just as grueling. Tommy was fading too, but Nathan and Olivia were wide awake as Oliver Olivetti discussed the last decade living within the ruins of Salt Lake City. Michael and Liberty seemed quite intrigued as well. Which said a lot because it was obvious they needed sleep, or charging or whatever it was that they did. Olivia hung on every word Mr. Olivetti spoke and held his hand at the table as she listened. Olivia had been pretty happy over the last few years, but seeing her dad still alive kicked things up another notch, almost to a fairy-tale level. Tommy saw a gleam in Olivia's eye, one he'd never seen before, and he got that warm-fuzzy feeling again. He looked at Nathan, and Nathan gave him a playful wink as Oliver went on.

In between stories of Olivia's youth, he claimed the only reason he and Olive, Olivia's mother, had survived the actual blast itself was due to the fact that their air conditioner was on the fritz. Tommy and Nathan didn't understand but Olivia knew exactly what that meant. She explained that being an older house, they had a deep fruit cellar, and it was always much cooler in there surrounded by its cement walls and thick, beam ladened ceiling. Olivia laughed and gave her dad a little grief as she always said he was too cheap to fix it. Oliver only smiled, because that little space was the source of many wonderful memories. And truth be told, it became his favorite spot in the house. He knew if he fixed the air conditioner, they'd lose their special gathering space. Oliver had even put a table and four chairs in the center of it. No television, no phone, nothing but talking, cards and board games, and that's how he liked it. It was down there that he, Olive and the couple from across the street were playing a card game called "Liverpool" when the bomb went off. (Which was ironic as Liverpool is where Olivia was at the time.) Oliver glossed over, his eyes got all misty-like, and he stated that a beam collapsed preventing the rest of the house from falling in on them while the cellar shielded them from the explosion. He then went from misty-eyed to heartbroken. "That's what killed your mother. The beam that protected us struck her on the head as it came down." Oliver then went from sad to angry, "And absolutely nobody came to help. Nobody! And as far as we knew we were the only survivors. We had no communication, nothing. All lines and cell services were dead. We were completely cut off." Oliver's anger grew even more, but now with an added look of creepy confusion to it. "Then they built that damn mote, and we knew we were never ... NEVER getting out."

Tommy could see the rage building up in Olivia's dad, and as though he were turning into the wolfman or something, Mr. Olivetti flipped the table over and stood up in a fiery fury. "Look out!" Tommy screamed, and Oliver began pulling at his head from its top with both hands! It made a wet crackling sound as the stretching bone and flesh separated. Olivia howled in terror as they were bathed in a shower of blood and an assortment of body fluids! He was a Velatian! Nathan leaped towards the alien to protect his wife. It pulled out a ray-gun that was stashed in its human skinsuit and disintegrated Nathan into a mere pile of Lizard King dust! Upon seeing her husband and father of her unborn child turned to a smoldering fine powder, she gasped and passed out. Tommy reached for his blaster but realized he had forgotten it in his other uniform. He looked to the twins for some help, but they were fast asleep. Defenseless, Tommy found

himself at death's door, staring down the barrel of the alien's weapon. He snarled one last time, just before everything turned to a blinding flash of white light.

"Tommy ... TOMMY!" At the sound of Olivia shouting his name, Tommy snorted himself awake and sprang up reaching for his blaster.

"Whoa, Tex!" Nathan yelled, and Tommy snapped himself out of the nightmare that ensued after he had nodded off at the table. "You all right?" Nathan added.

"Yeah, I'm fine," Tommy grunted. "Just tired, I guess. I need a smoke." Tommy excused himself, and as he headed towards the door, he intentionally walked right behind Mr. Olivetti and casually looked at the back of his neck. He was fine.

***

It was amazing how much the abandoned buried factories resembled that of an urban setting. Shops, restaurants, grocery stores, a ball field, theaters, you name it, they had it. The Salt Lake facility truly was a city of industry buried deep beneath the earth. Tommy found himself strolling the dimly-lit streets of the complex still in total awe. He walked down Runway Boulevard towards the runway itself where the top half of the Duke sat upright upon a tread crawler awaiting to live again. It was weird seeing the cowbot surrounded by a multitude of giant hanging exoskeletons, and Tommy shivered. He stopped and just stared. Due to the sheer ... amazingness of everything around him, he had forgotten his need for a cigarette. Upon remembering, he reached into the inside pocket of his uniform only to forget again. A flashing light similar to that of a flickering television was emitting from the monocle and cracks of the downed bot's head. It was hard to miss, with the light reflecting off the multitude of massive steel spider ligatures. He reached back into his uniform, but instead of grabbing his smokes, he pulled out his blaster and proceeded with caution. Somebody or some "thing" was in the Duke.

He went in through the bot's hip hatch as it was already open and entered the small lift that would take him to the head of the mech. Tommy didn't see this part of the Duke often, but every time he did it reminded him of duct tape. (Well, plenty of things reminded Tommy of duct tape as it was almost a fetish for him.) But this did in particular, as he once wrapped the bot's main organic thorium line in layer upon layer of the sweet, silver sticky stuff in the midst of a battle. He beamed with confidence when he thought about the ass-whoopin' they had put on Zargatron during that fight. Then his thoughts shifted gears on a dime, as they often did, and his confidence turned to fear when he thought about Annihilator. But before these feelings could play out any further, he had already reached the head of the mech.

Tommy held his blaster straight up alongside the silhouette of his face and peeked through the rear entrance of the cowbot's cranium. He rolled his eyes, sighed in relief and lowered his weapon. It was Dr. Takarada who was streaming an old episode of *The Love Boat* on the Duke's massive surrounding windshield. Tommy knocked softly on the oval frame of the hatch, and Dr. T nearly jumped out of his skin.

"Tommy-san!" He shrieked. "What is it you are doing here?" Tommy stepped down into the cockpit and eased his way along the side aisle that outlined the control room's theater-esque seating. But still being a little shaken up by his lovely dream, Tommy snuck a quick glimpse at the back of Takarada's neck as he sat in the seat next to him. The good doctor scowled and went all official, "I assure you General Taylor, I am quite human."

"Sorry, Doc, I guess I'm just a bit on edge." Takarada nodded and patted Tommy on the knee.

"I believe we are all a little on edge, Tommy-san."

"What are you watching, Doc?" Tommy asked, knowing damn well what Takarada was watching. Dr. T blushed and made up some lame excuse about how American television helps him with his English. Tommy believed him, but not really and acknowledged Takarada with a simple, "Sure, Doc."

Takarada then went on to explain that with all that was happening, he could not sleep. He turned off *The Love Boat*, and Tommy uttered a soft, "Thank God." As the glow of the stream diminished, the cockpit lit up, and there were open panels and tangles of wires piled up on the floor and protruding from the walls. Tommy knew what Takarada was doing (other than watching Captain Stubing and the gang) the second he looked in through the open hatch. Even though Dr. T. was taking a break, the smell of heat, sweat and solder permeated the cockpit. He was attempting to re-vamp the Duke's control center.

Tommy shuddered, "No more sleep-state ... right, Dr. T?" Tommy, as well as the other robotonauts, despised the sleep-state. That wretched system had a tendency to suck a little more life out of you every time you suited up to pilot the cowboy mech. Not to mention how you felt afterward, which according to Nathan was far worse than any tequila and cocaine-induced hangover.

Takarada shook his head. "No, no. No more sleep-state ... ever." Tommy was relieved, but Takarada was still worried. "It seems the Velatians couldn't get passed the Duke's internal operating system. Although they eliminated the need for the pilots to control the mech from an induced coma, they couldn't get past the need for the five distinct individuals to operate their designated part of the brain."

Tommy wasn't sure he was following, but figured it was Takarada's way of saying that the "sleep-state" had become an "awake-state," where the pilots did the exact same things they did before, only consciously. Takarada then, and quite abruptly, inhaled a large gasp of air through his mouth with a sudden epiphany. "That is why they used the members of the Vinyl Crush tribute band!" Tommy now knew for sure he wasn't following. "Don't you see, Tommy-san?" Takarada stated. "The Velatians could not change the mainframe of the Duke, it's too embedded. They simply changed the means of operating it. And without you, Nathan, Olivia, Michael and Liberty, they needed what they thought would be the next best thing, a tribute band whose members' only job was to pretend to be you. Tommy finally got it. It made sense. Takarada sprang up and said, "I know what to do, and it's simple because our evil alien friends have already done the work for us! I just need to change it from Velatian to human."

Now that was something Tommy did understand, considering what it was like having to try to figure out their crazy hieroglyphic language while in the thick of it. Takarada asked Tommy if he could stay and help, as this was going to take all night. And though tired, Tommy knew time was in short demand, so of course he agreed. Takarada said he needed to get his laptop and a few notes and asked Tommy to please remain here, promising that he'd be right back. Takarada didn't get a response and could only see the back of Tommy's head as he was leaning forward from his seat fumbling with the controls. Takarada didn't wait for an answer, and being as excited as he was to get to work, simply exited the cockpit to go get his stuff. Tommy continued to monkey around with the panel in front of him, and before long, he (like Dr. T.) had also figured out how to stream to the Duke's massive windshield. He knew it'd take Takarada at least twenty minutes if not more and decided it was time for a much-needed break. Tommy scrolled through the streaming selection, found what he was looking for, started the episode, took a quick look around, kicked back, lit up a smoke and got comfortable.

Even in the midst of all the craziness, Takarada was somewhat excited as he made his way up Runway Boulevard towards his compound (which was just a bed and nightstand within one of the old live-in barracks). This was the first "real work" he had done in quite some time, and though it was under horrific circumstances, he knew he could make a difference. He thought about the indecisiveness and fear he carried around for so long prior to all of this and cursed himself again for not acting sooner. Needless to say, none of this was his fault, but lately he had found himself battling the demons inside his head that tried to convince him otherwise. It was always hard for Kyoshi, being the "as a matter of fact" logical genius he was, to be burdened with something as troubling as a big heart. But maybe that was good as the world was in desperate need of men like Kyoshi Takarada. And even though he sometimes couldn't see it, everyone around him surely could.

Takarada, however, now knew how to get past this, and it seemed it involved something as simple as just "getting busy."

Because believe it or not, changing the Duke from its Velatian coding to human wasn't even his main concern. He grabbed his laptop and glanced at his hand-drawn images of the Duke. He didn't let on, and although "not letting on" is what caused the doctor so much pain to begin with, it seemed he still had a ways to go in trusting the process. He shook his head, crumpled up the drawing and threw it on the floor. As he walked out, the paper unfolded revealing that the Duke's legs were completely shot. He knew this but was hoping there was a way they could still utilize them in some fashion. Supplies were in short demand, and it's not like he could just waltz into your local "Giant Cowboy Mechs R Us" and put in an order of legs to go. As he glided down the stairs, he stopped dead in his tracks as though someone had just weighed his anchor into the wood of the wall. Or could he?

As the doctor was leaving his new quarters within the underground compound, a loud and rather important-sounding voice amplified throughout the streets. "Dr. Kyoshi Takarada, please report to the briefing center." Takarada grumbled and actually came pretty close to ignoring the page, but it just wasn't in his nature. Takarada entered the briefing center and saw it was Nathan Fox at the mic. "Nathan!" he said in a sharp tone sounding like an angry parent. It was funny, but even when Nathan would try to be serious, people usually thought he was messing around. Takarada barked that he didn't have time for his goofing out. Nathan assured the doctor he wasn't "goofing off" and said that a guest had just arrived and was eager to talk to him. Takarada turned when he saw Nathan was being serious, and before acknowledging his visitor, he bowed asking Nathan to please forgive him, and of course he did.

It was Dr. Chen Wang from the YETI Institute. He looked tired and road worn but was nonetheless happy to see his old friend, Takarada. Both men bowed, then shook hands and Dr. Wang skipped the pleasantries. "Kyoshi, I have gathered skin samples of the Annihilator from New York." Takarada's eyes widened. "I have not examined them thoroughly, but enough to get an understanding of what we are dealing with." This was good news indeed, Takarada thought. However, at the moment his mind was focused on the Duke. Besides, it was obvious that

Wang needed some rest. Takarada assured Wang they would promptly get on it tomorrow, allowing him to work and Wang to sleep. Nathan told the doctor where he could bunk down, and as he exited, Takarada found himself doing the same thing Tommy did. He put his arm around Wang, walked him to the door and snuck a peek at the back of his neck. He was fine.

Tommy was a little off as with the arrival of Wang, it took Takarada more like thirty minutes, and when he returned, Nathan was with him. They entered the smoke-riddled cockpit to the loud and chaotic screaming of Levi Ackerman shouting, "KENNY!" from an episode of *Attack On Titan* Tommy had been jonesing to see. Nathan, never really getting into the whole anime thing and not quite sure what he was watching, mimicked the moment and also yelled Kenny. Nathan, however, sounded more like Rocky Balboa bellowing, "Adrian!" and it didn't sit right with Tommy. Not knowing to never dis' anything anime when you're in the presence of a true fan, Nathan had the audacity to call Levi a poser! Tommy had a quick thought of shooting Nathan with his blaster but instead opted to not say a word and just shut it off.

Tommy asked Takarada what took so long, and he told him about the arrival of Dr. Wang. Tommy looked concerned and he asked Nathan if Wang was alone. Nathan said the topside guards reported he had two other guys and a pilot with him, but that was it. "They didn't even come down," he added, and in defense of his decision he said that he remembered Wang. It was a pretty hard name to forget, especially since he was coming from the infamous Bigfoot Institute. Tommy almost laughed, but his wheels were turning, so Takarada assured him Wang was human, and that he even looked himself. Tommy felt a little better, but frankly, it wasn't the possibility of them being Velatians that he was thinking about. It also wouldn't have mattered if the guards let them in or not. It was the questions like, did they practice the strict radio silence rules Jack had put into place? Or even more pressing, how did these men know they were at the abandoned base? And if they knew …

Chapter 21

Surprise!

Tommy had every right to be concerned as the attack came swiftly from above. Even though the factories of Cedar Mountain City we're as deep as, say, the Chrysler Building was tall, dust and debris showered down upon the compound with each explosion. It hadn't even been an hour after Dr. Wang's arrival, and though it wasn't intentional, they had inadvertently let on to our heroes' secret location through active radio communication. As the sirens wailed, Takarada, Nathan and Tommy hauled ass out of the Duke and beelined for the briefing center from within the subterranean facility. Jack burst out of his new quarters shouting, "God blind me!" and ordered that all topside entrances and launch bay exits were to be sealed. It was their only defense. Hopefully the emergency failsafe was still in place. The last thing they needed was for the elevators to open with a hundred armed Velatians charging in, or worse, having to harm the humans who were either military or E.I.O. personnel that had no idea they were being played. Noble's people took to the streets in a panic as he and Armstrong also made their way to the briefing center, which in a sense had become HQ within the base.

Olivia, Michael, Liberty and even Oliver Olivetti pushed their way through Noble's clan and met everybody in the briefing room. Takarada was trying to seal the points as Jack had ordered, but nothing was happening. Mr. Olivetti asked if he could help, but Takarada explained (as he frantically pushed button after button) that the process of sealing the points was done by activating a series of strategically placed explosions. He noted the blasts would bury all exit and entry points, and unless he had another way of detonating the bombs, there was nothing he could do. Armstrong came over, and he and Takarada pulled the front panel off the controls trying to locate the problem. Armstrong stated it was probably just years of deteriorating wire within the system. They were, however, able to get the topside guards along with Wang's men inside just before the thick, solid plates of steel slammed down barricading the top entrance. But that was about it.

Robert Jones led the attack from the air with an FU2 along with a few F-16 Fighting Falcon jets. They also knew the place to attack was the massive entry point where they brought the Duke in. It seemed that destroying the base was not their intent. They either wanted it for their own or for the toy surprises inside, namely the array of eight-legged exoskeletons constructed of titanium steel. They fired missile upon missile trying to bring the barrier that protected the long runway down with as little damage as possible. Tommy had the horrible thought that if they truly wanted in, they could just summon their pal, the Annihilator. That thing could lay waste to the entire area for twenty freakin' square miles. Liberty stated that the Velatians' scavenger nature would buy them some time as they will try to infiltrate with as little damage as possible.

KA-CHOOOM!

The briefing center rocked, even from three hundred meters deep, and everyone knew that if it collapsed, Earth's only hope would go with it. The two men and pilot accompanying Dr. Wang rushed in and over to where Armstrong and Dr. T. were tracing wires. Tommy wasn't even thinking about it but noticed the infamous "X" on the back of the pilot's neck. Radio silence nothing, they had a Velatian teamed up with Wang all along. Tommy got Nathan's attention and motioned the Lizard King over with a jerk of his head. He didn't want to pull out his weapon and just start shooting. After all, there was a chance that it truly was just a scar and nothing more. Plus, the briefing room was full of people and had become quite chaotic, so firing his blaster semi-haphazardly wasn't in the cards. Tommy nodded towards the pilot whose back was turned away from them, and Nathan caught his drift. They eased in closer, but almost as though he had a sixth-sense or something, he spun around, grabbed Nathan and put a gun to his head. Tommy, after seeing Nathan turned to dust once already, decided he could live without ever seeing that again and stopped in his tracks.

The Velatian ordered everybody into the corner, and if they didn't do as it said, it was going to turn Nathan into a Swiss Lizard King sandwich. Wang, not knowing that the Velatians assumed identities of their human victims, demanded an explanation from his pilot. The alien held Nathan tight within its left forearm, and with its right hand aimed the weapon at Dr. Wang's head. This action only infuriated Wang. He said that he hated to have to resort to measures such as this and fired him on the spot. The pilot laughed, and countered Wang's termination with a termination of its own by shooting the doctor in the head. It was surreal, and upon the gruesome sight, the room burst out into a cacophony of blood-curdling screams. Tommy hoped he was dreaming again, but he wasn't, as Dr. Wang collapsed onto the floor in a pool of his own blood. He was dead.

It tightened its grip around Nathan's neck and said that if they didn't open Launch Bay One, he was next. Obviously not knowing the hierarchy of main characters, the angry alien would have no problem seeing its threat through. Nathan yelled to Takarada not to open the mammoth doors that sealed the runway and to keep trying to blow the exit points. As much as he probably hated saying it, he added that in the grand scheme of things, he didn't matter, but what did was that the world held onto its only chance. Tommy looked surprised, but it was now clear to him, beyond any shadow of a doubt, Nathan Fox was a changed man. A few days ago, Tommy couldn't have cared less, but now he did, and he was at a loss at how to save his friend.

KA-CHOOM!

The briefing room shook hard as the latest explosion from above caused the Velatian to lose its balance. Not wasting even

a second, Tommy saw an opportunity as the discombobulated alien stumbled to regain its footing. Tommy lunged forward to intercept the weapon, but he wasn't fast enough, and the alien cocked its gun and started spouting off in its native tongue. Tommy couldn't save Nathan, and he watched in slow motion as the Velatian applied pressure to the trigger. Olivia screamed, "No!" and just as the hammer hit the firing pin the alien screamed in agony firing its shot into the air. The Velatian moaned in pain and rapidly shook its arm trying to break the grip of the razor-sharp teeth that were buried deep. Tommy cried out an "Atta girl!" and couldn't believe he had forgotten Suzy was still in Takarada's backpack! The wonder beagle brought the alien to its knees, and Nathan broke free. Tommy aimed his blaster at the Velatian, and Jack yelled, "Don't shoot!" as he knew the information it held was of the utmost importance. Tommy lowered his weapon, but the room still echoed in a small bang that sounded more like a firecracker than that of a Glock. The alien had taken its own life.

Suzy applied a licking technique to Nathan's face, because even though he got away, his head collided with the wall and was now on the floor in a daze. Olivia ran up to him, and Tommy was in shock seeing Suzy responding as though she actually cared for Nathan. He knew Suzy was capable of showing emotion, but the surprising part was the fact that she was showing it to Nathan. Tommy wondered if as soon as he felt nothing but good feelings towards Nathan Fox his emotions somehow transferred to Suzy. It was possible. After all, Takarada made her.

Another explosion rocked the buried foundation of the underground city, and one of the suspended spider skeletons collided with the ground! It hit with a tremendous crash and its sharp tarsi claws dug into the cement of the runway. While almost standing upright, it tilted and toppled over, pummeling a mobile crane to nothing but a pile of wood, cable and steel. Everybody felt pretty helpless as it was only a matter of time (and a small amount at that) before Jones infiltrated the base. Armstrong continued analyzing the mass of wires that led from the control panel of the main briefing room. But honestly, and as smart as he was, he still hadn't a clue. Takarada brought up the invasion on the big-screen monitoring system that consisted of six large screens mounted to the wall so they could all watch their demise in high definition. Tommy couldn't take it and screamed he was going to the FU2 to take out as many as he could. Jack shouted, "Absolutely not! You'll need to open the launch bay to get out, and you'll be blown out of the sky as soon as you exit. No, this is not the answer." Tommy was used to rebelling against the likes of Sir Jonathon, but figured he was right. He looked around the room and knew things were bad when he noticed Takarada tapping his index finger at an uncanny rate on the surface of the control panel. The room grew silent except for the sounds of war emitting from the viewing screens.

A brigade of F-16's each took turns launching missiles as they descended upon the massive mountainside gate. In a circular fashion, one would fire then rocket up, and the one behind it would do the same, almost like a deadly Ferris wheel. The blast-doors were built to withstand a nuclear explosion, but the constant barrage of heavy-duty rounds were taking its toll. Jones knew all too well what he was doing. The screens flickered with each hit, and finally they managed to blow a gargantuan-sized hole into the multiple layers of the four-foot thick metal and cement barrier. An invitation outlined in red-hot molten steel now awaited them. It was easily big enough for Jones's FU2 to fit through, and he instructed an escort of two F-16s to lead the way. Both jets zipped towards the opening, but just as they were about to enter, they exploded upon colliding with the putrid green force-field that was blocking their path. Jones screamed, "Pull up! Pull up!" and his FU2 narrowly escaped the same fate.

The briefing room cheered, and many knew what had just happened. Takarada looked over to Michael and Liberty, but was stunned to see they weren't holding hands, but also had their arms in the air as they cheered. Takarada turned from them and put his attention back on the viewing screen.

It was amazing as an assortment of brilliant colors burst in midair all around the jets and Jones's stolen FUJI fighters.

Reminiscent of the battle on their home planet, a multitude of aliens paired up looking like flying twin crosses while pelting an exuberant array of beautiful explosive orbs. It was the Noahmarians! A wide variety of exotic green and pink rays emitted from the mass of alien-occupied floating force fields, taking down the F-16s in single blasts. The Falcons returned fire, but their missiles were powerless against the Noahmarians, and soon they had reduced the fleet to only one jet and Jones's FU2. The floating orbs surrounded the last jet like an angry swarm of demonic bubbles, and all at once a thousand beams of light ascended on the final jet. Again, everybody cheered from the command center, and before the smoke could clear, both Jones and his FU2 had high-tailed it away.

Both Nathan and Tommy looked over to Michael and said they were wondering where he and Libs had gone after making their escape from the Liverpool cells. Even though they kind of knew. Nathan then smugly added, "I thought inhabitants from your planet weren't allowed to destroy." And Liberty simply replied,

"Well, we're not on our planet, now, are we?" Tommy curled his lip and smiled, kind of like Elvis, and though technically the response didn't make sense, he still thought it sounded cool.

As the cheers subsided, Armstrong shouted, "Eureka!" as he had discovered the rotted wires within the now decimated wall. Even though it was a bit too late, Jack nodded and still ordered that all exit points be sealed and fast.

"Michael, Liberty, get your people in here, NOW! If I'm right, we don't have much time." Armstrong pulled and reattached the fragile, frayed copper strands and gave Takarada a thumbs up. Takarada looked at the twins, they both nodded, all were in. He took a deep breath then hit the switch one more time.

BOOSH! KA-CHOOM!! BOOSH!

The summit erupted like a hundred volcanoes, and the explosives strategically buried the Cedar Mountain Range in a thousand tons of rock and earth. They were sealed in. Nobody was getting out, and there was only one thing on Earth that could get in.

Chapter 22

Time

There was no time for thought, only action, and Jack asked Tommy, Nathan and the gang to help corral everybody, including the Noahmarian refugees, to the bank of the launch bay's runway. He knew what they needed to do, but didn't know if they had five minutes, five hours or five days in which to do it. He pulled out his watch and prayed for the third option. Takarada knew too, but was more concerned about "what" he had to do as opposed to the time he had to do it in. He had been contemplating an idea he had on the chopper when discovering the Annihilator could move close to the speed of light. It wasn't much of an idea either, but it was a place to start. Takarada was eager to help. He knew there was nobody else on the planet that was as capable as him, Jack and the band. It drove him, but he was having a hard time focusing due to the sudden death of Chen Wang. Not because they were BFFs or anything, because in actuality (before all of this Annihilator nonsense) they hadn't talked in years. It was more about the surreal imagery that was now imprinted on his brain. There was a cruel contrast between the almost giddy Dr. Wang who believed he may have found something within the samples and the other Wang, the dead one.

It was hard to shake, and every time Takarada thought about it, the more his resolve died a little. But Kyoshi did know one thing. If Wang believed those skin samples could have somehow helped, then by God, Takarada would find the answer. His death would not be in vain.

Needing to be in the midst of the action, Takarada asked Armstrong and a few able-bodied people to please help him in setting up a makeshift lab alongside the runway. This way he could analyze the skin samples and search for an answer all while overseeing the necessary modifications to the Duke. Jack joined Takarada, and he conveyed his plans to Sir Jonathon in real time. There would be no opportunity to put it onto paper, to work out the finer details or anything like that, there was only time for one thing, results. A few hundred of Noble's people and about a thousand Noahmarians (who all looked like Michael and Liberty) crammed into the square of Runway Boulevard and awaited their orders. Takarada pointed at various areas of the bay while relaying to Jack what needed to be done. Jack held a bullhorn to his mouth, and his amplified voice designated men, women, children and Noahmarians to where Takarada believed they would be of the most use. There were two main points from which they needed to work in order to get the Duke back into action. Tommy was asked to manage one and Ramsay the other. But before everybody went off in all directions, Takarada brought his friends in close as he had an enormous favor to ask.

"We don't know how much time we have, but it is probably not enough, so this will be straight to the pointless. In this short duration, we will not be able to change the operating system of the Duke, so I am asking you to once again put your lives on the line. This plan will not work without you, as the robot will not work without you."

It was obvious where this was going. Every member of Vinyl Crush shuddered, then moaned, then scowled as they looked at the depressing sight of the downed bot off in the short distance. Jack almost lost it at the groaning and was on the verge of calling them a bunch of pansies, but didn't because he wouldn't want to get into that thing either. Takarada went on to say that he and Tommy-san had changed most of the controls to human, so no more weird hieroglyphics or buttons needing to be pressed in a series of four. That, however, was not the main concern, and Takarada added, "The sleep-state has also been removed, and the mech is now completely manual." There was a mutual sigh of relief, and at that moment Takarada knew they would not let him, nor the world, down. But then he trailed off and kind of mumbled that it would still need a total of five pilots to operate it. In other words, them. Nathan raised his index finger, took a breath to speak and before he could say exactly what Takarada knew he was going to say, the good doctor cut him off. "Yes, Nathan, that means everybody." Nathan didn't like that, Takarada also knew that it'd be a cold day in hell when Nathan allowed his pregnant wife to be put in harm's way to that degree. Takarada of course agreed. So, after a long and quite dramatic pause, Takarada added ... "Again, I need everybody. Everybody that is, but Mrs. Fox. I shall be taking her place in the Duke." It made sense, and all present agreed. Even though both her and Nathan had discussed this, Olivia, for a brief second, felt a need to retaliate. But she too knew it was the right decision.

Dr. Takarada believed he knew the answer, as it seemed it was decided among their discussion, but still felt he needed a solid confirmation. So again he asked, "Can I count on you?" Tommy stretched his arm forward, placed his hand out palm down and sighed, "I guess today's just as good a day as any to die. What do you say, guys, one last time?" No one hesitated, and Michael's hand was soon on top of Tommy's, followed by Liberty, Nathan, Olivia, Takarada and even Sir Jonathon's.

"Right!" Jack barked, and if you looked close enough, you could see a little teardrop in his eye. He repeated Tommy's sentiment, "One last time."

It was instantaneous, and the underground facility erupted into a fast-paced burst of endeavor. People and aliens alike scattered to their designated points within the underground factories, all eager to do their share. It played like an old black-and-white World War II newsreel touting determination as the facilities ignited in industry. Like beasts awakening from a long hibernation, the machinery came back to life from all areas of the bay. Lit up in an overcast of brilliant colors, the Noahmarians used their telekinetic abilities to move enormous objects in conjunction with the mobile cranes. Michael and Liberty guided orbs carrying steel, wire and even Noahmarians themselves from one end of the bay to the other. They moved with a fine precision, the same precision that also made the alien twins such great musicians.

However, something wasn't sitting right with Michael. Something was wrong, something was missing. He stopped, and merely being an extension of himself, Liberty rolled her eyes (something she had learned from Olivia) as she knew what Michael was doing. He reached into his pocket and pulled out a very special crystal he always carried with him. It was small, and Tommy always thought it looked like a miniature Everlasting Gobstopper, but it was far more valuable. This little crystal lit up in various colors, while at the same time Kashmir by Led Zeppelin blared throughout the entire launch bay. Tommy, illuminated in a shower of sparks from beneath the brim of the cowbot's large hat, lifted his facemask and screamed a frantic, "Freakin' Hell yes!" He smiled and felt a surge of hope, because in case you forgot, that's what music did for Tommy. It was the organic thorium that fueled his very veins. From thirty meters in the air, he gave a quick thumbs up to Michael (who probably couldn't even see him), flipped his welding helmet shut and went back to work.

It was a bit hard for Takarada to concentrate beneath the racket, but in a sense it was kind of comforting too. Jack and Noble made the rounds, visiting each small group and explaining their individual tasks. Some didn't understand their part, and Jack said they didn't need to. The big picture would explain it all. As he and Noble walked, Jack kept pulling out his pocket watch over and over checking the time. It wasn't about the hour displayed upon its hands, as the time of day or night had become irrelevant. It was about how much time had already passed. After the third or fourth time Noble became irritated and, breaking its little chain in the process, snatched the watch from Jack's hand. He looked at Jack and said, "This is the true amount of time we are promised," and crushed the watch within his mighty mitt. Jack remembered telling Olivia something similar, and though appreciative of the reminder, was a little pissed that Noble destroyed his favorite watch. "That was a gift from my deceased father." Noble sighed, feeling bad for destroying a family heirloom, and though his point was made he was now sorry and simply replied with a heartfelt, "Really?" And Jack said,

"No, I got it at ASDA in Liverpool for about twelve ruddy pounds." Noble didn't think it was funny but would never reveal he was glad it wasn't from Jack's father and came from the UK's equivalent to Walmart.

Time passed faster than usual, and Takarada and his new bestie, Armstrong, weren't any closer to finding an answer to understanding what made the Annihilator tick. It wasn't a living organism so to speak, but more like a mass of one-celled prokaryote mutations: billions, if not trillions, of simple bacteria forms held together by streams of fungi. He had never seen anything like it. Of course, this was a small sample, but if this were truly the case, this creature did not have the capability to bleed, because it had no blood. He wondered if Wang had figured out a way to attack the cells. This was far from the idea Takarada had earlier. Dr. T. was only thinking along the lines of merely slowing the beast down so it could no longer perform its disappearing act. However, he couldn't help but think that Wang found something more within the skin samples.

Armstrong was getting frustrated; he wiped his forehead and pulled his sweaty brow up from the duo ocular lenses of his old-school microscope. It was hot as hell, as closing the exit points cut off all ventilation. They still had plenty of oxygen due to the sheer size of the launch bays, but they also had no moving air or circulation either. Regardless, Armstrong at his wits end, chose to bitch about the twenty-some-year-old antique instruments they were stuck working with instead. "We must not give up, Professor," Takarada insisted, even though he was feeling it too. "The world is counting on us." Armstrong nodded, wiped his tired eyes and returned them to the viewing lens of his archaic microscope.

Even though he was a good cheerleader, Takarada was feeling the stress too, and the loud music, chatter and ear-damaging thunder of the factory wasn't helping. He was so tired, and everything around him started affecting his concentration. He tried to ignore it, but when Kashmir ended and Michael's crystal started blasting, "Nothing's Gonna' Stop Us Now" by Starship, Takarada lost it. It was rare for Dr. T. to lose his cool in any fashion, but you gotta' admit, there was a lot at stake. Besides, he absolutely hated Grace Slick, not to mention his head was pounding, overloaded with an influx of information but no actual answers. He picked up Jack's bullhorn that was still conveniently on the table in their makeshift lab and screamed into it, "Michael-san! Please silence the music or my head is going to explode!" All sounds stopped immediately. Dr. T. plopped down onto his stool and groaned. It was funny, too, that in the midst of all that was on the line, what now concerned him the most was that he lost his patience and hollered at Michael. As we all often do, Takarada replayed the words in his mind so he could somehow justify the guilt he felt. However, after the fourth or fifth time, the sentence kept growing shorter, finally stopping at and repeating, "My head is going to explode." Takarada sprang up from his stool, and forgetting all about the stupid guilt he was feeling screamed, "I got it!"

Armstrong, startled by Dr. Takarada's revelation, jumped back and struck a defensive Kung Fu pose. Realizing he looked like Daniel LaRusso, Armstrong lowered his arms, regained his composure and asked if Takarada would kindly fill him in. Takarada asked Armstrong to go back to his microscope and view the Annihilator skin samples he was scrutinizing earlier. He did and stated nothing was different. Takarada then asked Armstrong to magnify the image one hundred more times. He did, changing the small samples of dead skin to that of a whole new world, filled with a series of brown and green peaks and valleys. "Still nothing," Armstrong sighed.

"Exactly!" Takarada said. "It is not what is there, it is what IS NOT there," he explained. Now, Armstrong was pretty smart him-damn-self, but he had no idea what Dr. Takarada meant. Takarada removed the glass slide containing the sample from the scope and set it down on the table. Armstrong was still confused. Takarada grabbed a second slide, bent down and scraped it across the not-so-clean street of the launch bay from where their makeshift lab resided. He rubbed the two slides together with the contents of each sandwiched in-between, then

returned the original to the mechanical stage of the microscope. "Look now," he instructed, and Armstrong did, still seeing nothing. "Now," Takarada stated, "Magnify one thousand times." He did and gasped upon the contents of the slide. Takarada knew he would see it, there was no way to miss it. It only took one beat of his heart, and Armstrong understood, seeing what the doctor had done by adding some of our "Earth" the alien cells. He whispered a very low "whoa" upon the sight, affirming he was no idiot with just one word.

"Bacteriophage."

"YES!" Takarada echoed, "Bacteriophage!"

Dr. Takarada was chomping at the bit and again picked up Jack's bullhorn to summon all available personnel to their area. Armstrong congratulated Takarada, and though he didn't know the exact plan, he knew enough about science to get the general gist of the idea. As everybody gathered, Jack felt the need to remind Takarada of how busy they were, and that his little tea party better bloody well be worth it. Takarada, beaming with confidence, stated, "I assure you, Sir Jonathon, you will want to hear this." Takarada also knew most wouldn't understand his discovery, so he intentionally stalled until Ramsay, Olivia and Nathan could get there, because they would. Well, two outa' three ain't bad. Upon their arrival, Takarada opened the microscope up for viewing, and like a long-winded college professor discussing English Lit revealed his plan.

"Outnumbering the vast quantity of stars in the sky, there is a creature that inhabits our world, one you may not know even exists. It is estimated there are more than ten to the thirty-first power of them in existence right now on the planet." Olivia, Armstrong and even the twins gasped, but Takarada was losing the rest, so he dumbed it down a little bit. "That's ten million trillion ..." He paused, then added the final trillion for effect. "That's ten million trillion trillion of these tiny micro-beings, more than all other organisms on Earth, including bacteria, combined. And they are called ... bacteriophage!" As anticipated, he got nothing, except from the nerds in the herd. He sighed and dumbed it down even further.

"Okay, bacteriophages are among the most common and diverse entities in the biosphere. Bacteriophages are ubiquitous viruses, found wherever bacteria exist. And bacteria exist everywhere. Both Armstrong and I have discovered something we believe Dr. Wang already knew. According to the skin samples, it seems Annihilator is primarily made of bacteria and fungus." And of course, you cannot ever mention the word "fungus" in the presence of Tommy or Nathan, and now even Michael, without getting the infamous and old, "there must be a fungus among-us" line. Takarada never actually used the word "morons," because it was obvious he didn't have to, and he cleared his throat and continued.

If the Velatians did indeed create this monster, they did it by somehow stimulating both the bacteria and ...," he glared at the boys, "fungus by infusing them to life." Jack nodded. He was catching on, so was Noble. "As human beings," Takarada continued, "we are immune to bacteriophages, but viruses containing bacteria within our bodies are not. Nothing on this entire planet that has bacteria is. I believe that since Annihilator is primarily fused with bacteria" (he didn't even bother with the word fungus anymore), "this is how we can stop the beast." They erupted in cheers and applause. Really, all Takarada had needed to say was, "Blah, blah, blah, this is how we can stop the beast." That would have been more than sufficient.

Tommy, a little skeptical, asked Takarada two questions. "So, what will this do, and how do we do it?" Takarada took a deep breath and answered his first query because he knew the answer.

"Once a phage invades, they inject genetic material into bacterial cells, which then hijacks the host's cellular machinery to replicate the phage's genetic material and produce new phages." Tommy was sorry he asked, and Takarada, not having the time to explain, opted for drawing a quick (and not very good) picture instead.

"Man, that thing's creepy! It looks like a tall spider!" Nathan yelled.

Takarada flipped his sketch around and grinned, "I know, isn't it glorious?" And though this was a bit unsettling, they ignored Takarada's brief display of madness. He grabbed his trusty number two pencil and proceeded to show how a bacteriophage works, but in a kid's coloring book fashion.

"The tailed phages have three major components: a capsid, or head, where the genome is packed" (nobody even bothered to ask), "a tail, or sheath, that serves as a pipe during infection to secure transfer of genome into the host cell" (again, nobody even bothered to ask). He groaned, then drew a line down to the adhesive spikes and six tail fibers that gave it the appearance of a mutated arachnid and circled them. "This is how the phage locks onto the outer membrane of a cell. It then pumps its DNA into it causing new phages to manifest until it literally cannot hold any more." He stopped and scribbled over his sketch. "Thus, resulting in a million (or so) new bacteriophages bursting out and destroying the cell."

Both Nathan and Michael yelled, "Cool!" at the same time, and Takarada nodded, grinning in that same unnerving fashion.

Tommy then asked his second question. "Okay, that's great. So, how do we get the Annihilator to eat its broccoli?" And that's where Takarada didn't have an answer. But believe it or not, Nathan did.

"A bullet." Takarada was intrigued and asked Nathan to please continue. "We fashion a special bullet the size of a Buick and load it into one of the Duke's revolvers." Takarada liked the idea but stated it would be hard to penetrate the armor of the Annihilator. Nathan added that it must not be completely indestructible if Wang was able to get skin samples, but to be on the safe side, they could fire it into the eye or mouth of the beast. Takarada was indeed impressed with Nathan and agreed to the idea.

Tommy made one final observation and responded, "But what do we do with a million-trillion bacteriophages after they burst out of the Annihilator?" This time Olivia answered,

"They cannot survive out of their host. They'll simply die."

"Bloody hell, Kyoshi!" Jack triumphantly bellowed, "This is brilliant! Get us what we need and let's make a few of those virus-laced bullets if at all possible!"

Takarada crimped his lips together and nodded once in elated determination. It was indeed a longshot, but he was almost ecstatic to once again be filled with so much hope. It had truly been a while, and he felt his love of space and all of its mysteries coming back. For a brief second he thought about his father, which was odd considering he hadn't done so in quite some time. He could actually feel Hiroshi's presence. His eyes moistened, feeling as though his father himself was plucking his past fears and failures from his head and turning them to faith and hope. This was indeed a turning point in the life of Kyoshi Takarada. He also now understood that no matter what happened, and no matter the outcome, he would give all things his absolute best. His father would be proud, but then again, he had always been. Kyoshi never really understood what Tommy meant when he'd talk about the committee in his head, those self-destructive voices that would make you second guess yourself, doubt your own abilities and crap like that. But now he did understand and knew what he needed to do: he needed to fire that damn committee in his head. And that's exactly what he did, he fired those bastards.

Chapter 23

The Shaft

It was nothing shy of an absolute miracle, what had been accomplished in such a short amount of time. But then again, when you have that many determined people the likes of Kyoshi Takarada, and aliens lending an almost "magical" hand to the task, it's truly understandable. Fortunately, there was even a small amount of organic thorium left within the confines of the base's deep, dry cask vaults. Takarada and Armstrong both sighed at the amount of plutonium that still occupied the metal and concrete chambers. From the thick-plated glass shield, the stacks of silver ingots looked harmless, like mere bricks of gold waiting to be cashed in. But they weren't, as even taking a breath in their presence would cause instant lung-cancer and all sorts of other nasty things. Takarada held the green marble-sized ball of organic thorium in his palm and marveled at its power as Armstrong stared in awe. It was all they needed.

Tommy (sounding a little like Jack) instructed both doctors that this wasn't a field trip and that they needed to return to the launch bays. The plutonium vaults were even further down than the underground factories of Launch Bays One and Two, and for obvious reasons. They were completely surrounded by security systems that would close off all access and flood the area in cement should anything go awry. Chances are, Tommy thought, the cement had more than likely hardened within the pipes that held it, but he didn't want to test this theory. "Let's go!" he ordered, this time sounding exactly like Jack, and he herded the two men into the elevator.

The lift closed, and as they ascended, it was as though a bout of turbulence had interrupted their flight. Tommy guessed that they were fifty to sixty meters deeper than the runway of the underground factories. Takarada acknowledged his guess with a nod just as the elevator came to an abrupt stop. The lights flickered within, then shut off completely, only to be illuminated by the haunting green glow of the organic thorium within Takarada's turned-up palm. "Shit," Tommy whispered, and he panicked, pressing each and every button along the wall of the lift. The elevator jerked and again began to move, and he let out an elongated sigh of relief. Takarada then made a quick observation. "Tommy-san, I believe we are going back down."

"Shit!" Tommy again stated, but now at a level that was quite a bit louder than a mere whisper. He went back to doing a tap dance over the buttons, and the elevator stopped, but not because of anything Tommy had done. The turbulence turned to an all-out, constant tremor, feeling almost as though the earth was quaking in a trembling fury from the surface. It was. It didn't really need much of an explanation either, because all three men knew exactly what was happening. The great Annihilator had arrived.

Takarada believed the Velatians would offer everyone within the deep factories of the base the opportunity to surrender. He knew that they'd want to get their four-fingered, creepy, bug-like hands on the contents held within. The several hundred tons of steel, the vehicles, the remaining organic thorium, the Duke and all of that plutonium. There was no doubt they would take advantage of every single one of these resources for their own purpose and existence. However, it didn't take a genius to figure out that no matter what they said or what they promised, they would sooner or later kill each and every remaining human and Noahmarian. Dr. Takarada was sure this would buy them a little time as the aliens awaited Earth's capitulation.

Tommy took the butt of his blaster and pounded it against the thin outline of a hatch that resided on the ceiling of the lift.

After hitting it relentlessly a few times, it broke free and fell to the floor in a shower of cement, dirt and rubble. He pulled himself up on top of the elevator, stood and looked up. The sixty-some-meter shaft seemed to go on forever and climbed endlessly turning into nothing but black in just a few short feet. It seemed the E.I.O. still had safety measures in place, and a long, thin metal ladder ascended along the side of the heavily damaged, upward-climbing tunnel. Tommy knew he'd need to scale that damn thing if they were to survive. He pulled on the ladder, and as he did the earth once again shook, and debris hit his head. He was hoping he could climb up himself and send the cavalry back to rescue the doc and Armstrong. He gathered the launch bays could handle the strain, but the sheer weight alone of that infernal Annihilator was enough to bury the shaft with each footstep it took. It shook again and he knew that it was now or never, for all of them.

The sweaty hand of a long arm shot down from above, and Tommy yelled for either of the men to grab hold. They both knew what they needed to do, and neither liked it. Takarada went all noble, ordering Tommy to take the organic thorium and go up without them as Armstrong latched onto Tommy's hand. Tommy pulled up the professor and said, "Fat chance Dr. T.," as he again lowered his hand. Takarada growled but grabbed on, and Tommy pulled him up too. They wondered if the metal ladder running all the way up the shaft still did just that. Tommy decided it was safest for both Takarada and Armstrong if he took up the rear. Takarada placed the organic thorium into his pocket and volunteered to go first. He started climbing and boldly proclaimed that if he could walk up the stairs to the top of the Tokyo Skytree, this would be a piece of pie. Tommy didn't bother to mention that was almost twelve years ago and just told Dr. T. to talk less and climb more.

Jack reached for his watch that was no longer there while stating that Takarada and Tommy had been gone much too long. He, like Takarada, knew the Salt Lake City base like the back of his hand, and it was a twenty-minute trip tops to the vaults and back. They should have been back by now. He grabbed Nathan, and as they made their way to the elevators, the launch bay again began to tremble. Jack shook his fist in the air and cursed the Velatians. The Annihilator was taking pot shots at the slopes of the Cedar Mountain range with short laser bursts from its eyes. It wasn't attacking, not yet at least, as Takarada was right. The Velatians indeed wanted the treasures held within the confines of the base. It was obviously a show of strength, and every time it fired, the bay shook causing pieces of the high ceiling to fall like heavy rain upon the subterranean city. "Bleeding wankers!" Jack shouted as he and Nathan covered their heads and dodged debris as they approached the lifts.

Nathan pushed the "down" arrow between the two special elevators that descended to the absolute deepest bowels of the base. One opened right away, but unfortunately it was empty. It had never even left and probably hadn't been used in years. Jack and Nathan eyed the second lift. They knew. Jack spit into the palms of his hands and rubbed them together. "C'mon, Mr. Fox," he muttered, "let's see what we're up against." Jack grabbed one end, Nathan the other, and they pulled the doors of the lift apart. It opened fairly easy, and the two men stared down into the deep darkness. The top half was in shambles, and much of the emergency ladder that ran the length of the shaft was simply gone. Jack, however, could see a faint glimmer of green from way down below and exhaled in relief. He knew what it was, and he yelled down, exaggerating his already strong Liverpudlian accent. "I say old chaps, seems you're in quite the sticky wicket. Could you use a hand?" Nathan smiled, as it was rare when Sir Jonathon broke the ranks of his stoic character. But then again, a lot of things about Jack seemed different nowadays, but in a good way. Nathan thought about Sir Jonathon over the years and remembered when he had despised Jack. Now for the life of him, he couldn't imagine why.

Jack looked around. He saw a firehose encased in a square, red cabinet that was adhered to the wall. It read, "Break Glass In Case Of Emergency," and he did just that with the heal of his boot. He reached through the remaining shards and unraveled the hose until it was completely out. It was maybe a hundred feet, not nearly long enough, but it was all they had. "This'll have to bloody do," he sighed. Jack yanked on the hose, pulling it out of its housing, and proceeded to wrap the nozzle end around Nathan's waist. Nathan didn't even need to ask, it seemed he was going on a little adventure. Nothing like being "voluntold" for something as dangerous as this, and he then remembered why he used to hate Jack.

Tommy followed close behind Takarada and Armstrong as they crept like molasses up the long ladder one freakin' rung at a time. He didn't care though, as it had become unstable due to the explosions. It wouldn't take much for it to break free from the already damaged wall of the shaft. He heard Jack shouting but couldn't understand what he was saying. However, the light from above was all he needed to see. Tommy looked over his shoulder and spied the three long cables that dangled from the center of the shaft. He then looked down and couldn't see the bottom anymore. Though moving slow, they had still managed to move up the ladder almost thirty meters, or about halfway. Not an astronomical amount, but definitely enough to kill a person should they decide to take the plunge.

With the elevators being at the foot of Runway Boulevard, Jack wrapped the hose once around one of the cute, but redundant street signs and used it for leverage. Nathan went down the shaft feet-first with the hose tied just above his butt, while keeping his belly to the wall for balance. From the back, he looked like a climber scaling the steep slope of a mountain with both his arms and legs spread out wide. The deeper he went, the darker it became, and he fumbled around for any trace left of the ladder. So far, there wasn't any.

Even with the dust and debris still permeating the shaft, Nathan thought that as long as there were no more explosions, this should be (as Takarada would say) a piece of pie. But of course ...

BWOOSH!

Jack lost his footing but still managed to keep a tight grip on the hose suspending Nathan, and he bounced back and forth against the walls of the shaft. Jack pulled and tightened the wrap around the street sign, and though he dropped about ten feet, Nathan was fine, maybe a little bruised, but all in all fine. Below they weren't so lucky, and Tommy's decision to take up the rear of the ladder was validated when Armstrong fell backwards. Tommy locked his foot under a rung, held on tight with his super-robotic left hand and, looking like King Kong grasping the side of the Empire State Building, caught Armstrong at the cuff of his pants. He slammed into the wall, but Tommy held firm. Takarada watched from above. He was terrified but descended down the ladder. Tommy told him to stay put, but Takarada knew this was a two-man job, and frightened or not, he would rise to the occasion. He scaled down the side of the ladder easing past Tommy and held out his free arm to wrap it around Armtrong's waist. Tommy then did something he wasn't good at, he let go. Kyoshi held on using gravity to help maneuver Armstrong back into an upright position, and he clutched the rung just below Takarada's feet. "Holy crap!" Armstrong shouted, and he and Takarada laughed in that "I think we just dodged a bullet" kind of way. In all actuality, they had.

Nathan could see them clearly now and watched the whole thing by the green glow of the organic thorium housed in Takarada's front pocket. Jack lowered him a little further, and Nathan finally reached the top of the broken ladder. He locked himself in and untied the hose from his waist. Tommy was beyond happy to see him and gave Nathan one of those nods of approval that seemed to say it all. "Okay," Nathan stated, and it echoed within the long shaft. "Remember the old Batman show?" Armstrong smiled, and Takarada also grinned, but it was one of "those" kind of grins, and in a gravelly-induced tone, he acknowledged he knew the show with one word.

"Catwoman."

"Right, Dr. T., Julie Newmar … Catwoman," Nathan responded. "Well, they used to do a thing, and we're going to do it too. We're gonna' scale up this hose like it was the side of the tallest building in Gotham. Tommy, you go first, followed by Dr. T., then Armstrong, then me. When you get to the top Tommy, help Jack pull." Tommy and Takarada were stunned, and Armstrong hadn't known Nathan long enough to understand just how monumental this was, and the Lizard King summed up the moment with a loud, "MOVE!"

The Annihilator continued its assault on the mountains above, and the men pressed on and up as the shaft gave way a little bit more with each step they took. The street sign which Jack had wrapped the hose around was bending and on the verge of being uprooted from the asphalt of Runway Boulevard. Tommy pulled himself up from the lift's parted doors, took his place behind Jack and they pulled. The base rocked, but soon all men and the organic thorium were accounted for, and just in the nick of time. The final explosion literally sealed the shaft's fate in a cloud of black and white smoke erupting from the open elevator doors. Jack yelled, "Take cover!" and all five men dropped to the ground, covering the backs of their heads with tight interlaced fingers.

Tommy turned over, and when he saw a bright light approaching, he thought he was dead. He sat up, as did everybody else, and the gray debris that covered their bodies slid to the wayside. If he was indeed dead, then they were all on that one-way escalator to Val Halla as everyone was seeing it. The explosions ceased, and as the dust settled, the mysterious glowing ball silently and peacefully approached. Then in the next second, all was revealed. It was Michael and Liberty floating up the street in one of their pink, floating orbs. The force field dissipated only to be reconcentrated with everybody inside. As they glided effortlessly through the downpour of the crumbling structure, the twins stated that Ramsay had sent them to make sure they were all okay. Of course, all the men could ponder was, "Where were you five minutes ago?" knowing all too well how easily they could have just sent one of those damn orbs down the shaft to retrieve Takarada, Armstrong and Tommy. They, however, decided not to say anything and were happy just to be out of that stupid shaft and into some real danger. Tommy cracked himself up when he thought about their "out of the frying pan and into the fire" scenario. But one thing was for sure, there was no denying that worn out, tired look of triumph instilled upon Takarada's face. Tommy realized that what Dr. T. had done to help save Armstrong's life, and what it probably did for the good doctor himself, made it all worth the trouble. Although a floating orb would have been nice.

Chapter 24

Showtime

In all honesty, Jack was quite surprised in regard to the amount of time they had been gifted. Not from the Velatians of course, just in general. As he and everybody else congregated in the briefing room, Jack didn't really order, but more so stated in a polite way that it was time. Takarada, Tommy, Nathan and the twins descended down the stairs and walked that long line to enter the Duke for one final ride. As they left, Jones came through the static-induced screens mounted on the briefing room wall and laid down the law.

"It appears you have made your choice, and if you will not surrender peacefully, we are prepared to conquer the Earth. You have been given ample warning, and you are now out of time. If you wish to survive, you must ..."

CRASH!

A heavy porcelain coffee mug struck and shattered the main screen of the briefing room, in turn upsetting the vertical hold as well as the tint of the other monitors. Jones continued to spew his "superior species" bullshit having no idea the image of his face was not only scrolling up and down but was now blue and green.

"Bunch of bloody tossers!" Jack screamed. "Right, we don't need any ruddy orders or instructions from the likes of them. They've decided if they're not going to get what they want, they're going to use that wretched creature to annihilate this entire sector. Just like a bunch of bleedin' spoiled brat rock stars. They have no idea how much plutonium is buried here!"

They fled the briefing quarters, and Jack gathered the masses, ordering everyone to the runway. He picked up his bullhorn that was still residing on Takarada's table, and even though he wanted to make a speech, he didn't. "Right!" he hollered into the bullhorn almost louder than the device itself. "Noahmarians, create as many escape orbs as you can, filling them with as many people as you can. Pilots get to your choppers, I'll fit as many as I can onto the tread crawler and everyone head down the tunnel of Launch Bay One. Ramsay, you go first. Take the FU2, and when you reach the end of the runway unload your entire payload and blast us a new exit point from the inside of the mountain. We're leaving, and I mean right now! We only have one chance, and if the Duke can lure the Annihilator out to sea, we may have a bloody shot."

Robert Jones ordered the Velatian-commandeered FU2s and remaining jets to clear the vicinity, and before long they were out of sight. Annihilator took its place among the wreckage of the Cedar Mountains and burning patches of brush in order to fire its main weapon. Its body vibrated, and the sound of charging electricity echoed through the air as a shimmering red aura outlined the entire beast. It screamed, but before it could exhale its deadly pulse of power, the ground from where it stood crumbled. Annihilator broke through the surface of the Earth, sinking into the barren launch bay as though it were drowning in an enormous pit of angry quicksand. The ground hissed, then exploded in a ferocious geyser of steam, dirt and rock. And from the center of it, the Duke jettisoned straight up powered by two FU2 jet engines adhered to it in the form of a twin-flame-emitting backpack!

SHOOOOOSH!

The Duke spun and descended back towards earth feet first, all eight of them! As the bot touched down, steam burst from its new arachnid legs as they bent like massive shock absorbers to reduce the stress of impact. The sun managed to peak through the turmoil, reflecting off the mighty silver bot. It, and its newly acquired titanium steel limbs, glistened in a show of sheer majesty. Its eight legs stretched, giving the bot an extra ten or so meters of height, and like some kind of monstrous metal centaur, it stood. It was obvious the new additions had to be done fast, and if you looked close enough (especially wherever Tommy worked) you could even see thick rows of duct tape wrapped around some of the questionable welded joints. Oh, it was new alright, but not necessarily improved. Either way it was the Duke 4.0, and it was ready, willing and hopefully able to kick the Annihilator's ass back to wherever the hell it came from.

***

Armstrong filled the co-pilot seat as Ramsay prepared to execute a complete assault on the rock and gravel now sealing the exit of Launch Bay One. The FU2 was packed beyond capacity with people, and Ramsay announced over the craft's sound system, "Fire in the hole!" In other words, "Hold on to your butts!"

BOOOSH! SHOOM! KA-BOOSH!

In a brilliant display of sight and sound the wall of rock crumbled, blasting the large mouth of the buried launch bay and runway back open. The tunnel was flooded with light, and those upon the flat surface of the massive tread crawler jumped off and towards the smoldering exit. Men, women and children, all on foot, poured out of the new launch bay exit like a swift-moving river. From above, an assortment of helicopters, colorful levitating orbs and the FU2 itself followed. Jack jumped down from the crawler, and since it was no longer of any use, he simply left it behind. The Noahmarians, already floating to safety in people-packed globes, created even more forcefields to accommodate the tread crawler travelers. They couldn't stop; they needed to get as far away as possible. If there was such a thing.

A passing orb picked up Jack, and he took the lead, directing the unusual convoy westward. He had a destination in mind, and though he knew the choppers wouldn't be able to make the long journey, he figured he'd deal with that when the time came. But for now, there was only one place that made sense to him, and that was Japan. He wondered if that was even far enough, because if the Annihilator was to fire its primary weapon and all of that plutonium were to go ... Jack shuddered at the thought. He knew the force would be enough to completely knock the Earth off whatever of its axis was even left.

The Annihilator crashed through the high-beamed rafters of Launch Bay One, as the entire Salt Lake City base came down upon it. It landed on the buildings and briefing center, pulverizing them to mere kindling followed by a blanket of descending debris. The wonderful marvel that was the subterranean city filled with the earth of the surrounding Cedar Mountains, and soon the Annihilator was buried beneath it.

Both Tommy and Nathan screamed, "Yes!" as they watched from the Duke's wide-angled viewing screen. But somehow they knew it wouldn't be enough, and of course they were right. Even before the earth and rock had a chance to settle, the massive claw of the space-monster busted clean through it. Tommy pulled back on the jimmy-rigged and duct-taped thruster, and the Duke raised into the air. He wanted to get the hell out of there, but Takarada reminded him that the Annihilator needed to see them in order to follow them. Both Tommy and Nathan hated that plan, but they couldn't risk anymore countless deaths or the chance of it (as Jack would say) going all willy-nilly. Besides, this wasn't the place for round two, that was out at sea where its weapon could only do minimal damage. Takarada did suggest, though, that this may be the perfect time to fire one of those custom bacteriophage bullets into the beast's mouth as it pulls itself out of the ground. Tommy and Nathan hated that plan too, but it made sense.

Dr. Takarada pressed a series of buttons, and two three-foot-long virus-infused bullets loaded into the revolving section of each of the Duke's photon six-shooters. A circular-shaped bullseye appeared on the screen, and a bead of sweat rolled down Dr. Takarada's forehead. They waited, and though the hovering bot was less than stable, Takarada was ready. As anticipated, the Annihilator looked up and upon seeing the cowbot above, screamed its bug-like scream. The bullseye

blinked and beeped, then locked in, and Takarada fired. The deadly projectile blasted from the chamber and proceeded straight into the beast's open mouth.

Nathan yelled, "Direct hit!" and everybody cheered, even Takarada as he wiped his sweaty brow with the back of his hand. The mammoth space kaiju frantically shook its head, and Nathan noted that it looked more pissed off than usual. Takarada definitely agreed. "Okay Tommy-san, now we should get the hell out of here. I do not know how long it will be before the bullet takes effect." The Duke ascended, straightened its eight new appendages, and in accordance with their plan, rocketed towards the most unpopulated place they knew of, the middle of the Pacific. Hopefully there they could end this once and for all.

The FU2 engines mounted on the Duke's back spat twin trails of fire, and they hauled ass towards the ocean. Just like Takarada had predicted, the Annihilator was immediately hot on their trail. But like before, it disappeared, and soon it was directly in front of them. Tommy and Nathan pushed down hard on their twin steering mechanisms, and the Duke shot under the Annihilator, barely evading a catastrophic collision. The mech rattled, and everybody looked around wondering if their old robot friend would even hold. The ride was incredibly turbulent, as controlling each section of the bot's brain manually demanded more of a thought-on-the-spot reaction from the robotonauts. It wasn't like before when the cowbot acted upon their sleeping subconscious mind. But coma-induced sleep state or not, the reason it worked so well in the first place was due to their skills as musicians and anticipating what the others were going to do. Sort of how the drummer and bass player of a super-tight rhythm section can groove so well. Of course it depends on the individual's abilities, but a major part that takes these things to the next level is their musical connection. And that's what they had, at least Tommy, Nathan and the twins did. Tommy controlled the frontal lobe as Nathan manned the motor and sensory cortexes, while Michael and Liberty navigated both the temporal and sensory lobes. Takarada, being a newbie and all, was struggling a bit with the parietal lobe, but considering he designed the bot in the first place, it was coming rather fast. Plus, much of the parietal lobe is crucial for processing spatial awareness and integrating sensory input, so in a sense, it was right up his alley. But when it came to Dr. Takarada, what wasn't up his alley?

Tommy pulled hard left on his steering unit while Nathan pulled right. The Duke did a mid-air about face, and like a guitarist blowing all his cookies in the first set, they fired their most powerful weapon, the ROT beam. But now it was more like the NOT beam as sparks ignited from the control panels, causing the cockpit to go dark in an anticlimactic frenzy of nadda. Nobody could even see an inch in front of their faces, and they just sat there in the pitch black. "Well, that's not good," Nathan said in a rather calm demeanor considering their predicament, and Michael followed it up with a long and depressed,

"Dude."

CHOOOOOM!

In a blinding (and quite unexpected) flash of bright light, the cowbot's massive right-eyed monocle suddenly erupted, blasting a deadly green organic-thorium-fused ray!

KARAAAAM!

And they actually even hit it! They were stunned, as was the beast itself. Takarada wondered if the bacteriophages they had implanted in the bullet were taking effect. Unfortunately, Annihilator, more surprised than hurt, retaliated on the spot with two bursts of energy from its eyes. The beams pegged the bot in one of its brand new spider legs and blew it clean off! "We cannot fight it one-on-one like this!" Takarada yelled. "If we try, it will undoubtedly destroy us!" Michael and Liberty both knew what to do and stated together that they had reached the coast and were now taking the Duke far out to sea.

The cowbot bled from where one of its titanium legs used to be, leaving a trail of organic thorium upon the surface of the sea. It was gone. There was nothing anybody could do, so Tommy sealed the bulkhead that fed the green fuel to that particular appendage, and they carried on. Because sometimes, carrying on is indeed ALL you can do, and while losing a limb is never good, seven out of eight still ain't bad. Takarada waited for the

Annihilator to disappear at the speed of light and again reappear directly in front of them, or worse, appear in some highly populated region. But that, as of yet, still hadn't happened. He was 98.6% sure the bacteriophage virus would work, but that 1.4% of uncertainty was pounding on his brain and had him doubting. Liberty brought the monitors to satellite view and stated that the Annihilator had just disappeared. Takarada sighed while Tommy and Nathan prepared to dodge up this time with the Duke instead of down. They kept moving, travelling as fast as the bot could go, but with a keen eye on the viewing screen. Liberty then stated in a slightly excited, but still listless tone that it had again reappeared. Tommy and Nathan looked forward and screamed they couldn't see it, and she said they couldn't see it because it was still behind them. It was in and out, disappearing and reappearing while flickering like an old TV set, but its ability to hit the speed of light was clearly not working. Takarada's percentage rate shot up to 99 as the virus was indeed having some sort of reaction on the beast. It was definitely working and would've shot to an even hondo had he not been concerned about there being a deficient amount of the virus in its system.

It was obvious to Takarada that Jones and his Velatian goons were somehow able to control the monster. He wasn't quite sure just how, but he didn't really need to know. What Takarada did know was that if their precious little Annihilator was sick, they may keep it out of school until its better, and that simply would not work. One thing was for sure though, it could no longer travel at the speed of light. However, it could still outrun their cowbot bucket of nuts and bolts any day of the week.

BOOM!

The Annihilator, surpassing the speed of sound, rocketed over the Duke, and Takarada knew it was going to hightail it back to the dark side of the moon for some much-needed R & R. "Load the second bacteriophage virus bullet!" he demanded. Nathan did just that as Tommy locked onto the Annihilator like a heat-seeking missile, making it clear he was going to fire more than that, much more. The Duke's arms stretched straight out, and both barrels of its photon six-shooters were leading the way. Each of its seven remaining legs reared back, folding twice at their two joints while Tommy counted down … "Three … Two … One … Fire secondary engines!"

CHOOOOOOM!

Reminiscent of a squid using jet propulsion, the Duke's legs straightened into more of a streamlined position as an additional burst of power erupted from beneath its torso. Takarada loaded the second BVB (obviously he was tired of saying bacteriophage virus bullet) and stared at the bullseye superimposed upon the viewing screen. The ROT beam still needed additional charging to fire, but Tommy made damn sure the cowbot's blasters were ready to go. Michael announced that they were now traveling slightly above Mach 2, and that they would hit the coast of Japan near Kobe in a matter of minutes.

Takarada wrapped his right hand around his firing mechanism and didn't even realize his index finger was tapping faster than they were going. Nathan turned, first glaring at Takarada's finger, then at Takarada himself, and the doctor apologized. "No need to be sorry, Dr. T., just relax. You got this. Use the freakin' force, baby." Takarada would have bowed if he were standing, but he wasn't. So, without taking his eyes off the prize, he acknowledged Nathan with an awkward smile.

"Arigato, Nathan-san."

"Okay Doc, we need to come at it face-to-face if were gonna' shoot that thing into its mouth. I'll fire first, then you let him have it with the STD!" Takarada looked at Tommy's two heads as he had no idea what that meant, and Tommy shouted, "The bullet! That damn SVB, PVC, you know, that bacteria-filled thing!" Takarada understood, and taking Olivia's place within the Duke had a strong impulse to correct Tommy, but he wisely chose not to.

The exhaust trails emitting from the Annihilator made it hard to see through the fast-moving haze, but the computer was locked in. It was obvious the BVB was working, and the Annihilator was slowing down. Takarada didn't think it could even make it to the moon at this point. Michael and Liberty increased the thrust, easing them in for the kill. The Duke jettisoned over the Annihilator, swooped down and from an upside-down, back-facing-the-sea, midair position, descended upon it guns a-blazing! It was like a Fourth of July fireworks finale firing from the Duke's twin blasters! The Annihilator spiraled as the multitude of missiles exploded on and around it. Finally, it did exactly what they needed it to do. It opened its bug-like mouth and screamed, sounding like course steam blowing through a gargantuan twisted pipe. As before, the bullseye blinked and beeped, and Dr. Takarada fired. The bullet erupted from the chamber and disappeared into both the dusk and heavy clouds of smoke surrounding the creature. Nobody could see a damn thing, and they awaited a response from the computer. It was apparent that due to excessive smoke, radiation and such, it was having a difficult time locking in.

Takarada strained his eyes trying to see something. Although the viewing screens offered zero visibility of anything straight ahead, he could, however, see below. It was Osaka Bay, and the early evening lights of Kobe were rising with the full moon. He was sucked in by the bustle of the rush hour traffic, trains and coastal skyscrapers that made up the quaint city. Lost within his head, he imagined Kobe as a smoldering crater, but was pulled out of his thoughts by the one-word response from the computer ... "MISS."

Chapter 25

Big In Japan

As it had done so many times before on Earth, Noahmar and countless other planets, the great Annihilator descended feet first towards its destination with malicious intent. And even though the entire world was on alert, most people simply went about their daily routines. You can't really blame them though, as nobody wants to contemplate the harsh reality of a hurricane until it comes pounding at the front door. But in this case, boarded-up windows and heading to higher ground surely weren't the answers. There was nowhere to run, nowhere to hide and no evacuation route that could take you far enough away.

The giant creature hit harder than usual when it touched down on the edge of Osaka Bay next to the Kobe Port Tower. A popular tourist attraction, the landmark donned shops and restaurants topped off with a split-level observation deck offering spectacular views of the city and all that surrounded it. But what made the tower so unique was its hyperboloid shape and long burnt orange steel staves, intentionally giving it the look of a tsuzumi, a Japanese drum that resembled an hourglass. The behemoth seemed a little groggy, but make no mistake it still had plenty of piss and vinegar flowing through its bloodless body. It bent down and heaved the tower up from its cement foundation. The only things remotely holding it together were the thick pipes designed to give it the look of the drum. But gravity soon got the best of it, and it simply collapsed. The sirens erupted, and terrified people, half out of their minds, ran aimlessly in all directions. It looked down upon the masses and started picking off people one-by-one with short laser bursts emitted from its eyes.

It turned, setting its sights towards the heart of the city. An evening local train full of tired people anxiously scurried along, and the Annihilator cast its glare upon it. It trampled the remains of the tower and waded through the sea of buildings towards the elevated tracks, tearing down anything that blocked its path. It seemed they all led to one place, the Sannomiya Station, a large hub for trains and busses housed within a ten-story department store.

A packed Shinkansen traveling from Tokyo was fast approaching the station at a breakneck speed. This particular one was on a nonstop journey to Okayama and would simply be burning right through the Kobe Station on track three. Little did they know it was to be a one-way trip. The Annihilator raised its knee and brought its foot down through the web of wires onto the winding viaduct that supported a pair of elevated tracks. It exploded in a brilliant blast of electricity, and the bridge crumbled as though it was made of day-old gingerbread. The engineer slammed on the brakes, and the sparks of the metal wheels showered the street below. At 200 MPH, there was no hope of the bullet train even coming remotely close to slowing down, and it slammed unsympathetically into the leg of the great beast.

The engine ignited into a thunderous explosion of screams and steel as the decoupled cars sequentially launched into the air, one after the other. From the opposite direction, another local train that was approaching did manage to stop, and mobs of frantic people were filing out from both sides as well as the windows. The Annihilator screamed, smashed its way through the elevated bridge and yanked it up from the tracks. It became entangled in the cars and as though it were fighting a monstrous snake, lifted the train above its head and slammed it into a nearby building! It flexed its brawny, bug-like arms and bellowed in victory.

ZZZZZZZAPPPP!

Upon the Annihilator's chest a greenish ball of pure energy expanded and exploded with nothing more than a slight hum. In the slow-motion silence, the mighty space monster flipped backwards and collided with the street.

"Holy Crap!" Tommy yelled, "What the hell was that?" Takarada looked over to the twins and Michael simply stated,

"Oh, it's a little something that me, Dr. T. and Libs put together." Takarada didn't have time to go into the details, but simply stated he was able to merge the twin's power with the ROT beam and fire it through the Duke's monocle.

"Damn, Dr. T.," Nathan stated. "Remind me never to get on your bad side." And Takarada trying to be funny, stated that he already was.

The Duke wasted no time, landing in the ruins upon its seven titanium steel legs.

Steam hissed, escaping from all but one of its joints, and without hesitation, the bot charged in for an attack while the Annihilator was still down. The Duke aimed for its head, but the creature quickly rolled over, just missing the sting of one of the cowbot's new razor-sharp tarsi. The bot did, however, manage to pierce it in the back of its shoulder at the base of its wing. The Annihilator, who was undoubtedly not used to pain, screamed, and Nathan yelled, "I know that had to hurt!"

The Annihilator jumped to its feet, and instead of firing any of its assorted lasers or heat beams, opted for a right hook to the cowbot's kisser instead. The head of the Duke nearly sprang up from its shoulder like one of those Rock 'Em Sock 'Em Robots, and everybody in the cockpit violently jerked about. Nathan bitched about the seat belt rash he was sure to get, but had they not been strapped in, he probably wouldn't be alive to complain about it in the first place. The cowboy mech retaliated with a left jab, and the Annihilator tried to block by encasing itself within its wings as it had done before. But it appeared the monster was still a bit on the sluggish side, not responding quite fast enough. The Duke's fist broke through the armor at the chest of the monster, and if it could've bled, it would've. It made that weird crackly, crunching sound, similar to when you stomp (accidentally of course) on a large bug. The bot's hand dripped of a heavy, yellowish ooze as it retracted from the Annihilator's chest. The beast again went down, falling flat on its back. Tommy and the twins grimaced in disgust as Nathan and Takarada grinned in delight. Not missing a beat, the Duke clutched one of the abandoned passenger cars of the devastated local train from both ends. It bent deep at its knees (all of them) and pushed off the ground like an orchard jumping spider. As it landed, the bot's tarsi spread, imprisoning the Annihilator within its seven titanium legs. It held the train car from its middle as it pushed from the top, attempting to literally cram it down the creature's throat! Then in a flash, the Annihilator disappeared. The Duke, left with nothing but the train car, looked about for the monster, even though it was obvious. Tommy addressed Takarada with a puzzled, "Uhm, Doc? I thought we took care of that." Takarada sighed.

"I was worried that this might happen," he said in a very nonchalant fashion, and both Tommy and Nathan in a very "chalant" fashion looked at Takarada with bulging eyes.

"I do not believe the single BVB was enough. Though it seemed to work temporarily, we needed both of the laced rounds very muchly in order to accommodate for the Annihilator's size." Tommy and Nathan nodded, of course they knew. They knew as soon as the freakin' computer stated that wonderful one word, "MISS." But they tried to overlook the obvious, and since the Duke seemed to be holding its own quite well, they just figured the second bacteriophage virus bullet wasn't necessary. It was.

From out of the vast chasm where the speed of light exists, the Annihilator exited. It's double demonic insect wings extended and, body flexed, it reappeared high above the burning city looking as though it were being held captive within the circumference of the massive full moon. It was not happy. Takarada wondered if the creature, being able to perform its infamous disappearing act again, could once more fire its primary weapon. He didn't know if it ever lost the ability. He knew it took an immense amount of power for it to do so, so it simply made sense. But as of late, sense was in short supply, so there was no telling.

The Annihilator blasted twin red heat beams from its eyes, and like a tarantula, the Duke's front legs shot up, rearing the bot back into a defensive pose. The laser pegged the mech on its bottom where its new legs were attached, blowing yet another clean off. Still standing though, the cowboy bot retaliated with its new signature weapon that Nathan had dubbed, "The Kyoshi Twin Special."

CHOOOOOM!

But as a result of losing another leg, the bot was a bit off kilter, and the green-glowing ball surpassed the Annihilator, disappearing over the northern horizon. The kaiju continued to pummel the Duke, switching to its short burst beams. The inside cockpit of the cowbot was flashing, and fire was spitting from the seams of its newly duct taped electrical panels. But nobody was giving up, they'd come much too far to throw in the towel now.

Tommy announced that both of the photon-blasting six-shooters were fully charged, and the Duke drew its mighty silver revolvers from their stainless steel holsters.

FWAP! FWAP! BOOSH!

Two straight piercing lines of bright orange sucker punched the Duke from behind, and as the bot's back erupted, the sheer force pushed it face forward to the ground. The impact was tremendous as dirt, wreckage and thick dust erupted into the air. It was Jones and the Velatians themselves joining the attack from a FUJI FU2. Inside the cockpit of the Duke's cranium, warning lights beeped and buzzed, letting the robotonauts know unconditionally that the Duke was on its last legs, literally. Unlike the mech itself, the pilots were definitely worse for wear, but by some chance still remained unscathed, for the most part. But it looked like that was a temporary state, as the Annihilator advanced, and beams from the FU2 riddled up and down the back of the mech.

Takarada swelled with great pride as the fires within the cockpit of the dying Duke illuminated his drenched forehead. He wiped the heat and sweat from his face with the bottom half of

his untucked shirt and sat back in his chair. He looked at Tommy, Nathan and the twins, and his eyes watered up. He couldn't imagine a better or more honorable death. He just wished they could have stopped the Velatians. Tommy, on the other hand, was more angry than sad and cursed the Velatians for the underhanded tactics they used to rob people of their bodies, lives and dignity. He then cursed human beings for their ignorance to not see through the changes that had been taking place. "People are so stupid," he thought, and how freakin' crazy was it that everybody assumed that the bad guys were the good guys and the good guys were the bad guys. It infuriated him. He then cursed himself, because even he was blind to it all, and it was right under his nose, Jones, the state of the E.I.O., the Goku, everything. His fury grew inside of his heated head, and all he could do was think of Suzy, and he wished she was there with him in these final moments.

Nathan unstrapped his safety belt and stood up. "We're not licked yet! After all we've freakin' been through, it's not going to end this way. No way in hell!" he stated with each word growing louder than the one before it. "THINK!" he shouted, "I've gotta' wife and an unborn baby out there counting on me!" Nathan, like Takarada, started getting emotional. He asked if they knew the Serenity Prayer, and when no one responded, he recited it.

"God, grant me the serenity to accept the things I cannot change, the courage to change the things I can, and the wisdom to know the difference."

"Okay, I've accepted a lot of things over these last ten years, but I'll be damned if I'm going to accept this! I didn't come face to face with the eight eyes of an 'effing twenty-story spider to call it a day now. I DO NOT ACCEPT THIS!" he shouted. Takarada stood up, slammed the base of his clenched fist down upon the console and agreed.

"Yes, Nathan-san! The courage to change the things that I can! I have not overcome these weaknesses to simply give up when the going gets touched!" Michael and Liberty, who had suffered more than anybody, also stood up in defiance of their demise. Tommy rolled his eyes and told Nathan that his "Triple

A" bullshit wasn't going to save anybody this time. Nathan fired back,

"That's where you're wrong, Tommy, because it's not about A.A., it's about life." Nathan pulled his sobriety medallion (the one he never left home without) and flung it hard and fast like a little frisbee at Tommy. Tommy didn't even blink and caught the bronze coin in one move within the palm of his robot hand. Although he'd seen and even held the medallion many times before, he had never really seen or held the medallion before. This time he actually read it, and in the addition to the Serenity Prayer it also said, "To Thine Own Self Be True." He squeezed his eyes shut, tightened his grip on the coin and it seemed the message was slowly infiltrating his thick skull. He looked at Nathan, his best friend, smiled like Han Solo and then shouted, "God, grant me the serenity, the courage and the wisdom to know the difference of how to kick some freakin' Velatian ass!" Nathan nodded. It wasn't quite right, but either way he liked it. But what he really liked was the newly found fire erupting in Tommy's gut.

Takarada got in on the excitement stating he may have something else that could be of great importance and mentioned a small detail he had been contemplating. "I have been thinking," he said in the midst of the sparks and flashes, "There is an area at The Goku that has been off-limits ever since its inception. Truthfully, in my state of mind over the last few years, I did not care enough to give it any real concern. But knowing now what the Annihilator is, and what the Velatians are, I believe if we can somehow get to the Goku, we can stop this, completely." Now Tommy was completely on board.

"Well, Doc, what do we do?" and Takarada responded with,

"Without the bacteriophage virus, we cannot win. There is only one thing we can do. We either get to The Goku or we die tithing."

The burning cockpit vibrated in hope and determination while Tommy eased the thrust forward ever so gently. The Duke's back engines coughed and backfired, but the mech, like themselves, wasn't ready to call it quits quite yet. The busted up and brittle bot lifted into the air sort of like an old man trying to pull himself up from the cushions of a deep comfy chair. But before anyone could cheer, the Annihilator swung around and latched onto one of the Duke's skeletal steel legs preventing the spider-bot from making its escape. Michael and Liberty grabbed hands in a gallant effort at generating more power. Unfortunately, it was of no use, and the cowbot again hit the ground. The Annihilator placed its big beefy foot onto the back of the bot to prevent it from trying to make another run for it. Its red eyes widened, and both it and the Velatian-occupied FU2 open fired on the Duke in a shower of destructive heat rays. It seemed that this was the end.

Chapter 26

Goku And The Rokkos

If you've ever witnessed an evening sky permeated with the shimmering glow of a thousand kamifusen, you truly know what a miraculous sight it is to behold. Also known as Japanese flying lanterns, the ancient art of the illuminated paper balloon, especially in large numbers, is rumored to bring prosperity and good luck. From a distance, a myriad of kamifusen is exactly what it looked like as a countless mass of Noahmarian orbs floated down from the heavens. Like a million stars held within the invisible walls of a traveling galaxy, their numbers only seemed to double as they reflected off the waters of Osaka Bay. Many of the multicolored orbs broke off from the multitude and descended upon the Annihilator like a swarm of angry fireflies. The flying spheres flickered and as the glow of their outer shells pulsed, a deadly ray of white light extracted from each one. The Annihilator let go of the Duke's limp and lifeless body and went into a defensive mode protecting itself from the array of incoming beams. For the moment, it seemed the legends were indeed true, because this was nothing but a mammoth stroke of luck for the Duke and those inside of it.

Following close behind were Ramsay, Olivia and Jack in the FU2. Olivia's dad was also aboard sitting close to his daughter, radiating with pride as she navigated the flight plan of the ship and prepared it for battle. Noble, his daughter, Armstrong, Ann and Bruce, always sticking close to their fearless leader, also chose to ride in the craft. The rest of his clan had the earthly pleasure of taking up the rear in the second fleet of Noahmarian spheres. As was their original plan, they needed to get the Annihilator and the Velatian jets away from the city. Jack knew he couldn't get Jones or the Annihilator back out to sea, so he needed to push the fight inland towards the Rokko Mountains. The best way to do that was with the Duke.

Tommy and Nathan were taking turns trying to kick the back hatch of the cowbot's cockpit open when the twins simply disintegrated it in a nice shade of pink. Nathan pulled himself up and looked out from the back of the bot's head. It was next to impossible to see from the Annihilator's dancing cloud of debris as it ducked and dodged the swarm of pesky Noahmarian orbs. It was thunderous. Nathan slipped back in through the hatch and asked the twins if they could put the recently departed door back. They couldn't.

Jacks large head appeared in multiple places of the cracked surround screen within the cowbot's cockpit, and though he was breaking up he made a brilliant observation. "Bullocks," he groaned. "Seems you are all in a bit of a sticky wicket. Can you by chance get airborne?"

Takarada answered, "I believe we could manage, especially if Michael and Liberty are able to offer some assistance." Jack nodded, then responded,

"That thing hates the Duke, and to destroy it I think the Annihilator would chase that blasted robot to the ends of the earth. Jones on the other hand knows not to follow it out to sea, and if they're controlling that bloody monster, I don't think it'll go either, even if it wants to." Jack paused, "I need you to lead it due north to the Rokko Mountains. If that bloody thing fires its main weapon, it's fairly unpopulated." At that moment Tommy knew that Jack knew that the bullet didn't work. He realized this was more of a suicide mission as opposed to trying to stop the Annihilator. Stopping the Annihilator couldn't be done. It was too strong, too fast and too powerful. It truly was the destroyer of worlds. As they had done before, the Noahmarians were putting up a tremendous resistance, but as soon as that thing used its big macdaddy power pulse, all bets were off.

Jack stated that he could not order anybody to do this, because even though he was in charge, technically he wasn't. But

thank God he was. He stated if anybody wanted to jump ship, he wouldn't blame them. Not that there was anywhere to jump ship to mind you. Nathan pushed Takarada aside and demanded to speak to Olivia. Jack summoned her to the comm, and the first thing she did was let Nathan know he looked like crap. He laughed, a little. His smile then disappeared, and he went all serious. "Get away from here, get away from this thing, its gonna' turn this whole area to nothing but glass." With those words, Olivia realized they weren't coming back, and tears started flowing down her cheeks. Jack stood behind her and, putting his hands upon her shoulders, eased her away from the comm. This was the most serious Jack had ever seen Nathan Fox. The only other time he saw him even remotely close to this level was way back at the beginning when all Nathan cared about was himself. Jack sat back down at the comm, and as Olivia's father comforted his daughter, Nathan made Sir Jonathon promise. "Damn it, Jack, I'm serious, promise me you'll get Olivia, her father and everybody else the hell out of here." Sir Jonathon had no idea how to juggle all of this, but of course he agreed.

As Jack wondered how he was going to make good on his new promise, Takarada cut in emphasizing the importance of getting to Hiroshima and The Goku. Jack started feeling the pressure and began to stress out because in addition to everything that was going on, he couldn't figure out why they now needed to go to the Goku. Dr. Takarada cleared his throat and muttered four words, "To kill the queen." And Jack exploded.

"What do you mean kill the queen? Sounds like a ruddy punk rock song! What does the bloody queen have to do with all of this?" Takarada waited, and though Jack was pretty smart him-damn-self, it still took him a second. Like Kyoshi had done earlier, Jack put two and two together, and it definitely equated to the sum of a queen. He knew Takarada was spot on. "Right," he barked, "We'll just add it to the bloody shopping list." He stopped to think, and though he no longer had his huge walrus mustache, he stroked his chin with his thumb and index finger as though it were still there. He was not keen on separating the troops of what he believed was Earth's only defense against both the Velatians and their monstrous stooge. The last thing he wanted to do was scatter his people (and aliens) willy-nilly all over the planet. But some of the world's most prolific and successful battles demanded this action for even a remote chance of victory. As much as he hated the idea of splitting up, a two-front war was his only option. And though the battle was here, right now in their very midst, another would surely wage when they arrived at the Goku ... to blow it up. Jack laid out his plan, instructed Michael and Liberty to spread the word to their alien brethren and gave the order to go into action.

Jack ordered the rear flank of floating Noahmarian spheres consisting of Noble's clan, the pilots that ditched their choppers and the aliens it took to fly each orb to Hiroshima. That way they'd be out of range when the Annihilator did finally fire its weapon, but also close enough to the Goku should they need assistance. The Annihilator seemed to have forgotten all about its new archenemy, the Duke, as it was quite preoccupied with the front flank of attacking alien orbs. Jack instructed the FU2 to set a course for Hiroshima, but stated they had to take care of a little business first. Olivia was beyond devastated, but she also had a job to do, not because she was ordered to, but because it was necessary. Ramsay asked if she was up to the task, and that part of Nathan that now resided inside of her gave Olivia the strength to do what needed to be done. Though she was quite far away in her thoughts, she wiped her eyes and replied, "Yes, we're locked and loaded." Ramsay put the pedal to the metal so to speak and rocketed upwards with the FU2. Jack's stomach turned upside down. It'd been a while since Sir Jonathon had been in an actual air battle. He held in his lunch and strapped in with a, "Bloody hell."

Jones's escort of twin F-16 Falcons had been ordered to patrol the area and had no idea what was coming. The first jet came into sight, and Ramsay didn't even bother to use the computer targeting system. She placed her thumbs over the red buttons on each side of her U-shaped steering mechanism and waited precisely for the right moment.

BAP! BAP! BAP!

From the front cannons of the FU2, a barrage of bright orange dots stitched across the evening sky, and the first F-16 didn't know what hit it. It erupted in mid-air, exposing their intent. The second jettisoned in from behind a trail of 20mm bullets, and Ramsay nosedived straight down. The Falcon came about, and Olivia prepared the next round for firing. Like the perfect pass of a football, Ramsay spiraled dangerously close, passing the F-16 and temporarily blinding it with the twisting vapor trails of the FU2. She turned hard right, and as she blasted the jet full of holes, Olivia launched two missiles. With a quick tip up of its left wing, the F-16 was able to dodge the first flaming projectile. But what saved it was also its undoing, and like a swinging pendulum, its right wing grazed the second oncoming missile. The jet burst in a series of dual explosions, and the FU2 soared beneath the falling flames of debris. Jack sneered and murmured, "Bleeding wankers," from under his breath, then set his sights upon Jones, who was nowhere to be seen. However, Sir Jonathon was almost certain to where he had gone and staying true to his word shouted, "Set a course for Hiroshima and punch it."

The Duke sputtered and cacked out a succession of deep, congested coughs from its battered engines. Both Tommy and Nathan grimaced as they pulled back on their helms. Takarada increased the flow of organic thorium to all turbojets as the twins stood by. He was hoping not to have to tire them out by using their telekinetic abilities, not yet at least. The cowbot shook hard like a chilly chihuahua, and small bursts of flames flashed from its engines. Both Nathan and Tommy bellowed as they buried the forward levers of the propulsion drive deep into their housing units. Takarada wouldn't have believed it had he not been there himself as the small crackles of flames from the bot's engines ignited into large bursts of thrust. The mech's cockpit felt like the inside of an incinerator and shook like Nathan the day after he quit drinking, but by God, it was airborne! Tommy always said there was something special about the Duke, but this was different, almost magical. He felt his chest heat up and placed his right hand over his heart, over his pendant. He didn't know for sure, but had a strong feeling

Akira was there, helping in some way. She was, after all, a Yokai princess, and in this strange world of gods, monsters and aliens, who's to say?

The Noahmarians had succeeded in pushing the Annihilator north, but not very far, and it was still fairly close to the Kobe city limits. That is until the cowbot rocketed overhead on its way towards the Rokko Mountain Range. Jack was right, that thing indeed hated the Duke and instantly forewent its fight with the swarm of alien orbs in order to pursue the mech. Michael announced that the Annihilator was closing in, and all were a little surprised that it hadn't used its vanishing act to surpass them. But then a cold thought entered each and every one of their minds, it was saving its power.

Jack's giant head once again appeared on the screens of the Duke's shattered windshield letting the pilots know that he, Olivia and the others were already over Hiroshima. Nathan sighed and thanked Jack. "Don't thank me yet my boy, because this is where the fun really starts." Nathan knew what that meant. He also knew that Olivia would more than likely be tagging along for the ride. However, he chose not to fight Jack on it because he did indeed make good on his promise. They were all out of the Annihilator's range, and no mission (even if it meant blowing up an entire enemy base) was nearly as bad as dealing with Mr. Tall, Dark and Scary. Tommy, thinking about his friend Toshiyuki, reminded Jack that not everybody at the Goku was necessarily a skin-suited, soul-sucking Velatian. Jack acknowledged Tommy and stated that he had already started the evacuation of the base. He knew that would mean the probable escape of many, if not all of the aliens, but was confident once the queen was dead, they soon would be too. Nathan chimed in and backed Jack up saying that as soon as the queen bites it, Jones and all the other minion beetles would simply drop dead. Takarada didn't believe this to be the case, and Nathan backed up his hypothesis by proudly professing it had to be true because he saw it in a movie. Jack, not wanting to deal with Nathan on this, simply ignored him and assured Tommy they would do their best. Tommy knew Jack, and knowing his best was pretty damn good, felt he couldn't ask for anything more.

It was at least twenty miles of winding narrow mountain roads to the nearest village from the secret E.I.O. base located at Mount Gokurakuji. From above Jack could already see people (and probably aliens) fleeing in a panic. The FU2 simply hovered past the guard stations, stone walls and tall barbed wire fencing that kept trespassers at a distance. Most of the guards were gone so there was no resistance there. Jack fired up the comm to let Tommy know that the guard shacks had all been abandoned and that there was no sign of his friend Toshiyuki. He waited, but there was no response.

Tommy saw the incoming communication, and even though Jack nor anyone else on the other end could hear, shouted, "Sorry, but we're unable to come to the phone right now," as the Duke ducked, dodging the incoming fist of the Annihilator's right mitt. Nathan followed up by pulling up on a lever that did "who knows what," and followed Tommy's comment with a,

"Please leave your name and number at the beep."

After being around Tommy and Nathan for so long the stupid rubs off, and of course Michael had to get in on it too. So, in his best falsetto voice, Michael mimicked a long "BEEEEEEEEEEP," as the creature kicked the Duke square in the chest. The cowbot stumbled, but thanks to its remaining six legs, wobbled like a Weeble but didn't fall down. Instead, it dug into the ground, sturdied its stance and fired a Kyoshi Twin Special from its monocle. They didn't miss this time, and the green ball expanded around the Annihilator like a forcefield, silently exploding from within.

The beast staggered about for a second, and Takarada screamed, "Silent but deadly!" as the Annihilator fell flat on its face. It seemed even Takarada wasn't immune to the throes of the stupid as apparently it was rubbing off on him as well.

***

Like NORAD in the U.S. or the Olavsvern base in Norway, all E.I.O. complexes constructed within the confines of a mountain only had two to three exits and entrances. Some varied, but they usually consisted of at least one burrowing runway where jets and other assorted craft could come and go from a massive hangar within. They were also equipped with one main roadway entrance for troops, trucks, tanks and such, protected by an immense vault-like door designed to keep intruders out. It was that very three-foot-thick semicircle of steel guarding the Goku that blew into a million pieces after Olivia fired two missiles into it from the FU2.

Even though Jack and Ramsay had never been to the Goku, they both knew there was a self-destruct protocol for each E.I.O. base for desperate times such as ... well, this. Jack looked deep through the dim smolder of the long tunnel and contemplated their next move. He decided only a small team would go in, and that Olivia would stay with the others aboard the FU2 which was a freakin' fortress itself.

Like Rambo gearing up for first blood, Ramsay, Jack, Noble and Armstrong grabbed any blaster, bomb or blunt object they could carry, strap on or fit into their pockets. They wasted no time whatsoever and, stepping over the remaining glowing pieces of steel, they warily entered the insects' lair.

The evacuation siren within the abandoned base was still tweeting in triplets, and the inside of the Goku was dark except for the soft, red glow of the emergency lights. With their backs up against the wall, Jack led the small group single file down the burrowing shaft.

ZAP! PING!

It started with one bullet ricochetting off the metal frame of the tunnel and grazing the side of Armstrong's arm. They hit the ground as a multitude of rounds sizzled overhead. Ramsay without hesitation reached into her bag of tricks, pulled out a plasma grenade, removed the clip with her teeth and chucked it without really looking. The bomb exploded, but she didn't wait for the dust to clear and immediately tossed another.

CHOOOM!

She, without any concern for herself, then stood up, swung one of the two machine guns she was toting around and screamed to the flickering of 800 rounds per minute. Jack,

Armstrong and Noble, the world's biggest man, watched in terror as little five-foot Ramsay went all Scarface shouting, "Say 'ello to my litto' friend!" as she pushed forward. The alarm stopped, and as the echoing bullets subsided, the men (who were still on the ground) just waited in the silence. "Are you coming or what?" Ramsay shouted, and they jumped up, following her from behind like three frightened ducklings.

The Goku went deep, not as deep as Salt Lake City as they weren't harboring any plutonium, but still pretty deep nevertheless. Jack knew it would be quicker if they separated, as there were two prime targets within the base they needed to hit, quicker maybe but definitely not safer. For that reason alone, Jack would have preferred that they stick to each other like glue, but time and circumstances dictated the opposite. He told Ramsay and Armstrong to hit the main control center in order to start the self-destruct sequence. Jack indicated that if it was like the FUJI or the Liverpool branch, no code or safety protocol was necessary. Just break through the thick glass with the butt of your gun, press the big red button and run like hell. "Then with a bit of luck," Jack stated, "we can all meet at the FU2 in approximately twenty minutes for a spot of tea." So, they went their separate ways. Ramsay nodded and looked at Jack as though she were never going to see him again, and she and Armstrong left for the control center. Jack watched her go, sighed and he and Noble headed towards the basement, because that's where all scary things happen.

Instead of the elevator, they opted for the emergency stairs that led down to where Jack was positive the queen was kept. He was doubtful they ever had the element of surprise after blowing the front door off, but after Ramsay went postal, he knew for sure. He also didn't want to get trapped like rats in a cage, because once in the lift there would be absolutely nowhere to run. The descent down was long, moist and red, and Jack knew beyond the shadow of a doubt what awaited them. Noble, as quietly as he could, kicked the locked emergency exit door, knocking it clean off its hinges. Jack gave him a dirty look, and Noble shrugged his shoulders, took the lead and they crept down the hall. They quickly but cautiously maneuvered each step, and when they came to another hallway on the right, Jack grabbed Noble from the back of his shirt and whispered, "Whoa." Sir Jonathon pulled Noble backwards, eased around him and peeked down the long, narrow hallway. Just as he had thought, there were two armed Velatians standing guard in front of a set of double doors. "No time to dilly-dally," Jack stated, and he turned the corner and pumped the enemy aliens full of lead with the small submachine gun he was packing. The guards went down, and Noble rolled a grenade ahead of him and Jack, blowing the doors wide open. Both Jack and Noble stopped dead in their tracks, and as their jaws each hit the floor, Jack uttered an aghast, "God blind me." It was the queen, and she was pumping out foot-long Velatians in the form of yellow, wormlike larvae at that very moment. The queen's quarters were of a brown alien foliage that was beyond disgusting. Noble grimaced at the indescribable stench, doubled over and vomited. Jack placed his hand upon the back of Noble's shoulder, gazed at the queen and waited to be devoured. But it seemed giving birth to possibly hundreds of Velatians a day made her somewhat apathetic, and she simply paid no attention while continuing with her royal duties. Robert Jones, on the other hand, felt quite the opposite as he and his cronies stormed in through the lingering haze of Noble's grenade.

The first thing Jones did was make sure his precious bug queen was still intact, and upon seeing she was, turned to Jack. "Well, well, well," he hissed, "Looks like you're in quite the sticky-wicket, Sir Jonathon." Jones laughed, obviously amused with himself.

"I don't know you sir," Jack snarled, "You are not the Robert Jones I once called friend. You murdered him." Jack shifted his glare to Jones's men, "And who knows how many other humans you and your cohorts have killed." Jones smiled and said,

"No matter how many it is, it's not enough." Jack's heart broke, and he quietly asked Jones if Iscariot was part of their plan. Jones, knowing it didn't matter, simply replied with a conceded, "Of course." Jack looked down in pure anguish and wondered if Iscariot had been turned as well. Jones slithered up close to Jack and placed his index finger on Sir Jonathon's nose.

"We've been here a long time, Jack. Much longer than you can imagine." He stopped as though he had just had a brilliant idea. "Say Jack?" Jones asked, "Ever seen a Velatian? I mean up close and personal?" Jack just stared at the alien with a stern look of disgust on his face. "I'll take that as a no then," it seethed. "Well behold our glory!"

Robert Jones, almost verbatim to Tommy's dream, dug its fingers into its skull and pulled. Its human head split straight down the middle and opened up that of a red-eyed, gloss-black scarab. It was there Jack realized where the Annihilator got its stunning good looks. The skin and hair that disguised the Velatian flopped to the ground like two sides of a rubber mask drenched in chocolate syrup. They (also like the Annihilator) didn't bleed, but their skin suits sure did.

Both Jack and Noble remained completely still as they watched in horror. Neither one looked scared, just pissed off. Jones twitched like the overgrown insect he was and asked Jack what he thought. "I must say, Robert, I'm not sure if I like it, but it is quite the improvement from your wigged-out Ziggy Stardust days."

Jones, or whatever his name was, had no idea what that meant and turned to his fellow Velatians and cackled out something in their native tongue. They responded like the true brownnosing bug-like minions they were and chirped in unison as though Jones had just said the funniest thing in the world (or any world for that matter). Of course he had no idea what was said, but Jack started laughing too, quite hysterically as a matter of fact. Now Noble was a little concerned and gazed at Sir Jonathon convinced he had lost his mind. "Yes, jolly good one indeed," Jack chuckled. "Now I've got one for you."

Jack stepped back, ripped his shirt open from both sides and let Jones and the other Velatians in on his little joke. Jack was packed! Loaded to the teeth with enough explosives wrapped around his body to blow any bug, their queen and its litter of larvae straight to hell. It was hard to tell what a shocked Velatian in its true form looked like, but the other guards looked terrified. "What do you think Jones? Good one huh?" Sir Jonathon giggled as he used his body like a pointed weapon to maneuver Jones and his Velatian lackeys away from the door. Jack eased forward, in turn forcing the aliens up and against the pulsing larvae-filled ovipositor that stuck out from the queen's abdomen. They created a Velatian shield with Jones in the center of it, and they would defend the queen to the end. Which was much closer than they could imagine.

Sir Jonathon moved back towards the center of the lair and told Noble to run like he never ran before. As Noble turned and headed towards the door, he told Jack to hurry up. That's when he realized Jack wouldn't be coming with him. Sir Jonathon eased towards the pack of Velatians, and Jones screamed for Jack not to be a fool, that he would die too. Jack calmly admitted, "I've died before, one more time shouldn't make any difference." He sneered at the Velatian one last time, and with half of a grin stated, "You always did want to be a Beatle, Robert. I'm glad you finally got your wish you son of a bitch." Jack grabbed the trip wire of his bomb-ladened cummerbund, pulled, and the lair ignited in a brilliant flash of white. And just like that, the queen, the larvae, Jones, the rest of the Velatians and Sir Jonathon himself were all but a memory.

Chapter 27

And In The End

Ramsay and Armstrong hauled ass out of the Goku's roadway entrance with a squad of trigger-happy Velatians on their tail. They managed to get up the flight stairs of the idling FU2, and as Armstrong dove in, Ramsay turned and fired on the enemy aliens from the open door. Armstrong caught the fresh photon blaster that Ann threw at him, and they both joined Ramsay at the hatch, raining down upon the Velatians with a shower of bullets and beams. Ramsay looked to her left and saw Noble's daughter with her nose pressed up against one of the portholes indicating that he and Jack had not returned. Another squadron came out of the black of the tunnel with their guns blazing, only to be followed by another ... with bazookas! Olivia could've easily blown them all away from the helm with one little missile, but didn't want to risk taking out Jack and Noble should they return. Soon it wouldn't be an issue anyhow because in less than sixty seconds the Goku would be nothing but a smoking crater.

A plethora of explosions, photon rays and machine gun bullets decimated the side of the FU2. Though the craft was pretty dang rugged, it wouldn't be able to withstand this constant barrage of firepower too much longer. Ramsay bit her lower lip. They needed to go, but she didn't want to leave Jack and Noble behind. She looked at Noble's daughter still adhered to the window, then looked at the other forty or so people crammed into the FU2. She shook her head, sighed and shouted, "Take off!"

The engines of the FU2 accelerated and it slowly began its ascend. "Wait!" a frail little voice screamed. "I see my daddy!" Olivia saw him too from the windshield. It looked like he was injured but was being assisted by a few of the actual human E.I.O. guards that were still alive. She didn't see Jack anywhere. With their guns pointed outward, the Goku soldiers moved as one with Noble protected in the middle. One of the guards was Tommy's friend Tokiyushi. He was battered and beaten to a pulp, but alive nonetheless and quite angry. Without regard for himself, he unloaded the contents of his machine gun into the oncoming bazooka brigade. Multiple lines of smoke trails rose into the air due to their firing shells going up as they fell down. Ramsay, Armstrong and Ann duck-walked down the flight stairs, grabbed Noble, then beelined back up and into the FU2. The Goku guards followed while continuing their assault on the Velatians, and with about four seconds to spare, the hatch door slammed shut and they were airborne.

It was more like an intense earthquake than an explosion when the Goku self-destructed. Oh, the bombs went off in a thunderous roar, but it was though the mountain hiccupped as opposed to just outright exploding. The ground lifted like a big, forested bubble, but the weight of the mountain kept the brutal fires contained, and it simply caved in. The Goku was gone, and it seemed everybody within the confines of the base was also gone, including Jack.

***

The Duke hit hard after being hurled into the side of the Rokko Mountain. Like a tightly-wound spring, the bot used its six legs to push itself off of the steep slope fists-first and right into the Annihilator's face. The creature went down backwards, but almost like an all-star ninja wrestler, rolled with the impact back into an upright stance. It swung around and pegged the cowbot with a bright burst of its translucent beam. The Duke again went down, and a battalion of the Noahmarian fighting orbs took over. They shot their single rays from their floating orbs pummeling the Annihilator relentlessly. But they were losing power, growing weak from the long battle and the beams were no longer having any tangible effect on the beast.

Michael and Liberty watched from the broken monitors within the Duke's cockpit as the orbs of their fellow Noahmarians began to basically evaporate, leaving the exhausted aliens at the mercy of both the behemoth as well as gravity. Some had enough power to grab the hand of their twin and float down, while others simply did not. Takarada felt horrible as he watched countless Noahmarians plummet to their death. He didn't think it would help in any way, but he turned to offer condolences to Michael and Liberty, only to see they were no longer there.

Michael and Liberty, holding each other's hand, mimicked the twin cross formation of the past fighting Noahmarians and apparated high above the Duke. Tommy, Nathan and Dr. Takarada watched as the twins used each of their free hands to shoot one lifesaving green beam after another. To achieve even more power, the twins reverted to their true form of a single entity, as did many of the other Noahmarians they had just saved. Though they were of a humanoid form, you may remember they are made of pure energy encased within in a thin membrane, two lives within one shell so to speak. Like they had done before when they defended Noahmar, the two beings within one form grabbed the hand of the next reverted form quadrupling their power. Some offered true resistance as they shot their destructive multicolored orbs, while others simply could not carry on. The Annihilator then introduced yet another weapon, generating one long constant beam of light that blasted from between its two antennas. The extending ray went long and far, and with the precision of a deadly scalpel, methodically took out every Noahmarian that was still in the air, including Michael and Liberty.

Each heart of every man within the cockpit of the Duke burst in unbelieving agony. "No! No! No!" Nathan moaned. "That DID NOT just happen!" But it did, and like Sir Jack, Michael and

Liberty were gone, just like that. Takarada wept as an uncontrollable flow of tears rushed down his face. Tommy just stared. Like the others, he was devastated beyond belief. His sorrow, however, turned to extreme anger, and he cursed with all of his soul this wretched and merciless thing known as Annihilator.

Though they could no longer use the Kyoshi Twin Special, they could still use the ROT beam itself. With all that had happened with the Duke, Tommy didn't know if it was even safe to fire their most powerful weapon. Even though it was cleaner, the organic-thorium-fused ray was stronger than any missile within the planet's nuclear arsenal. He knew that if it didn't work, nothing would, and that scared him the most. Like Noahmar and countless other planets, Earth would become just another statistic in the grand scheme of things. He hated that more than he feared the possibility of it not working. Tommy smashed his teeth together and hit the button. At the same time the Duke's monocle fired the powerful ray, the Annihilator's fist collided with the right side of the bot's steel-plated face. The beam malfunctioned only managing to shatter the thick plated lens of the mech's monocle. It exploded into a countless number of red shards, but the ROT beam itself never fired.

The mighty Duke in all of its cowbot majesty still stood. It was dead as a doornail and simply being supported by the long extension of its six legs, but either way it still stood. A sharp wind of smoke and glass whistled in through the hole that now occupied the majority of the Duke's head. The organic thorium fumes were now seeping into the already battered cockpit, and Tommy didn't expect to live much longer, nor did Nathan or Kyoshi. Through the Duke's brand-new observation skull, the three men found themselves face-to-face with the Annihilator. They all despised it with such loathing, and Takarada believed no man should ever be held subject to this kind of intense hate. Nathan knew he'd never see Olivia again or meet his unborn child, and he couldn't stand the strain of them being alone in this new world order. Tommy thought about his parents, SCOTT and even Suzy, but mostly his beloved Akira. At first, he prayed silently, asking Akira if she could somehow do something. But in his anger, he didn't even know if she had helped them at all in the first place as everything that happened could be logically explained. He started doubting the astonishing feats of all that had kept them alive, chocking it all up to mere coincidence. It seemed his hope and faith in something greater than himself had, like the twins, departed this realm. Either way, it was time to die. The three men stood side by side from within the crumbling cockpit and stared back. Takarada grabbed Nathan's hand, Nathan grabbed Tommy's and they all held tight.

The Annihilator's chest expanded, and it breathed in all the smoke-ladened air that surrounded the area. It clenched its fists, stretched its arms out wide and began to pulse. It swelled more and more with each of the three men's heartbeats and almost appeared to smile at them as it fired its main weapon. Tommy snarled and screamed a defiant, "Fuck you!" as everything erupted in a frenzy of flesh and guts.

The Duke went down, and though it seemed futile, Takarada, Tommy and Nathan instinctively held on, bracing themselves for the inevitable fall. The bot's head stayed connected as it toppled down to the ground tilting upward, giving them, in a sense, a ground-level, floor seat to the show. It was almost beautiful and something no one on Earth and maybe many other planets could ever claim to have witnessed. From the expanding stomach and chest of the Annihilator, trillions upon trillions of illuminated bacteriophages exploded from the inside of the behemoth and swarmed up towards the heavens. There were so many in fact that the entire Kobe region lit up in the light of their soft glow; it was nothing shy of amazing. The empty husk of the creature, supported only by the bacteriophages themselves, seemed to turn to mere dust as the last of the virus escaped.

None of the men moved or even spoke a single word, they simply laid there in the wonderful silence. Tommy realized he was clutching tight to the pendant around his neck, the very one Akira had given him so long ago. He reached over to offer Nathan a hand, who in turn offered Takarada the same courtesy. They pulled themselves from the battered ruins of the Duke and watched as the long trail of bacteriophage climbed to the stratosphere.

Amidst the wreckage, Takarada, Nathan and Tommy saw the multitudes of injured aliens scattered about the fields that outlined the Rokko Mountain range. Takarada's chest jumped, as for a second he thought he saw Michael and Liberty among them, then remembered that's what they all looked like in their Earthly form. The death toll was unimaginable, as was the damage. All the wars, plagues and catastrophes of the planet combined didn't come even remotely close to this.

Takarada gazed up and, quite by accident, watched as the last of the bacteriophages disappeared from sight. They didn't simply die off as both he and Olivia had thought, and he wondered if he had created some sort of new strain or lifeform. Overwhelmed by a sheer sense of awe he looked to the skies with a new hope. He looked further, eager to get lost within its majestic and mysterious plains, the ones simply known as space. He felt at home and pondered the chance of even more life from beyond the above. He welcomed the possibilities. If there ever was another war between the heavens and Earth, he would approach it with a brave face and act accordingly. He would never give up. The eternal night that surrounded our planet was becoming less and less vast. Takarada now understood that it was these mysteries, these challenges, that brought Earth and its inhabitants closer to discovering the secrets of the galaxy. Dr. Kyoshi Takarada breathed in the air and smiled. The great Annihilator was dead.

Chapter 28

Epilogue

Shakespeare wrote that "A coward dies a thousand times, but the valiant taste of death but once." And though this may hold true for some, there are many of brave character who have encountered the reaper, or in Japanese folklore, the Shinigami, not once, but twice in their life. This may be hard to understand, but for some in this world, life does not truly begin until after it is over. For Sir Jonathon this was not his first death. It was also nothing shy of an absolute kiseki that after taking four bullets to the back, Sir Jonathon would live to die another day many years later, a proposition many of us would jump at should the opportunity ever arise. Because Jonathon, along with his gruff demeanor, round glasses, permanently un-straightenable tie and of course, that giant walrus-like mustache, left this harsh world with an abundance of treasures, wisdom, fulfilment and true friendship. Yes, he was indeed a warrior, a courageous senshi, but he was also a surprisingly gentle man. In the end, I truly believe that Jonathon realized something many never will, even if they had ten lifetimes to do it in, that the love you take is equal to the love you make.

Takarada backed up from the microphone and sat down in between Tommy and Nathan on one of the folding chairs lining the back of the stage. Nathan patted him on the back and gave him a "well done" kind of nod. Takarada hated crowds and gazed at the mass of people that had gathered on both sides of Mathew Street. He knew Nathan was much better at addressing large audiences than he was, but reading Jack's eulogy was something he wanted, no, needed to do. Regardless, he was glad it was over. He folded the piece of paper that was in his hand and shoved it deep into the front pocket of his trench coat. A sharp December breeze blew, and Dr. Takarada raised his collar to shield his face from the sting of its kiss. At the foot of the recently erected temporary grandstand, Liverpool's lord and mayor raised his hand in the air signaling the conductor that it was time. With a short blast of his whistle, the gold instruments raised, and the musicians donning their bright red jackets, hats and bibbers burst into song. It was a not-so-rousing arrangement of Jack's favorite tune, "In The Midnight Hour," by Wilson Pickett.

Tommy couldn't help but groan at the start of the hokey rendition, and Takarada turned, giving him a stern look. It wasn't that Tommy disliked the song either. On the contrary, he loved it. It was however ... well, let's just say this particular version. But in the band's defense, it was quite cold outside and blowing into the metal mouthpiece of any instrument would be extremely hard with a pair of frozen lips. As they marched off into the distance it began to snow, and Kyoshi looked down the long block. He couldn't help but laugh to himself, and though it wasn't confetti or paper, it still looked as though Jack would finally get his much-deserved ticker-tape parade.

As the music faded, it was replaced with a completely different kind of sound, the cry of Nathan's son. Olivia held up Jonathon Thomas Fox and told Nathan it was his turn to change the baby's diaper. As Olivia handed Jonathon Thomas over to Nathan, Ramsay handed Michael Kyoshi, who also needed changing, to Olivia. Tommy got a hefty waft of the baby's business, crinkled his nose and stated, "Save the world, and what do you get in return? A big, stinky diaper."

Nathan rose to his feet, smirked and replied, "If you're lucky, Tommy. Only if you're really, really lucky." He headed down the flimsy stairs of the stage with his child in his arms, and Olivia did the same with the other. Tommy watched the four of them walk off, and once again he found himself a little bit envious of

freakin' Nathan Fox. But he was also extremely happy for both him and Olivia. Somehow, he knew they'd make it. They were too different from each other not to. Nathan yelled back that he and Olivia would see him later at the Cavern Club.

Takarada, Tommy and Ramsay followed suit and headed down to the street from the stage. Ramsay was still crying from the service slash celebration, and Rose stood waiting for her at the bottom of the stairs. Rose put her arm around Ramsey as she patted her eyes with a tissue. Her tears turned to that awkward, crying kind of laughter, and she said they were going to have to pass on the Cavern Club. It was a long flight back to Sydney, and they were heading out in the morning. He hugged her for a long time, and when they finally separated, Ramsay put her palms against his face in the same way that a loving mother would. She scrunched his cheeks together, then kissed him on the lips. He made a retaliatory face, but knew she was concerned about him, and he begged her not to worry.

Truth of the matter was Tommy had been somewhat happy over the last year, much more than he'd been in a very long time. Of course, he grieved over the loss of Jack, the twins and for all of those who lost their lives during the last war. It was truly horrific, and if there was any way he could change things, he would, but he couldn't. It was like drilling through cement, and once it infiltrated his thick head, he finally began to understand that stupid "Serenity Prayer" that Nathan was always going on about. He also started to get that whole "To Thine Self Be True" thing too, and it was time for him to follow his heart.

Over the last decade Tommy had saved thousands of lives, and though he wrestled with walking away, he was no longer interested in being General Taylor. And with the exception of the acoustic album he was going to record with Nathan, he wasn't too keen on being Tommy Lynn Taylor the rock star either. He liked being Thomas (although Tommy was okay too) Taylor whose passion was playing fingerstyle guitar. He didn't need to be labeled by what he did, not anymore.

He knew Ramsay meant well, and it was apparent she just didn't want to see Tommy alone and miserable. But it wasn't the case. He wasn't. After the Velatian war and nearly being pummeled multiple times by the Annihilator, Tommy realized he'd never be alone. Akira was with him. It was hard for him to explain, and most would probably think he'd lost his mind (and maybe he had), but it had become obvious. He had no desire whatsoever to be with anyone else, none at all. And no matter what anybody said or thought, he now knew in his heart that it was Akira that had saved their lives so many times. Maybe it was for the sake of the planet, or maybe it was because even from the great beyond, Takamagahara, Heaven or wherever the hell it was that Yokai Princesses went, she was keeping a faithful eye on him. He knew in the end, he would be with her again, and Tommy could wait the short time on Earth for an eternity with Akira. So for now, he was content. He hugged Ramsay one final time and invited her and Rose to visit him and Suzy in Imizu sometime. She said she would, and Tommy had a hunch she would too. Especially since she was going to be spending so much time in Japan working with Takarada rebuilding the FUJI. He reminded her it was only a three-hour trip by bullet train and was going to hold her to it.

As they walked away Takarada waved, reminding Ramsay he would see her in a few weeks in Tokyo. Another cold whisp of wind blew, forcing Tommy's collar to lift. Kyoshi turned to fix the turned-up lapel of Tommy's jacket and forced out a proud but not necessarily genuine smile. This wasn't the end of their friendship, but it was indeed the end of an era. And as hard as it was, they both needed to turn the proverbial page and move on. Tommy put his arms to his side and bowed, and with all sincerity, he congratulated Dr. Kyoshi Takarada, for being appointed the new commander of the E.I.O. Takarada returned the gesture, and though he played it down, they both knew there was no one better suited for the job. "I'm glad you are living in Japan, Tommy-san." Takarada stated. You will always be welcome at The FUJI or anywhere that I may be, because family is not about where, it is about who." Tommy took a deep breath in a poor attempt to stifle his tears.

"Man," he admitted in an unsteady voice, "this is way harder than I ever thought it would be." Tommy caught himself gravitating towards his old norm and volunteered to help get things squared away with the Noahmarians and the people of New Salt Lake City. It had been over ten months since the Annihilator went up in a bacteriophage puff of smoke and almost that same duration since he saw Kyoshi last. Takarada assured him that all of this was well under control and reminded Tommy that what he needed to do was keep concentrating on his new life. Takarada hated to say it, but it needed to be said. Truth is, Takarada would have loved for Tommy to come with him, be his Number One and help in the rebuilding of both the FUJI and the E.I.O. he was one of the few people he really trusted. But even though Takarada said no to Tommy's offer, he did, however, add an, "At least for the time being," for good measure.

The crowd was thinning, as was the snow, and Takarada looked up towards the heavens.

It was kind of peculiar, and maybe even a little cheesy, but a ray of sunshine managed to find its way through the thick overcast above, and shine down.

"Let me tell you something, Tommy-san. Sir Jonathon had mentioned often that life is about living in the moment, always stressing that there are no guarantees for tomorrow. I have always agreed with that philosophy, and working with Sir Jonathon and the E.I.O. over the years I have seen and experienced this first-hand. I mean, look how many friends and loved ones we have lost in these wretched wars alone." Takarada stopped for a moment as it was obvious he was getting choked up. "I wasted many days of my life living in a fictitious future filled with thoughts of impending doom, and those are days I will never get back. It is time I could have spent with friends and loved ones while enjoying all of the subtle, and not so subtle, beauties of life. Enjoying the things that are forever surrounding us, at this very moment. I no longer want to waste this most precious of commodities while on some never-ending objective, telling myself I will be happy once I reach my goal. I feel now, Tommy-san, that is more like putting happiness on hold as we wait or strive for something we may never reach. It is not about living happily ever after as the fairy tales state, it's about living happily where you are right now, wherever that may be." He looked at Tommy and made a profound realization.

"Imagine if another Annihilator attacked or, God forbid, something worse. We would do everything in our power to defeat it, just as we have always done. But did you notice while we were fighting the beast we weren't thinking too much about tomorrow? Not because we dreaded it, but because we simply did not think it was coming. Mark my word, something far worse than Annihilator is imminent, but until then I'm not going to live my life in fear as I await its arrival. I will not be afraid. I'm going to cherish every moment because I now believe that the journey is just as important as the destination. And when it, or they, or whatever does show up, we'll do exactly what Sir Jonathon Winston would have done. We'll rise to the occasion, do our absolute best and give the ruddy bastards what for!"

The End

ANNIHILATOR: Big In Japan Book III is dedicated to the life, career and memory of the beloved actor, Akira Takarada. To me, Akira Takarada was the definition of class, and I was privileged to meet him on many occasions. Takarada-san was never anything less than the quintessential gentleman that he portrayed in so many of his films, and he absolutely adored his fans. My son even appeared in a French kaiju documentary receiving a heartfelt hug from Takarada-san after a 35mm presentation of the original Gojira! While writing *Big In Japan*, I always imagined Akira Takarada whenever I wrote about Dr. Kyoshi Takarada. So much so that I finally built up the courage to contact him. Going through the proper channels, I was able to ask him if I could use his likeness for Alan's illustrations in the upcoming books. Sometimes when we meet our heroes, we are left empty and often feel letdown. This, however, was not the case with Akira Takarada. I am honored that he agreed, and I am forever grateful to him. I have included a copy of the letter I received from his offices in Japan before the release of *Big In Japan Book II: POWER*. It warms my heart whenever I read it.

Again- Takarada-san ... This one is for you.

Dear Timothy,

I am back in Japan and assist Mr. Takarada with international communication.

A few days ago, Mr. Takarada forwarded me a copy of your email asking for permission to use his likeness in your novel. Mr. Takarada thinks it is "OK" as far as it does not infringe on any copyright or characters from other stories/movies.

Before you publish your next novel, please send a copy of the character to see what he looks like and some extracts of the novel.

By the way, "Kiyoshi Takarada" is Mr. Takarada's father's name. So, he was pleasantly surprised you picked up that particular name for the character.

Best regards...

A note from Tim

As Doctor Kyoshi Takarada stated in this book, *"One of the only constants in our lives that stays the same is change."* It's inevitable, and the last few years of my life have been absolutely filled with it.

Beyond writing and playing music, I've found myself called into something I never expected: serving as the director of a nonprofit ministry that helps men and women battling addiction. And not just the usual suspects like drugs and alcohol, but the daikaiju-sized struggles that can make life feel unmanageable, or let's be honest, a living hell.

They always say to write what you know, and I'd be lying if I said this latest chapter of the *Big In Japan* saga wasn't shaped by that calling. But what a blessing it's been. As someone who is also in recovery, I've been gifted with a life I once thought impossible, a life filled with a loving wife, amazing kids, a ton of friends, anchored in faith, hope, and love. Honestly, I don't know if I could ask for anything more.

That said, one thing that *hasn't* changed is my lifelong love of all things kaiju, tokusatsu, anime, and Japanese culture. That passion is as fierce as ever. In fact, two chapters of this book were written while adventuring through Tokyo on our most recent trip to the land of the rising sun.

Over the last decade, I've had the privilege of producing and performing on a variety of music projects, both with bands and solo artists, and I've even managed to release two albums of my own. I've also penned a few "kaiju-esque" short stories and articles for *Mad Scientist* and *G-FAN* magazines.

To all my fellow travelers:

Enjoy the journey, live in the now, don't be afraid of criticism, don't give up, and keep the faith.

A note from Alan

When we first started *Big in Japan*, I thought I was just drawing a fun adventure about giant monsters, guitars, and friendship. Turns out, I was creating a mirror, and it's kept reflecting back at me in strange and wonderful ways ever since. Like Tommy, I've played on stages and wrestled with identity. Like Suzy, I've chased mystery. Like Takarada, I've asked big questions with trembling hands. And along the way, I've poured everything I know about music, comics, film, faith, and failure into this series. It was the first thing I did out of art school, but I learned more making it than I learned at SCAD.

These stories started as a love letter to kaiju and tokusatsu, but they became something deeper: a reflection of our fears, our joys, and the wild hope that transformation is always possible, even in the face of annihilation. I've spent the last two decades working as a writer, musician, professor, and illustrator. I've scored films, drawn comics, taught college students, led worship, and stayed up too late dreaming about what happens next. What a gift it's been to keep telling this story.

I still believe in monsters. But more than that, I believe in the people who face them.

Let's keep going.

www.ingramcontent.com/pod-product-compliance
Lightning Source LLC
Chambersburg PA
CBHW021958010726
47494CB00003B/795